THE PRODUCER'S DAUGHTER

LINDSAY
MARCOTT

THE PRODUCER'S
DAUGHTER

Copyright © 2013 by Lindsay Maracotta

All rights reserved.

Published in the United States by Crooked Lane Books, an imprint of The Quick Brown Fox & Company LLC.

Crooked Lane Books and its logo are trademarks of The Quick Brown Fox & Company LLC.

The Library of Congress Cataloging-in-Publication Data is available upon request.

978-1-61129-075-2

Cover design by Tricia McGoey

Printed in the United States.

www.crookedlanebooks.com

Crooked Lane Books
2 Park Avenue, 10th Floor
New York, NY 10016

Second Edition: November 2015

10 9 8 7 6 5 4 3 2 1

ACKNOWLEDGMENTS

My deepest thanks: to P.D. Graves for brilliance and expertise; to Nancy Yost for perspicacity and tenacity; to Dyanne, Ronda, Vid, and Susannah for thoughtful reading and unflagging encouragement.

1990

The elfin-eyed Danish au pair Sabina Larsen, called Bina for short, came sneaking back into the Pasadena mansion where she was currently employed at just after two a.m. on a mid-September morning.

Some three hours earlier, she'd wriggled like a herring out the narrow window of her maids' quarters room and nimbly scuttled over the iron railings at the back of the sprawling property. Her boyfriend Jamie, who played bass with a grunge band called Fukaduk, was waiting for her on the street, idling his beat-up old Nova. They cruised to a couple of clubs in Old Town, knocked down four or five Heinekens, then parked under a burnt-out streetlight for a vigorous quickie in the Nova's vomity-smelling backseat. Dropping her back at the house, Jamie had pleaded to come in with her. "I swear to god, Been, I'll split before dawn. Nobody'll find out."

"I can't let you. It's too risky."

He kept begging, and she kept saying no way, until finally in a huffy fit he'd flung the used condom over the iron railings and peeled off with a sharp squeal of his crap-car tires.

He was a pig, really, Bina thought, hoisting herself back into the property. Maybe she ought to dump him.

She located the condom limp on top of an azalea bush like a tiny, shriveled corpse and hurled it onto the road; and then she made her way tip-toe through the garden path back to the house. In the pale glimmer of a crescent moon, it looked enormous, almost monster-like—way bigger than it did during the day. Painted the green of forest moss, it had a kind of Japanese design, curling eaves and carved wooden beams thrusting out; so what was it doing here in the land of sunshine and orange trees and cheeseburgers with a side of fries?

Her room was on the side of the house facing an asphalt service alley. The window, she was relieved to see, was still partially opened. She set a knee onto the sill and slithered back through the opening, but caught her foot and tumbled with a heavy thump onto the floor inside. She froze for several moments, listening.

Gingerly, she picked herself up and switched on the light.

She could not afford to lose this placement. She'd been sacked after six weeks from her last job minding the three kids of a moneybags Santa Monica lawyer, because Mrs. Lawyer had informed the agency that Bina was a messy slob and had a fresh mouth. Okay, maybe that was sometimes true. But the *real* reason was that Mrs. Lawyer was, like, forty-five, with a bony ass and a chin so sharp you could cut hard cheese with it, whereas Bina was twenty-two, with those sly, green, elfin eyes and a plump, high, little behind that Mr. Lawyer could never keep his own baggy old eyeballs off of.

Well that wasn't her fault, was it?

Still, the agency told her she had only one more chance, and if she screwed this one up, they'd cancel her visa and ship her on the next cheap-shit Icelandair flight back to Copenhagen, where the weather sucked, and any little notion she'd been cradling of maybe breaking into the movie business she could kiss bye-bye.

She began to quickly undress, shrugging off her black and white striped Emporium jacket and boy's Fruit of the Loom undershirt, peeling her maroon jeans down to her ankles and kicking them off. Stupid she was to have risked this placement by sneaking out—particularly when it was such a fabulous super one. Only one child in her charge, a four-year-old girl named Hannah—and a quick, funny little imp she was! A little bit of a temper, maybe, but loving, too. Bina was already quite fond of her.

But best of all, Hannah was the daughter of Warren and Pamela Doran. The *famous* Warren Doran, who had produced and directed *Wildwood Murphy and the Secrets of the Forgotten Palace* when he was only twenty-seven, and then started the company WildFilm which made one blockbuster movie after the other—including, of course, two more *Wildwood Murphy's*. And Pamela . . . Well, her maiden name was Sebring, as in Sebring mattresses and Sebring pillows, and her family fortune was worth god only knew how many millions. Plus Bina did not have to worry about Pamela going all jealous-berserk, since she was the most drop-dead beautiful woman

Bina had ever seen: tall and willowy, with lemon-colored hair parted in the middle over a delicately diamond-shaped face. And her eyes— the pure, silvered blue of a glacier lake. Some people called them cold; but Bina had discovered that if you cracked through that layer of glacial ice you could find yourself tumbling, almost drowning, in great sea-depths of feeling.

Now Warren, on the other hand, wasn't what you'd call hand- some, Bina reflected, stepping out of her sex-fragrant panties. On the short side, with corky dark hair and a wide, kind of rubbery, mouth. But there was this intensity about him, a fiery, live-in-the- moment quality that was far sexier than a lot of so-called good- looking guys Bina knew. Jamie, for instance, with his poodle eyes and sharp little nipping teeth . . .

She balled her panties and in disgust pitched them across the room.

The Dorans, Pamela and Warren, had been on the cover of *People* magazine, and Bina had sent a copy to all her friends and family back home. THE HEIRESS AND THE MOVIE KING was the headline, and underneath: "The New Hollywood Royalty." They were posed on a red carpet, stunning in tux and gown, looking young, glamorous, madly in love.

At least Bina was certain that Warren was madly in love with Pamela. You could tell by a thousand ways, how he glanced down a long dinner table, picking her out with a kind of startled pleasure; or the way he lightly grasped her arm, the most tender of touches right above the elbow, to guide her through a door. With Pamela, though, it was harder to tell. She treated Warren the way she treated everybody, even her daughter Hannah—with a pleasant and sort of unshakable composure, which again was why some people called her cold. Except for that one time two, maybe three weeks ago: Bina woke up in the middle of the night and heard them, Pa- mela and Warren, someplace down in the house, Pamela's voice normally so musical and cool and low rising up and up the scale to a witchy screech: "Don't touch me! Don't ever touch me, you fuck- ing goddamn son of a bitch!"

Then a shattering of glass. And then Warren, murmuring low: Bina strained to make out his words but couldn't, just the tone of them, patient, reassuring, fatherly, even.

And in the morning it was like nothing had happened. Not a glance or a word. Not even a splinter of glass to give away the night before.

Bina wondered if she'd dreamed it. Or maybe Pamela had just

drunk too much of that expensive Scotch the Dorans kept in crystal decanters. Bina had an uncle like that, a sweet man until he got going too much with the *akvavit*, and then suddenly an ogre!

But that had been that, and Pamela and Warren just continued on living their fabulous life of Hollywood royalty.

And, oh, it was fabulous! Everyone came to pay them court. The most glittering of stars attended their parties and Bina got to meet them when she brought little Hannah down: There'd been Harrison Ford, jaunty but at the same time kind of shy; and Jessica Lange with Sam Shepard, and fast-talking Eddie Murphy with his looping laugh. Goldie and Kurt had come, and Jack and Anjelica, and Demi Moore, so exquisite, no wonder Bruce Willis was wild about her.

And most thrilling for Bina, Jackson Brandt, who played Wildwood Murphy in all three of the movies, Bina's favorite films of all time. He was always so charming, even flirting a little, despite his wife being there. His wife was a tall and skinny ex-supermodel, kind of a sourpuss who never seemed to appreciate that she'd snagged the sexiest man alive.

So strange to realize it was over a month now since Jackson Brandt had perished in that car crash on the Pacific Coast Highway. Shocking to the whole world, of course. Warren Doran had been quite disturbed and upset, and even Pamela had betrayed rare feelings of deep emotion. Bina herself had cried for hours and hours when she'd heard the news.

Leaving her clothes in a tangled heap on the floor, she padded naked into her old and ugly bathroom. This was an historical house, over a hundred years old, which was ancient for this country. Owned by Pamela's daddy. Yesterday, a group from some society had come through to gawk at the woodwork and chandeliers and hear about the presidents and millionaires and once even a prince of England who'd slept here. Bina thought wistfully of the Dorans' home back in Brentwood, all modern and high-tech, with marble surfaces and walls and walls of glass. But Warren was off on location in Vancouver, and Pamela said she felt safer here in Pasadena in the home she'd grown up in.

Which seemed kind of crazy. Pamela's daddy, who was some kind of an old playboy, was away sailing in the South Pacific. Pamela's mama lived in Salzburg with her third or maybe fourth husband, an Austrian baron. So except for a servant couple who slept in the gatehouse, the three of them—Pamela and little Hannah and Bina—were rattling around alone in this big old mansion which anybody, obviously, could sneak in and out of. Whereas the Brentwood house was bristling with alarm systems and motion detectors and a private security car that drove by every half hour, keeping everybody safe and sound.

No, it made no sense.

Bina lowered herself gingerly onto the historical wooden toilet seat that had once left a nasty splinter in her butt and peed at some length. Her vagina itched: she wiped vigorously, and then sniffed the tissue. If she'd caught a fungus, that bass player would wish to god he'd never been born.

She flushed, went to the sink, swiped a toothbrush over her teeth. Maybe it was the sight of her naked breasts bobbing in the mirror's mottled glass, but she suddenly flashed on her last conversation with Warren, the day before he left for Canada. The child, Hannah, was down for her nap, and Bina was using the break to catch some sun rays by the pool, stretched out on a chaise in her bikini. Warren emerged from the garage, twirling his car keys on his finger like a cowboy with a pistol.

"Hey there, kiddo! How's it going?" He always spoke to her easily, as if she was a friend, not an employee, and her ideas and opinions counted as much as those of anyone he knew, studio heads and movie stars included. "Everything hunky-dory?"

"Everything is swell with me."

He perched on the edge of another chaise and regarded her for some moments, not in a drooly Mr.-Santa-Monica-Lawyer way, but thoughtfully, as if totting up and appreciating the sum of her. And then he'd said, "You know, a girl like you could do far better than being an au pair."

Her heart had begun to beat quickly. Was he going to offer her a part in his movie?

But then he began to talk about a woman named Elizabeth who was a great friend of his. A beautiful, refined, and extremely smart lady who, Warren said, handled only a very select number of girls. "You'd be amazed at who they are. There's a girl who was on the cover of the Victoria's Secret catalogue. Another one, an actress, you'd recognize her immediately. And a Brazilian girl, gorgeous, she was a runner-up for Miss Universe." These girls, he told her, made thousands of dollars a week, and their clients were strictly A-list, the biggest and richest names in the industry.

Bina had lain perfectly still, listening while he talked. The world suddenly seemed to be filled with birds: a hummingbird churned past her ear like a monstrous insect; a trio of crows lifted from a sycamore; a mockingbird on the roof of the pool house scrolled through its repertoire of trills, whistles and song hooks.

It was impossible, but Warren seemed to be suggesting she become a whore.

And yet there was nothing in his voice to suggest he was talking about anything dirty or against the law. Just the opposite—he could have been suggesting milk and cookies. He spoke pleasantly about girls who'd saved enough money in a few years to set themselves up in glamorous businesses. Other ones who'd even married the A-list clients. It was hard to get to Elizabeth, he said, many well-qualified girls tried but didn't have the connections. "I could give you an introduction," he told her. "Strictly as a favor, you understand. Just get the ball rolling for you."

Then he'd slapped his knees and sprang to his feet. "Well. You think about it."

And Bina had thought about little else since.

Now she rinsed her mouth, spat, then padded back into the bedroom. She gave a start. The little girl, Hannah, was standing at the foot of the bed.

Lort! Bina whirled and snatched up her jeans and jacket and scrambled to put them back on. Hannah was a smart little kid. If she babbled anything to her mother about Bina having no clothes on, it would be Icelandair for Bina before she could blink twice. Maybe even arrested; you never knew in this prudish country.

Jeans zipped, she turned back to the child who was gazing at her with an unnerving seriousness. She was wearing the pink, bunny-footed pajamas Bina had put on her earlier that evening, and her left thumb was jammed in her mouth.

Bina crouched down and gently removed the thumb. "What are you doing awake, dumpling?"

"Mommy's sick."

"Did you wake up Mama? That's very bad, Hannah. You know you're not supposed to do that."

"She won't wake up. She's sick."

Bina stopped the child's thumb from migrating back to her mouth and grasped her hand. "Come, dumpling, let's go upstairs. And tip-toe, ja?"

They crept up the narrow back staircase to the second floor. Bina paused at the door to Hannah's room, the first on the landing. "Back into bed now, okay? I'll go see Mama."

The child nodded. Bina continued to Pamela's room at the end of the hall. Not the largest bedroom in the house, but so much the prettiest, with a wide, six-sided bay window overlooking the rose gardens and the lozenge-shaped pool. The door was cracked open and there was a light burning inside.

Bina rapped lightly. "Pamela? It's me, Bina. Sorry, are you awake?"

No response. She pushed the door open further.

The long body lay on the bed twisted into a kind of question mark. Blonde hair over the face, like a broom attempting to sweep off the ugliness of contorted features. Bloody vomit everywhere, on the bedclothes, the carpet, on walls and furniture; and on the carpet, a bright green canister marked with a drawing of a winged insect.

Bina's knees buckled and her stomach heaved. She tried to shout but no sound would come. She staggered, dry-heaved again, then turned and found the little girl Hannah standing behind her.

It was Hannah who began to scream, because Bina had grabbed her by her rough, dark hair and was dragging her by it down the hall.

ONE

Once again, Hannah was dreaming about the magic shoes.

They were gossamer thin, the color and sheen of old silver dollars, nestled in a box lined with pale green tissue paper. They didn't seem to be any label she recognized: neither Tod nor Chanel nor Louboutin; still, she knew they were special, that they possessed magic properties; and reverently she removed them from their nest and slipped them on her bare feet, first the right, then the left. She began pacing, back and forth, up and down, and it was like skipping over clouds. She could travel anywhere in these magic shoes, as far away and as high up in the air as she pleased.

But something was wrong. She was no longer skipping above the clouds, she was slogging through something thick and cold. She was terrified of looking down, but she felt compelled to, and when she did, it was just as she dreaded—her feet were being covered by some dull, gray substance, like the dried lava beds you see in Maui: layer upon layer, until she couldn't move at all.

She jerked awake shouting: "Help me!"

"No wa-a-ay."

Her dorm-mate, Teresa Ojeda, a chunky teenager, lay snoring: a quick nasal snort on the inhale, a long harsh breath through the mouth on the exhale, and it sounded like "No wa-ay, no wa-a-ay." A crushed pearl light gleamed in the high slit of a window, illuminating the cement block walls and bare fixtures of their dorm room.

Every morning, for the past fourteen months and five days, Hannah had opened her eyes to that first faint gleam. For the first several seconds, she'd remain entangled in whatever dream she'd been having; but then the elements of the dream would scatter. And with the strengthening light, reality would seep into her like wet cement.

She was in prison. The Peachrock Women's Correctional Camp, deep in the Mojave Desert. She was serving a sentence of twenty-two months for grand felony theft.

They could call this a dorm room, but the beds and desk were bolted to the floor; and outside that slit of a window—beyond the rec court and the dung-colored stucco of the administration block and the slopes of sparse, barely blooming succulents—was a high fence made of barbed wire.

But suddenly a feeling of elation swept over her. She punched the air jubilantly with her fists. "Whoo!"

The other girl stirred awake.

"Hey, Teresa!" Hannah called to her. "I'm getting out today!"

"Awesome," Teresa murmured.

Her release was scheduled for two p.m. The past week had been a carnival of forms and documents to sign, medical exams and psych interviews, and lengthy confabs with her lawyer. She'd given away most of her possessions—the little stashes of imported olives and anchovies and macadamia nuts; the soaps and moisture creams from Neiman Marcus; her terry cloth robe and slippers, and her foam pillow—items that counted as lavish luxuries in this place—and donated her books, F. Scott Fitzgerald and Trollope and George Eliot, to the barebones prison library. The few things she was keeping—a Spanish textbook, some handmade mementos from other prisoners she'd been tutoring, an ebony-framed photo of her mother—she'd stuffed in a black plastic trash bag secured with a rubber band.

Seven weeks ago, she'd been up for parole, but a random dorm search had turned up contraband in a slit in her mattress—a folded pocket knife. "It's not mine," she'd protested. "I've never seen it before!"

Yeah right—it's what everybody said. Her parole had been rejected.

Then a miracle. The State of California, perpetually broke, granted early release to hundreds of non-violent offenders. Hannah Sebring Doran—daughter of the famous producer Warren Doran; former celebutante; felony shoplifter—was among them. She was still half-fearful that someone would come in and say wait, it's a mistake! You're not getting out after all! Since lunch, she'd been pacing the dorm room, her thoughts racing.

All her life, people had envied her. It was true that she'd experienced an early trauma in her mother's suicide, but she'd been too young to really remember it; and after that, such privilege! Growing up between a showcase home in the most exclusive part of Brentwood and a lavish Pasadena estate. Traveling the globe. Rubbing elbows with movie stars and moguls and socialites. A parent as charismatic and successful as Warren Doran, showering her with every indulgence.

Every indulgence except the one she really craved—his undivided attention. For Warren Doran, his movies always came first. No, she told herself acidly—make that first and second. Everything else, including his daughter, placed a distant third. He was rarely home, constantly jetting around the world raising money for his films, or producing his films on distant location sets, or attending their foreign premieres. When Hannah was brought to visit on sets, she'd be assigned bit parts to keep her occupied—she had her SAG card before she was eight. At her father's parties, her role was to charm fading actresses and, when she was older, to flirt with (and occasionally seduce) the hot young actors and screenwriters Warren was attempting to hire.

But her father continued to be remote. The day she won her first tennis tournament, Warren was tied up at a studio meeting. While she was giving the valedictory speech at her prep school commencement, he was partying in Cannes. During most of her freshman year at Yale, he'd been on a shoot in New Zealand. Her sophomore year, there was a Parents Weekend scheduled, and this time her father swore he'd come: "Wild horses couldn't keep me away!"

It wasn't wild horses. It was an actress. Some brainless, self-obsessed star he'd been wooing for his next movie was having a meltdown, and he'd had to rush to her side. "I've got to talk her through this. You understand, don't you, honeybun?"

Something snapped. "You bastard!" she'd yelled. "You don't give a shit about me, do you?" He'd sighed with exaggerated patience. "You're not a little kid anymore, Hannah. You need to grow out of these temper tantrums."

An idea revolved in the back of her mind—if it was vapid, brainless celebrities her father responded to, then screw it—that's what she'd become. She stopped attending classes, then dropped out of Yale and returned to L.A. Having turned twenty, she had a huge allowance from her mother's estate. There was a crowd of kids she'd grown up with—a wild crowd, kids with rich parents and money to burn, who hung out with the edgiest young stars and their entourages—and it was easy enough to hook back up with them. And over the next three years, she'd fashioned herself into a fixture in the tabloids and the celebrity gossip sites. Doing all the things celebutantes were supposed to do: you drop a small fortune on stare-at-me clothes from the boutiques on Robertson and Melrose Place and another fortune on hair and nails and waxings; you get your name linked with a member of Vampire Weekend and then a Calvin Klein underwear model; you walk a pot-bellied pig on a leash into Nobu and jump into the fountain at the Music Center and sign a line of handbags patterned with dead mice. On the way, you become Very Best Friends with other girls who were hot on the paparazzi radar and then you have very public spats with those Best Friends and even more public make-ups with them.

It was an act. The Act was easy to pull off, but increasingly hard to keep up—except, she discovered, after a couple (or three, or five) Grey Goose martinis; and then it became less like an Act and more like a natural things. She became used to seeing her name and face flash by on screens. She had Twitter followers by the tens of thousands. But the gratifying thing was that her father seemed to finally take notice. He began inviting her to more of his parties, introducing her around with a new sort of pride. She was mildly famous. She was now an official asset.

Right up until the nightmarish afternoon a year and a half ago, when she was arrested and led in handcuffs to the Beverly Hills precinct and booked on a charge of grand felony theft.

Warren Doran had been in Rome but caught the first plane back. He'd arranged by phone for a lawyer—a partner in a top Century City firm that specialized in celebrity defendants—and within hours of her arrest, Hannah was out on bail.

Three weeks later, she and her father met with the attorney in his glossily-appointed twenty-third floor suite. A silky guy in custom-made suits who billed twelve hundred bucks an hour. "I've negotiated a deal with the D.A," he announced. "Twenty-two months at the Peachrock minimum-security camp facility. You'll be up for parole in less than a year."

"But I'd have to go to jail?" Hannah had paled.

"If we take this to trial and get a guilty verdict, you could be facing a maximum of four years."

"That's insane!" she insisted. "It was a mistake. I didn't do it on purpose!"

"And that's what we would argue to a jury," the lawyer said smoothly. "But let me explain to you, Hannah, how the prosecution will spin it. They'll point to a young woman with an income of three quarters of a million dollars a year—an income she did not have to lift a finger to earn. They'll ask the jury why this wealthy young woman would steal a necklace she could afford to buy. And they'll offer reasons. First, they'll present credit card receipts to show you'd already blown most of your income for the year. And second, they'll suggest that for spoiled young people like yourself, the rules just don't seem to apply. You feel free to park your BMW's in handicap zones. Entitled to cut directly to the head of a line. And if you see something you want—even a two hundred and twenty-five thousand dollar diamond necklace—and you find yourself inconveniently low on funds, well then you feel entitled to simply take it."

"That's not true! You're distorting everything."

The lawyer's voice became raw silk. "The decision is yours, Hannah. But in my experience, juries are an unpredictable bunch. I'd strongly advise you to accept the deal."

Shaking, bewildered, Hannah had turned to her father. "Dad? Do you think I should take it?"

"I think you'd be foolish not to, honeybunch." Warren Doran had spoken softly, but his eyes had been twin pools of black ice.

The deal required that she allocute to her crime; and so she stood up before a judge and declared that at or around 3 p.m. of October 2 of the year before she had been present at the establishment of Charles Gray Jewelers and had deliberately secreted a necklace into her handbag and keeping it concealed, she had left the establishment.

It was a lie. She had done no such thing.

She was not a thief.

Even now, it made her stomach clench to remember that look in her father's eyes. He'd believed it! she'd realized—all those hateful things the lawyer had been saying—he thought they were true. All the time she'd spent trying to win his approval—even twisting herself into someone she wasn't, a caricature of a celebrity—and she'd only succeeded in driving him further away. What an idiot she'd been! There was one thing prison taught you—if you go in seeking approval, you're bound to get kicked.

That was over. From now on, no more act. She'd be taking control of her life. She had heaps of money—okay, why not *do* something with it? She'd been nurturing a plan. An exciting plan— the kind of audacious, big-picture project her father would understand. Something that would really make a difference in people's lives, the way she'd felt she'd made a tiny difference to the women she'd tutored. She could hardly wait to get going on it—just thinking about it caused her spirits to soar.

She'd force her father to see her in a different light. Maybe she would never succeed in getting his true admiration.

But she'd damned well win his respect.

"Doran!"

Hannah was yanked from her thoughts by the sound of her name. It was Johnstone, the C.O. who vaguely resembled a bottle-blonde Rosie O'Donnell. One of the better C.O.'s: irritable and no rocket scientist, but neither was she a petty tyrant, like so many of the others. "Move your ass, Doran. We're kicking ya out."

Hannah grabbed the black trash bag containing her possessions. "It's about time! I was starting to think you couldn't stand to let me go."

"We can stand it fine. Come on, let's hustle."

In brisk lockstep, they traveled down concrete corridors painted the color of a bad smog day that even in the middle of a desert summer would retain a chill. And at the end of each corridor, a security checkpoint, buzzers and locks and touchpads and more buzzers and cameras staring with their inflamed single eyes.

Always and everywhere cameras.

Finally, they arrived at Receiving and Discharge where a raucous throng was already congregated. A party atmosphere: some two dozen women, shouting and whooping in excitement. Bumping hips and fists; slapping high-fives. A C.O. was bellowing: "Straight line! Form a straight line!" but nobody seemed to be paying attention.

"Hey, Doran, can ya believe it, we're gettin' out!" A woman with glistening corn-rows knocked a hip against Hannah's. Another younger woman who'd been one of Hannah's tennis students held up a palm: "*Vamos, niña!*" and Hannah slapped it jubilantly and replied: "You go too, girl!"

She went through the final steps. Surrendered her prison I.D. Collected a check for her work hours ($967.62). Received a carton containing the clothes she'd been wearing when she'd arrived. A shock of recognition: The dove gray Marc Jacobs jacket and pleated ivory linen shirt; the charcoal Ralph Lauren trousers.

The jacket was rumpled and reeking of someone else's body odor. The shirt had sweat stains in the armpits. And her shoes—a pair of black Chanel ballet flats—had been replaced by a size ten pair of metallic gray sneakers.

"Something wrong?" The prisoner in charge of personal effects was a woman from another dormitory. Hannah only knew by her last name, Costano. She had rusty freckles and large yellow-brown eyes.

"My shoes are missing. Somebody switched them for these."

"You wanna make out a complaint?"

Elements of Hannah's dream suddenly drifted back to her. "Hey, Costano," she said impulsively. "What do you think? Do you think these sneakers could be magic shoes?"

Costano narrowed her yellow eyes. Then gave a half-grin. "Sure. Why not?"

"Okay, then. No complaint." Hannah took the box and changed quickly in a curtained area. When she came back out, most of the women were already in street clothes. The party atmosphere had dissipated and many of them were standing anxiously by the exit. On the outskirts of this group, she saw two women she hadn't noticed before, one older, one younger. She tensed.

Valentina Rostov and Zizi Howell. They were the first two prisoners Hannah had met.

"Hello, Hannah. I am Valentina Rostov."

It was her first venture into the social room, two days after her arrival at Peachrock; she stood tentatively in the back, clutching a Louise Erdrich novel, overwhelmed by the din of the blaring t.v. and the other prisoners' raised voices. The woman, Valentina, who had spoken to her was of an indeterminate age, possibly forty, possibly fifty, at least six feet tall, with overblown, rather smeary features and a furious mane of orange-red hair. She must have been a knockout when she was younger.

"We are all knowing who you are, of course," she continued. A pronounced accent, Russian or possibly Bulgarian.

Another, younger woman appeared at her side. Pretty, cocoa-skinned, with gamine features and a giggle bubbling on her lips. "I'm Zizi," she introduced herself.

"My darling girl, Zizi Howell." Valentina curved an arm around her.

"We like to call ourselves the R.B.'s." Zizi fluttered her round dark eyes and giggled.

"Arbees?" Hannah said. "Like the fast-food place?"

"No, like the letters R. B.? It, like, stands for Rich Bitches?"

"We are the only upper-class chicks in this dog pit. You are definitely going to want to hang out with us." When Valentina Rostov smiled, her features smeared almost to a blur.

Valentina was originally from Moscow and was in for solicitation of prostitution and Zizi, who came from Inglewood, was serving time for swiping a Porsche from a valet stand in Venice

Beach—though they'd known each other some years before when they'd both worked as call girls for the renowned Malibu Madam. "Betsy Bell, very famous madam, you know," Valentina had declared, with what seemed like pride.

There were other prisoners who came in and out of the R.B.'s orbit—a Santa Barbara housewife who'd pushed her yacht dealer down a steep flight of stairs; an Orange County gym teacher who'd seduced a tenth grader—but the core of the clique remained Valentina and Zizi. They made no secret of being lovers: they openly kissed and petted each other.

At first Hannah was glad to be taken under the R.B.s' wing. They showed her the ropes, soothed and flattered her, and their constant chattering was distracting. They always had tidbits of intimate gossip about the rich and famous, fed to them from mysterious friends on the outside. Valentina received regular gifts of superb Beluga caviar from one of those friends and was generous about spreading it around. And Zizi had a talent for mimicry—celebrities, the guards, other prisoners—that could make Hannah laugh.

It was unsettling, though, that they seemed to possess a vast amount of information about Hannah herself. Valentina could rattle off details about her—the amount of her trust income, the décor of her home, and even about her grandfather, Jonas Sebring—things Hannah thought nobody had known except herself. "How do you know all this stuff?" she demanded.

Valentina blew a scornful puff of air. "Please. You are a famous girl, Doran. Everybody is knowing your life."

Maybe so, Hannah reflected. For the past few years she'd been flaunting her life in public. It was scary to think how much information was available, when every manicurist, and publicist's gofer, and maitre d' was a potential snitch to *The Star* or Perez Hilton. Who knew what she'd let slip in unguarded moments?

But why, she wondered, were the R.B.'s so interested in such trivia?

It stopped mattering, though, because Hannah soon began to draw away from them. Valentina, she'd realized, was cunning, selfish, and greedy. And if Zizi never meant any real harm, she had no ethical mooring either—she'd do whatever she wanted, right or wrong, without a flicker of conscience. Instead, Hannah enrolled in classes—Spanish conversation, Victorian lit—and volunteered to coach tennis to young women from the streets of Juarez and Compton on the dilapidated prison court.

Had the R.B.'s taken her withdrawal as a snub? Because Hannah suspected that the contraband that had kept her from parole—the pocket knife inside her mattress—had been planted by Valentina, or by Zizi acting on orders from her Russian squeeze.

Suspected—but had no way of proving it.

Her instinct was to avoid them now. But in a few more minutes, they'd never see each other again. *Why not part on good terms?*

She approached them with a peace-making smile. "Hey, guys! Can you believe it? We're all getting out together!"

"Yes, a fantastically coincidental event." Valentina spoke in a mocking tone.

Zizi bobbed her head gleefully. "First thing, we're gonna go to Dan Tana's to have filet mignon, and I'm going to order pink champagne. Why don't you come with us, Hannah? We're really gonna party!"

"No, not possible," Valentina said quickly. "Our plans are made."

"No problem," Hannah said. "I've got plans of my own. I just wanted to say good luck to you, and . . . well, thanks for all the Beluga."

"We ought to thank you!" Zizi giggled.

Hannah shot her a quizzical look.

But then an ear-splitting rasp announced the release of a lock, and Valentina, with Zizi in tow, shouldered past Hannah to join the surge to the exit. A pair of guards opened the steel doors, and the women spilled into the yard. Dressed in street clothes, mostly jeans with sweatshirts or hoodies, they looked oddly more uniform than they had in their motley prison-wear.

Another guard opened the chain-link gate. Hannah took her first step of freedom, breathing deeply the clean hot air of the late April desert. She watched the women disperse. Some boarded a white van that would ferry them to the bus station in the nearby town. Others romped towards husbands, mothers, friends waiting in cars and trucks.

She waited until she saw Valentina and Zizi disappear into one of those cars. Not the flashy model I'd expected their pick-up to be—it was an ancient maroon Cadillac with a Texas plate that read NO REGRETS.

Instinct made her wait until it had securely vanished from sight.

And then, clutching her trash bag, shuffling in her magic plastic sneakers, Hannah headed for the black limousine purring softly at the side of the road.

TWO

I got a tip. Hannah Sebring Doran is getting let out of jail today."

"Yeah, so?" Veteran combat photojournalist Mitchell J. Arpino, one hand fiddling with the mounting of the Nextel walkie-talkie on the dash, the other hand groping through the metallic jumble in his equipment bag, steered his eight-year-old Corvette with a knee through the hilly core of Bel-Air.

"It's. An. Exclusive!" Ajay Nayar, the voice on the walkie-talkie, was the sole proprietor of A&J Celebrity Shots; he had a way of sounding when excited like he was being squeezed to death by a snake, a cobra or whatever—each word like a last gasp. "Luxury condo building called the Bougainville. Highland and Wilshire. Around sixish. You need to stake out the street."

"Old news is no news, dude. Who's going to care?"

"I think there'll be interest. Her daddy's a big-time producer, right? And I'll bet you were conceived on a Sebring mattress, bro."

"It was probably a Beautyrest, *bro*, and what my parents screwed on thirty-one years ago ain't no news either."

"Come on, get me some snaps. My source is exclusive, right outta the parole office." Ajay had paid informants everywhere, like some sort of mega-nark. If a celebrity sprained a pinky toe or had a wiggy Pap smear, he'd know about it within the hour.

"Who else you got on it?" Mitch asked. Ajay usually sent his shooters out in packs, three or four. They'd surround the celeb like coyotes centering a stray cat "I'm short. It's just you. Good opportunity, my bro."

"Pass. I don't want anything to do with that chick."

"So how come?"

"I've got my reasons."

"What reasons?"

"*Reasons.*"

"Come on, spill it bro."

Mitch grabbed the steering wheel with both hands. "Okay. About two years ago, right? I was working a launch party at a penthouse suite in the Peninsula. For some new aftershave. Smelled like ball sacks if you asked me, but nobody did. I'd gotten everybody I'd come for, and so I wandered into a room where nobody else was and went out on the balcony for a smoke. A couple of minutes later, Hannah Doran appears. She's startled—didn't expect to find anybody else. I offered her a cigarette, and we got to talking and then laughing about stuff. And I'm feeling like we've got kind of, I don't know. A rapport . . . "

"A rapport?"

"Yeah. Like there's this spark between us. I'm thinking . . . Well, shit, never mind what I'm thinking. Then all of a sudden, she pops back into the room and slams the sliding door shut and locks it. And I'm out there all frigging night, until the maid finds me the next morning."

Ajay spluttered a laugh.

"Not funny, man. It was cold. The wind was blowing like a gale force and I was wearing just a T-shirt. I had nothing to eat. Had to piss off the balcony. And then sometime around dawn it started to rain. And I mean in buckets."

Ajay was beside himself with glee. "Priceless, bro!"

"Yeah. MasterCard freaking priceless."

"Come on, what had you done? You hit on her, right?"

"No. I mean, we kissed . . ."

"I knew it! Whoa! You overstepped, bro. You're lucky she didn't push you over the rail. One of her famous temper tantrums."

Mitch dismissed such luck with a grunt. "Anyway, like I said, nobody's gonna care if she's out of jail or not. Her producer daddy's a has-been. The Flop King."

"You gotta keep up with the blogs, dude. Warren Doran is back. He's redoing *Wildwood Murphy* for Constellation. A whole new trilogy, with a monster 3D budget."

"You can't make *Wildwood* without Jackson Brandt, and Jackson Brandt is dead and gone to legendary-film-star heaven. Probably taking turns doing Marilyn with Elvis."

"The blogs speak, and they say Denny Brandt is going to fill his daddy's shoes. He's set to play Wildwood."

"Oh, yeah?" Mitch, who had resumed navigating with his knee, suddenly gripped the wheel with his right hand to negotiate the swing onto Roscomare. "That's interesting, because it just so happens, I'm on to something with Denny right now."

"Really?" Ajay gasped. "What? A sighting? Where the hell are you?"

"I'm up in the hills, and I've gotta concentrate. I'll call you in an hour when I've got something."

"Yes! Call!" Ajay gasped.

Mitch turned off his phone just in case anyone was making a sweep for cellular activity in the area. It wasn't possible to be too paranoid right now, because what he was about to do was A: probably illegal; B: definitely unethical; and C: pandering to the lowest common denominator that drove about ninety-nine percent of media content these sorry days. The last of which wasn't a crime, he allowed, but ought to be.

Technically speaking, he was a member of the paparazzi. Having once been a legitimate combat photographer, he saw definite parallels. This was a war, no doubt about it. The enemy was on all sides: the celebs who'd just as soon see him dead; the cops who hated his guts; and most of all the other paps, who'd willingly, even cheerfully, draw blood—his or anyone else's—in order to grab the money shot.

He'd been at it for over three years now, and that practically made him a grizzled vet. Most kids who jumped into the game—now mostly Colombians, Afghanis, Israelis, Persians—they burned out in the first few months. Couldn't take the pace and the pressure.

Mitch veered off Roscomare onto a side road, swerving to let a truck barrel past. As he did, he caught a glimpse of his face in the side view mirror: strong bone structure courtesy of a distant Creek Indian ancestor; somewhat too-snubby nose; a reasonably firm chin currently adorned by a didn't-get-around-to-shaving-this-morning stubble. Dark curly hair with too many cowlicks to qualify as Byronic and therefore fell under the category of "mop." Not bad-looking. Except for an inquisitive, slightly sardonic, expression in his brown eyes, his was the kind of medium-rugged face that might belong to an actor in some Law & Order spin-off. Or a guy modeling duck waders for L.L.Bean; or maybe a middle inning reliever for the Angels . . .

No, strike the last one. To Mitch's lifelong regret, he'd never exhibited any special athletic prowess.

But he had been bestowed with one singular talent, which he

thought of as The Eye. Given his first camera at the age of twelve—a basic Minolta SLR—he'd felt instantly that it was a logical and necessary extension of his own optic nerve. Framing, focusing, capturing the vital image in a split-second—these seemed like natural reflexes.

He fell in love with the work of the great photojournalists of the past. Was amazed by how Dorothea Lange and Walker Evans could capture the Great Depression in a single face. How Weegee, the New York City press photographer, could document an entire crime in one flash photo.

This was what he wanted to do, Mitch realized—to tell great stories with a camera.

For his MFA thesis at Roski, he shot a portfolio of preteen kids who sewed diaper bags in a sweatshop in downtown L.A. Thirteen hours a day for a few scraps of tortilla and a flea-infested straw mat. They were essentially slaves. When the school exhibited the portfolio, the sweatshop was busted, and the kids put in decent foster care. Mitch had broken his first story.

He was hired by the *L.A. Times*. Paid his dues by shooting brush fires and Cinco de Mayo parades. Got transferred to the New Delhi bureau and then embedded with a Marines combat unit in Afghanistan, patrolling the treacherous provinces north of Kabul. War, he discovered, was the ultimate story. He was following in the footsteps of Robert Capa, the greatest of all combat photographers.

Five months in, he caught some shrapnel: it gouged a thigh and just missed his jugular, leaving a star-burst scar at the base of his neck (it would prove almost as seductive to women as a long lens). But it abruptly ended his foreign posting.

No way he was going back to covering fires and parades. At night, when the slivers of metal still raw in his leg and neck made it hard to sleep, he began thinking of those Mexican kids sewing diaper bags. He'd seen ten and eleven-year-old prostitutes soliciting on the back streets of New Delhi and Bangkok and Jakarta. There had to be millions of kids forced into slavery in every corner of the globe. When he'd recuperated enough, he dug up a grant from a children's charity to do a book and accompanying documentary to be called *Underaged Slaves*, with the promise of more funds to follow. He began to shoot in Thailand.

Fast-forward nineteen months. He was in Haiti where kids orphaned by AIDS or the quake were routinely sold as "servants." He had a bad case of turista, bowels liquefied. He'd maxed out three credit cards, and the local he'd hired as soundman had vanished with half of his equipment. He called the charity to plead for more cash.

The charity was bust. It had sunk its entire endowment into an investment fund that turned out to be a Ponzi.

Back in L.A., Mitch crashed on a friend's couch while fruitlessly job-hunting. Newspapers and magazines were firing or folding—nobody was even hiring stringers. Five weeks later, he was nursing a mojito at Hyde Lounge, mulling over his nonexistent options, when the scrawny, hyperactive guy at the bar next to him struck up a conversation. This was Ajay Nayar. Successful paparazzo—had recently jumped ship from one of the major agencies to set up on his own.

"Most agencies will steal the balls from right under your dick," he told Mitch, manically swirling his Coke Zero with a straw. "They'll insist on buying all rights to your shots for a flat fee. You get no taste of the upside. But me, I'll cut you in for forty percent of all future sales. I sell one of your shots to some German or Dutch tabloid for twenty thou, that's a quick eight grand in your pocket, bro."

Forget it. Mitch was a photojournalist, not some sleaze of a celeb-hound.

But Ajay was persistent, and Mitch began to feel a tug: Why the hell not? He was living in the heart of L.A. surrounded by privilege and money. High school kids driving Beemers. Pricy clubs packed with spoiled slackers.

Why not grab a little for himself?

He started slow, getting his sea legs by taking part in the paparazzi gangbangs outside Kitson when one of the Kardashians had been sighted, or racing the pack after Britney or Miley. Then he began prowling solo, working from a combination of instinct and tips on the ever-streaming web feeds. He developed the requisite capacity for stealth and the willingness to bend the rules. Shooting red lights and stop signs; going the wrong way on one-way streets. Camouflaging himself in a tree or in the brush on hillsides. Effecting disguises; sniffing out the unguarded entrances.

And he had the advantage of The Eye. The skill to frame and focus in a split second. The ability to choose a good shot from a worthless one under intense pressure. He began netting ten, twelve thousand a month.

But it was getting tougher. There were too many shooters now. Any tweener with a camera phone could score if Zac Efron or Lindsay Lohan happened to show up in the vicinity. And many of the paps who worked for the bigger agencies were nothing more than thugs. There were increasing incidents of violence, free-lancers getting stomped. Mitch had begun to stow a can of Mace in his camera bag.

He was almost thirty. It was time to get out. Back to his real life's work.

If he could just nail one really big money shot. One that would pay out a hefty six figures. Like, for instance, the first and exclusive photo of an A-list star's baby.

Or an A-list star's corpse.

Or, really, an A-list star doing anything freaky, self-destructive, or in the nude.

Hence his current plan: he'd been driving up here yesterday around 4 p.m., beating traffic on Sunset by taking Roscomare up through Bel-Air to Mulholland. Passed a private lane that was well known to the paparazzi—it was shared by a few gated estates, one of which was occupied by Denny Brandt, the red-hot young actor and son of the legendary Jackson Brandt, along with his girlfriend, the romantic comedy princess Cristina Townsend. They'd recently gotten engaged, an event sealed with a flawless pink diamond ring, 8.6 carats. Rumored to have cost three quarters of a million dollars.

Crissie was never shy about flaunting herself to the media: close-ups of the pink diamond on her finger had scintillated like a newly-discovered galaxy on the front page of every tabloid. Her fiancé was a different matter. Denny Brandt was known in paparazzi terms as a "shark"—a major star who eluded being photographed. Didn't go out much—and when he did, always kept his head down or obscured his face with hats and scarves and shades. A clear shot of him would be worth a bundle.

As Mitch had passed the private lane, several construction crew trucks had come barreling out. On an instinct, he pulled a U and drove back up the lane. Pay dirt! A third home was being built on a lot adjacent to Denny's. The wood framing was complete, the flooring and interior staircases were in, but no walls yet. A couple of guys were padlocking the gates on the chain-link fence surrounding the construction.

Mitch approached them. A conversation in halting English and mangled Spanish. He handed out a few benjamins, and a deal was struck.

Now he stopped a good way down the road. The Vette was not what you'd call a stealth car. A C5 coupe painted Road Hazard Yellow, with a 350 h.p. roar. Bought for peanuts from an Israeli who'd been loosely connected to E! Online and for unspecified reasons had to suddenly blow town. Mitch was aware that to some people the Vette made him seem cooler than he actually was; and to others, it just made him seem like a dick. He justified it by telling himself its speed gave him a crucial edge when it came to chases. But the fact was, he loved the damned machine. A baby rocket that went 0–60 in 4.7 seconds.

Which, considering, it actually got pretty good mileage. Maybe should get a bumper sticker pointing that out.

The gate was padlocked shut. Mitch selected one of the cameras from his bag—the Canon with the long lens, 17–85mm., its body wound with dull gray electrical tape for protection—and the three inch PocketPod tripod. He proceeded up to the chain-link fence. It was 4:36: all work had ceased, and the crew had cleared out. He circled the fence to the back where there was a smaller gate behind a line of Port-O-Sans.

As promised, it was unlocked.

He walked quickly into the construction site. Climbed a staircase to the second floor. Skirting piles of sheetrock and lumber, he headed to the eastern exposure and gazed out from the edge.

Denny Brandt was in town. It stood to reason that he'd come in or out of his home before the end of the day. Mitch stretched out on the flooring, fastened the Canon to the mini-tripod, then propped himself on his elbows and peered through the long lens. An unobstructed view to the grounds next door.

Christ, man. He drew back, hesitating. He was doing something he swore he'd never do—lurking outside a residence. Doorstepping, it was called in the trade.

Then he thought of Denny Brandt. Arrogant bastard, born into Hollywood royalty. Everything handed to him on a platter.

And Crissie Townsend. Known for squashing underlings like bugs. Screaming fits when she didn't get exactly her own way. The relentless pursuit of her own fame.

Screw it! He peered back through the lens.

Something suddenly whizzed over his head and slammed into one of the framing beams behind him.

Jesus! It was an arrow! The point lay deeply embedded in the wood of the beam, the shaft and fletching still quivering.

Another one whizzed by, missed the beam and sailed on through the open framing.

What the hell? He glanced wildly back at the other house. Someone had appeared on the ground floor patio. Shit, it was Denny

Brandt! He was wearing one of those short Japanese robes called a hapi coat, and he was bare-legged and barefoot. And he was threading another arrow into an antique-looking crossbow.

"Hey!" Mitch yelled. "I'm up here!"

Denny Brandt drew back on the bow and let loose the shaft.

Mitch flattened himself. *Tha-wunk!* The arrow struck a far beam. *Holy jumping god, this was serious shit!*

He grabbed his equipment and scrambled rapidly across the flooring. Adrenaline pumping, he dove for the stairs, skidded down them on his ass. A pocket of his jeans caught on a nail head, momentarily fixing him in place. He yanked hard. The pocket tore. And then he was off in a sprint, propelling himself out of the framework and back through the Port-O-San gate.

He stopped in his tracks. Two men were standing beside his car. One was very big, the other was very small. Both wore shades with titanium frames, opaque lenses.

Maybe, Mitch thought wildly, he could hide in one of the Port-O-Sans and stay locked in until the coast was clear. But they'd already spotted him; and the big one was huge, a Samoan or Hawaiian, circular face, looked like a Thanksgiving parade balloon packed with meat—could probably pick up the toilet and shake Mitch out like grit from a shoe. He was strangling a baseball bat by the neck, a composite-type DeMarini Voodoo.

"Sir? Excuse me, sir." He spoke with that phony-deferential tone that was the hallmark of security muscle everywhere. "I'm going to have to ask you for that camera."

"No way."

The Samoan stepped forward, swinging the bat from his fist in a little pendulum motion. Mitch took his measure: despite the guy's size, he could probably drop him with a feint and a left hook. But there were two of them. And the small guy, all vintage Afghan Whigs T-shirt and greaser rattail, was toting a pair of heavy gauge pliers.

Mitch clutched the camera like an infant to his breast. "Look, guys, be reasonable. I'll delete the shots, okay?"

"Gotta take it, sir."

And now Denny Brandt materialized from the private road connecting the two properties. He was still wearing the hapi coat, but his feet were now slapping in yellow rubber flip-flops.

Mitch had to give him credit—Denny was one hell of a handsome dude. Lot of stars, the camera loves 'em, but when you see them in person, they diminish—they're actually way shorter than you think or there's something sort of freakish about their faces, a lopsided lip, or a lantern jaw. But not this movie star. Not old Denny Brandt. A buffed and perfectly proportioned six-footer, with that shag of auburn hair cut to achieve maximum fabulousness. And just a touch of Irish wildness in the famous brown-black eyes that kept him from too pretty.

Mitch decided to take the offensive. "Are you out of your mind? You frigging tried to kill me!"

A corner of Denny's mouth lifted sardonically. "If I wanted to kill you, you'd be one dead son of a bitch right now."

"You shot frigging arrows at my head! I could have you arrested."

"Would you like me to call the police, sir?" smirked the Samoan.

Mitch hesitated. Sure, call the L.A.P.D. Like they were really going to believe that Denny Brandt had ambushed him with a bow and arrow. Like hell they were—particularly since Rat Tail Boy was now scrambling around up in the framing, busily prying all the evidence out of the beams with those pliers.

What was more likely to happen, what would *absolutely* happen, is that Mitch would be hit with charges of trespassing, invasion of privacy, insulting a movie star, god only knew what else.

He shook his head. "No cops."

"Good choice," Denny said. "JoJo, would you please dispose of the camera?

"You got it, Denny."

The Samoan snatched the Canon still attached to the mini-pod, flipped out the memory card, dropped the equipment and whacked it with the DeMarino.

"Fucking hell!" Mitch wheeled on Denny. "I'll sue you, you crazy asshole!"

"Be my guest."

Denny had been sued twice, Mitch recalled, both times by paps: one whose jaw the star had busted; the other after Denny had taken a baseball bat (possibly the very same DeMarini the Samoan was now twirling in his gigantic fist) and whacked the hell out of the photographer's Mustang. Both lawsuits had come to nothing.

"I suggest you leave now, sir." The Samoan manufactured another deferential smirk.

"One more thing," Denny said to Mitch. "I've got a head for numbers. I see a license plate once, I never forget it. I've got yours in my head, meaning whenever I want, I can always find out every single detail of your life."

"What's that supposed to mean?"

"Whatever you want."

Mitch stared into the star's eyes. Black and wild, almost wheeling wild. But with a clear intelligence behind them. Denny had gone to Yale, he recalled—or was it Harvard? When you were the best-looking human being on the planet, it made it easy for people to forget you also had a brain.

"Yeah, whatever," Mitch said.

He picked up the battered hunk of metal that used to be his Canon and climbed back into his Vette. Pulled a screeching K-turn and ripped out of the lane.

Okay, that was a total bust, but maybe it was also an omen. A sign from the universe. He'd sold his soul, and it was high time he started getting it back.

Forget chasing the quick buck. Find a real story. Something he could sink his teeth into.

He flashed on Ajay's tip: Hannah Doran released from jail. When she'd been sentenced, Mitch hadn't exactly cried. He'd been nursing that grudge.

But he remembered being amazed that she had quickly accepted a basically crappy deal, without seeming to even consider going to trial. She had no prior offenses. The surveillance tape from the jewelry store had been obscured by other customers, so there was no hard proof of a deliberate theft. In a town where celebrities literally got away with murder, she should've gotten a slap on the wrist. Token jail sentence, or possibly even probation, with a side of community service.

So . . . why did she leap at a two year stretch? And why hadn't she been sprung way before this on probation? Was there something else there? Like maybe the shoplifting charge had been a cover for something bigger? Or she'd been covering for somebody else—one of her BBF's or a boyfriend?

Or maybe there'd been nothing. It was all exactly as it went down.

Only one way to find out. He buzzed Ajay.

"It didn't pan out with Dennistina. Give me the Doran address again."

THREE

I t was Hannah's father who'd sent the limo to pick her up. A classic Warren Doran touch: *You get the best of everything. You just don't get me.*

For one wild moment, Hannah had thought it *was* her father emerging from the car with his customary exuberant step. But no, it was just the navy-jacketed driver, springing to open the back door for her.

As they pulled away, she'd caught him sneaking peeks at her in his rearview mirror. Did he recognize her? She could imagine him later telling his wife or his buddies: "Hey, guess who was my afternoon pick-up? Hannah Doran! Remember? Rich party girl, got nabbed pocketing a diamond necklace from some fancy-schmancy store in Beverly Hills? It was all over the t.v. back then. Hangover Hannah they called her? I had to haul way the hell out to the desert, the women's pen outside of Barstow."

It didn't matter. That was the past. In the future, she was going to turn all that around.

But thinking about it—that awful nickname—triggered a replay in her mind of the day of her arrest. She tried to untangle the events that were still a blur. It had been October, hot and tinder dry, a wildfire raging somewhere to the south of the city. She'd been out until two the night before, a party on the roof of the Standard, slugging back far too much Grey Goose, not getting home until 4 a.m., and that day she'd been dragged to lunch at La Scala with two of her best friends, Cristina Townsend and Lorian Merrick. Crissie, her sitcom still at number one in the ratings, had landed her first movie role, a romantic comedy opposite the red-hot actor Denny Brandt, and she was babbling on about it, and Lorian, who played at being a publicist, was waxing enthusiastic. Hannah, her head throbbing, picked at the avocado in her chopped salad.

And then Shawn appeared. Shawn Serafian, the man she'd recently fallen in love with—an artist, great-looking in the way Hannah particularly adored, all slouchy and hollow-cheeked, with a tousle of unkempt dark hair. "Just sold an acrylic to a collector from Palos Verdes!" he crowed. "Seventy thou—didn't even haggle!" He ordered champagne, and Hannah hadn't wanted to step on his celebration, so she let him pour her a glass and drank a few toasts, and then let him top the glass off.

Then Shawn left to go back to his studio. Crissie began wheedling Hannah and Lorian to walk over with her to Charles Gray, the exclusive jeweler on Rodeo, to help her select a piece to wear to the Emmys. "Come on, guys, you *know* I can't make these kind of decisions by myself."

From that point, everything got progressively fuzzier. The small shop was crowded, four or five other customers besides the three of them. An Asian salesgirl with magenta hair laying necklaces and pendants on a strip of deep black velvet. Crissie, always the princess, trying piece after piece, draping each one around Hannah's or Lorian's neck, rejecting them all, demanding to see others.

Hannah suddenly feeling so violently ill she staggered out into the fresh air.

Somehow she made it back to the valet at La Scala and got in her car and began to drive; but at the corner of Wilshire and Fairfax, she had to pull over and throw up. And that's where the cops showed up: a vertiginous revolving of lights. She had the blurriest of memories of a policeman foraging through the caverns of her Prada bag, triumphantly pulling out something sparkling. A necklace—a double strand of diamonds and cabochon rubies set in filigreed white gold.

Retail price: two hundred and twenty-five thousand dollars.

After her arraignment, with reporters swarming and leaping like sand fleas, she'd blurted something about the Mascara Fizzes and feeling sick and woozy. The media had had a field day with it: *A HANGOVER MADE HER DO IT!*

And maybe it had, she thought now, watching the dun and sage-colored desert speed by. But in the dozens and dozens of times she'd tried to reconstruct the scene, she had never been able to picture opening the clasp of her bag, dropping the necklace in, and fastening the clasp again.

Could she really have been that hungover?

The desert out the window began to give way to outer urban—low-rise office buildings; clustered tracts of identical tile-roofed homes; artificial patches of irrigated foliage. Then the car was negotiating a metallic tangle of intersecting freeways, and her excitement grew as the downtown L.A. skyline rose like Oz on the left.

They crept in rush hour traffic down Cahuenga, then onto Franklin, paralleling the densely-settled Hollywood Hills, the famous, dopey Hollywood Sign peeping in and out of view. And now they were winding through the neighborhood of Hancock Park, sycamores furred with new leaf, and tall, feather-headed palms flanking the graceful old mansions. Hannah's heart skipped as she caught sight of her building—an Art Deco wedding cake called the Bougainville, built in the Thirties and reminiscent of the glamour of the era.

She was home!

The car glided into the building's portico. The concierge, galvanized by the sight of a limo, shot out from the adjoining office. Eddie—he'd been head concierge here since practically the Jurassic period. Hadn't changed much—just gotten puffier, his face a strawberry soufflé rising badly between his cap and collar. He snapped the door open smartly.

"Hi, Eddie," she said.

He gave a startled skip backwards. "Sweet lord in heaven! Hannah?"

So it was "Hannah" now? In the past, it had always been "Miss Doran" this and "Miss Doran" that. But fair enough, she thought. "Yeah, it's me. I'm back." She grabbed the trash bag and slid out of the car.

Eddie's gaze took in the bag, the garish sneakers, the crumpled clothes. He was nearly rigid with astonishment. "Nobody told me you'd be coming," he managed.

"Nobody was told. I didn't want any fuss."

"No reporters or nothing, huh? I gotcha." He grinned and rocked back a little on his heels. "Nothing like last time, huh?"

She didn't mind that he didn't leap to open the lobby door, as he would have in the past. She'd spent over a year having to wait for some CO to release a buzzer or turn a key in the lock. It felt delicious just to be able to open a door for herself.

She entered the lobby, noting changes. That potted fern was

new. A bench with velvet cushions had vanished. At the reception desk, a young man she didn't recognize.

Eddie followed her in. "Hey, your people changed your locks. For security reasons. I got your new keys in the office. Hold on a sec, I'll get 'em for you."

Lugging her black trash bag, Hannah crossed to the ornate brass cage of the elevator and pressed the button. The lift began its slow descent from an upper floor with a familiar clunk. *I'm home,* she thought with almost bewilderment. *I'm really home!*

"Hannah!" somebody called.

She turned. A guy walking toward her, black jeans, baseball cap, shades. Canvas bag slung over a shoulder. In one hand, a blur of gray shooting light.

Without thinking, she hurled the trash bag at him. Another lesson from Peachrock: you react first, think later.

She heard him give a yell as the bag hit him. The knots became untied and the contents flew out and scattered over the marble floor. At the same time, the elevator cage rattled open, and she threw herself in, hitting the top button. The elevator rose with a jolt.

How did he know? she wondered. *And how many others would there be?*

The elevator opened at the penthouse floor, directly in front of her door. She didn't have the key, she realized. She gave a growl of frustration and hit the door with the palm of her hand.

And then Eddie erupted from the service elevator down the hall. "Jesus, god, I'm sorry. He must have sneaked in when Michael was on the phone or something."

"Is he still here?"

"Nah, he beat it. But, boy! You sure got him good! Bet he never saw that one coming." Eddie eyed her with a certain admiration. He was holding a few of my scattered things—a couple of cards, the photo of her mother, Pamela—and a silver key ring. "Here's your keys and some stuff I picked up. I've got Michael getting the rest. I'll bring it up."

"A little later, okay, Eddie? I'll call down and let you know."

"Sure thing, Hannah. Just call down and let me know." Eddie headed back to the service lift.

Hannah turned the double locks and pushed open the door and stood frozen on the threshold. The duplex had an eclectic Moroccan décor, and the profusion of beautiful objects and jewel colors was for a moment so dazzling she had to shut her eyes.

Then she went in, kicked off the ridiculous sneakers and wriggled her toes on a soft carpet. She dropped down and made snow angels on the carpet, scissoring her arms and legs. She leaped up onto a couch and bounced up and down. She jumped off the couch and began wandering through the rooms, picking up items, staring at their shapes and feeling their heft. Making sure it wasn't only a dream.

Maybe it was the past year that had been a dream: the Peachrock camp, and the C.O.'s, and the cement block corridors, and Valentina Rostov and her R.B.'s. . . .

All just a bad dream.

She scampered up the floating acrylic staircase to the second floor and went into her bedroom. She tumbled onto the canopied bed, feeling like Goldilocks, finding the bed that was just right. The incredible luxury of a soft, thick mattress! She leapt off it and went into the master bath—another bit of heaven with its rain forest shower and sunken Jacuzzi tub.

She caught her reflection in a mirror. Yikes! Her shoulder-length brown hair scraggly as an old hippy's. Her skin dull, her lips pallid. These rumpled, smelly clothes. No wonder Eddie had seemed so taken aback.

She knelt to the sunken tub. Turned the taps on full blast and poured in half a bottle of bath oil, infusing the air with the scent of lemon verbena. She peeled off her ruined garments and prison-issue bra and panties and immersed herself in the steaming foam. There'd been only one rust-stained bathtub in her Peachrock dorm's communal bathroom, in a stall with a door off its hinges—she hadn't had a bath in complete privacy in over a year.

She closed her eyes, moaning with the bliss of it.

And then her eyes shot open.

It was crazy, she knew. But she suddenly had the feeling that she was being watched.

⊃⥎⤶

Mitch Arpino regrouped himself back on the street. In the past few hours he'd been shot at with arrows by a maniac movie star and then whacked with a Hefty by a jailbird heiress. But what the hell . . . he reflected philosophically. Just another glamorous day in the life of a paparazzo.

But he wasn't done here. Not by a long shot. If anything, this had raised even more questions. Why was Hannah Doran coming home from a longish prison stretch all by herself? Where was her daddy? Her dozens of fancy friends?

Something else ticked at him. He lifted his camera—the Olympus 18x Zoom he used for close-up work. Flipped back through the shots he'd gotten of her. Zoomed in on her face closely. Yeah—there was some hint of resemblance to someone else he knew. Or rather, someone he'd snapped recently, possibly in close-up . . .

As he headed to his car, his mind shuffled quickly through a portrait gallery of actresses, models, American Idol contestants, Grammy winners, TV talking heads . . .

Nope, came up blank.

And then he noticed the SUV—a dusty green 4Runner parked at the red curb directly in front of Mitch's Vette. A guy with a fat, square face behind the wheel. A handicap placard dangling in the windshield. Another shooter—it had to be. The handicap sign was no doubt a counterfeit. A lot of paparazzi used them—a cripple sticker they called it. A trick of the trade Mitch despised: his mom had M.S—the simplest errands were already a huge deal for her without some ass-wipe hogging her designated parking spots.

So Ajay's exclusive source wasn't so damned exclusive after all.

Mitch went up to the 4Runner's window. Fat Face was reaching for something out of a cooler on the back seat. In front beside him, Mitch could see a headset, a pair of military binoculars. And a couple of photos, unmistakably of Hannah.

He thumped his fist on the window. If the sitting jump were an Olympic sport, Fat Face would have grabbed the gold.

Handicapped, my ass. Mitch shot him the finger.

The guy turned the ignition and floored it.

Mitch watched him speed away. He was suddenly seized by a realization: Fat Face was no paparazzo. He was a cop. FBI, L.A.P.D. . . . .

But a fed or an L.A.P.D. cop wouldn't be working solo.

A private dick, then.

Mitch's entire being prickled with heightened sensation. Definitely a big, fat, juicy story here. He stared back at Hannah Doran's building, at the top, the penthouse floor. "I'll be back," he muttered in a lousy Schwarzenegger imitation.

It still nagged at him: who the hell was it that she reminded him of?

⁂

Disgraced ex-L.A.P.D. officer Roger Lopez, working surveillance outside the Bougainville condominium building on the corner of Highland and Palmera, was in the process of removing a box of Almond Breeze unsweetened chocolate non-dairy beverage from the cooler on the seat beside him, when a thump on the window made him jump.

Outside, some asshole in a Nike swoosh cap, shooting him the bird.

What the hell?

He scrambled to turn on the engine and pull out, looking back at Nike Swoosh in the rearview mirror with an unease that bordered on alarm. He wondered if he'd been made by his subject—the girl who occupied the penthouse floor, the one he was being paid to listen in on. And if so, was this a signal—some joker the mark had sent out to let him know that *she* knew he was there?

Or was it just some civic-minded asshole who objected to him parking at a red curb?

Either way, it was nothing he was interested in reporting back to his boss. Don't ask, don't tell. Rule number one in this business.

He cautiously circled the block, made sure Nike Swoosh had taken off. Then he parked again, shook the Almond Breeze like a canister of dice, opened it and chugged it down. Since working private security, he'd packed on forty pounds. The wife had stuck him on a low carb diet, ordering him up stuff from a website called Carbs Begone. It was working okay—he'd dropped maybe five, six pounds. Except now he was in this thing called ketosis, meaning his sweat smelled worse than cat piss and his breath could blast paint off the side of a battleship. When the wife started moaning, he'd said "Hey, you want fat or you want stink. You choose."

He flipped the empty box back into the cooler. He was still unnerved by Nike Swoosh.

This whole job unnerved him. When Lopez first started working private surveillance, it was for Marco DaSilvio, the notorious Hollywood private investigator, since convicted on sixteen counts of racketeering and conspiracy. It was from DaSilvio that Lopez had learned what a snap it was to spy on anybody, just a few easy tricks to get inside a home or office and plant your bugs and maybe a couple of pinhole cameras. Any moron could tap a phone: you just needed to know how to get into the phone company's neighborhood "b-box" and locate your mark's cable pair; and after that, about sixty bucks worth of Radio Shack equipment would get the job done.

DaSilvio was just a cartoon goon—forever shooting his blubbery mouth off about the celebs who hired him to get the dirt on their ex-wives or the head of some rival studio. The spy with the loose lips, that was DaSilvio.

And yeah, sure, some of what he'd done was illegal. There was invasion of privacy. Some small time intimidation tactics had been employed. But nobody got hurt really, except in the wallet—and DaSilvio's marks had been folks who could definitely afford to lighten up in that department.

But the guy who'd recruited Lopez for this assignment was a fish of a different color. Thirtyish. Close-cropped hair. Almost nondescript. Called himself Cherry. Stripper name. Weird.

"So what's the interest here?" Lopez had asked. He had to know something about the perimeters—the scope of a job. What to hone in on. Nine times out of ten, it was a cheating spouse, catch 'em in the act.

"Protecting an investment." The guy, Cherry, stared at Lopez.

Before getting kicked off the squad, Lopez had worked eight years in the hellhole of narcotics. He sure as shit knew a killer when he saw one.

Maybe he should bag this job. Get out while the getting was good. But the money was significant, and he was a couple of months behind on the payments for his Tuscan villa-style three bedroom out in Simi Valley.

Somebody was gonna take the gig, so it might as well be him.

Through his earpiece he picked up sounds of life coming from up in the penthouse condo. He grabbed a zero carb onion bagel from the cooler, tore off the cellophane wrapper with his teeth and, chewing with gusto, he settled back to listen.

FOUR

The rumor that Alicia Chenoweth, senior executive vice-president of Worldwide Production at the family-friendly motion picture studio Constellation Pictures, had once been a hooker in the stable of the Malibu Hills Madam, was a rumor that everyone in Hollywood had heard, and everyone had repeated, and everyone knew to be totally false.

Absurdly false, in fact. Bossy, motherly Alicia, with her just-this-side-of-dumpy body and deceptively sweet face . . . The former schoolteacher who'd steered such PG movies as *Santa's Little Helpers* and *Ferdie the Green Dinosaur* . . . Granted, she had fabulous tits and a tiny waist, and those short legs of hers were pretty damned shapely . . .

But still . . . Alicia?

Please! It was just one more of those silly Hollywood urban legends that continue to make the rounds long after everybody knows they're nonsense—like the actress whispered to be really a hermaphrodite; or the actor with a gerbil up his famous butt.

The fact that the rumor happened to be true would have flabbergasted most of the people who'd so gleefully passed it along. But true it was: for several weeks, at the age of twenty-one, Alicia Joanne Chenoweth had been a working member of Madam Betsy Bell's notorious establishment.

And at the moment, as she stood waiting for the elevator in the fifth floor of the Constellation production building, she had the strangest impulse to reveal this early item of her résumé to the intern who'd just come creeping up to her.

"Hey, uh, Alicia? Cody Takish needs to see you in his office, like in, uh, ten minutes?" The intern was a junior at USC, but looked about twelve.

"What's it about?" she said sharply.

The kid looked like he was about to wet his pants. "I, uh, I mean his assistant didn't tell me. She just said it was, like, urgent."

Little boy, Alicia was tempted to say, *I was turning tricks for the Malibu Madam when you were still in diapers, so you don't have to be in awe of me.*

She did not say it, of course. She had never told anybody, and never would. "Okay, thank you, Adam. You can tell Jacqueline I'll be there."

She turned and marched back into her dazzlingly beautiful office and buzzed her assistant: "Rollie, call Mommy and Me and tell them I'll be about thirty minutes late."

Then she sat rather primly down on the azure blue leather couch, and folded her shapely legs beneath her, and, gazing out at her panoramic view of the San Fernando Valley, considered how much she despised Cody Takish, president of Worldwide Production, the thirty-six-year-old weasel who happened to be her boss.

For her fortieth birthday, with two failed marriages under her belt, Alicia had gifted herself with a vial of sperm from a top-rated Santa Monica fertility center. The sperm had been manufactured by a six-foot-two, hundred and ninety-seven pound, cardiac surgical resident. Light brown hair, hazel eyes, no family history of genetic disease. Black diamond skier. Jazz clarinet player. Jewish on his mother's side. Nine months to the day after she was inseminated with this uber-sperm, she gave birth to a pair of hazel-eyed baby girls, whom she named after two of her favorite movies, *Laura* and *Shane.* From the moment she first cradled them in her arms, her passion for these miracle babies exceeded anything she'd ever felt for a man.

Cody Takish knew she'd be leaving at precisely this moment to be with her daughters at Mommy and Me. He could have called her in at any time during the day to discuss whatever matter had crossed his trivial mind. But he'd waited until now, knowing she'd be anxious to get going. Thinking he could ram anything he wanted down her throat.

Think again, you little turd.

She focused on the hazy expanse of the Valley. Miles and miles of little ranch homes, each with its carport and patch of yard. In some alternate universe, that's where she was living, in one of those ranch homes. Teaching second grade. Married to the wrestling coach. A five-year-old Prius in the carport and a minivan on the street.

And that would have been her life, except for that one night when she was twenty-one years old. She'd been finishing up her teaching degree at Northridge State, waiting tables on weekends at a local Marie Callender's, sharing an apartment with a wild child named Marcy.

That night, a Wednesday, Marcy had said, "Hey, want to come to this really cool party with me?" and Alicia, who should have been studying, impulsively said, "Sure." They drove high up into the scorched hills east of Malibu, to a house built like a concrete box. Some surly men in mirrored dark glasses stopped them, and Marcy had spoken some password—"tuna salad" or "tapioca pudding"— some deli food was all Alicia could remember, and then they were permitted to pass.

Inside was the strangest place Alicia had ever seen. Black shag carpeting covered the floors and the furniture was gold. Jungle plants flourished in huge Chinese pots and ornate birdcages hung from the ceiling. The cages were empty—the only bird was a large blue parrot who strutted around freely, squawking lyrics from "Papa Don't Preach."

There was a kind of cocktail party going on. The women were all young and gorgeous, dressed in the glitter-trash styles of the late '80s. The men came in all ages and all degrees of attractiveness. A few looked like scruffier versions of movie and t.v. stars (they *were* those stars, Alicia would find out later). Others—older, stockier, wearing suits or sports jackets—looked like they ran powerful companies (they did). Still others were a type she couldn't place, youngish with wiry builds and a hyped-up quality like roosters on speed.

Marcy immediately shot off. Alicia huddled in a corner, gulping a strong margarita, grateful when one of the wiry guys began chatting her up. He was a kid trying too hard to be cool, all *Spinal Tap* shag, and a *Miami Vice* two day stubble, and Aviator shades even though the lights were low. He talked nonstop and fast in a Jersey accent that made her giggle. She had liked him.

Then a lady approached. Fiftyish—by far the oldest female in the room. Pink lace dress. Slightly crepey cleavage set off by a demure string of pearls. Black hair lacquered into a Jackie Kennedy pouf. She shook her head curtly at Jersey Boy and he immediately slunk off. Alicia remembered thinking just that: *He's slinking off!*

The lady squeezed Alicia's hand affectionately. "My heavens, a pretty little child like you should not be in a corner hiding your substantial lights under the proverbial bushel." Her voice was both gravelly and Southern sweet—molasses poured over uncooked grits. "My name is Elizabeth, folks just call me Betsy, and this is my humble home. My, what bewitchin' eyes you have, I just bet you could slay a man dead with one tiny little glance from those instruments of destruction . . ."

After prattling on like this for several moments, she said: "Why don't you come and let me introduce you to one of my most charmin' and dearest old friends. His name's Henry, and I know he's just dyin' to meet you."

Henry was seventyish. Wiry, balding, with a shapely white goatee and sharp little eyes. An old goat. And he was indeed charming in a roguish, billy goat-like way. Alicia drained her margarita, and then another, and the disco music throbbed with a rich and insinuating beat; and the Old Goat gave way to other gentlemen, all in their sixties or older, who twinkled and teased and leaned close enough for Alicia to smell their boozy breath. And then here was Betsy back again, all aflutter. "Darlin', you made quite a hit with my friend Henry. If you're agreeable to the suggestion, he would very much like to continue the evening."

In the years following, Alicia would tell herself it was because of all the tequila she'd drunk. Or because she'd been so young and naïve she really didn't understand what she was agreeing to. And that anyway she had liked Henry—he seemed like a man who, except for his age, she might be dating anyway.

But she'd always be kidding herself. The real reason she had accepted his proposition was because she was being crushed by school loans and car payments, and the tips for schlepping pot roast and Boston cream pies at Callendar's sucked. And she'd known perfectly well what she was agreeing to.

There were several bungalows behind the main house and she accompanied Henry out to one of these. It was dark inside except for the glow of one small lamp and frugally appointed: a waterbed with black satin sheets; a bed table; more of that black shag carpet that looked like fungus.

And Henry had been sweet, really. Took great care to make sure she was comfy. "Are you warm enough?" he murmured. "Shall I pull the sheet up? Would you like another pillow?" Almost like a parent putting a child down for the night, except for the fact that they were both naked and he was lying on top of her. And the sex—well, maybe because she was drunk and dozed off a bit in the middle, but it seemed to be over in an instant. The funny thing was that afterwards he stayed for quite a long time, just lying beside her and talking. About his experiences in the air force during World War II, and his sailboat that he docked in the marina, even about his grandkids. It was like the roles had been reversed—she was now the parent indulging a chattery child.

Sometime after midnight, he dressed, kissed her on the cheek and left. Alicia returned to the main house, and Betsy handed her a rose-colored envelope containing six crisp hundred dollar bills. "And darlin', Henry would adore to see you here next week."

And so the next Wednesday Alicia found herself going back to the concrete house. The same scene. The gorgeous, glitzy young women, the eclectic mob of men. Pulsing music, the squawking parrot, strong drinks. But no Henry.

She looked for Jersey Boy. He wasn't there either.

Betsy made other introductions and told her another gentleman "wished to continue the evening." This one was slightly famous, a rising young comedian. He was one of the hyped-up types, and Alicia was reluctant, but Betsy was so sweet-talking and wheedling, that finally she agreed. In the bungalow, the comedian babbled nonstop, a rambling, incoherent monologue. Suddenly he yanked down his pants, roughly pushed Alicia to her knees and forced her mouth to his erection. It was mottled purple and smelled like cheese. In revulsion, she pulled back. He slapped her and she screamed. Then he took a step and crashed face down onto the bed. He lay sprawled unconscious, jeans and underwear bunched at his ankles, pink ass bobbing as the water bed sloshed and wobbled. Alicia ran out of the bungalow and back into the party, where she hunted down Marcy and in near hysterics demanded to go home.

Despite several calls from Betsy Bell, she'd never gone back.

In the annals of flesh-pedaling, it really wasn't much. Hardly Irma La Douce. Or Jane Fonda in *Klute*. Just an immature college girl acting like a fool.

And that would have been that, except, just after graduation, she got a job offer in the p.r. department of the movie theater chain, Luxor Theaters. Twice the salary of a beginning teacher. She assumed it had come through her school's job placement office, until she caught a glimpse of the company's president.

It was the Old Goat.

His name wasn't Henry, it was Ronald. After several weeks, he approached her. Casually: the big boss graciously exchanging a few pleasantries with a new hire. Then she began to be sent to his office on various pretenses, and he'd keep her there for increasingly long periods of time, resuming the monologue he'd begun on Betsy Bell's black satin sheets.

And every once in a while, late at night in his locked office, they'd have a friendly fuck on the tweedy sectional couch.

Then she got hired at Constellation and never saw him again. Several years ago, she'd read that he'd died at his desk of a massive coronary, and she'd felt a few pangs of regret. But she couldn't deny that she'd also felt a greater amount of relief.

So here she was. In possession of this glamorous office, pulling down seven hundred thousand a year, plus bonus and perks galore, rather than out in that little Valley ranch house. If she had to do it all over again, would she do it differently? Refused to repair to the bungalow with the Old Goat? Or said no to the friendly fucks on the tweed couch?

Honestly, she didn't know.

She waited exactly eleven minutes, then presented herself to Jacqueline, Cody Takish's assistant, who waved her in to Cody's vast office suite. He was on the phone. It was one of his favorite ploys—to keep you twiddling your thumbs while he leisurely concluded a call to someone obviously more important than yourself.

She took a seat opposite his custom-made Lucite desk. There was a painting on the wall behind him. A Georg Baselitz: it looked like a portrait of a seated man that somebody had mistakenly hung upside-down. Another one of Cody's tactics—if he caught you peering at it with confusion, he'd pounce: "That's a Baselitz upside-down painting," he'd inform you triumphantly. "It's meant to hang that way!"

Needless to say, he'd hired a former curator of the Getty to buy his art for him. Left to his own resources, Cody Takish wouldn't know Baselitz from Bozo the Clown.

Several minutes ticked by before he hung up. "Oh, hey, Alicia. Thanks for stopping in."

"Could we make this quick, Cody?" she said. "I've got my kids waiting."

"Quick as we can." He reminded her of a gingerbread cookie: a round face baked to a golden brown on tennis courts; tiny eyes like raisins; lips pale and thin as icing. "It's about the *Wildwood Murphy* deal. I've got some concerns."

Alicia felt a shiver of apprehension. She was the one who had championed this remake of the Eighties' blockbuster. She'd gone out on a limb, arguing that it would become a hugely profitable franchise for the studio. A cash cow, well worth the staggering—okay, obscene—amount of money it would cost. It was supposed to be a solid green light—the studio's tent pole release of next summer. If for any reason it should get derailed, she could hear the gurgle of her job—hell, her entire career—going down the toilet: *glug, glug, glug.*

She kept all apprehension out of her voice. "Talk to me, Cody."

"I just want to go over a few things before we make the pay-or-play offer to Denny Brandt."

"The offer is all set to go on Friday. What more is there to go over?"

"I think Friday is being a bit premature."

Premature? she silently screamed. *We've only gone over it fifty-two times in the past three months.*

"How so?" she asked.

His iced-on lips formed a perfect gingerbread man O. "It's the numbers that keep tripping me up. You've got this movie budgeted at 170 million dollars. In the current financial climate, I'm just not sure that's going to fly."

You weasely little roach! You told me you had sign-off on that number!

"I'm surprised to hear that, Cody," she said evenly. "I thought you were comfortable with that budget."

"I'd be a hell of a lot more comfortable if we knocked it down to a hundred and sixty-five."

"I'm not sure we're going to be able to do that. You're familiar with the script—it's nonstop action, loaded with CGI. This budget is tight as it is."

Cody assumed a long-suffering expression. "God, Alicia, it sounds like you're angling for an even higher number. I wish you wouldn't always be so out of control like this. You've put myself and the studio in a bad position."

I have? When we've discussed this budget for months?

It took every ounce of control to keep the rage out of her voice. "Okay, where do you suggest we tighten up? Should we cut some of the big effects? How about we lose the army of shape-shifting mummies? Or maybe the avalanche of diamonds? I mean, hey, if we get rid of *both* those scenes, we'll save a bundle."

"You've got to be joking, Alicia. We're shooting in 3D. Do you really want to cut out the most spectacular 3D scenes in the movie?"

"No, Cody, I don't. I'm simply trying to point out that this is by necessity an extremely expensive movie."

"There's expensive, and there's out of control." He clasped his hands behind his neck, made a pretense of deep thought. "I think maybe we should take a hard look at the above the line costs. Fifty million? That's just insane."

"Not really, Cody. That includes the star, the female lead, an A-list director . . ."

"Okay, whoa, hold on a sec. Let's look at the star. Fifteen million dollars against fifteen points of gross to Denny Brandt? I mean, Jesus, Alicia. These are tough times—all the stars are cutting their upfront salaries. Let's go ahead and make that pay-or-play to him, but for ten million, not fifteen."

She let out a sharp laugh. "He'll tell us to go to hell."

"Come on, a chance to step into his daddy's boots? He'd screw a buffalo to do this movie."

"I think you're wrong about that, Cody. Denny was very reluctant to take on his father's signature role. It's one reason we had to offer him so much, to coax him into doing it." Now it was her turn to furrow her brow in a pretense of deep thought. "We could get that number down by passing on Denny and going with another star. Mark Wahlberg might be available. Josh Brolin . . ."

Cody's face now smoothed into the oh-so-patient expression of someone dealing with a congenital idiot. "Not going to happen, Alicia. As you know, I commissioned a research study on this project. It shows that Denny Brandt is the only star who can make this movie fly."

Yeah, and I was the one who told you to commission the study, asshole.

"I'm aware of that, Cody," she said calmly.

He reached for a glossy green bound report and ostentatiously thumbed through the pages. "Here . . . It shows that with Denny playing Wildwood Murphy, sixty-one percent of the movie-going public is definitely interested in seeing this film. And that's *before* we even start shooting, never mind marketing it! With any other actor in the role, it drops down to about twenty percent."

Yeah. And if you hadn't blabbed about this report to all your agent pals, it would have been easier to negotiate with Denny in the first place. "I'm aware of those percentages, Cody."

"We need Denny Brandt," he pronounced officiously. "Your job is to get him at the right price."

No, my job is to see your head under the wheel of a flatbed truck as it's slowly backing up.

She took a deep, calming breath. "Okay, look. I'll stall the offer to Denny, and in the meantime, I'll see how much I can cut elsewhere."

A long sigh whistled like leaking gas through the gingerbread

O. "I've been over this budget with a fine-tooth comb. This morning, I had a lengthy sit-down with Martin, and he totally agrees it's too high. But except for Denny's salary, I don't see much wiggle room anywhere else.

In a sudden flash, Alicia saw precisely what Cody was doing. Wow! She should have caught it immediately. He'd set a very sweet trap for her.

He'd gone to Martin Drake, the chairman of the studio, and planted the bug that Alicia was over-spending. If she didn't get the budget down, she'd be in deep shit with Martin.

But if she were to go to Denny Brandt's people and make a lesser offer than what they'd pre-negotiated, there would be a nuclear explosion. Armageddon time!

And Alicia would be Ground Zero.

And then Cody Takish would step in and soothe all the exploding tempers and close the deal—at the original higher price, of course, telling Martin that Alicia had really left him no choice. Making himself the hero. The only person who could *really* get things *done*. The Boy Wonder, indispensable to the studio.

And as for herself . . .

Glug. Glug. Glug.

She shot a glance at the Baselitz painting. The face of Upside-Down Man seemed pinched with desperation. *You and me both, kiddo.*

"Okay, Cody, I think I understand your concerns perfectly now. Here's another idea—maybe we can shave some off the producer's fee. WildFilm is also taking fifteen million up front. Maybe I can renegotiate with Warren Doran and get him to knock that down."

Cody tipped back in his chair. "Dream on, Alicia. In case you've forgotten, Warren controls the remake rights. He doesn't have to give up a nickel, and believe me, he ain't going to."

"The least I can do is try. I'll stall the pay-or-play to Denny Brandt and set something up with Warren. But now I've really got to scoot—I'm late for Mommy and Me."

She got up and turned and headed briskly out of the office, hoping she looked even marginally more confident than she felt. For reasons she'd never been able to identify, the charismatic and always affable producer Warren Doran was one of the few people in Hollywood she was afraid of.

FIVE

A bell was ringing. Hannah scrambled out of the tub and snatched a robe from a hook and stood dripping, naked, in total confusion. For the past year, her life had been regulated by bells and buzzers and whistles; for lock in and wake up; for bed check and rec period and for just because; but which bell was this?

Then she realized—it was just a phone. The house phone mounted on the wall beside the bidet. *She was home!* Squirming into the robe, she picked up the receiver.

"There's a Mr. Miller here to see you. Says he's a friend." Eddie's voice was wary. He was taking no more chances of letting interlopers in.

Thad Miller, her father's junior partner. "Yeah, thanks, Eddie. Please send him up."

The robe she'd grabbed was a man's robe—the abandoned property of her ex-boyfriend, Shawn Serafian. For a second, she imagined she could detect his scent in the terry cloth, a mixture of aftershave, acrylic paint and tobacco. It triggered a dizzying wave of longing and desire.

She reminded herself of the way he'd dumped her. By text—the day before she had to surrender herself to Peachrock.

The hell with Shawn Serafian! He was slime, not even worth thinking about.

She stuffed the robe in the waste basket along with the prison discards, then hurried to get dressed. She grabbed a bra and pair of panties from a lingerie drawer and a fresh a pair of royal blue Juicy Couture sweats from a shelf. Her skin was rosy from the hot bath, and the color of the sweats accentuated the smoky gray of her eyes.

She ran a comb through her damp light brown hair and checked the mirror again. Definitely an improvement!

The door double-chimid impatiently and she ran bare-footed downstairs as her front door chimed.

"Hey, babe! Welcome home!" Thad Miller stood in the vestibule, beaming. He was tall, with a narrow build, handsome in a sort of forgettable way. He wore a snappy leather jacket and beige cords. His light hair had receded just a touch, and—perhaps to counter that—he had grown a trendy short beard.

"Thad!" Hannah exuberantly flung her arms around his neck. "I'm so glad to see you!"

"Whoa!" he chuckled. "So . . . Wow. Welcome home."

"It's so great to be back. You can't imagine!"

She noticed suddenly that there were two men hovering behind him, young Latinos in uniforms emblazoned with carrots and carrying white cartons marked LARCHMONT FINE FOODS.

"I brought some provisions," Thad announced. "I thought you'd probably just want to kick back tonight and cocoon, rather than have to go out on the town."

"You thought exactly right!"

She led them into the kitchen with all its expensive, gleaming appliances that she had rarely used. While the delivery men unloaded the groceries, Thad straddled a stool at the counter.

"So how does the place look? Everything spic and span? I kept your maid coming in once a month to do the dusting and scrubbing and etcetera."

"It looks amazing. Like paradise."

"Good. Terrific. So, okay, these groceries . . . Well, I didn't know your exact tastes, so I told them to throw in a range. Milk, for example. There's whole, one percent and soy. Several different kinds of breads, one is non-gluten, F.Y.I. And, well, cheeses and juices, snackables. Pre-cooked stuff for the freezer. You'll see. Anything else you want, this place will deliver. I opened an account for you, you just got to call 'em. Also, in one of these drawers . . ." He pulled himself on the rolling stool along the counter to a drawer at the end. "Yeah, here. A selection of take-out menus, Thai, Indian, Italian, Chinese. Or if you want something more gourmet, there's this service, they'll pick up from any restaurant in town."

Classic Thad Miller—micromanager to the extreme. The perfect second banana to a Big Picture ignore-the-details guy like Warren Doran.

"Okay, now what else?" He drummed his fingers on the counter top. "Your car. The lease was up last month, but I extended it. Had it serviced, it's running tip-top and the tank is full. Your license is good, right?"

She nodded. "It's one of the things they had us organize before release."

"Cool. Oh, and I got you a new iPhone, in the charger there on the counter. The number's unlisted. Your old one got posted on the net, and you wouldn't *believe* all the whack jobs who thought they desperately needed to get in touch with you."

The delivery men had finished. Thad slapped some bills in their hands and they filed quickly out. Hannah moved to the phone and took it out of the charger.

"I want to call Dad," she said. "Where is he, anyway?"

"In Vegas. Holed up with our money people. You can try, but I doubt if he'll pick up. I've tried him six times today."

"That's it? Just in Las Vegas?" Anger flashed across Hannah's face. "I thought he was out of the country. Why couldn't he be there for me today?"

"Hey, he's got to give these guys a hundred percent. If it had been anything less important, you can bet he'd be right here now instead of me."

She replaced the phone in the charger. "You don't have to cover for him. I know he's still furious with me. He almost never came to visit, and when he did he could hardly keep it off his face."

"Oh, hey, not furious. Maybe disappointed. He feels you let him down. He tried to give you every advantage and you threw it all away."

"But I haven't. And I'm going to prove it to him." She sat down on the stool beside him. "Thad, I'm glad you're here, because I want to talk to you about something."

"Shoot."

"There's something I'm thinking about doing. Something I'm really passionate about. I think Dad's going to be really impressed. In fact, I *know* he is."

Thad smiled indulgently. "Let's hear."

"I want to start a foundation."

"A what?"

"A charitable foundation. With my trust money." Her face lit with excitement. "A few months ago, I had some mail forwarded to me and there was an appeal from this place called The Sunlight Center. It's downtown, it's for the homeless—it's a shelter, but not just, it's also got programs, and a food kitchen, and a thrift shop that employs people who need jobs. I got in touch with the guy who started it, Benny Davis. You know, the actor?"

"The guy who played Dr. Toke Taylor in all the *Wildwoods*? I thought he was dead."

"No, god, no! He's very much alive. Anyway, the center is in trouble. It's had a hard time raising money in the bad economy. It might have to start closing a lot of its facilities. I promised Benny I'd start contributing. But then I thought, why can't I do more than that? I've got a huge inheritance. I could structure a foundation to keep it going, and also get involved with it! Eventually maybe even help it expand! Become a model for something that could be done in other cities . . ."

"Whoa!" Thad threw up his hands. "Back up a sec. I don't know what you've promised this Benny guy . . ."

"Nothing really yet. I'm going to go down, have a look around, talk to him. And I need to talk to my trust managers, of course. I never paid much attention to my money before. But that's going to change. I want to take more control of my funds."

"Great. Excellent. But Jeez, Hannah, you're still in reentry. You've only been out for what? A few hours? You need to kick back a little, especially before you go jumping into anything radical. Relax, get a massage, a mani-pedi. Buy some new outfits."

She shook her head impatiently. He wasn't getting it. "I'm not interested in any of that stuff. And it's not jumping into anything. I've done a lot of research on the center. Benny's had commendations from the mayor and a congressman, and there are hundreds of articles and blogs written about the center. You can look it up yourself."

"Yeah, I'm sure. I believe you. And if you want, I'll help you out with all that. In fact, I'll be thrilled to. I'm just saying, you need to take first things first. For instance, you've got to meet with your parole officer, right?"

"Tomorrow. Yes."

"And what about going back to school? Weren't you going to apply to UCLA?"

"I already have. For the fall semester. I can be in school and still be involved with the center."

"Okay. But just promise me, first things first."

"Okay," she conceded. "Maybe you're right, I probably need to settle in for a day or two. But I'm really serious about this, Thad. You'll see."

"I hear you, babe. Speaking of money, though . . . I need to get your credit cards reissued. Until then, I left you some cash. Twelve hundred bucks, in the drawer with the menus." He got to his feet. "Well then. I think that about covers it. I should take off, leave you in peace." He hesitated. "Unless you want me to stick around?"

For a moment, she was tempted to say yes. The penthouse suddenly seemed huge, empty, even with its profusion of stuff. She remembered how she'd felt spooked in the bathtub, the feeling she was being watched.

It might be comforting to have company. And there were those feelings that had been aroused by Shawn's old robe. . . . Thad was an attractive guy. At the moment, he seemed more attractive than he ever had before . . .

She caught herself. No, it would be a mistake. She knew intrinsically that it would be.

"Thanks, but I'm okay," she told him. "But I really appreciate your coming and . . . well, for everything you've done."

"Totally my pleasure. If you do need anything else, give a holler. My number's stored in your phone. You can call me twenty-four seven."

He left and she lingered in the kitchen. The sight of the groceries being unloaded had made her realize she was hungry. Starving, in fact. She pulled open the heavy door of the SubZero, gazed at the laden shelves. Fresh food! She began wolfing down bunches of purple grapes, large hunks of Danish blue and Camembert cheese, a fistful of arugula. She ripped open a brick of Irish butter just to inhale its creamy aroma, then finished with a long swig of freshly-squeezed grapefruit juice, letting rivulets run down the sides of her mouth. She felt she'd never had a more delicious meal.

Then she went to the iPhone. She hesitated a moment.

Then she called a number in Pasadena that she knew she shouldn't. It picked up on the second ring. "Hello. Jonas Sebring speaking."

She'd known her grandfather would answer the phone himself—he threw a fit if he wasn't allowed to. "Hi, Nonny. Guess what? It's me, Hannah."

"Hello, my darling! How are you today?" He sounded overjoyed to hear from her. It meant nothing. Since his Alzheimer's had become full-blown, he greeted everyone like that.

"I'm fine, Nonny," she said. "I'm really terrific. I've been away for a while, but I've come back."

"That's wonderful, my darling. Truly splendid."

She pictured him, a frail, absent old man rattling around the enormous house that his own grandfather had built in 1908. "I can't wait to come and see you, Nonny."

"Please do come, my darling. You're very welcome to visit. It'll be my privilege to see you."

"Maybe in a few days. I'll have to get permission to go up there."

"But you need to come home now!" he said.

"I *am* home, Nonny. My own home. That's where I'm calling you from."

Jonas Sebring raised his voice. "You need to come home right *now*, Pamela."

Her chest tightened painfully. "It's not Pamela, Nonny. It's me, Hannah. I'm your granddaughter, can you remember?"

"You don't have to stay there!" His voice grew high and agitated. "Goddamn it, Pamela, stop being so goddamned stubborn! He doesn't own you, for godsake! Come home right this instant, do you hear me?"

"Nonny?"

He began to shout incoherently. There were voices in the background—his caretakers, the Filipino couple, Gloria and Tomas Esposito, who lived in the gatehouse of the Pasadena estate. Hannah could hear them trying to soothe him as he yelled louder and more violently.

"I'll come see you soon, Nonny," she said, though he was no longer listening. She hung up before one of the Espositos picked up.

She'd known her calling would upset him. It had been selfish to do it. But she had been just craving to hear his voice.

She gave a start as the phone in her hand jangled—a ring tone version of "Girls Just Wanna Have Fun." Thad's idea of cute.

She wondered if Gloria or Tomas had pressed Return Call. She answered tentatively: "Hello?"

"Doran?" A woman's voice, sibilant, barely audible. "Is that you?" A discernable accent.

"Valentina?" she ventured.

She heard: "Oh, crap!" and the line went dead.

Hannah pressed RETURN. She let the other line ring for what seemed like forever.

There was no answer.

⊰⋇⊱

Listening in on a cell was even easier than tapping a land line— any moron could do it. Having recorded both calls to and from the penthouse, Roger Lopez yanked open the passenger-side door of the 4Runner. Now that it was dark, he had the luxury of peeing at the curb rather than utilizing the jar he kept on board for the purpose.

Instinct told him that his employers would be more interested in the second of the two calls. Whatever, he thought, unzipping; they weren't going to share their thoughts, no matter what. And that was perfectly fine with him.

※

The bright, noisy chaos that defined the Rustic Canyon Mommy and Me play group always gave Alicia's spirits an enormous lift, but the activities were almost over by the time she got there now. *Thank you, Cody, you conniving little turd.*

She collected the twins and bundled them into their car seats in the nanny's Volvo. As she headed to her own car parked at the end of the crowded curb, someone called her name: "Alicia!"

She tensed. It was Marcia Rossler—formerly Marcy Cook, the wild child who'd been her apartment mate back in college. Like Alicia, Marcy had traveled a long way since then—married to the head of one of the largest talent agencies, mother of three. Gone was the purple Mohawk, the black thigh-high boots and Madonna-wannabe bustiers: now she was all Ralph Lauren linen and demure blonde bob—the very image of a posh Westside soccer mom.

But Marcia Cook Rossler was one of the few people who could positively connect Alicia to those parties in the Malibu Hills. And vice-versa of course. Not that either ever would tattle on the other, since they'd both have a vast amount to lose; but by tacit agreement, they avoided one another.

Marcia sidled up close and dropped her voice. "I just wanted to give you a head's up. I ran into Betsy Bell this morning. At this place on Barrington that does my nails. I was waiting for my regular girl to be free and Betsy came in and sat down right next to me. I nearly had a heart attack!"

Alicia felt a chill. Roughly an hour ago, she'd been thinking about Betsy Bell for the first time in ages, and now this! A coincidence, no doubt, but a damned spooky one. "I'd heard she had some incurable disease, cancer or something, and retired to Miami."

"I think it's Parkinson's. She's got the shakes. And she did retire, but to Texas, some little town she originally came from. She said she'd mostly given the business over to one of her girls, a Sabina somebody? But she still keeps a hand in. That's why she's in town, she told me. To take care of some business."

"So you actually talked to her?"

"She started talking to *me*, almost like it had just been maybe a week since we'd last seen each other instead of what? I don't want to *think* how many years. I couldn't just ignore her, could I? Except for the shakes, she hasn't changed a bit. It's kind of freaky, actually. That plastic-fantastic hair, remember? And that fakey Blanche Du-Bois way of talking? And she stinks of smoke. She probably still smokes those tiny cigars, do you remember?"

Alicia nodded with a shudder. "Thanks for telling me. I'll keep my fingers crossed that I don't run into her too."

"No, wait, there's more. She mentioned you."

"She did?"

"Yeah, well first she asked about my husband—she wanted to know if Bobby represented Warren Doran, the producer, you know? I said no, I think he's with Morris or ICM, and she said oh, I just thought if he did, I could pass along to Warren my congratulations about his daughter. I said, what about his daughter? And Betsy said she's being released from prison today. Hannah Doran, yikes, I'd forgotten all about her. What did they used to call her? The Martini Girl or something?"

"Hangover Hannah." Alicia muttered it more to herself than to Marcia. "I didn't hear anything about her getting out."

"I guess it was supposed to be very hush-hush. They didn't want any media. Remember when she was arrested, what a freaking media zoo it was? But anyway, that's when your name came up. Betsy says she reads *Variety* religiously and she likes to follow the careers of the girls she's helped out."

"Helped out?" Alicia said acidly. "Is that what she calls it?"

"I know, it's sick. And then she said how she read that you were in charge of the new *Wildwood Murphy* movie that Warren Doran's producing, and how she'd picked you out right from the start as a girl that was going places and blah, blah, blah. But then I got called for my pedi, and I was so glad to get away from Betsy I practically flew out of the chair. I'll bet you can understand."

"Yeah, I can."

"Forewarned is forearmed." Marcia gave an ominous lift of her brows, then turned away.

Alicia continued on to her car, her thoughts in turmoil. It was alarming that Betsy Bell had kept tabs on her through all these years. She reminded herself that she was a fairly public figure, that it wasn't difficult for anyone to keep tabs on her—and that poor old Betsy, suffering from a progressive disease, probably needed to still feel connected to people of significance. But it was even more alarming to know that the Malibu Madam's business still continued—Alicia had assumed that Betsy had packed it all in a decade ago.

Her thoughts shifted to Hannah Doran. She'd interned for Alicia at Constellation during the summer after her freshman year at Yale. Alicia remembered her as a smart, focused young woman who'd asked a lot of questions—meaningful questions about the way the studio worked and why certain decisions were made—listening thoughtfully to Alicia's replies. She'd been astonished when Hannah dropped out of Yale and begun morphing into a preposterous sort of Paris Hilton doppelganger. Even more by the whole "Hangover Hannah" affair: it hardly seemed to jibe with the focused young intern Alicia had known.

It struck her suddenly that in the entire time she'd been working with Warren Doran, he had never once mentioned his daughter. And not a peep, certainly, about Hannah getting out of jail. If it was true that he'd wanted to keep it hush-hush, he'd definitely succeeded.

Why then, Alicia wondered, would a semi-retired madam living in the Texas boonies be the first to know?

SIX

The delicious odors wafting from inside Chinois on Main made Mitch Arpino's knees weak. His lunch had been a gobbled fish taco from a food truck and he was still feeling peckish. But the baby shower for the hip-hop diva that was taking place inside the restaurant could go on indefinitely, and a shot of the diva with her baby bump could bring in a nice check, so he could do nothing but wait for her to emerge and keep salivating.

And yawn. Which he did, strenuously. He'd been up half the night researching Hannah Sebring Doran. In fact, he had left a perfectly warm girl in his bed—a big-eyed, horoscope-quoting, reality-show-aspiring waitress/actress named Kirstie who'd served him his fried free-range chicken plate at Cheebo—the kind of girl who couldn't resist a guy with a big camera; in short, the kind of girl Mitch had totally sworn off of, but every so often suffered a relapse . . . Anyway, he'd left a perfectly warm and naked woman to get up and hunker over his laptop for nearly three hours to read up on Hannah Doran's life story.

Beginning with her parents, Warren and Pamela. That golden couple of the mid-Eighties. He'd hunted up the old *People* magazine cover story: *The Heiress and the Movie King*: a gushy, hurl-inducing piece of puffery. The photos intrigued him, though. The golden couple splashing in the Malibu surf, gracing a movie premiere, cooing over their darling little daughter. Mitch had been struck by Pamela's luminous beauty. She was almost freakishly beautiful, and she radiated that particular glow of a woman deeply in love.

No way to fake that. It was the real deal, baby. Mitch trusted his eye on that one.

But then a few months later, she sayonara's herself by chugging down a wasp pesticide. Had to be a hell of an excruciating way to go.

Made no frigging sense at all.

Mitch cruised through a few of the reports on the suicide. Pamela had died at the Pasadena estate she had grown up in. Poignant detail. Discovered by a not-quite-five-year-old Hannah and a Danish nanny named Sabina Larsen—the latter apparently so traumatized by the incident that she'd lost her ability to speak English and needed an interpreter to give her account.

Warren Doran had been on set somewhere out in the desert and couldn't be contacted immediately, and Hannah's only other blood relative, Grandpa Jonas Sebring, was yachting in the Pacific, so little Hannah had spent a night in the custody of Pasadena Children's Services until Warren could get back to retrieve her.

According to subsequent interviews, Warren had no clue why his wife had pulled a Madame Bovary. "We were so happy," he had repeated in every statement. "She had everything to live for. We had a perfect life, we were uniquely blessed. I'm just stunned, I can't believe it even happened. I have no answers."

Later there were insinuations of a drinking problem. Bouts of black depression. The usual.

But Mitch kept flipping back to those photos of Pamela in *People*—the glow, the ecstatic radiance of her expression. It was genuine, he'd stake his career on it—no way was it just an act covering up some underlying despair.

Then later years: many shots of Warren Doran with a variety of new women, all of them fashioned on the Pamela model, but none measuring up to the pure, thrilling beauty of the original. Not much on Hannah. A shot of her at twelve with her grandpa, Jonas Sebring, at some skeet-shooting event in Santa Barbara. Another at eighteen, graduating top of her class at her fancy-schmancy private school. And then the following year, Hannah on the steps of an actually ivy-covered building at Yale participating in some protest over cutbacks in minority scholarships.

Then she dropped out of college and hit the celebutante scene, and after that, she had about umpteen million pages on Google. She'd bobbed up at every notable party and premiere, dressed to the trendy nines. There was bratty behavior: public tantrums, bogus feuds with other celebutantes. Her name affixed to a short-lived novelty line of handbags. Her face featured in an ad for a local sports club. All of it dutifully reported and chewed over in the tabloids.

Culminating in a torrent of ink and pixels after she was caught pocketing a two hundred and twenty-five thousand dollar piece of bling.

He read the interview after her arraignment. Talking about the hangover that had supposedly scrambled her brains.

Wouldn't have been a bad defense, he mused. Defendants had beat worse raps on stupider excuses.

But then a few weeks later, she cops a plea for a nearly two year stretch at the Peachrock state facility. Still puzzled the hell out of him.

In the morning, after sending Kirstie-the-waitress off with a distracted hug, he'd leapt to the phone and called a pal—Kenny Wozensteig who was clinging by his fingertips to a job on the city desk at the *L.A. Times*, and who owed Mitch big for a tip concerning a married senator who'd been sneaking out of the Westwood W in the small hours of the morning. He asked Ken to troll his law enforcement sources, see if there was any interest in Hannah Sebring Doran.

"There's a name ripped from the headlines of yesteryear." The ever-snide Wozensteig. "Isn't she in jail?"

"She's been sprung."

"Yeah? And what's it all to you?"

"No comment."

"Okay, now I'm interested. When do I get more?"

"Depends on what you dig up."

Mitch, who still had to pay his substantial rent, had been checking the Twitter feeds—Perez Hilton, TMZ—some hours later and had just picked up the item on the Chinois baby shower, when Wozensteig called back. No heat on Hannah Doran. Considered a low risk parolee. "So what have you got on her?"

"Nothing. Just fishing."

"You pull anything out of the water, you got my number."

"You're on speed dial, Wozensteig."

Mitch had gathered his gear and headed out to Santa Monica to stake out the expecting diva. First, though, he'd swung by Hannah's co-op building on Highland. He looked for the P.I. in the green 4Runner. Nowhere in sight? Was he off the case?

He stared at the building. Impregnable with its doormen and porters. He'd have to find another way to get to Hannah.

He continued on out here to Chinois where he'd been cooling his heels ever since. This goddamned shower was going on forever. The freaking diva could have *had* the baby by now. There were about twenty shooters gathered by now, along with civilians who'd gotten the word and had their digital cameras ready. The value of any shots was going down by the second.

His text tone buzzed. Message from Ajay Nayar:

ibis hotel launch party tomorr 9pm
cn u cover?

Mitch hated doing events. Large hassle, small return. But what the hell: he needed the cash. He'd heard the investors in the Ibis were all celebs, so they'd be out in force.

He texted back:

ok on it

⁊⁊⁊

The parole officer's name was McAuliffe; he was a burly forty-something with a sparse brown moustache that looked like the residue from a slurp of coffee, or maybe a prankster's satire of Hitler. He seemed to radiate contempt for Hannah and she could guess the reasons: first, for the unmerited twist of luck that had set her free; second, because she'd been designated a "high profile" case and permitted to use a special entrance to the offices instead of clocking time in the packed and agitated waiting room. He wore the expression, half glowering, half smirking, that Hannah recognized from so many of the C.O.'s at Peachrock: *You might think you're some hot-shit royal princess who craps diamonds and pees champagne, but right now, baby, your ass belongs to me.*

But I don't think that! she wanted to blurt out to him. But like those C.O.'s, she knew his mind was set. Nothing she could say or do would change it. She could only take the path of least resistance.

She'd marched obediently through the preliminary routine. Peeing in a bottle. Getting photo-capped—her identifying marks, the lightning bolt scar on her left shin, her one tattoo, a starfish paddling across the swell of her left buttock, photographed for circulation to every police force in the state. And now she sat in a pose of respect while McAuliffe barked out the conditions of her parole.

"You may not own, use, or have access to firearms, ammunition, or any knife longer than two inches, except for kitchen knives that shall not leave your place of residence. You *will* submit to random anti-narcotics testing. You, your home, and any property under your control, can be searched without a warrant and without prior notice to you. All of this clear?"

"Yes, very clear," she said.

"You're on a fifty mile leash. You don't go one step further without a written pass, you got it? You wanna spend a night away from home, you call me first. You move, you check in with me ahead of time."

"I want to go visit my grandfather in Pasadena this weekend. It's under fifty miles, but I'll probably want to stay overnight."

"You call it in."

She nodded. "I will."

"You got any kind of job lined up?"

"Not a job exactly. I've applied to go back to college. And there's a homeless center I'm planning to get involved with."

His expression went bored. "Yeah, okay, fine. Just remember, you always keep me in the loop." He grabbed up a ringing phone and snapped: "McAuliffe."

The interview was over.

Hannah breathed a sigh of relief. She went out the back door she'd come in and headed quickly to the adjacent parking lot. She was still unnerved by the anonymous phone call of the night before. The more she'd thought about it, the more she was sure that the accent had been Russian and the caller her former prison mate Valentina Rostov—and the thought now crossed her mind that perhaps Valentina or her lover Zizi Howell might also have a parole appointment here. She scanned the lot, half-expecting to see the vintage Coupe de Ville with Texas plates that had ferried them away from Peachrock. It wasn't there.

She continued to her own car, the silver blue Mercedes SLK 350 whose lease Thad had extended. There was an unwashed green van parked several cars away and a stocky man leaned against it eating a candy bar. As she came closer, he leaped inside the van. She felt a stab of alarm. *Get a grip!* she told herself. The phone call and the encounter with the photographer had obviously left her jumpy.

She jumped again at the sound of her cell phone. *Valentina?* she wondered.

She glanced at the caller I.D. WARREN DORAN. The sight of her father's name gave her a rush of emotion.

She slid into her car and pressed TALK. "Dad?"

"Hey there, honeybun. How's it going? Everything good?"

Breezy as an ocean beach. Like she'd just come back from a

weekend at the Golden Door instead of fourteen months in prison. "Everything's fine, Dad. It's about time. Where are you?"

"Still in Vegas. I've got my money people here and we're dotting all the i's."

"When are you getting back?"

"Tomorrow morning, crack of dawn, on their plane."

"So I'll see you tomorrow, then."

"That's going to be tough, honeybun. These people are coming in with me. I've got wall-to-wall meetings and in between I'll be holding their hands. But things are okay, right? Thad's seeing to everything you need?"

"Damn it Dad!" she burst out. "I can't believe you're pawning me off on Thad Miller! Are you avoiding me?"

"Of course not, Hannah. Don't be dramatic. I really am absolutely up to my ears. But tell you what. My guys are leaving Wednesday, so Wednesday night, come over to the house, okay? I'll clear my schedule. We'll put all this mess behind us and start all over again."

"Can we? I mean, start all over again? Because that's what I really want to do!" She cursed herself for sounding too eager. In a calmer voice, she added, "I've got so much to tell you, Dad. Wait till you see how I'm getting my act together. You're going to be amazed."

"I'm sure, honeybun." He already sounded distracted, voices in the background summoning him. "Come at seven, okay? You'll meet Tracy, my new lady."

Thad had neglected to mention anything about a new lady. "You've got a girlfriend? Since when?"

"A couple of months. You're gonna love her. You two are going to get on like a house on fire. Listen, honey, I've got to run. See you Wednesday, I'll have bells on." Then he was gone.

Damn it! Hannah pulled out of the lot, her emotions raging. She felt like calling him back and telling him to go to hell. And yet at the same time, she could hardly wait to see him. Of course, he was still furious with her, she reasoned. And maybe he had reason to be. She hadn't proven anything to him yet. That she really was turning her life around.

But she would prove it. And very damned soon.

She pulled out of the lot and drove randomly, not wanting to go home yet. The day had begun with a thick high fog stoppering the sky, but now an emerging sun lent a glitter to the air. Everything seemed bejeweled: even the pavement was dusted with diamonds. *I'm free!* For the first time, it began to seem a reality. Her spirits began to bounce back.

She turned onto Beverly Boulevard with its boutiques and cafés that had once been her familiar haunts. Partly out of nostalgia, partly from the need to test her new sense of freedom, she parked and began to walk. There'd been changes. Several storefronts had FOR LEASE banners strung across the windows. Others had morphed into new businesses. Didn't that gardening shop once sell Art Deco antiques? And that Fifties' motif coffee shop—it used to be the Café Luzita, a tapas place that had been the toughest reservation in town.

But here was something that was the same—the etched steel door of a boutique called Wave. Used to be one of her favorite boutiques—at least once a month, she and a group of her very best friends would descend on it, scooping up cashmere camis and ruffled shirts and peep-toe stilettos. On an impulse, she pushed open the heavy door and nearly collided with a woman staggering under the burden of an enormous heap of black garments.

"Omigod! Hanny?" The face that peered from behind the black heap belonged to Lorian Merrick, one of those former best friends. "Omigod, Hannah, is that really you?"

"Lorian?" Hannah let out a laugh. "I can't believe it!"

Lorian still looked the same—like a pretty snake, tiny face swaying on a long, slender neck, with a hood of black hair slicing across her eyes—but she'd acquired braces on her prominent teeth, bright pink braces almost the exact shade of her lipstick, like a fashion accessory you could snap on and off to match your outfit. She called herself a publicist, but she was more accurately a sort of professional friend of the rich and famous: agreeable and attractive, she ran gofer errands and exercised her genius for throwing inventive parties, in return for small payments and generous mooching privileges. "I can't believe it's really you!" she rattled on. "I mean, when did you get out? How come nobody knows? Why haven't you called me?"

"I haven't called anybody yet. It all happened so quickly, my release and everything. I only just got home."

"Everybody's gonna freak when they find out! I just can't believe it! Wow, your hair, it's so much darker and, like, wavy. There's this new colorist, Mioni, she does everybody, Kim and Drew and Scarlett and everyone, and I can get you an appointment, even though she's usually got like a six week waiting list. She'll get you back to normal in no time."

Normal. For a moment, Hannah turned over the word in her mind. Maybe it was true—that she could link arms with Lorian Merrick and everything would blink back to the way they were, and none of the nightmare events in between would matter any more.

A pager buzzed on Lorian's hip. "Omigod, that's Crissie! I'm bringing outfits for her to try on and I'm already late. Wow, wait'll she hears! Hey, did you know she's with Denny Brandt now? They got engaged!"

"Yeah, I heard all about it on *Entertainment Tonight*." The t.v. in Hannah's dorm rec room had blared constantly and had conveyed the news about Cristina Townsend's engagement to Denny Brandt, sealed with the huge pink diamond ring.

Lorian gave a sheepish smile. "I guess we all should've kept in touch with you more. I was going to come back and visit again, but time gets so crazy . . ."

"It's okay, I really didn't want visitors," Hannah assured her. "It only kind of made things worse. But I do want us to all get together soon. You, me and Crissie."

"Yeah, Hanny that would be great. Except getting Crissie to do, like, lunch or anything these days is almost impossible. You thought she was high maintenance before, you wouldn't believe her now! The queen bee of all time!"

"But I need to talk to her. To both of you. I need you to help me figure out some things."

Lorian looked shifty. "What kind of things?"

"About what happened that day I got arrested. It's all sort of a blur in my mind. Maybe you two can help me put it back together."

"I don't know. Things have changed. Crissie's such a huge star now. Everybody wants a piece of her and Denny. It gets complicated."

"But you can arrange it, Lorian. You're still close to her, aren't you?"

A struggle raged on Lorian's face. "I've got an idea. There's a launch party tomorrow night for this new hotel in, like, Silver Lake? It's called Isis? I'm helping out with the party, so I can invite people." Lorian balanced her bundle of clothes on one hip, dug into a messenger bag that rested on the other and drew out a glossy white card. "Cris will be there, you can ask her yourself."

Hannah glanced at the card. "You sure she'll be there?"

"Totally. A lot of the investors are celebrities, Denny's one of them, and *everybody* is gonna be there. It's going to look kind of lame compared to those parties I used to do before—we've had to cut back on everything. Hey, remember the one I did for Verizon at that empty temple in Koreatown where I actually got Lady Gaga to show up and do a number? God, that must have been like over two years ago!" Her pager buzzed again. An angry queen bee. "Cris is going to strangle me if I don't get this stuff to her. I'll put your name on the list for tomorrow, Hanny. See ya, okay?" Juggling phone, clothes, flapping bag, Lorian backed out the etched steel door.

Watching her leave, Hannah flashed on the one visit Lorian had made to Peachrock. She'd come with Crissie Townsend and a third of Hannah's Very Best Friends, Tasha Merrick. They'd obviously thought it was going to be a lark, visiting a women's prison—like a scene from a B-movie, sexy-tough broads in tight-fitting jump-suits. They'd dressed à la punk in thousand dollar distressed-leather bomber jackets and grunge jeans from Theodore; and they'd brought gag gifts: a stuffed panda dressed like a convict; a pro makeup set with false moustaches and putty; a book entitled: *How To Profit From Your Upcoming Incarceration.*

The three of them, Crissie, Lorian, and Tasha, sat rigidly on plastic chairs, looking shell-shocked. The visitor's room reeked of cheap candy, dirty diapers and B.O. with an overlay of drugstore perfume, and it reverberated with strident voices and a baby crying at the top of its lungs. The panda had been slit open and the stuffing checked for weapons. Most of the makeup set items had been confiscated. The gag book, though, had made it through in-tact. The three of them made chit-chat, Lorian desperately cracking jokes. The dose of antidepressants Hannah had swallowed that morning seemed to put a window of thick glass between herself and them, but still she was ex-travagantly glad to see them: she wanted to throw her arms around them and beg them never, ever to leave.

A woman sitting nearby began loudly praying to the Virgin of Guada-lupe. "Shut up you old cunt mouth!" another woman yelled and a second baby started howling. A toddler who'd been crawling around the floor grabbed at Chrissie's mocha suede boots with sticky palms, and Crissie leapt to her feet. "These are brand-new!" she screeched. "Not anymore," Tasha giggled. The buzzer rasped for the end of the visitors' hour and the three of them, Tasha, Lorian, and Crissie, fled with undisguised relief.

Her cell phone ringing jolted Hannah back into the here and now. The I.D. read: PRIVATE PARTY. She answered, already knowing who it would be.

The Russian's voice was a whisper, scarcely audible. "I need to meet with you, Doran."

"What do you want?"

"No talking now. Where can we meet?"

Hannah noticed that the saleswomen now had her on their ra-dar. She glanced at the white card she was clutching. "If you want to speak to me, I'll be at a party at the Isis Hotel tomorrow night. On Silver Lake Boulevard."

A click, and the other line went dead.

"Wave," spoke Roger Lopez into his recording device, as he watched Hannah emerge from the boutique. He'd followed her from the parole office and parked his 4Runner a discreet six car lengths away. "Beverly Boulevard, number 7331."

He'd been ordered to report on any stores that Hannah Doran went into, especially any expensive ones. He didn't know nothing about this Wave, but from the looks of the fancy front door, he suspected it fit the ticket.

At home, Hannah found an envelope slipped under her door. It contained a notice from her condo board. Her maintenance payments were two months overdue.

Impossible. Irv Waterson, who'd been her business manager since she turned eighteen and began collecting income from her trust, was a fanatic about paying bills on time.

She called his office. A secretary informed her that Mr. Waterson was out of town. And no, the secretary could not look up the status of Miss Doran's bill since the office no longer handled Miss Doran's account. "The administrators of your trust transferred it, oh gosh, nearly a year ago."

Hannah was stunned. She hung up and called Thad Miller.

"Yeah, we're using our own accounting guys now," he said breezily. "Frankly, babe, your affairs were getting pretty messy, what with all the legal bills. Waterson's a good man, very old-school and all that, but he was slowing down, he's all but retired. So Warren thought, and I agreed, that it would be more efficient—and, by the way, cost you a hell of a lot less—to manage it through our own guys."

"Why didn't anyone tell me?" she demanded.

"According to your dad, you never took much interest in finances."

"Well I am now. From now on, I plan to be highly involved."

"As you should be." He cleared his throat. "Okay, I feel kind of embarrassed telling you this, since I just bragged about how brilliant we are over here. But before we actually go into production, we've been doing a massive upgrade of our computer system. There've been glitches, a lot of stuff has been offline including your files. But we're getting straightened out. I'll be honest, it's one reason I didn't leap at your idea last night. About that place of Benny Davis's . . ."

"The Sunlight Center?"

"Yeah. This is why I didn't seem so enthusiastic. Why I didn't want you to commit yourself right off."

"How long is this going to take?"

"Should've been up and running perfectly by now. We've been as inconvenienced by it as you are. But I'm gonna kick butt in accounting and make sure that payment of yours is taken care of. Anything else I can do for you?"

"Maybe," she said. "Did you give out my number to anybody?"

"Absolutely not. Why, the media sniff it out already? Goddamn vultures."

"No, not the media. Somebody I used to know."

"Beats the hell out of me how they got it. But these days, it's hard to keep anything private, it's all out there. You want the number changed again?"

"No, it's not necessary. Not yet."

"Cool. So just keep taking it easy. Enjoy yourself, catch a movie, do some more shopping. I'll let you know when everything's sorted out."

Hannah hung up, feeling even more uneasy. Her father put such enormous trust in Thad Miller. She was beginning to wonder whether that trust was justified.

And another thing occurred to her: what had Thad meant by "more shopping"?

What made him think she'd done any at all?

SEVEN

The private G5 jet taxied to a stop on a runway of the Santa Monica airport at 7:45 in the morning. Warren Doran, world famous producer of motion pictures, emerged from the cabin with the flair and attitude of visiting royalty. His plush cashmere pullover was the color of sable, and the ermine of a custom-made shirt peeped out at the cuffs and collars. In lieu of a scepter, he clutched a silver BlackBerry; and his head was crowned with a cap that displayed the rearing mustang familiar to millions as the logo of WildFilm Pictures, the company Warren Doran had founded and controlled.

The two men who emerged behind him were by all comparison nondescript: close-cropped hair; well-cut conservative dark blue suits. They were the owners of the G5 jet. They climbed briskly into an idling black Eldorado and drove away.

Warren's personal assistant, Benjamin, a recent graduate of Dartmouth with a faded ski tan and an intellectual squint, was waiting for him in a BMW M3 sedan, one of the four cars in Warren's personal fleet. Benjamin retrieved a small leather bag from the jet's steward, then got back behind the wheel, while his boss slid democratically into the seat beside him. They did not chat: Warren was already absorbed by his BlackBerry.

After a short drive, they whisked through the gates of Warren's contemporary Brentwood mansion. He went inside, while Benjamin docked the sedan in the six car garage and then took off in his own more modest vehicle.

Rather to Warren's relief, Trudy, the thirty-one-year-old Australian ex-bartender turned Victoria's Secret model who currently shared his abode, had already departed for Pilates. He headed to his private gym and clocked twenty minutes on the treadmill. Then he steam-showered and changed to a fresh outfit similar in both casualness and costliness to the one he'd arrived in. His chef had already whipped up a fruit and powdered supplements smoothie and was flipping the three egg white omelet that Warren had requested despite the two breakfast meetings he had scheduled back to back this morning. Others at these meetings would have to talk through mouths full of muffin and cantaloupe, while Warren would hold the advantage of taking nothing but the occasional sip of espresso.

He downed his food while skimming stories in *Variety* online. "Killer omelet, Anton!" he bellowed to the cook, who popped out from the kitchen and took a mock little bow. Reaffixed to the Black-Berry, Warren set back out, driving himself in another of his cars, a Lexus hybrid the color of morning mist lit by sun.

Nobody watching him cruise out of the nine foot high wrought iron gates would suspect that he was flat broke.

But he was.

He had made five films in the past seven years, and all five had tanked except one, a little caper flick that had broken even. He'd hit an Evil Streak. That was his term for it: Evil Streak. At some point or another, everyone—actor, producer, director, studio boss— would skid into one. It didn't matter how enchanted your career had been until then: eventually the spell would turn against you.

And it could happen in an instant. One minute you're whizzing along in a golden coach, and then *shazaam!* Suddenly you're just squatting on a pumpkin.

If you were lucky, the evil streak would last for only two or three projects. Unlucky, and it went on and on, burying you alive in a landslide of vicious reviews, empty theaters, red ink.

His last movie was supposed to be the one that broke his evil streak. A big budget adaptation of *A Tale of Two Cities*—the kind of arty crowd-pleaser that should be guaranteed to sweep the Oscars. A celebrated director, an A-list ensemble cast, with cameos by everyone from Ian McKellan to Jack Black. It couldn't lose.

Except that it did. The reviewers yawned. Ticket-buyers were few.

The Oscars were its last hope: he'd dumped another thirteen million into an Academy campaign: a blitz of double page trade ads, glossy mailers, junkets for reporters and editors.

It won two Oscars—for Best Costumes and Best Sound Editing.

Who the hell goes to see a movie for the sound editing? Nobody, that's who. He lost nearly sixty million bucks.

After this fiasco, the media pronounced the death of WildFilm. All of Hollywood vibrated to the same buzz: Warren Doran was over. All the people who had slobbered all over him when he was on top—they were the same ones now drooling at the prospect of feasting on his corpse.

They were going to be disappointed, those frigging vampires. He was about to come roaring back, and in a way that would drive stakes of awe and envy through every single one of their gloating, sucking, vampire hearts.

Thanks to the two men in navy blue suits.

But at the thought of them—so quietly tailored, so neutral in expression and nondescript of feature—Warren felt something like iron fingers grip his stomach, squeezing out a searing bubble that traveled up behind his breastbone and burst in a scorching flame in the back of his throat. He rummaged for the packet of purple pills in his pocket and swallowed two with a swig of Evian.

But he couldn't stop thinking about them, the men in navy blue, and his first meeting with them five months ago in a blond-on-blond boardroom overlooking the garish skyline of Las Vegas. It had been Thad Miller who had arranged the meeting: Thad's father had been Chief Accountant for the father and uncles of these men and had been trusted by them, and that trust had filtered down to Thad. Thad had sat at the end of the long blondwood table, a thick stack of glossy-covered reports and binders choc-a-bloc with charts and numbers in front of him, looking respectful.

Warren had been at the head of the table. He sprang to his feet to deliver his pitch.

"Gentlemen," he began. "I have unearthed buried treasure!" He allowed just the breath of a beat for dramatic effect. "And I'm here to give you the opportunity to share it."

As a producer, Warren Doran wore many hats. One of them was salesman. He was a superb salesman. After the éclat of that introduction, he began to verbally tap and leap and spin, creating a swirling sense of excitement in the room. His every intonation said "listen to me!" and his every gesture commanded "have confidence."

This unearthed treasure, he explained, was a movie made in 1985 called *Wildwood Murphy and the Secrets of the Lost Palace*. "You know it. I'm sure you've seen it, maybe even more than once. Everybody knows it, and everybody's seen it. Wildwood Murphy, the million-aire daredevil, collector of rare artifacts and secret Nazi-hunting spy. It was a blockbuster at the time. Movie magic! The two sequels were even bigger blockbusters. Everybody's seen those as well.

"Bringing back the Wildwood Murphy franchise is guaranteed to rekindle movie magic. Think Batman! Superman! Indiana Jones! Characters that audiences already know and love and line up to see time and time again." Warren spread his arms, like a prophet invoking divine authority: "It's the Holy Grail of the film industry, gentlemen—a hit franchise! A movie that will keep pumping and pumping out money through another two, three, however many more sequels we want to make."

He paused for a sip of the sparkling water in the etched Waterford glass in front of him. Letting the men in navy blue take this all in.

The younger of them who was called Alex, the one who smiled a lot, showing small, pointed, blazing-white teeth, folded his hands on the table and smiled. "So what's so buried about this treasure, Warren? You were the one who made the movie in the first place, weren't you?"

"That's correct. I produced and directed the first *Wildwood Murphy*. I'm a first-rate producer, but I've got no patience for directing. You're on set from before sunrise to after sunset and everything moves like frozen molasses. Too slow for me. I've always hired A-list directors since that first time. But I did manage to hang on to the rights to *Wildwood Murphy*. The studio was asleep at the wheel in that regard."

"And so?" said Alex. His manicured fingers drummed a little tattoo on the table.

"Okay. I've brought the project to Constellation Pictures, the studio that released the original three movies. They immediately leapt on it. They see the potential as much as I do. They're still kicking themselves in the ass for letting the rights get away, and they're desperate to bring the franchise back under their own banner. Now the preliminary budget to make the first one is one hundred and seventy million dollars. The studio's willing to split the cost of production with me and take care of all the rest—marketing, prints and ads, distribution . . ."

"Back up a second," Alex interrupted. "You say you own the rights, so why have you waited until now? Why didn't you do this five, ten years ago?"

"Good question. And there's a very good reason. A remake would have been a no-brainer except for one detail—the character of Wildwood Murphy is deeply embedded in people's minds with the actor Jackson Brandt. When he and his motorcycle went into the Pacific Ocean, it sure seemed like he took Wildwood with him. R.I.P. Over and out. What nobody could have predicted, though, was that his son, Denny, would grow up to not only look like his father, but become an even greater superstar. Denny Brandt is a white hot nova of a movie star. And he's agreed to take the role." Another pause for dramatic effect. "Gentlemen," Warren continued. "Wildwood Murphy has risen from the grave!"

At the bottom of the table, Thad Miller nodded vigorously.

Warren continued to tap and spin. He described the mouthwatering sums that the franchise could expect to generate. He spoke of mind-boggling box office numbers, both home and abroad. Of DVD sales and hefty payouts from HBO and eventually network t.v., and lucrative product tie-ins—to Burger King and Pop Tarts and M&M's—and the millions more to be raked in from licensing the characters to toy and video game manufacturers. . . . "The sky's the limit. We might spin off an animation series, a Broadway musical. Not to mention soundtrack CD's, an app or two . . . hell, maybe even a ringtone . . ."

Alex cut in again. "This all sounds quite interesting, Warren. But splitting the cost of a hundred and seventy million dollar movie means you need to raise eighty-five million up front. That's a significant amount of money."

"It definitely is. But in return, I can demand—and get—twenty percent of the gross revenue. That's twenty cents of every dollar that comes in to the studio. A conservative estimate for how much cash this franchise will pull in worldwide is two to three billion dollars. That's *conservative*. The sky's the limit from there. So eighty-five invested, we're looking to get back four, five hundred million, and possibly a shitload more!"

Now Warren sensed he had their rapt attention.

"Let's hear the risks." The elder of the men in navy blue who was called Tom did not speak much, but when he did it was gruffly and to the point. "What's the downside?"

"Let me explain it this way." Warren gestured out the plate glass to the gaudy Vegas skyline blinking and flashing beyond. "What is it that insures a profit for a casino?"

"House advantage," Tom said.

"Precisely! House advantage. The odds of every game, blackjack, roulette, craps, the slots, they're all stacked against the player in favor of the house. Maybe it can be as little as half a percent for blackjack, maybe you can get up to fifteen for an Any 7 bet on the craps table. The house advantage means that over the long run the casino will always turn a profit. But let me ask you this. What if by some bizarre streak of luck—some weird, crazy, evil streak a casino gets a run of super high rollers, say maybe a dozen in a row, and they all win big. Seven figures, one after the other. Nothing shady, it's just sheer dumb luck—they're doubling down, they're maxing out the odds bet, and it's all paying out. *Shazam!* Suddenly that casino is thirty or forty million bucks out of pocket."

"Impossible," Tom grunted.

"Or next to impossible," smiled Alex. "The odds of that happening are astronomical."

"Exactly. Okay, so with Denny Brandt playing the role of Wildwood Murphy, we've got a built-in house advantage. Audiences all over the world will already know about the movie and be dying to see it—and before we even shoot one frame! Reviews won't matter a rat's dick, it's not that kind of audience. Lousy economy won't matter either—they'll scrape up the nine, ten, fourteen bucks for a ticket. Maybe a nuclear war might keep people away, but gentlemen . . ."

And Warren had spread upon them his most dazzling, most confident, most winner-take-all smile: "What are the odds?"

Warren's part of the show—the bedazzling striptease—had concluded. He'd turned the meeting over to Thad Miller, and Thad distributed charts and binders, and for the next hour he directed everyone's attention to this fact on such-and-such a page or that number in such-and-such column. And by the end of the meeting the men in navy blue had agreed, pending legal vetting, to commit the entire eighty-five million dollars.

The deal was finalized, and WildFilm Productions had cashed a five million dollar advance.

Warren had just spent the past few days with them in Vegas bringing them up to date, assuring them that everything was on schedule. They'd flown back with him to L.A. on separate business. At the thought of them, at this very moment checking into Shutters, another burning bubble popped in Warren's esophagus. He'd skipped over several significant risks of the project—not least of which was that lunatic of an actor, Denny Brandt. One crazy fuck of a loose cannon. Well, okay, most actors were pretty certifiable—but Denny was in a class by himself. Capable of blowing the whole thing to shit if he hated the color of your socks.

If Denny walked before signing, this movie was toast; and Warren would have to face the men in navy blue. They'd want their five million back, and with high interest.

And most of that money had already been spent.

No worries, he assured himself. Denny was going to be signed

on Monday, and then Warren could go ahead and sign up a direc-
tor. The hottest directors all over town were lining up begging.
Once one was on board, the film was an official green light.
Absolutely nothing to worry about.

He breezed through both breakfast meetings, the first at the
clean, well-lighted, Nate 'n Al's, the second in the plush recesses of
the Belvedere. At five minutes after ten, he swung into his reserved
parking space behind the converted warehouse in Venice Beach
that housed the offices of WildFilm Productions.

Fabulous offices. When rumors that he was in financial trouble
began to rumble through the industry, Warren had responded
promptly by remodeling his offices. A trendy Malibu architect had
created a kind of cross between a high-tech Silicon Valley campus
and the Cirque du Soleil. The cost of the renovation had been
huge, but it had done what it was supposed to do—shut up the
loudest quacking about WildFilm's impending doom.

Never let them see the hole in your pocket.

As he wound his way around cubicles that looked like Bedouin
tents fashioned of Plexiglas, he was greeted by a succession of
young, eager, and stunning-looking employees. He liked having
pretty people around him. Eye candy was one of the perks of being
in this business.

"Got a sec, Warren?" His junior partner, Thad Miller, flagged
him down.

"What is it?"

"Talked to Hannah. There's a bit of a hiccup. She suddenly
thinks she's Bono or whatever. Concocted some scheme to give away
her money."

"What?"

"Remember Benny Davis?"

"That cokehead?"

"He got shot, got crippled and dried out. Started some homeless
center downtown. Wants to set up some foundation and start pouring funds into it."

"Jesus Christ almighty. Are you going to take care of that?"

Thad glanced at his watch. "I'm on my way right now to start
the ball rolling."

"Make sure you get it covered." Warren continued on to his office. His daughter, Hannah, unexpectedly released from jail was another wildcard—and possibly the most dangerous one of all.

His assistant Benjamin squinted up from his desk. "Oh, hey,
Warren. Alicia Chenoweth wants to do drinks tonight, six-thirty at

the Four Seasons. She said it was extremely urgent, so I cleared the time for you."

Alicia! There was such a tight vise in Warren's chest now that if he didn't know better he'd think it was the prelude of a heart attack.

✂

The smell of greasy, over-cooked food instantly propelled Thad Miller back to his childhood. Las Vegas before it became the province of celebrity chefs—when it was the paradise of $4.99 all-you-can-eat prime rib buffets. Herds of Middle American lard-asses in Bermuda shorts and polyester polos stuffing their faces before waddling out to lose twenty times the cost of their bargain meal at the slots or the roulette wheel. Until he was a teen, Thad and his mom had dined at one of these buffets nearly every night while his dad ate filet mignon with his bosses—the Miltons and the Stevos and the Little Mickeys. Not just the smell—everything in this dive transported him back to that time: the dingy fluorescent light; the plastic chairs; the stack of Lotto cards on every table.

His dad, a CPA, had sported the title Chief Accountant to a variety of bland-sounding corporations. But in reality he'd been just a stooge for the guys on top. Thad had degrees in both law and accounting, and in reality he was just a stooge for *his* top dog, Warren Doran. Or at least that was how Warren treated him.

In actual fact, he had saved Warren's ass; and though Warren had grudgingly promoted him to partner, he still used Thad as an errand boy. But that was going to change. Thad was about to save Warren Doran's ass, round two—and after this time, he was going to start demanding all the respect and status he deserved. Hell, he could even picture a day when he'd be running WildFilm and Warren would be *his* glorified gofer.

In the meantime, Thad continued to act out his expected role. Meaning, while Warren took power meetings, Thad sat in a mid-Wilshire greasy spoon called Chubbie's, picking at a veal parmigiana hero. The "veal" consisted of some ground-up parts of a cow—eyeballs, hoofs, gristle—glued into a patty, engulfed by mystery cheese and watery tomato sauce.

With two fingers, he tweezered a gooey string of cheese from between his front teeth and thought wistfully of the gnocchi gorgonzola at Madeo, his favorite place for Italian in L.A. When he lunched at Madeo with Warren, they were bowed to the best table, fussed over by the waiters, and offered free delectables by the maitre d'.

But when Thad ventured there on his own, he got shuttled to a table near the kitchen and the level of service never rose above the briskly professional.

Things were going to change, people. Bet on it.

He glanced across the noisy room. The flabby guy with the bad moustache and fancy watch was draining his third cup of coffee. Thad watched him swipe a rough paper napkin across his chin and reach for the check that made a little tent beside his plate.

It was about time! Thad didn't have to pretend to eat this glop anymore. He got up and went over to the flabby guy's table. He hovered in bumpkin style—hands behind his back, feet shuffling. "Um, hello. You're Richard McAuliffe, right?"

"Yeah." McAuliffe darted a suspicious look.

"I don't know how this works exactly. I, um, have some information about one of your parolees."

"Which one?"

"A recent one. Hey, you mind if I sit down?"

McAuliffe shrugged. Thad dropped into the chair opposite him. McAuliffe's fancy watch was an Omega with a gold face— pricey but not in the Rolex or Patek class. On par with the Audi sedan McAuliffe was driving. A click too expensive for a guy in a parole officer's pay class. He wasn't maxing his credit cards—Thad had run a credit check and McAuliffe showed a respectable 758, so it had to mean he was on the take. Looking the other way on minor infractions. Or maybe feeding the media items about high-profile clients. Meaning the odds were good he'd be receptive to certain suggestions.

"The parolee I'm talking about is Hannah Doran."

McAuliffe's ears pricked up. "And you are . . . ?"

"I'd rather remain anonymous."

"If you wanted to leave an anonymous tip you could've called my line."

"Oh yeah, is that how it works?" See, I don't know any of this."

"What's the tip?"

"Something I saw. Jewelry, brand-new, had a price tag. At her place, her condo, you know? She was bragging about how she snatched it. Like, I don't want to get into any trouble with her people. But you're allowed to do searches, right?"

"Compliance search."

"Right. The point is, I think she's kind of sick, and I'd really like her to get help." Thad shrugged. "That's it, I guess." He stood up. "Sorry for interrupting your lunch. Anonymous tip on your phone line, I'll remember that." He gave a self-deprecating laugh, started as if to turn away, then swiveled back. "Hey, do you ever go to Vegas?"

"Me? Sure, I guess. Sometimes. Why?"

"I, um, kind of represent one of the casinos and, well, here . . ." Thad pretended to fumble in the pocket of his jacket and drew out a thick envelope.

"What's this?" McAuliffe said warily.

"Kind of a promotional thing. Three day weekend, everything comped. Deluxe room, all meals and drinks. Tickets to a couple of shows—that *Mystere*, by Cirque du Soleil, it's great stuff, I really recommend it. And a voucher, a grand's worth of chips. Enjoy!"

At the door, Thad took a quick look back over his shoulder. McAuliffe was greedily rummaging through the package, realizing he'd struck gold.

Outside, Thad crossed the street to an SUV idling at the curb: black Escalade with Vegas dealer plates. Windows blacked out. He climbed in the passenger seat, nearly choking on a miasma of marijuana smoke.

Thad's boyhood friend, Conrad "Cherry" Morrison sat behind the wheel sucking on the j. He looked exactly the same as for as long as Thad had known him, which was since the seventh grade: He still had the same hard, ordinary features, but the red hair that had inspired his nickname was faded to a dark reddish-brown and was clipped Marine-short. His denim jacket straining across his wide shoulders

Thad and Cherry Morrison had grown up on what you might call the opposite sides of the same track: both their dads were associates of various Vegas mobsters, Thad's as an accountant, Cherry's as a high level enforcer. A knucklebreaker with status. Cherry, as a tough kid, fascinated a nerd like Thad. Thad had followed him anywhere Cherry let him and copied him slavishly. He played the same ultra-violent Xbox games as Cherry, and twitched to the same heavy metal bands, and cheered on the sidelines when Cherry beat the crap out of some loser.

They'd lost touch after Thad enrolled at Nevada State and Cherry checked into the state pen (for pistol-whipping a clerk during a 7/11 holdup). Then, after all these years, Cherry Morrison had popped back into Thad's life. It was back in Vegas, right after that first meeting to pitch *Wildwood* to Tom and Alex Cantorella: Thad was waiting for his car at a valet stand and there's a furious honking and squealing of tires and up bombs a '99 Camaro—and lo and behold, it's his old boyhood pal, Cherry Morrison at the wheel! Cherry seemed happy to see him, and what could Thad do but go have a couple of shots and hash over old times?

And then Cherry showed up in L.A., and at first Thad tried to shake him. Then the problem of Hannah Doran's unexpected release from prison presented itself, and it occurred to Thad that Cherry could be useful in solving it. It was Cherry who'd clued Thad in about parole searches and how Hannah's P.O. McAuliffe was known to be open to a little grease; and it was Cherry who'd steered Thad to Roger Lopez, a P.I. willing to bend a law or two or three.

In retrospect, hooking back up with Cherry Morrison had been fortuitous indeed.

Cherry flicked the butt out the window. "So?"

"He took the packet. So I don't know."

Cherry grinned. "Relax, Thad boy. It's a done deal." He reached out and pinched one of Thad's ears between his fingernails. "It's all good."

"Ow!" Another thing Thad had forgotten: Cherry Morrison loved to hurt things.

Watching Warren Doran enter a room, Alicia always thought of that old Carly Simon song about another Warren—Warren Beatty, supposedly: *he walked into a party like he was walking onto a yacht . . .* The difference being that with Warren Doran, it was like he was *always* walking into a party—the most inexpressibly thrilling party imaginable—and he was the charismatic host, the one who had especially invited *you*. His step was fluid and self-assured, and he made eye contact with everyone. But once he got around to you and his warm brown eyes locked on yours, you felt that you were the one he'd really been looking for, the one and only person in the room who really and truly mattered.

Now, sitting at a back table in the Windows Lounge of the Beverly Hills Four Seasons, she watched him thread his way through the other tables, performing his party host ritual. Alicia gripped her glass of St. Emilion a little tighter. She had run the same gauntlet—kissed many of the same cheeks and shook the same hands—but it was taking Warren quite a bit longer. All eyes would remain on him as he joined her at her table.

Good. Alicia wanted eyes on them. You never knew how people in this business were going to react to bad news. They could become emotional, abusive, both verbally and physically. Once, someone she'd had to fire had burst into tears and begun banging his head against her desk. Another time someone had fainted. And a young Irish actress, told she was being replaced, had clawed at Alicia with a full set of acrylic fingernails, leaving a bar code of blood across Alicia's cheek.

She was reasonably assured that Warren Doran wouldn't scream, rake her cheek, nor bang his head on the table. And god knows he wouldn't faint—certainly not in a room full of A-list observers.

It would be later, out of public view, that he'd stick the knife in.

"Alicia! My god, you look absolutely sensational!" Warren had finally reached her table and his brown eyes were smiling at her. "What a stunning suit. That shade suits you. Violet, would you call it? It gives you a bloom, like a teenager, it really does."

In spite of herself, Alicia flushed with pleasure. "Thanks. You're looking very well too, Warren."

"Oh, I do what I can to stay presentable." He ordered whatever Alicia was drinking. They exchanged some industry gossip, who got a new deal where, what company was on the verge of going belly-up. "And how are your kids, the enchanting Laura and Shane?" he asked. "Still crazy over *Dora the Explorer?*"

"More than ever. They're lobbying hard for the Magical Welcome Dollhouse."

"They turn five pretty soon, right?"

How does he do it? she marveled. "Yeah, in a month. Speaking of daughters, though . . . I heard that Hannah just got home. You must be ecstatic."

"Over the moon." He reached for his glass and in doing so knocked it over. Red wine streamed across the glossy dark wood surface of the table top.

A movie moment, Alicia thought. Did he do it on purpose to stop any more discussion, or was he so rattled that it was an accident?

A pair of waiters scuttled over to mop up the spill, apologizing that all other tables were occupied. Alicia waited until everything was cleaned up and a new glass of St. Emilion brought for Warren, and then she pounced. "There's something we need to discuss. There's a problem with the *Wildwood* budget."

"Oh?" Warren casually—too casually—selected a few nuts from the bowl on the table and popped them in his mouth.

"Cody Takish wants to go back to the table with Denny."

Warren munched an almond, his eyes fixed on hers. "What do you mean?"

"I mean just that. He wants to renegotiate. Cody wants to knock down the pay-or-play offer to Denny to ten million."

"That's a joke, right?"

"No, Warren. I'm serious. Everyone's into deep cost-cutting now, you know that. Cody wants to look like a hero by announcing to Martin Drake that he's slashed the *Wildwood Murphy* budget. To do that, he wants us to get Denny to lower his price."

"Is he fucking out of his mind?" Warren realized he had blurted this too loudly and that eyes were shifting in his direction. He lowered his voice, "You know what'll happen if we try to squeeze one cent off the deal. Denny will shit missiles! He'll go nuclear! He'll unleash every single one of his psycho agents, and they'll torch your studio to the ground. And Denny Brandt will be the one to light the freaking match!"

"I know, Warren. Christ, I know. It's Cody. I said the same thing, and he just gives me his arrogant, little-know-it-all crap."

"We'll be dead. He's going to blow up the whole project."

"You don't have to tell me. I mean, god, I'm frantic about this!" Alicia stared down at her glass in a calculated pause, then lifted her eyes back to his. "There's only one other way I can think of."

"And that would be . . . ?"

"It's not what you're going to want to hear, but just hear me out a second. What if you stepped up and offered to lower your own participation? Take a cut of maybe five percent."

"Not going to happen," Warren said sharply.

"For godsake, Warren, you'd still stand to make a killing on this franchise. Think about it. The alternative is being left with nothing."

"I've got investors to answer to." His words were like razors. "I've sold them on these numbers. You think I can go back and tell them oops, my fucking bad, the studio's changed its mind?"

"Hey, I completely understand. It's tricky, it's an embarrassment. But I know *you*, and I think you could sell them on this new turn of events. That's your strong suit, isn't it? Because what other choice have we got? Both our asses are on the line." She maintained unwavering eye contact. "I think you'll agree with me that whatever it takes, we've *got* to make this movie happen."

She watched as something terrifying moved across his face. For one moment she thought she had miscalculated—that in public or not Warren Doran was capable of going completely and violently out of control. She braced herself, her pulse racing.

To her profound relief, the murderous impulse vanished from

his features. He brought his glass to his lips, took a deliberate sip, smiled wryly. They *had* to conspire with each other: Alicia realized he understood that. The best bedfellows in Hollywood were made by the shared potential for getting screwed—much more than the potential for mutually making money.

"Yeah, I agree. That's the bottom line. This movie has got to happen," he said. "Let me work on this. Stall Cody for a few days— tell him we've found another way, whatever you want to say. I'll think about what to tell my people."

"I could murder the little prick. I really could."

"Yeah, but that would be justice," Warren said. "And there's no such thing as justice in this town."

Alicia laughed but couldn't suppress a feeling of deep unease. He had backed down too quickly.

What, she wondered, could he be planning?

EIGHT

M itch Arpino could hardly believe his eyes.
     From the ranks of the paparazzi penned behind the scarlet
ropes outside the Isis Hotel launch party, he watched Hannah advance up the red carpet. He'd been wracking his brains for a ploy to
get to her, and here she was, delivered up like a gift from the gods!
He shouldered his camera (a Canon Digital Rebel XS 10.1MP, purchased gently used from Samy's Camera this morning) and edged
nearer to the rope.

She looked better, he had to admit. Had a bounce, a shine to
her. She wore a short black Armani, maybe from a few seasons
back, but classic in its simplicity. Hair pulled back in a clasp. Earrings that were simple silver drops.

Somebody suddenly recognized her. "Hey, Hannah! Hannah
Doran!"

Mitch was shoved brusquely aside by one of the few
female paparazzi, a gangly Israeli chick in clingy fatigues, looked
like Olive Oyl with a camel toe. Pathetic amateur: knew she
was supposed to protect her rig with tape, but not when to
stop—she'd taped up not only the camera body but half the lens
as well.

With a strategic thrust of his shoulder, he sent Ms. Oyl hurtling
against two scruffy Afghanis from Buzz Foto who, like a well-
rehearsed comedy duo, stepped efficiently apart to let her go sprawling onto the pavement. Mitch darted into his former position and
threw up a hand.

Hannah almost hadn't gotten out of her car. The sight of the paparazzi propelled her back to the media circus after her arrest. But a valet had already opened her door, and there was a long line of cars waiting behind her, and so she stepped out onto the red carpet. Maybe they'd no longer care. Or they might not recognize her—a bit older, a few pounds heavier, her hair no longer pale blonde, and wearing a fairly simple little black dress.

No such luck. It began almost immediately. "Hannah! Hey, Hannah Doran!" The chant. Persistent. Possessive. "Hannah, look over here! Hey, Hannah, when did they let you out? This way, Hannah, turn to me, how about a face?"

She had the urge to turn and run.

But they'd love that, she knew. Distress. Fear. Those were the emotions they fed on. But she was damned if she'd give it to them. Instead she stopped and faced the snapping lenses with the most glittering smile she could muster.

"Hannah, what was it like in jail?"

"Hey, Hannah, do you have to go to rehab?"

"Have you seen your father? What does Warren think?"

She didn't respond to the questions, but turned cooperatively this way and that, keeping her poise as the cameras clattered and flashed.

And then suddenly she saw him—the photographer who had surprised her in her lobby. At first she wasn't sure it was him, and then she was. He was a bit different from the rest—a few years older, a little more rumpled. A lot more sardonic-looking.

She stared at him defiantly. Letting him know that she wasn't backing down.

And then he got swallowed up in the roiling mass of other paparazzi, and she lost sight of him. She continued to the door, where a kid in guyliner made a show of scrutinizing his clipboard for her name before letting her in.

꧁꧂

That look she'd shot him made Mitch's blood boil.

It was a challenge. He never backed down from a challenge.

The questions were spinning in his mind; Why had she taken the lousy plea? Who had she been covering for? Did she know about the P.I. staking her outside her condo building . . . ?

He had only one choice—he had to sneak into that party. If he got caught, he'd be banned from working all rope events like, maybe, forever.

But what the fuck . . . He hated working events.

An old-time movie. It was Hannah's first impression inside the hotel. Everything in black and white, the décor, the outfits, even the faces of the strangers around her; everything slightly flickering, slightly speeded up.

No, not all strangers: faces from the past began to formulate. Faces with eyes that shifted right past the girl with light brown, slightly wavy hair and four-year-old Armani. Then some of those eyes darted back to her, narrowing quizzically or widening with surprise. One or two people gaped as if they'd seen a ghost.

She made several rounds of the main room searching for Lorian Merrick and then veered out to a terrace that wrapped around a green-lit swimming pool. And then she froze. There, suddenly, clustered on a semicircle of Chippendale sofas, was a little group made up of people she'd once considered her closest friends.

There was Lorian Merrick's snaky head, a flash of the rose-colored braces in her grin. Beside her, Tasha Golden, who was half Persian, but looked like a pampered Eskimo, all bobbed nose and glossy black tresses. And Cristina Townsend, with wavelets of strawberry-colored hair half-obscuring one eye—even from a dozen yards away, Hannah could see the huge pink diamond on Crissie's ring finger.

And Denny was there, of course. Denny Brandt, incandescent with fame, sitting directly across from Crissie, legs sprawled far apart to allow maximum crotch exposure.

And others. The tubby gossip columnist, Barron Hope, mouth ceaselessly flapping. A British socialite known as Baby, so thin you could practically floss with her.

And oh! Hannah's heart skipped: there was Shawn Serafian, her ex-lover, slumped like a rag doll on the end of one of the couches.

Lorian suddenly spotted her. "Guys, there she is!"

For one wrenching moment, nobody moved.

Then Tasha Golden squealed and leapt up and threw her arms around Hannah, and Crissie Townsend, with just a little more restraint followed suit. And then everyone was talking at once, yelling over the din of the crowd and the music: "When did you get back?" "Why didn't you *call*?" "Are you going to move or stay in your old place, because I know this incredible place at the beach that's for lease . . ."

"Hey, Hanny, did you have to become some girl's bitch?" the gossipy Barron Hope smirked.

"Jesus, Barron, *you're* the frigging bitch," Lorian snapped, "don't pay any attention to him, Hannah."

Tasha piped up: "Hanny, I know the most *amazing* stylist, she dresses Reese and Cameron and everybody, and I can arrange for her to take you shopping. I mean, that dress is *sweet*, but you must be dying to get new stuff"; and Crissie said, "If you're talking about Regan Silverton, she's over, her taste totally sucks," and the socialite Baby stage-whispered in Hannah's ear: "Denny nailed Regan Silverton once, that's why Crissie hates her," and then Baby and Crissie exchanged death rays.

"Yeah, but really, Hanny, you've got to build your image back," Lorian declared. "Start being seen in the right places. All the new clubs. Ooh, I know the most fabulous image consultant, I can arrange a lunch for you guys."

Someone thrust a glass in Hannah's hand and she somehow found herself sitting haunch to haunch with Denny Brandt.

His blue-black eyes were blurred. His auburn hair was wreathed in cigarette smoke. "So you're back?" he drawled.

"Very observant," she grinned.

"So are you okay?"

"I guess." She shrugged. "I survived, at any rate."

"I'm not surprised. In fact, I'd have put odds on it." He rattled his glass. "Want another drink? You're a vodka girl, right?"

She set the glass she'd been clutching on a table. "No, I've mostly cut it out."

"How virtuous." Denny eased a Camel from a pack and tilted the pack to her.

"Thanks, no. I quit that too."

"What gives, Doran? Did getting locked up turn you into a nun?"

"Not quite. I've still got a few vices left."

He leered. "Oh yeah? Any I should know about?"

"Denny, give me a ciggie." Crissie Townsend leaned forward, protecting her territory. Her death ray was now aimed at Hannah.

Which was funny, Hannah thought, because she was probably the only woman on the planet that Crissie didn't have to be jealous of. Not that Hannah wasn't aware of Denny's stunning physicality—you'd have to be a corpse to be immune to it. But ever since they'd first met—at Yale, when Denny was already a star of the drama department and Hannah a freshman and a mutual friend had fixed them up, thinking it would be a no-brainer: the son of the legendary Jackson Brandt, and the daughter of Warren Doran, the guy who'd made Jackson Brandt a star—there'd been a strange sort of friction between them. Maybe, Hannah thought, that if opposites attract and likes repel, it was because she and Denny were *too* much alike. Whenever they'd met in the years following, she often noticed something he said or did, an unconscious gesture or a quirk of facial expression, and it would be almost like looking in a mirror; and at that point she wouldn't know whether she felt like kissing him or pushing him away.

He seemed to feel it too, this peculiar push-pull. But the push always won out.

But she wanted to put all that behind her. The past was the past, and she was starting over. "Hey, I heard the news," she said with a smile. "That you're going to be the new Wildwood Murphy."

Denny took a quick drag of his cigarette and blew a thorny crown of smoke into the night air. "It could be."

"That means you'll be working with my dad."

"Only if he's smart enough to finally close my deal."

"He's smart enough. If he wants you, he'll get you."

"He not only wants me, he needs me. Bad. Who else is he gonna get to play Wildwood?"

His arrogance made her temper flare. "You really think you can fill *your* daddy's shoes? Jackson Brandt was a *real* movie star."

Denny's smile broadened. "The truth? I'm gonna be even better."

And then he did something strange—he stuck out his tongue at Hannah.

And she immediately stuck hers back out at him.

For some reason, they often ended up doing this, she realized. Like they were just a couple of kindergarten brats.

Crissie sprang instantly to her feet. "Denny, I'm bored. Let's go back inside."

"Cris, wait!" Hannah said. She'd made a mistake—her goal had been to talk to Crissie and now she was driving her away.

She started to get up, but somebody grabbed her wrist. She watched Crissie and Denny sail back into the hotel, towing a flotsam of entourage in their wake. Then she turned to the person who'd restrained her and with an electric thrill saw it was Shawn Serafian.

"Hey, baby." He'd been drinking heavily: his voice was slurred and his eyes barely focused.

She could feel the others watching them intently. She worked to keep her voice as light and devoid of emotion as possible. "How are you, Shawn?"

"Hanging in, I guess. You look good. The brown hair and all. More like who you really are."

"Yeah?" she said lightly. "And what would that be?"

"Brainy, you know? You were always more of a serious person than you let on."

God, she'd forgotten how stunningly sexy he was. The long green eyes that deepened to the color of moss when he made love . . . His luxurious mop of coal-colored hair, a few veins of silver now glinting at the crown and temples . . . She felt a tug in the pit of her stomach.

Shawn reached for Denny's abandoned pack of Camels. She noticed the way he placed the cigarette between his lips just slightly off of center. The way he cupped just his fingers, not his entire hand, while he lighted it; and the slight curl of his lower lip when he exhaled. It was startlingly, achingly, familiar. She had the irresistible urge to touch him.

She reached out and let her fingers lightly brush the back of his arm. "You look good too. You haven't changed a bit."

"The hell I haven't. I'm going gray." His mouth twisted in a sardonic grimace.

"It suits you. It's distinguished." She allowed her hand to rest on his arm. "I read some articles about you. They said you're one of the hottest artists around. The price of your work has gone through the roof.

"I've been lucky." He sucked a deep drag of the Camel. "So . . . I guess you must hate me, huh?"

She took a breath. "Any reason I shouldn't?"

"Yeah. Yeah, I know. I fucked up, I realize that. I just hope you don't totally hate me anymore."

He took her hand in his. Firm, warm. She nearly choked with longing.

She forced herself to remember the agony of discovering his treachery. She pulled her hand away. "Maybe I really just pity you, Shawn. You're a coward. The minute things got hard, you ran away."

He looked at her. A lock of dark hair tumbled into his green eyes. In spite of herself, she felt another spasm of desire.

"I wish you'd had the guts to break up with me face to face," she went on. "Or at least make a call. How can you expect me not to hate you?"

He narrowed his eyes, puzzled. He lifted the Camel to his lips again. His hand was shaking, she noticed.

"I don't mean that," he said. "I mean, yeah, that all was shitty. But I meant about before that, for putting the stuff in your drink, making you sick and shit. It was a stupid, lousy thing to do, and I'm sorry I did it."

The blaring music combined with the shrieking crowd was so deafening that Hannah couldn't be sure she'd heard him right. "What do you mean?"

"You know, at lunch that day."

"No, I don't know. I really don't have a clue what you're talking about."

He stared blearily at her, making an effort to focus. "I thought you'd figured it out. You got so dizzy and sick right after taking that drink, I thought it was pretty damned obvious. I just thought you knew."

Suddenly she did know. "You doped my drink. At lunch, the day I got arrested."

He took a deeper drag on his cigarette, his hand quaking hard.

"Why?" Hannah demanded.

"Shit, I thought they told you by now."

"Told me what?"

"There was a guy. He said he did interventions, he said your friends were worried about how much you were getting drunk all the time and they'd hired him to do an intervention on you. He said if I helped him with it, he'd give me half what they paid him. Six thousand bucks. He gave me some powdery stuff in an envelope, said it would make you throw up, and after that you'd hate the taste of alcohol, and you'd lay off it."

Hannah stared at him, almost blinded by mounting rage. "Who was the guy?"

"I don't know. Some average Joe. He came up to me the night before—don't you remember, we were at that thing at the Standard? I was totaled. I'd have had no memory of him even asking, except the next day I found the envelope with the powder and the cash in my pocket."

"You goddamned bastard!" she hissed.

"Hey, it was supposed to be a win-win. I was getting ready for that show at Image Space and I was really stressed, and I guess doing a lot of blow. I got into a kind of hole. Look . . ." His voice was a whine. "The show was gonna sell out, I was going to make a ton of money, I just needed some to tide me over. And what the guy said was it was going to stop you from getting fucked-up drunk all the time. It was all supposed to work out. How was I to know you'd do something insane like go out and steal a diamond necklace?"

She slapped him hard across the face.

Tasha Golden gave a little squeal, and Barron Hope giggled.

"Hey, you guys!" gasped Lorian.

"I didn't know," Shawn whimpered.

Hannah gazed around this little clutch of people she used to call her friends. Which of them—or was it maybe all of them?—had been in on this? Maybe they really had thought they were doing her a favor. But none of them had uttered a word about it during the nightmare that followed. Not one word that might have helped in her defense.

Shaken, she got to her feet and headed back inside.

"Hey, Hanny, are you going?" called Tasha Golden. "It's still like way early."

Lorian leapt up and grabbed her arm. "Hanny . . . ?"

Hannah jerked it away. "I suppose you were in on it too?"

"In on what?"

"The intervention. You were at that lunch, Lorian. You were the one who probably set it up."

"I swear to god, Hannah, I don't have a clue what you're talking about."

"Maybe you were even the one who slipped the necklace in my bag. To teach me some kind of lesson. Do me another favor."

"Hanny, you're talking crazy . . ." Lorian stepped toward her.

"Just leave me alone, okay?"

Hannah turned and bolted inside. *They were monsters, all of them, she thought wildly. Grinning, treacherous monsters! How could she have been so stupid to consider them her friends?*

The party was packed now. She pushed her way through, hoping to catch Denny and Cristina. More than ever, she needed to talk to Crissie and it could be her last shot at it. She thought she glimpsed Denny's shaggy head near the bar and started towards it. Then stopped suddenly.

The figure of Valentina Rostov, leader of the R.B.'s at the Peachrock Women's Correctional Camp materialized in the crowd.

She wore a spangled yellow dress and her scarlet hair was piled in a furious beehive. She walked in her characteristic way, head jutting forward like a bull preparing to charge.

Hannah pushed forward through the crowd to intercept her. Her eyes swept Hannah head to toe. "A little black dress," she noted with a smirk. "Very understated."

"What do you want, Valentina?" Hannah said.

She gave a look of mock hurt. "Not very friendly, Doran."

"How did you get my cell number?"

Valentina's eyes shifted. "Puh, I can get anybody's cell number, Putin, Hilary Clinton, Oprah, I don't care. You think yours is hard?"

"Could you get Putin's in just a couple of hours?"

Valentina smiled her smeary smile. "This is just like you, Doran. Always making jokes. But are you thinking you are sent to Peachrock by a joke? You think you are put in my dormitory by some funny accident?"

"What does that mean?" Hannah demanded.

"Oh, now I have your serious attention."

"Yeah, you do. What are you talking about?"

Valentina lifted her shoulders. "To get more is going to cost you."

She wanted money. Of course—Hannah should have known. "If you want anything from me, you're going to have to be more specific."

There were suddenly voices raised over the din of the music. The crowd began to surge, and there was more shouting. All around, people were pulling out phones and security men were charging from all directions.

Valentina glanced around with alarm. "This is not good. We will have to talk sometime else." She took out a cell phone, put it to her ear and strode off towards the exit.

Hannah tried to follow, but the Russian's long legs gave her too great an advantage. By the time Hannah emerged from the hotel, a car had swooped up to the entrance and Valentina jumped in.

Not the antique maroon Caddy Coupe de Ville that had collected her from prison.

A sleek Bentley sports car, the color of licorice.

And Zizi Howell, ex-Peachrock prisoner, was at the wheel.

⁊⁘℮

Mitch jogged back to his car parked front of a mini-mall sushi joint. He kept several changes of outfits in the trunk: he exchanged his Nike cap and funky safari jacket for a Paul Smith black blazer, dark gray linen shirt, and a pair of German eyeglasses with nonprescription lenses and black steel frames. He stowed the big Canon and took out a VuPoint Pen Style digicam, which he clipped onto the inside pocket of his jacket.

He sprinted back to the hotel. Damn, it was an ugly building.

He marveled at how closely the architect had succeeded in making it look like a packing carton. Though for all Mitch knew, maybe that was deliberate—an ironic reference to the boxes that homeless people camped out in. Budget chic, right?

Word of a celebrity event had obviously spread in the past half hour, inflating the crowd of rubberneckers in front to a dense little mob. Mitch easily insinuated himself among the rubberneckers and bided his time. A white limo pulled up. The crowd surged in expectation. Mitch drew a deep breath and bellowed: "It's Leo! Leo DiCaprio!"

The name went viral through the crowd: "Leo's here! Leo!" The surge swelled to a tidal wave, which heaved its way toward the limousine. Mitch expertly swam against the current and reached the door. The kid checking the list barely gave him a glance.

Okay, he was in. The crowd was hopped-up, restlessly milling. The music sounded like amplified cats in heat. Lights flashing and spinning. If you were an epileptic, you'd be having a grand mal.

He let the current swirl him past the three-deep bar, around the perimeter of the main room. Then spotted Hannah, on one of the fancy sofas out on the pool terrace.

He started toward her.

Shit! She was with Denny Brandt and his murderous entourage. Mitch edged to a more oblique sight line. Crissie Townsend was there too; but why was he getting the feeling that it was Denny and Hannah who were actually together?

The more intently he watched, the more the feeling grew. Not that they were making goo-goo eyes at each other—in fact, they actually seemed to be squabbling. But it was something more subtle—something about their body language, maybe. It seemed to echo each other's. Like a real couple's would . . .

Suddenly, they stuck their tongues out at each other. Jesus! It seemed like an intimate gesture. More so, somehow, than if they'd stuck their tongues down each other's throat.

Crissie was tugging Denny away. Mitch looked back at Hannah. That thing that had been nagging at him—who was it that she reminded him of? He suddenly had an idea. It left him thunderstruck!

But now Hannah was snuggled up next to that pretty boy of an artist she used to go with, what's-his-name? Sloan, Shawn, Sharon . . . Whatever. His work still sucked.

La plus ça change. The more things change, the more they stay the goddamned same.

He watched them getting cozier and cozier, Pretty Boy now practically in her lap.

Then suddenly she slapped Pretty Boy in the face.

What the hell?

Mitch continued watching as Hannah sprang to her feet and raced back inside the hotel. He followed.

She stopped in her tracks. A tall, slutty-looking chick was moving toward her. Not young. Nasty features, high dyed-red hair. Russian was his bet. Hannah obviously knew her—was heading now to meet her.

So what was this all about? A totally new twist.

He took out the VuPoint and shot some footage as the two women came together. Too bad it was so dark. He moved forward, trying for a better focus, and knocked hard against somebody's elbow.

"Sorry, man," he said.

The guy swiveled. To Mitch's profound dismay, he found himself staring into the wild blue eyes of Denny Brandt.

"You!" Denny spluttered. With a feral growl, he swung at Mitch's head.

Mitch ducked, successfully, to his astonishment. He returned a left cross that, to his further astonishment, connected with Denny's face. He felt the sickening crunch of breaking bone accompanied by a sharp pain in his knuckles.

Denny roared. Blood poured from his nose, no longer the chiseled appendage of classical statuary, but now a crumpled ruin slumped in the direction of his left cheekbone. Mitch stared in fascination at the sheer quantity of blood that issued from it. Like a spigot turned on full force. His own jacket was spattered with blood, his left sleeve soaked through to his skin.

Then multiple hands were grabbing his shoulders and a fist slammed him in the stomach. With a "woof," he doubled over, dropping the digicam, dimly aware that Denny was screaming: "Call the cops! I want this shithead arrested!"

Another fist caught the side of Mitch's head and he went down. Just before blacking out, he considered the irony that, because of tracking a jailbird, he'd probably be going to jail.

Unless of course he was killed first.

For some reason, it all seemed kind of hilarious.

NINE

Hannah had spent a sleepless night, obsessively turning over the events of the Isis party.

She thought of Shawn Serafian. It was so clear to her now that he was a coward and a leech. The thought of him touching her now made her want to throw up.

But she couldn't get out of her mind what he'd told her—about being paid to set up an intervention and spiking her drink. He could be lying. Shawn would say or do anything to promote himself and his career. But what would he gain by lying about something like that?

No, she was certain it was true. It all added up.

One of her friends was behind it, he'd said. Lorian Merrick was the obvious suspect—it was just the sort of stupid-with-good-intentions-stunt she might pull. Hannah pictured her, with her tiny cobra head and rosy braces. Insisting she'd known nothing about it. Lorian was practically incapable of lying—she'd fidget and giggle and end up blurting out the truth.

Plus, she was continually broke. No way she could have coughed up six thousand bucks to give to Shawn.

Okay, so if Lorian hadn't set up the intervention, then who? Crissie?

Never. Crissie Townsend was almost pathologically cheap. She was the queen of being comped. She'd never even pick up a Starbucks tab, let alone spring for a six thousand dollar intervention.

And among all the many others Hannah had so casually called her friends, how many would really have cared whether she got sober or stayed fall-on-her-ass drunk?

Certainly not six thousand dollars' worth of caring.

Her thoughts turned over to Valentina swaggering her way through the party. Her insinuation that they'd been thrown together at Peachrock for a purpose. Obviously wanting to squeeze money from her. Valentina was never to be trusted; yet Hannah couldn't entirely shake the idea she had something important to tell her.

She finally fell into a doze at dawn. When her phone jangled just before eight, she jolted awake and snatched it up.

"Uh, hi, my name is Bethany? And, um, Lorian Merrick said you were looking for a personal assistant?"

Hannah grogglily told her that Lorian was mistaken, she didn't need an assistant. When she hung up, the phone immediately rang again and continued nonstop through the morning: she'd given the number to Lorian and maybe one or two others last night and it seemed to have circulated with the speed of light. The callers were gallery and boutique owners and the managers of day spa managers and bistros and they gushed with delight at her return. Lorian herself didn't call. And neither did Crissie Townsend.

Breakfasting on a cup of espresso, she tried to get hold of Crissie Townsend on any of the half-dozen phone numbers she had for her. Each time she was stymied by a gatekeeper—an assistant or secretary. Hannah had once cushioned herself like that. But that was back in the days when her name alone could tunnel immediately through Crissie's defenses. Now it didn't even get her past the first line.

On an impulse, she tried Shawn Serafian and got his voice mail. The call was almost immediately returned by a gravelly-voiced woman who identified herself as "Mr. Serafian's attorney" and informed Hannah that Mr. Serafian would take legal action if Hannah tried to "implicate him on any misdoings" or proceeded to "harass him further."

With an effort, Hannah refrained from telling her what precisely she *would* like to do to Mr. Serafian. She channeled her frustrations into gulping a second cup of mud-black coffee.

She didn't have time to pursue things further. She had other plans for the day.

She went upstairs to her bedroom and opened the triple doors of the closet. Its motorized racks were jam-packed with garments. Thousands and thousands of dollars worth of clothes, trendy items from boutiques like Wave crammed in beside classic pieces from Chanel and Valentino. She began pulling things off the racks, choosing the most expensive designer things, until she'd accumulated a large stack. She carried the stack down to the garage and loaded it in her Mercedes, then programmed her GPS to an address downtown.

It directed her to a destination on the outskirts of Skid Row—a long, low, stucco-clad warehouse with peeling mustard-colored paint. A faded sign over the rolling doors read: THE SUNLIGHT CENTER. She pulled into the asphalt yard in front and parked beside a large truck with a ramp descending from it. A smell of food—chicken, okra, black beans—issued from inside the truck. Some dozen people were occupied around it, most carrying foil-covered trays. A woman called to Hannah: "Help you?"

"I'm looking for Benny Davis."

"Inside somewhere. He could be in one of a dozen places."

"I've also brought some things to donate."

The woman spoke into a walkie-talkie: "Pick-up!"

Two burly men came dashing out of the warehouse and began scooping the garments from the backseat. Hannah followed them inside, looking eagerly around. It was a sharp contrast to the desolation of the neighborhood—in here, everything was bright and everything seemed to be infused with purposeful energy. Dozens of volunteers bustled about. Some were affluent-looking, but the majority were ragged or eccentrically-dressed and obviously recruited from the streets.

Hannah followed the men through a huge space filled with long aluminum dining tables covered with flowered yellow oilcloths. They continued past a partially divided-off section that served as an auditorium. She glimpsed other rooms—workshops, classrooms. Somebody was practicing a clarinet from somewhere invisible.

Then they went through a wide opening in back into a brightly-lit thift store. The two men deposited Hannah's donations on a table in the thrift shop, and immediately people crowded around to inspect them. "Hey, Benny, come and look at this stuff," someone yelled.

Like a biblical sea, the volunteers parted as a middle-aged African-American man rolled up briskly in a wheelchair.

Benny Davis. Former character actor, made famous by his role as Dr. Toke Taylor, the science-brain sidekick of Wildwood Murphy in all three of the films. He'd been magnetically handsome back in the Eighties, small but powerfully built, with a bristling corona of black hair and intense, hooded black eyes. Several months after filming the last of the trilogy, he'd been shot in a mugging after leaving a Hollywood club late at night, and it had left his legs paralyzed. For some years, he'd disappeared from public view. When he resurfaced, it was as an advocate for the homeless.

Hannah stepped forward to greet him.

"Is that my girl Hannah?" he boomed. "Well just look at you! Last time we met, you were just an itty-bitty thing."

"I didn't know we'd met before," she said with surprise.

"Sure. You couldn't have been more than four years old—so no surprise you don't remember."

"Was it with my father?"

"No, actually you were with your mama."

One of the workers who'd been sorting through the clothes interrupted. "Check these things out, Benny. They're gorgeous."

"Let's see what we got." He rolled up to the table, picked up a silk cocktail dress. Glanced at the label. "Dior, huh? Pretty classy. Don't know what you paid for it, but the top price we can sell stuff here is about eighteen bucks. And how many of my folks you think can wear a size two?"

Hannah flushed. "I didn't think of that. Should I take it all back?"

"Hell no. I know a gal who's got a consignment shop in Culver City. She'll sell this stuff to starlets and shoot us back half the profits. If that's okay with you."

"That's definitely fine with me."

Benny assigned a volunteer to pack up the clothes, then turned back to Hannah. "Let's you and me go to my office and talk turkey."

His office proved to be a rickety roll top tucked into a far corner of the thrift shop. Its writing surface was obliterated by overflowing files, dog-eared papers, mugs filled with Bics, pencil stubs, paperclips, loose change. The inner sides of the desk were measled with pink Post-its. "So . . . What do you think so far?"

"What I've seen is amazing. So many people and activities. More than I'd imagined."

"This warehouse is just a part of it. The dormitory's over on Alameda, it was an old insurance building we converted to a hundred and sixteen SRO's. There's the preschool and daycare a couple blocks away. And we've got an outreach program—we get health services and food directly to the folks out there in tents. But you know this stuff."

"I read about it, but it's different to actually be here. The energy is amazing."

"Lots of enthusiasm. Never enough money. So let's cut to the chase. How much can you give and how soon?"

"I can't give you an answer this minute. In the next couple of days, I'll know more."

His eyes bore into hers. "I've been through this before. Rich kids wanting to play do-gooder. They all think they're the next George Clooney. But once they see there's no miracles, they get bored and take a hike."

"That's not me. I'm in this for the long haul, I promise. It's just that it's going to take a few days to get my finances straightened out. There are different people handling it now and things need to be straightened out."

"What about your father? Is he okay with your plans?"

She bristled. "This has nothing to do with my father. It's my money. I'm doing it on my own."

He grunted. Then glanced at a clock. "I've got to go manage the lunch serve. If you want, I can have somebody take you around to the other facilities."

"Let me help!" Hannah said. "With serving lunch. I can at least be useful."

He stared at her for a moment, in a way that made her squirm. Then he relented. "Okay, go get yourself a pair of gloves from the truck. You can be on salad."

಄

When he'd finally come swimming back into consciousness, Mitch's first thought had been he was dead.

Except by some extreme cosmic fuck-up he'd been dispatched to the wrong afterlife: *this* one was populated by angels with bald heads, brown skin, and bling so shiny it would boil a mere mortal's eyes, plus a girl angel with carmine lips so luscious, they answered that old philosophers' question once and for all—was there sex in heaven?—with a resounding *oh yeah*! No harps though—just a sucking R. Kelly-ish sound track, which Mitch, to no avail, tried to will away.

He could only conclude that this was a celestial reward for hip-hop artists mowed down before their time.

As proof of this hypothesis, the face of an actual hip-hop artist floated into view—perpetual-chart-topper, multi-Grammy-winner, Jazz-M.O.—and he was smiling beatifically at Mitch. A diffused golden halo, like an afro made of light, set off an otherwise bald head.

Weird: Mitch didn't remember hearing that Jazz-M.O. had bit the dust. Maybe it had happened concurrently with Mitch's own demise and their souls had somehow become intertwined and that's how he'd ended up in Jazz-M.O.'s paradise . . .

As Mitch was working out this rather complex theory, he became conscious of a searing pain in his gut. He groaned. The angels began to laugh. Sadistic bastards. Maybe he wasn't in heaven after all. Maybe he was in rapper hell. Which would explain the R. Kelly sound track . . .

"You gonna be in some motherfuck world of hurt tomorrow morning," spoke the head of Jazz-M.O., and it laughed too.

Then it had all started to come back to Mitch. After getting slammed by Denny's Samoan muscleman and blacking out, he'd regained consciousness several minutes later, dimly aware that he was lying on the floor in the middle of a fist fight. The rapper's posse must've intervened, stopping Denny Brandt's security from beating Mitch into Puppy Chow. And then the rapper's posse and the movie star's security had begun wailing on each other. Mitch's first thought had been for his VuPoint video pen: he'd crawled on hands and knees through the melee and miraculously located it among the stomping feet. Stowed it in his pocket; and then the posse was hauling him up and dragging him by the armpits out of the hotel.

He must have blacked out again, coming to in the backseat of this limo.

Ironically, the same white stretch limo he had used to effect entrance to a party that had almost landed him in a bed in the nearest available ICU.

The Jazz-M.O. posse had seemed grateful to Mitch for having provided entertainment in what had otherwise been a fairly dull evening. They'd wanted to continue the love, proposing (as far as Mitch could tell) to bring him back to the rapper's Hollywood Hills castle. Do some lines, round up some more fine ladies. Check out some cuts from Jazz-M.O.'s latest work in progress . . .

"Can't do it guys," Mitch had said. "I'm already in a motherfuck world of pain."

They laughed like he'd just cracked the world's most hilarious joke.

"So where you living, my brother?" Jazz M.O. had smiled beatifically again—though his halo had proved to be just glare from on-coming headlights on his shaven pate. He'd been kind enough to drop Mitch off at his bungalow in Studio City, with a fistful of Percocet 512's as a parting gift.

Bless you, oh sainted angelic Jazz-M.O.

Bless you, oh Percocet 512.

He'd lost the entire morning to painkiller oblivion, interspaced with dreams in which he heard fists pounding on his door—possibly the police coming to arrest him for assault on a celebrity. At around one, he managed to struggle out of bed, stiff, aching, but amazed and relieved not to find himself in handcuffs. He checked his messages: about a dozen, all from Ajay.

He fortified himself with a Percocet and called his boss.

"The fuck?" Ajay squealed. "I've been hearing all over town you attacked Denny Brandt! Like, that you hit him with brass knuckles or a blackjack or something."

"Wait up. He swung at *me*, so I swung back and punched him in the nose. Then his goons started beating on me, and some other guys hauled me away. End of story."

Ajay gave a grunt. "You get any pics?"

"Sorry. It's a tad difficult to shoot when you're having the crap beat out of you. And, by the way, thanks for asking if I'm okay."

"Oh yeah. You okay?"

"I'll live." A spasm of pain racked him. "I hope. Any word on how Denny is?"

"They took him right over to Cedars and reset his nose. I hear it'll be back to Greek god soon as the bandage comes off."

"He threatened to have me arrested."

Ajay gave a snort. "Sure, and tell the world he got busted up by some pap? That'll be the day."

True, Mitch reflected: it was always the paparazzi that sued Denny Brandt for battery, not vice versa. He felt a relief of sorts. "Just give me another couple of days, okay? Then I can get back to work."

"No can send you out, bro. You're toxic. At least for the time being."

"Shit, A. I need the cash."

"Sorry, dude. You want to prowl on your own, send me shots I can use and I'll use them. But you're officially suspended from this agency."

Mitch let loose a torrent of invectives and slammed down the phone.

Damn, that hurt! He treated himself to another half Percocet, then called his next door neighbor, Sandra, an adorable widow in her seventies who liked to fuss over him. She drove him to Valley Presbyterian, where he was X-rayed, assured there was no permanent damage, had his midsection taped, but was refused more Percocet. Then Sandra ferried him to the mini-mall where he'd left his car. Another minor miracle—it was still there, in front of the sushi joint. Not even a ticket. He sent Sandra off with heartfelt gratitude, then blew twenty-eight bucks on assorted sashimi takeout and returned home.

While devouring ahi cake and seaweed, he ran the footage

from the VuPoint on his Mac. A grainy twenty seconds. Couldn't make out much of Hannah, but a decent image of the mysterious slutty-looking redhead. He froze a still and emailed it to his *L.A. Times* pal, Kenny Wozensteig.

Another tidal wave of pain. A dose of Percocet and another hour of blissful sleep.

He wasn't quite awake yet when he answered the phone. Kenny Wozensteig had been talking for several minutes before Mitch identified him. "Whoa, back up a sec, man. I've gotta get my head clear."

"One of those nights?" Wozensteig cackled.

"You wouldn't believe."

"Aren't you getting a little old for that shit?"

"I'm way too old. But I gotta make a living. So did you get an I.D. on the girl?"

"Valentina Rostov. Forty-eight years old, native of Moscow, entered the U.S. illegally, surprise, surprise, best guess twenty years ago. Last official address, Peachrock Women's Correctional Facility. Just sprung a few days ago as part of the state's early release for nonviolent offenders."

So she was a prison bud of Hannah Doran's. Fascinating to know.

"So what was she doing hard time for, this Ms. Rostov?" Mitch asked. "Russian mob-related?"

"I'd be willing to bet she's got many close, personal friends in the Rusky mob. But she herself was one of Betsy Bell's employees."

"That's it? A Malibu Madam hooker? A little long in the tooth, isn't she? And since when do they give working girls more than a slap on the wrist?"

"Rostov was a little higher up in the organization. A procuress. She cruised the clubs and recruited young gals for Betsy—and I mean young. She got nailed in a sting—a couple of baby-faced undercovers posed as fifteen year olds, and Ms. Rostov scooped them right up."

Underage prostitutes. Jesus!

"Want to tell me what your particular interest in this lady is?" Wozensteig inquired.

"Nothing. I was working a party, and she looked kind of out of place. So I was just wondering, is all."

"Yeah, I'm really buying that," Wozensteig said acidly. "You ask me about two Peachrock parolees, this one and Hannah Doran. Obviously there's a connection."

"Still no comment."

"Maybe I'll start doing a little digging on my own."

"Be my guest. But there's nothing, really. Just my idle curiosity."

Wozensteig gave a snort. "Yeah, right. Take care of yourself, Arpino. You sound like hell."

Mitch hung up and ruminated on Wozensteig's info. Russian-born corrupter of little girls very anxious to have a word with Hannah Doran. And Hannah seemingly anxious to talk to her. If this Rostov had reverted to her old ways . . .

Well, Hannah was too old to be of recruiting interest.

And too rich to be tempted by anything else Rostov might have to offer.

So what was the Russian's panting interest in her? More than ever, his gut told him there was a real scoop here.

Actually, his gut was screaming maniacally at him that he'd better go lie back down. Half an hour, he told himself.

The minute he hit the bed, he was out like a light.

Her first meal in the Peachrock common dining room, and Hannah could feel all eyes on her, the celebrity rich girl newcomer. She kept her head down as she picked up a tray from a stack. It was covered with hard globs of gum, dried out grains of rice, smears of petrified condiments. She turned to exchange it for another, but the woman in line behind her had already grabbed a tray, and Hannah could see that it was just as disgusting. She continued to the serving station, received a plate of shredded beef, reconstituted mashed potatoes, and canned string beans, and a slice of white bread. "You want some butter for that bread?" The prisoner who was serving her slapped a scoop of butter onto the bread slice. A dead cockroach congealed in it. Hannah gave a scream. Everyone around her began to laugh.

Despite the sedatives and antidepressants, a red rage overtook her. She threw the tray on the floor.

Someone grabbed her by the arm. It was Zizi Howell, one of the duo who called themselves the R.B.'s, the Rich Bitches, who'd introduced themselves in the rec room the night before. "Fuck that bitch, you don't gotta eat here," Zizi told her. "We make our own food upstairs." She led Hannah back to their dorm, a shabby kitchenette on the second floor. The other R.B., Valentina Rostov, was stirring a pot on a minute stove.

Valentina smiled broadly. "I have a welcome treat for you, Doran." She twisted open a small glass jar of cornichon pickles. It wasn't cornichons. It was caviar—the eggs were larger than any Hannah had ever seen and a pale, translucent gray, like fine sea pearls. "Genuine Beluga," Valentina said. "Five thousand dollars an ounce. I have friend who is sending it to me with my every month package. Lucky for me, C.O.'s are too stupid and ignorant to know what it is, otherwise they are stealing it fast."

"A generous friend," Hannah said with astonishment.
Zizi giggled.
Valentina made a sharp sound, and Zizi shut up.
"We are needing spoons, darling," Valentina said to her.
Zizi extended her wrist and snapped a spoon from up her sleeve.
"Magic," she said. "Do you want to see some more?" She passed her hands crosswise over her chest and then held out her opened palms. Nestled in the left was a neon blue cell phone. "Magic," she said again, and a laugh bubbled at her lips.

"Speed it up!" Benny Davis snapped at Hannah. "There's still a lot of folks to come. We don't have all day."

"Okay, Benny." She shook off the memory that had been triggered by the trays sliding past her station and concentrated on her task of serving salad. The line of clients seemed endless. Some of them smelled more pungently than the food. Some refused any salad. Others wanted salad, but only if they knew precisely what dressing was on it, or else they were quite specific about no shred of lettuce touching any other item, the chicken or black beans or sticky rice. One explained quite matter-of-factly that plants stayed alive inside you and took over your mind cells. Some appeared furious to be here; others smiled as sweetly as if they were at a quilting bee. Some seemed to be existing on a different, and possibly more vivid, planet.

The majority of them said some version of "thank you."

At first, Hannah tried to look at each client in the eyes and say a nice word. She knew how much a little thing could mean—a gentle touch of the hand, a kind glance.

"You're putting on too much." Benny Davis barked like a drill sergeant. "We're gonna run out before the end of the line. Start rationing."

"Got it!" She began dishing up smaller portions.

After the first hour, her shoulders were aching. By the end of the second, her serving arm was cramping. Despite cutting back on the portions, she did run out of rice and could only grimace in apology to the remaining dozen people.

Finally the last client had been served, and Hannah helped clear the trays to the clean-up crew inside the truck. Then she went in search of Benny. She found him smoking a cherry-colored pipe in front of the rusted green and white bus with a wheelchair access.

"Hard work, isn't it?" he said.

She stretched her shoulders. "Harder than it looks."

"I'm impressed you stuck it out."

"Did you think I wouldn't? Where do you think I've been the last fourteen months, the Maui Four Seasons?"

"Oh yeah, I forgot. You be some bad-assed hardened criminal now."

"You got that right," she snapped back.

It was the first time either of them had mentioned her prison term and it seemed to clear something in the air. "Hey, Benny?" Hannah ventured. "Could I ask you a question?" He twitched an eyelid. She took that as an affirmative. "I've been thinking about what you said. About how you'd met me when I was little with my mother."

"Yeah?"

"Where was it?"

"On the set of the last *Wildwood* movie. It must have been what, '89, '90? We were shooting in Arizona, out there in the Painted Desert. She came out for maybe about a week, and she brought you with her."

The ghost of a memory flickered. A cactus that looked like a person pointing to the sky. Running on white sand. A boy tickling her.

"So what was she like?"

"Your mama?"

"Yeah. My father will never talk about her. My grandfather used to sometimes, but usually just about when she was a little girl. And everybody else who knew her only tells me how beautiful and elegant she was. I can see that for myself in the pictures I have of her."

"So what do you want to know?"

"Anything. I mean . . . Did you like her?"

"Like her?" Benny tilted the stem of the pipe, considering the question. "I don't know if that's the right word. Your mother was . . . like a candle in a shadowy room. People got drawn to her. You couldn't help it, you just wanted to get near to that glow. Except maybe some of the actresses. Even during when she was pregnant with you and had a belly big as a beach ball, she could out-shine them."

"Did she seem unhappy?" Hannah pursued. "I mean, on the last set when she showed up with me, did she seem upset about anything?"

'I don't know." His tone was unconvincing.

"But you could tell there was something wrong?"

"Jesus Christ girl!" he exploded. "How am I expected to remember back then? I hardly knew your mother. She pretty much kept to herself. I can't answer these questions!"

"I'm sorry. I just . . . All my life I've been trying to make sense of what my mother did. Why she killed herself. She had an amazing life, everybody said so. My father worshipped her. Everybody did."

"So what do you think? You were such a rotten little kid, you drove your mom to drink bug poison?"

"No! Of course not."

"Look. Maybe there *is* no sense to it. Bad brain chemistry, who knows? Or maybe it's true that some movies are just plain damned cursed. You know, like what they say about the *Poltergeist* films. Five of the cast members died young. That little girl who was in it, dead when she was only twelve. The older one, Dominique Dunne, twenty-two when she was killed by her boyfriend. Some people think it's the same deal with *Wildwood*. Jackson's dead, and that girl who starred in the second movie, Emma Lockhart, dead of a brain tumor a few years later. Ken Motolla drowned less than six months after directing *Shamans*. And the writer, Ron Tobias—died choking on his own vomit after some tequila binge, didn't even make it to thirty. And look at me . . ." He shrugged. "Half dead."

Hannah shook her head. "I can't accept that my mother committed suicide just as the result of some curse."

"No, I don't suppose you can. But I'm sure as hell not interested in chewing over shit that's been over and done with years ago. You okay with that?"

"Yeah," she said. "I'm okay with that."

For now, anyway, she added silently.

❧

Roger Lopez pretended he didn't recognize the woman who'd hoisted herself into his 4Runner, but he did. She went by several names, Pettie, Patsy, Petunia Pig; and in certain circles she was as famous as they come, the freaking Meryl Streep of shoplifting. She could cruise into your Bloomingdale's or your Saks Fifth Avenue and in less than fifteen minutes jack about twenty K worth of merchandise, secreting it in the lining of her coat, the hem of her pants, a handbag with a zillion hidden compartments, up her pussy, you name it. Lopez might even have collared her once upon a time, he couldn't remember for sure.

He had cash for her. Five crisp Franklins, secured by an orange paperclip. She reached greedily for them.

"First the goods," he said.

"Okay, okay, okay." She rummaged in her bag of a zillion compartments. Her jaw was clenched so hard it was a frigging miracle it didn't snap in two. Being a meth-head really took it out of you.

"You got it or don't you?" Lopez demanded.

"Jeepers fucking H on a cross Christ almighty! I got it, okay, okay?"

Lopez backed off. Tweakers could go from irritated to enraged in the blink of an eye. Chances were excellent she hadn't slept in maybe a week.

From one of the bag's million compartments, she yanked out a strip of sparkle. "Got it got it got it. Like you wanted, store called Wave on Beverly Boulevard. No problem, easy job."

Lopez took the bracelet and examined the dangling price tag. $2,750. Didn't look like diamonds or emeralds, more like pieces of colored glass—rose, green, pale yellow—but the fancy price tag would definitely do the trick.

"I could fence that for more than five hundred, you know," Petunia Pig said with a shifty glance at him.

"I don't think so."

"Yeah, I totally could. Couple of places."

"You can try. Or you can take this like we agreed."

He held out the clipped bills. She snatched them and bolted out from the vehicle.

Lopez jiggled the necklace, letting it dance and play in the sunlight slanting through the dusty windshield. Pretty thing. The wife loved stuff like this. Too bad he had to let it go.

He slipped it into the pocket of the blue polyester phone company uniform he was wearing. Helped himself to a GoLower Nut Bar (3.3 net carbs). Then settled into a stake-out across from the garage exit of the Bougainville building. Just after noon, the silver blue Mercedes SLK pulled out with Hannah Doran at the wheel.

Lopez slung a tool belt around his hips and checked to make sure he had the key ring he'd been given. A small remote on the ring opened the garage gates. On foot, he headed into the garage and got into the elevator. He pressed PENTHOUSE. The elevator didn't budge: Hannah Doran had locked her floor. He was ready for this contingency: he turned a small key in the slot beside the button, and the elevator ascended eleven floors. Two more keys on the ring unlocked the double Schlage deadbolts on the penthouse door. He stepped inside.

His impression didn't change from when he'd been in here before to plant the bugs. Big place. Killer views. He wasn't mad about the décor, though. You'd think somebody in her income bracket could afford more leather. And what's with the no drapes?

He deliberated briefly over where to hide the bracelet. Didn't have to be rocket science. He lifted the cushion on a couch, stuck the bracelet under it, plumped the cushion.

Then he made a fast exit, locked the locks, got back into the elevator and hit GARAGE. Didn't budge. He tried the little key in the slot, but it didn't fit. Meaning to go up from the garage, you needed still another key, which nobody had given him. Why two different elevator keys? People were getting too damned paranoid these days.

He'd have to exit through the lobby.

No big deal—nobody was gonna give much notice to a telephone guy going purposefully about his business.

⁂

After the long nap, Mitch still ached, but in a manageable way. The sashimi hadn't been exactly filling. He showered, rewound his bandage and gingerly got dressed. Then he drove to Art's Deli and wolfed a pastrami on pumpernickel together with a mound of German potato salad, an extra-sour pickle, and three refills of black coffee.

Welcome back to the human race.

While he ate, he phoned his parents who still lived in the same Sacramento suburb where he'd grown up. "Your mom's having a lie-down," his dad told him. "They gave her that Tysabri treatment this morning and it just leaves her so wiped out. Hey, you know that stuff is made from mice?" His mom had been getting the drug intravenously once a month, and his dad always said the same thing. In the five years since Mitch's mother had been diagnosed with M.S., his dad seemed to have aged a couple of decades.

"Yeah, I know, Dad. Bioengineered from mice antibodies."

His dad chuckled. "I should start calling her Minnie."

He usually said that, too.

"I'm gonna come up real soon, Dad, I promise. And tell Mom I'll call her later. If she's up for talking."

By the time he got back in his car, it was late in the afternoon. Time flies when you're having fun.

He sped over Laurel Canyon and then down once more to the Bougainville Apartments. He had no real plan—he was just winging it. He parked on the street—legally, for a change. Then—still winging it—he went into the building. A piece of luck: it wasn't the doorman who'd tossed him out before. A younger Latino now manned the reception desk.

"Mitch Arpino, here to see Hannah Doran." He said it crisply, with authority.

The guy called the house phone. "No answer. You want to leave a message?"

Leave a phony name on the wild chance she'd give a call?

He had a better idea. He took out one of his business cards and scribbled: *V R is extremely dangerous. I can help.*

He asked the Latino kid for an envelope and sealed the card in it.

The elevator across the lobby pinged. The doors opened and a guy in a Pac Bell uniform stepped out, tool belt jangling,. Holy shit! It was Fat Face Guy, the P.I. in the green 4Runner with the phony handicap sticker. He flashed a thumbs up at the Latino kid and walked briskly out the door.

Mitch scrambled after him. "Hey! Hey, you!"

Fat Face shot him a nervous glance and quickened his steps. Mitch caught up to him. "Hey, you! Who do you work for?"

"I work for Pacific Bell, mister. Can't you read?"

"Don't give me that crap. I saw you the other day. You're staking Hannah, right?"

The guy's eyes widened. He broke into a trot.

The green 4Runner with the cripple sticker was parked once again at a red curb. Mitch wondered why he hadn't noticed it right away. His brain must be a bit fuzzy from the Percs.

Fat Face dove into the vehicle and clicked the door lock. Mitch banged on the window. "Hey, asshole, I want to talk to you!"

He sprang out of the way as the guy hit the gas. He ran after the 4Runner, still yelling, until he was racked by an intense wave of pain in his gut. He doubled over and vomited up a yellow-gray mash of pumpernickel, pastrami and potato salad.

Guess you can't have your guts pounded on and expect to be doing wind sprints any time soon. He resolved himself to another night of laying low.

TEN

Hannah stood in front of her closet again, this time frozen with indecision.

She'd be seeing her father in a just a couple of hours and could already feel his eye on her. Measuring her up to all the gorgeous women who'd passed through his life. Particularly measuring her up to her mother. She'd possessed an effortless chic—she'd been as stunning in jeans and a white T as in a Givenchy gown. Warren Doran could let his daughter know how far short of that standard she fell with just a lift of an eyebrow.

She wasn't dressing for him, she reminded herself. She was done begging for his approval.

The thought freed her and made it easy to choose an outfit. She paired an apricot cashmere cardigan with a soft black skirt, accessorized by black suede pumps and a liquid-looking white gold bracelet that had belonged to her mother. She brushed her hair to a shine and clipped it in a low ponytail. Darkened her lashes and applied a soft peachy lipstick.

Maybe the light was particularly forgiving in the room, but she was starting to think she looked rather pretty.

She grabbed a purse and headed out to the elevator. Eddie, the concierge, was just emerging from the service lift, holding an envelope. "Yo, Hannah. Just coming to put this under your door."

Not another late payment notice, she hoped. She opened the flap. The envelope contained a pale green business card:

MITCHELL J. ARPINO
A & J CELEBRITY SHOTS

Two phone numbers and an email address. And a message hand-written on the bottom:

V R is extremely dangerous. I can help.

V R—Valentina Rostov, it had to mean. Hannah felt a thrill of alarm.

Was it from him? The paparazzo from the lobby—the one who'd also been outside the Isis Hotel? Was it a trick? Some attempt at blackmail?

Or something genuine?

She couldn't think about it now. She dropped the card into her bag and then headed into the elevator.

From three blocks away, she could hear music blaring. Don't let it be from Dad's house, she prayed.

But she knew it would be: it was music from the 1940's, all creamy horns and wa-wa saxophones—her father's standard party repertoire. And indeed, when she pulled up to the house, it was ablaze in lights, the horns and saxes leaking from every window and door. Other cars were turning into the drive, and a pair of young men in red jackets were stacking them in the motor court.

Of course! What had she been expecting? A sentimental little reunion, just the two of them, all cozy in the breakfast nook? And she'd sob and say, "I'm sorry, Daddy," and tears would well in his eyes and he'd confess, "I'm sorry too that I was never there for you, but I promise I will be from now on," and they'd fall into each other's arms, all happy-ever-after?

Idiot! Even before her arrest, she could barely remember any time in her life when she'd been alone with her father. He always had people around him—domestic staff and WildFilm employees, business associates and social pals, and girlfriends and the friends of friends and the hangers-on of girlfriends' friends . . .

Why did she imagine anything would be different now?

She surrendered her car to one of the red jackets, then walked to the front door of her childhood home. It was a huge, white, geometric structure, a modernist style that had gone out of fashion for a time in the Eighties but had now come roaring back in style. Inside, a crowd that was typical for one of her father's gatherings: famous faces mingled with studio bigshots in the center, while less illustrious guests—the budding stars, the midlevel execs, the friends of friends—milled on the sidelines.

"Oooh, you must be Hannah!"

Hannah turned to see a woman fluttering towards her who

looked enough like Pamela Sebring Doran to make the hairs on the back of her neck prickle. Though this Pamela had a high-pitched voice with an eager, Australian accent. "I'm Tracy! I've been dying to meet you! I've heard so much about you, I feel like I know you already!"

Up close, the resemblance to Hannah's mother diminished. Tracy had Pamela's classic nose, but a bandage across the bridge proclaimed it had been recently reconstructed. The long, pale blonde-streaked hair approached, but didn't quite achieve, Pamela's silvered shade. And Tracy's blue eyes were a bleached denim, not Pamela's sapphires trapped in ice. And no surgery could ever replicate Pamela Sebring's flawless cheekbones.

"I've heard lots about you too, Tracy," Hannah told her. A polite lie.

"Oooh, I'm so glad. I know we're going to be super great friends." She swooped in for a hug, and Hannah caught the scent of Chanel Number 5. It had been her mother's signature perfume, she knew—a contrast to the showy Opiums and Poisons that were the rage in the Eighties. It evoked in Hannah a dim memory of a garden full of white flowers, a pair of long, cool arms encircling her.

For a moment, she wanted to strangle this chirping woman who had usurped her mother's scent and her mother's features.

But it wasn't Tracy's fault. Her father tried to remake all his women into a version of Pamela. And Tracy seemed better than most of them, if a lot more talkative: "I found the most scrumptious caterer, everything authentic American, grilled cheese and sweet potato fries, and ooh, hot oatmeal cookies with iced milk shooters . . ."

"It sounds amazing," Hannah interrupted. "But I wasn't expecting so many people."

"Oh, you know your dad. A real party animal. Once he starts inviting, he can't stop himself."

"Where is he?" Hannah asked impatiently.

"Oh, silly me, I should have taken you right away. He's in the den room making cocktails. He can't *wait* to see you!"

Tracy grabbed Hannah's hand and led her through the crowd, hailing every other face: "Looky, it's Hannah, the guest of honor!" and continuing to chatter nonstop. And then they were in the den with its wall of sliding glass doors giving onto the wide gardens and the pool. And there, suddenly, was Warren Doran.

Hannah felt her heart quicken.

He was standing behind the black marble bar, whirring up a froth in an old-fashioned green glass blender. He wore a loose, sea-blue linen shirt and perfectly-tailored black jeans. His hair was maybe a fraction thinner, the lines radiating from the corners of his eyes a bit more pronounced, but he still looked thirty-eight.

He had always looked thirty-eight.

A little crew of women bunched around him, hanging rapturously on his every word. He said something, grinned boyishly. The women tossed back their heads and laughed.

The blender went *shwhirrr.*

Then he glanced up and saw Hannah. And for a moment, his face went blank. Not a trace of emotion displayed on it.

She froze, not knowing how to even proceed.

Then suddenly he was grinning and beckoning to her with a cupped hand, all exuberance and welcome. "There she is!" he boomed over the wailing saxes. "Hannah! Honey Pie! Come on over here!"

"I'll leave you two to catch up," Tracy said kindly.

Hannah approached her father. He was holding the martini shaker between them, almost like a kind of armor. They both hesitated. "Dad . . ." she began.

He put the shaker down and held out his arms, and she bolted forward. She felt a slight restraint from him as he hugged her. That was okay—it was too soon to ask for more.

"How are you, Dad?" she began.

"Me? I'm great, honey pie. Fantastic! Couldn't be greater!"

"You look terrific. Really."

"Thanks, I'm feeling tip-top. You look swell, too, honeybun. Simple elegance, you can never go wrong." He turned to the group of women clustered around him. "Hey, everybody, let me introduce my daughter, Hannah!" He pronounced names. There was a babble of voices: *Wonderful to meet you, Hannah; Warren, you didn't tell us she was so attractive . . .* Hands squeezed hers, strangers embraced her.

Her father turned back to the bar.

Shwirrrr went the blender.

"I'm making strawberry daiquiris!" he announced. "In honor of my daughter, Hannah. Always been your favorite, right, honey bun?"

The first time he'd made one for her, Hannah had been about twelve and it was just strawberries and crushed ice, a slushy in a crystal tumbler, but over the years the drinks had acquired the requisite alcohol. It had become their tradition—that she was crazy about his strawberry daiquiris. Their only tradition.

"Yeah, I love them," she answered.

He handed her the frosty glass and she took her first taste of alcohol in over a year.

"Like you remember?" he beamed.

"Exactly. It's perfect."

"Go get yourself some chow, honeybun. Grab some of those Kobe beef sliders before they disappear. Tracy sure knows how to put on a good spread, doesn't she?"

"Yeah, I will, in a minute. Dad, I want to talk to you first."

"Of course. Shoot." Warren fastened the top on the cocktail shaker and began shaking vigorously.

"I mean, somewhere quiet. I wasn't expecting all these people. You told me you were going to clear your calendar."

"Of work, yeah, and I did. This isn't work, honey bunny. It's your coming home party. Once everybody heard you were back, of course they wanted to see you." He uncapped the shaker, poured the foaming liquid into a glass and poked a finger to stop the foam from overflowing the rim.

"I don't even *know* most of these people."

"Of course you do. You've met most of them before."

"It's not the point. I've got a lot I want to talk to you about."

"And we're going to have lots of time to do that. But right now, this is a celebration. Eat, drink and be merry! Have some fun! Be with people your own age!" His eyes swept the room. They settled on a thin, slouching kid with a Fu Manchu. "Look, there's Noah Post. You went to school with him, right? I'm hoping to get him for my new *Wildwood*—you've heard I'm relaunching the franchise, haven't you, honey? There's a part as a young jewel trader Noah would be perfect for . . ."

He was trying to slot her back into her old role—luring in the young actors for whatever movie he had in the works. "Noah Post doesn't interest me," she said. "I came here to see you."

Somebody gripped her by the elbow. "Excuse me, Warren, mind if I borrow your daughter for a moment?" A short, fortyish woman with a pretty face framed by chunky enameled earrings. It took Hannah a moment to place her: Alicia Chenoweth, the Constellation Studios executive in charge of her father's new movie.

"Sure, absolutely, Alicia," Warren said heartily.

Alicia led her to a sofa in a quieter corner of the room. "I was just on my way out but wanted to say hello. I hope you remember me."

"Of course I do," Hannah told her. "That summer I interned for you was one of the best times of my life."

"How are you doing now?"

"Okay. A little overwhelmed, I guess."

"I can imagine. But I really wanted to tell you that I think you look absolutely lovely. This is the way I remember you from that summer, a girl with shiny brown hair."

"I had it done back to my natural color before reporting to prison." Hannah shrugged wryly. "I figured the salon services there were not going to be great."

Alicia chuckled. "You've got the most lovely gray eyes, but they were lost when you had blonde hair. Now they really pop. The first thing I noticed when I saw you come in."

Hannah shook her head self-consciously. "I think I put on a little weight. All my clothes are too tight."

"Only because you used to be practically anorexic before. You look much better now. You've got a bloom. You must be doing something right."

"I did quit smoking. And drinking. At least, mostly." She displayed her glass. "My first in way over a year."

"No refills." Alicia took the glass out of her hand and placed it on a nearby table. "Remember what a bossy bitch I am?"

Hannah grinned. "I do remember that most of the interns were terrified of you. But I figured you had to be pretty tough to get where you were. There were some V.P.'s who just liked to throw their egos around. But when you were harsh, it was always for a reason."

"Was I harsh with you?" Alicia pulled a face.

"Only if I was dragging my butt and deserved it."

"That couldn't have been very often, because I remember being very impressed with you. I picked you out as a girl with enormous potential. And I still think so. You just wandered off the right path. And maybe . . . well . . ."

"Maybe getting locked up was the best thing that could have happened to me?" Hannah couldn't keep an edge of bitterness out of her voice.

"No, of course not! It was a terrible thing, maybe even an unjust thing. I just meant that maybe you could start all over again. Do it better this time. Do you have any plans?"

"Yeah, I do. I'm going back to college in the fall, but there's something else. Something I'm pretty excited about it." Her face became animated. "Have you ever heard of the Sunlight Center?"

"Sure. Benny Davis's baby! I went to a benefit for it a year or two ago. It's supposed to be a terrific facility."

Hannah nodded eagerly. "I've started volunteering there, and I'm hoping to get really involved. I mean, with funding and administration. I think it's something that I could make a real difference."

"I'm sure it is. From everything I know about it, it's perfect for you! Something you could really sink your teeth into. I always wondered . . ." Alicia regarded her intently.

"Wondered what?"

"What made you change? I mean, why did you drop out of Yale so suddenly and become the opposite of everything you seemed to really be?"

Hannah glanced at her. There was such a depth of warmth and maternal concern in Alicia's brown eyes that she had the sudden impulse to throw herself into her arms, be cradled and comforted. "It was a stupid thing, really," she admitted. "There was a parents' weekend. My father promised to come, and then he stood me up. He'd done the same thing a hundred times before. I don't know why this time it felt different. I thought, I don't know . . . If I came back to L.A. and made myself into somebody more interesting and glamorous . . ."

"Then maybe he'd pay attention to you?"

Hannah gave a short laugh. "We had to do group therapy at Peachrock, and the therapist asked me if I thought that's why I stole the necklace—to get my father's attention."

"Do you think it's true?"

"No, I don't." For a moment, Hannah was tempted to confide everything in Alicia—about the drug Shawn had put in her drink, and her suspicions that one or more of her friends had set her up. Who better to give her advice than Alicia?

But Alicia was glancing at her watch, getting ready to leave. "Listen, Hannah, it's hard to be the child of a famous parent. I see the casualties all over town. I worry about it with my own daughters. Not that I'm particularly famous, but they will grow up knowing privilege."

"So you have kids now?"

"Yes, twins. Shane and Laura. They're four going on five, and I guess I'm one of those over-protective middle-aged moms. I get frantic if I leave them for too long. Which is why I've got to scoot. I promised them I'd be home before they went to sleep." She leaned and kissed Hannah tenderly on the forehead, like a mother to a favored daughter. "You're going to be fine, Hannah. I have total confidence in you."

From the corner of an eye, Warren uneasily observed his daughter getting chummy with Alicia Chenoweth.

He'd made a mistake. He had not sufficiently prepared himself for the sudden appearance of his daughter. Particularly for the change in her appearance—looking so much more like she had when she was younger. For one horrible second, it had brought back feelings he thought he had long suppressed. Feelings of rage and powerlessness. Memories of people long dead.

He wondered if he had given any of that away.

A flame erupted in his esophagus. He grabbed a miniature melted cheese sandwich and stuffed it in his mouth. This so-called simple food cost a fortune. For all these teeny-tiny burgers and bite-sized peach cobblers, they could have had filet mignon. But at least the bland cheese and bread helped soothe down the acidic bubble.

Things were at a crucial point. He could not afford to make any mistakes. Yesterday, at the Shutters bar, he had floated the prospect to the men in navy blue of dropping down their cut of the *Wildwood* deal. He had spun and tapped and twirled as fast and as furiously as he could. Movie deals were made up of many different entities that were always in flux, he'd assured them. You gave up a little here, you collected more there.

In the end, there'd still be buckets of money for everyone.

The professional cordiality had drained from their eyes. It was replaced by a hard, steely gaze.

Taking a page from Alicia's book, Warren laid the blame entirely on Cody Takish. "The bastard is making a power play. Unfortunately, he's crazy enough to blow the whole project apart and if he does, nobody wins. And that is what we've got to prevent, by whatever means necessary."

They didn't say yes and they didn't say no. They were due at a meeting in Vegas. They made some polite noises and left abruptly for their plane.

That look—flat, cold—in their eyes was beyond frightening: it had tortured Warren for the rest of the day and night, prevented him from sleeping, causing him to start awake at every rustle and creak in the night.

He'd go see Cody Takish first thing tomorrow. He'd get on his knees if he had to. Promise him anything, a cash bribe, suck his dick, whatever. And if Cody wanted Alicia Chenoweth to be thrown to the dogs, then so be it.

Tracy's brassy laugh suddenly sliced through the music. She'd commandeered the young actor Noah Post and the kid practically had his nose down her cleavage. Good for business. Tracy was almost right, he reflected. That prima donna of a Beverly Hills surgeon had sculpted her nose perfectly, and her hair was the correct shade of pale blonde. The breasts were maybe half a cup size too large, but those too could be corrected. Her single greatest defect was that voice. She never stopped talking. She was vocal even during sex. She talked dirty. She talked nonsense. She wouldn't shut up.

He glanced back at Alicia and Hannah again. Hannah, the wild card, the one factor that could really wreck his universe. Thad Miller would take care of things, he assured himself. Thad always did.

He watched Alicia tenderly kiss his daughter. Maternally.

He grabbed his own drink—a Ketel One martini—and went to join them. "So what are you two cooking up?" he said jovially.

They both looked a little startled at his approach. "I was just leaving, Warren," Alicia said, getting to her feet. "We'll talk first thing in the morning."

"We certainly will, Alicia." Warren leaned solicitously to his daughter. "Honeybun, I didn't mean to neglect you. Come with me—there's still a lot more folks I want you to meet."

⁂

For the rest of the evening her father had stayed glued to her side, though they were never actually alone—he was always waving over new people, gathering a little crowd. Hannah's brief chat with Alicia Chenoweth had somehow been reassuring—she was able to play her part of the charming, poised young woman with great potential. An asset to her father. Another frozen daiquiri had appeared in her hand, and despite Alicia's orders, she finished it.

Driving home, she realized how stupid she'd been to have the drinks. She was not going down that slope again. No way! But once again, she'd fallen under the spell of her father's enormous charm. If it pleased him to make her daiquiris, she'd been charmed into drinking them. And he'd promised they would spend more time together: "Alone, just you and me, as soon as I can catch my breath."

Did she believe him? She flashed on the look on his face when he'd first seen her. The absence of any expression. Somehow it had been worse than if he had shown anger or disgust.

What did it mean? she wondered, as the elevator opened onto her penthouse floor. Had she disappointed him so terribly that he could hardly still consider her as his daughter?

She turned the double keys and opened the door. There were lights blazing throughout the first floor. Maybe she was still buzzed from the daiquiris because she couldn't remember leaving so many turned on.

Then something moved on the couch, and she let out a shriek.

ELEVEN

Valentina Rostov had kicked off the stiletto-heeled sandals that had been killing her bad back, and she lay sprawled on the couch, an embroidered silk pillow mashed under her head, big bare feet propped on the opposite arm. Her black dress, made of a slippery fabric, was scooped deep in front, its brief skirt hiked just short of her panties. A near-empty bottle of Skyy vodka and a cocktail glass sat in easy reach on the floor beside her. A saucer overflowing with cigarette butts floated on her stomach.

"Christ god, Doran," she said hazily, "don't be so jumpy. It's only me."

"How did you get in here?" Hannah snapped.

"That sweet little man who guards the door downstairs is letting me in. It's about time you are getting back. I am waiting for a million hours." The Russian's lipstick, a vivid orange, looked like it had been applied in a moving car: it made her smeary features look even smearier.

Hannah strode to the phone. "I'm calling the police."

"Don't be a stupid ninny. You're just a couple of days out of prison, and here you are in your own home with one of your fellow prisoners. Do you want police checking this out? Who knows what I am hiding in my bag? Maybe narcotics, I don't know."

Hannah glanced at her warily. She moved away from the phone. "What do you want?"

"I'm not going to hurt you, Doran. I just want to talk to you in privacy. But you are a celebrity, if you go someplace, everybody watches you. Everybody listens. So tell me, please, what else am I supposed to do?" Valentina reached for the cobalt blue bottle and swirled the dregs. "I'm so sorry, darling, I drank up all your vodka, it is the only thing I can find. So nice and frosty in the bottom of your freezer drawer. But you must only drink Russian vodka, darling, not silly designer type."

Hannah dropped into a chair. "All right, let's talk."

"First things first. I want some money. In cash."

"Yeah, I figured that. What do you need it for?"

Valentina gave a snort. "Everybody always needs money. I had a friend who was paying me lots of money. Both me and my darling girl Zizi. But now that I am out of jail, I am no longer convenient to her. We are both of us now just a nuisance to her. Zizi and I are wanting to get out of town. Far away out of town."

"You're going to break parole? You could get in a lot of trouble."

"'You could get in a lot of trouble.'" Valentina repeated Hannah's words in a mocking singsong. "I don't give a shit about parole. Parole is nothing. There is much more trouble for me than breaking my parole."

"So how much do you want?"

"Fifty thousand dollars."

Hannah gave a startled laugh. "Are you kidding? What makes you think I'd give you that much?"

Valentina directed a smug smile at Hannah. "Why is it, do you think, Doran, that when they go searching your dorm room at Peachrock, they are finding a little knife inside your mattress?"

"I already know why. You set me up—you and Zizi."

Valentina gave an assenting shrug of her shoulders. "Yes, okay, but my point is, who do you think was putting us up to it?"

Hannah shot her a startled glance. "What do you mean? I thought you were just trying to get back at me. Because I didn't want to hang out with you and your R.B.'s anymore."

Valentina's face went slack with scorn. "You're a stupid, stupid girl, did you know that? Do you think I am wasting so much of my time because a nothing, pathetic creature like you doesn't want to play with me anymore? Is your head really so swelled up?"

"So why did you do it then?" Hannah demanded.

"Ah ha, now you see, I have something to sell. And you've got something to buy. Oh, there is so much you need to know, darling little girl. You think you went to prison by accident? Oh, once I tell you things, you are going to think fifty thousand dollars is a cheap price, I can promise you."

A wave of nausea slammed over Hannah. "Why should I believe anything you say?"

"You always were knowing something was wrong, isn't that true? Me, I'll tell a lie if I need to, I don't care. But let me tell you, stupid girl, I'm not lying to you now."

"Did it have something to do about an intervention? About putting something in my drink to make me sick?"

"You think I'm giving away my information for free? Darling, you know me better. But I will tell you one thing for free. Whatever it is you think you know, forget about it. There's a million times more."

Hannah stared into Valentina's eyes. She saw greed, stubbornness, a swaggering sense of superiority. But beneath all that, ill-concealed by her mocking bravado, there was also a deep degree of fear. "Okay. I'll give you what you want. Fifty thousand dollars."

Valentina sat up eagerly. The cigarette butt-laden plate on her stomach overturned on the couch. "Oops." She began plucking the butts off the cushion with a drunken meticulousness.

"Leave it," Hannah said.

Valentina tried to brush off ashes, grinding them further into the fabric. "Now look what I've done. What a mess I am making. Don't worry, I will clean it all up." She tried getting to her feet, weaving a little.

"Stay there. I'll get something to wipe it with."

As Hannah disappeared into the kitchen, Valentina fell back down onto the couch. She hazily thought of Zizi waiting all this time outside in the Rolls Royce convertible she'd stolen from a Century City mall parking garage this afternoon—a trade-in for the Bentley she'd boosted a couple of days before. Silly girl, Zizi. Valentina had wanted her this time to take something a little less show-offy, maybe a Honda or even a Hyundai, something that wouldn't scream "Whoo, hey everybody, look at me!" but when it came to automobiles, Zee was a dumb little snob. And anyway, Zee said, just so long as they didn't get attached to any one car, the way Zee so stupidly had done with that Porsche Carrera she'd gotten herself locked up in prison for, but instead keep switching them everyday, they'd be okay.

Still, Valentina felt jumpy. She needed to get what she came for and then get the hell out. She lapped up the last drops of vodka in her glass, squirmed, then attempted to pick up the rest of the cigarette butts, succeeding only in wedging one further down between the cushions. She tried to dig it out, and her fingers closed on something hard. Instinctively, she knew it was a piece of jewelry.

Yes, she was correct. It was a bracelet made of sparkling stones with a solid gold clasp. Very pretty. And it still had a price tag on it, in the four figures.

That dumb rich bitch, Valentina thought scornfully. So careless with her valuables and probably didn't even give a damn.

She glanced furtively toward the kitchen. Hannah was emerging with a damp cloth in hand. Valentina tucked the bracelet into the cleavage of her bra and stood up unsteadily, wedging her feet back into the shoes. The bracelet made a satisfying lump between her breasts. "So we are all clear, then?" she said.

"Yes. I'll just need some time to get the cash."

"Oh, please. Everybody knows you're filthy rich."

"Not quite yet. Most of my money is locked up in a trust."

Valentina shot a glance around the sumptuous penthouse. "So who is paying for all this?"

"I get an allowance, but it's controlled too, and right now it's gotten screwed up. I have to get things straightened out before I can get you any kind of money."

"Then get your things straightened out. By tomorrow. Four o'clock."

"That's not enough time."

"I have no more time," Valentina said sharply. "I am coming back here tomorrow at four o'clock."

"No, not here! I don't want you coming back into this building."

"So where, then, please?" Valentina said scornfully.

Hannah racked her brain: The city was teeming with eyes: where, outside her own home, had she ever experienced solitude? "There's a cemetery in Hollywood, it's called the Forever Cemetery—it's on Santa Monica, off Gower. It's never very crowded. If you drive through it to the opposite end, there's a lake with a little Greek temple on an island. We can meet up there. "

"A cemetery. Beautiful, darling. Very James Bond, very cloak and dagger. Okay, we can meet like spies at four o'clock. But remember, if you're not there, I am leaving, and you are never finding out any of these things you definitely need to know. You understand?"

"Making yourself understood has never been your problem, Valentina," Hannah said sharply.

"Okay. Beautiful." Valentina ineffectively tried to smooth the creases in her dress, gave up and wove her way to the door. She paused at an array of photographs on the console table and picked up a photo of Hannah's mother. "I know who this is. Pamela Sebring."

"Don't touch that." Hannah lunged to grab it away.

"Oh, I see, she is your icon. Your perfect Madonna, pure as driven snow. Well let me tell you something else, darling Hannah. Your worshipped and adored Madonna was not so pure as snow after all."

"Shut up! You don't know anything about her."

"Oh, and you are thinking that you do? You are thinking she just said one day 'oh my heavens, life is so boring, there is nothing good to watch on t.v., I think I will just swallow this little bit of poison and die'?"

"Just shut up!"

"No problems." Valentina put the photo down and tottered out the door.

Hannah stood trembling for a moment. It suddenly seemed that nothing in her life was what she had thought. Had any of her friends really been her friends? And what did she really know about her mother? Who was she? Why did she choose to die?

And what, if anything, did Hannah truly know about herself?

She struggled to control her emotions, but it was impossible. She sank into a chair, pressed the cloth she was still clutching to her eyes and, doubling over, began to cry convulsively.

※

Roger Lopez, behind the wheel of the green SUV with the handicap placard dangling from the mirror, lit into the popcorn chicken that had come with the KFC Variety Big Box Meal. He was still shaken from his run-in with the guy in the Swoosh cap—same dude who'd banged on his window the first night on this job. Because of his nerves, Lopez had been stuffing down carbs to beat the band as he recorded the conversation up in the penthouse across the street. He washed down the popcorn with a slurp of Pepsi. All was silent for a few moments up there. And then a lot of boo-hooing.

He took notice of the person coming out of the building's front door. It was the tall whore-faced redhead he'd observed go in some hours before. Fifty to one it was the babe with the Russian accent he'd been listening in on.

Pulling on his soda straw, he kept eyes on her as she walked up the street, booty swinging in that short black dress. She got into a sweet Rolls convertible, with a hot little black baby behind the wheel. The two of them, redhead and black baby, stuck their faces together for a big wet kiss. They swapped tongues for a while, then drove off.

Lopez noted the incident on his Microcassette, trying to keep the smirk out of his voice. Then he began tackling the mashed potatoes with gravy. He'd polished it off and was working on the biscuit and crispy strip, when up rolls an SUV. Blackest frigging vehicle Lopez's ever seen. No chrome, blacked out windows. Even the Nevada dealer plates murky with splattered mud.

The killer-eyed guy named Cherry jumps out. Lopez hands over both the recorded conversation upstairs and the cassette with his dictated notes. Reports about the redhead and the black baby locking lips.

"Nice." Cherry's grin stretches nearly all the way back to Nevada.

"The big one, the Russian—she was up there with the Subject," Lopez continues. "She tried to shake the Subject down for fifty grand. Subject resisted. Russian says she knows stuff."

"Stuff, huh?"

"Uh, yeah. Hints that the Subject's ass got sent to the pen because of a set-up. She'll tell all once she gets the cash."

Cherry begins whistling tunelessly. Everything about this dude gives Lopez the creeps. He hands him the recorded microtape. "It's all on here. They're meeting up at some cemetery tomorrow."

"We'll see about that," Cherry says.

Lopez doesn't even *want* to know what that's supposed to mean. "So we're good for tonight, then?"

"We're good." Cherry looks at his watch. It's blue plastic, like a kid's watch. "I'm off," he says. "I got some people to meet."

⁂

Cody Takish, the youthful president of Worldwide Production of Constellation Studios, and his wife, Marilyn, had been snapping at each other since the drive home from dinner at Toscana. She bitching that she did not appreciate the snide, shitty way he'd talked about her "dabbling" at interior decorating, how dare he mock her profession in front of all the others at the table? And, by the way, don't think she hadn't noticed Cody drooling over that teenaged Silicone Wonder that Howie Brenner had tried to pass off as his date, as if everyone didn't know Howie was a closet fag, just ask his two ex-wives. And Cody had replied yeah, sure, you and all your friends adore thinking you're married to a bunch of queens because it's better than the truth, which is when it comes to fucking, your sagging tits and cellulite asses are a total buzz kill, baby.

From these opening salvos, they'd escalated into full-scale war, lobbing deadly missiles of insults and accusations at each other; until finally Marilyn had swallowed a double dose of Lunestra and dropped off into a deep, softly snoring oblivion.

Cody stomped down to the media room and poured himself a stiff scotch. Then he reconsidered and rolled a joint of an amazing high-potency grass that had been hand-carried from Humboldt County specially for him.

He slumped in a leather swivel chair, inhaling deeply, staring at the t.v. Letterman drooling over Anne Hathaway. Bet *her* buns don't make you think of cottage cheese.

Pleasantly stoned, he dozed off.

A crash of shattering glass directly overhead jerked him awake some hours later and propelled him off his chair. Earthquake! During the last big one, he'd been yanked out of a sound sleep by the sound of his chimney crumbling, furniture crashing all over the house. Nearly caused him heart failure.

Stay calm. Don't panic.

After a moment, he realized there was no shaking or rolling. Not a quake. It had just been one fuck of a loud crash and then silence.

So what the hell?

He crept gingerly back up to the ground floor. "Marilyn? Did you break something?"

Couldn't have been Marilyn. Once she took her Lunestra, Armageddon couldn't wake her. It was probably Graciela, the live-in housekeeper. Getting up to furtively raid the refrigerator without turning on lights.

But there was nobody in the kitchen. Nor in the dining room.

"Graciela?" Nervous now, Cody edged down the hall toward the living room.

Even in the dark he could see that one of the tall arched windows facing the garden was shattered. He felt a jolt of fear. He assured himself that every window and door in the house was wired to the alarm, and that Marilyn, a safety freak even in the middle of a drag-out fight, would have been careful to arm the system when they returned. A broken window would immediately notify the private security company, and a patrol car would already be on its way.

He snapped on the light. Jumped. The person who had smashed the window was still in the room!

A guy in a blue jeans jacket. He appeared to be sort of stroking one of Cody's most prized pieces of art—a heavy glass sculpture that resembled an undulating sea creature, by the famous artist . . . well, Cody could never remember the name of the artist, but his dealer had told him the piece was now worth three times the twenty-something grand he'd paid for it.

"Don't touch that!" he snapped.

The intruder looked blankly at him. He grasped the sculpture in his hands and raised it.

The doorbell chimed.

"That's my security people at the door," Cody said smugly. "So if I were you, I'd put that back. It's a valuable piece of art."

The guy hoisted the sculpture a little higher.

"Are you goddamned deaf?" Cody strode sternly over to him. "I said, put that down!"

This time the intruder did exactly what he was told, putting it down hard on the top of Cody Takish's skull.

TWELVE

Pick me up, Mommy!"

Shane, the elder of Alicia Chenoweth's twin daughters by six minutes, wrapped her arms around her mother's legs as Alicia was trying to roll up a pair of opaque black stockings.

"Not now, sweetheart, Mommy needs to get dressed."

Shane continued to cling to her. "I want you to pick me up!" Her hands were gluey with oatmeal. Alicia firmly detached herself from her daughter and yelled to her nanny: "Marianela! Can you please come and get the kids?"

On the opposite side of the bedroom, Shane's sister Laura, wearing nothing but sunshine-colored panties, was trying to walk in the Cole Haan pumps Alicia was planning to wear: she shuffled a few steps, toppled over and howled.

"Marianela!" Alicia snapped the tights at her waist, then went to the howling Laura, with Shane toddling after her. Cradling Laura, she glanced at the clock. 7:55. She was due at 8:30 at a meeting with Cody and several of the higher-ups. Barring a miracle, she was already going to be several minutes late.

Marianela, a hollow-cheeked young Peruvian with bobbed raven hair, appeared in the room. "Something is wrong with the stroller, Alicia. I can not make it to go open."

Alicia noticed that her tights were now smeared with oatmeal and would necessitate a change. If she didn't have another pair in black, it would mean a total change of outfit.

"I want to watch t.v.!" Shane scrambled over to the Sony that was tuned silently to *Good Morning, America* and plopped herself down directly in front of it.

"I wanna watch t.v.," echoed Laura and shoved Shane aside. Shane slapped her sister's shoulder and Laura returned a swat to Shane's arm.

"Girls, stop it please! Marianela, would you take them to finish their breakfast so I can *please* get dressed."

Marianela managed to coax the twins back to the kitchen. Alicia began peeling off the smeared tights, one eye on the television. It seemed that George Stephanopoulis had been co-opted by a local breaking news story. An aerial shot of a fancy neighborhood, big houses with sprawling grounds. One house directly in center view, a white L-shaped contemporary with a long, rectangular pool; seen from the vertiginous three-quarter angle of a helicopter's vantage, it reminded Alicia of Cody Takish's place.

She rummaged through a drawer in the built-in bank, fishing out another pair of tights. The on-screen image flashed to a covered body being wheeled on a gurney through a throng of television crews, caught-in-the-moment dog walkers, bathrobe-clad neighbors. A crawl began at the bottom of the screen: STUDIO BOSS DEAD IN SANTA MONICA HOME INVASION.

Alicia felt a tingling in her fingertips.

The helicopter camera zoomed in from above on the white contemporary. "My god!" she whispered. It was definitely Cody's house. His pool was edged with fountains shaped like dolphins spouting water from their parted snouts, and yes, there they were—dolphins, clearly identifiable.

She dove for the remote and turned up the sound. A man in the uniform of a private security firm was being interviewed: "We've been seeing this, a lotta break-ins all over the Westside. Don't matter if there's a security system—they smash a window, grab whatever's handy. In and out before we even arrive. I guess Mr. Takish just happened to be up at that time and unfortunately caught them by surprise . . ."

Alicia suddenly became aware that her cell phone and every extension of her house phone was ringing.

During her twenty-five minute speed to the studio, Alicia frantically reviewed her options. Cody dead! It couldn't be true. But if it was. . . . If Cody really had been suddenly . . . well, removed, things might now go her way. A cold thought, but a reality.

On the other hand, if the studio quickly replaced him, it could be worse for her. The first thing a new hire does is sweep out all their predecessor's projects. Cody had swiftly and efficiently cleaned house when he came in.

There was only one move that guaranteed a win for her. A highly risky move, but she was desperate enough to attempt it. Turning into Constellation, she rehearsed what she intended to say.

Everyone had gathered in the conference room. It looked like a war room. A grim tribunal sat around the table. Dick Landower, the silver fox who was chairman of the parent corporation, presided like a general. He was flanked by two lieutenants: Martin Drake, chairman of the studio, a man whose eyeballs were constantly in motion; and Lois Dubosky, overdressed head of worldwide marketing and distribution. Various other senior executives slumped in seats. Faces were ashen. Shaky hands brought cups to lips and picked from the platters of scones, muffins, and bagels arrayed on the table.

"I'm in total shock," Alicia proclaimed, pouring herself coffee.

"We're all in shock," said the chairman, Dick Landower. "This is a stunning and completely unforeseeable tragedy."

"It's *farcockt!*" exploded the marketing chief Lois Dubosky. "He was what, only thirty-six? It's a terrible, *farcockt* thing."

Everyone muttered in agreement.

"Lois, does Publicity have a handle on the memorial arrangements?"

"Full page in both *Variety* and the *Reporter* tomorrow. We'll be making a substantial contribution in his name to cerebral palsy—Marilyn is on the board of the Southern California Association. We haven't been able to talk to her yet—she's under heavy medication."

"Was she assaulted too?" one of the V.P.'s ventured.

"No, thank god, she was upstairs asleep," Lois said. "The intruder didn't get up there."

"Do we have the full story on what happened?" Alicia asked.

"Pretty much," said Martin Drake, eyes darting left and right. "At around three in the morning, somebody smashed through a window of the ground floor of his house. According to the police, it's been the M.O. of a rash of burglaries on the Westside recently. They figure Latin American or Russian gangs. These guys don't give a damn about setting off alarms. They grab whatever valuables are in reach and are gone before the security or the cops arrive. Poor Cody just happened to be up at the time. The cops figure he heard the window breaking and went to investigate. Caught them trying to steal his Chihuly and he attempted to stop them."

"His what?" demanded Lois Dubosky.

"Dale Chihuly sculpture. Made of glass. Very heavy. The robbers bashed his head with it."

Cody killed by a Chihuly. Alicia suppressed a snort.

"He's sort of a hero, isn't he?" mused Dick Landower. He ran a hand through his silver locks. "He was defending his home and his family."

"Absolutely!" declared Martin. "He went down like a champ."

He went down, at any rate, Alicia thought.

"Cody always was a fighter," somebody contributed. "Never one to back off."

"I think we should observe a minute of silence to meditate on Cody Takish's life and valor." Dick Landower bowed his head.

Alicia stared down at the polished surface of the exotic rosewood table, and in its loops and grain she conjured a picture of Cody Takish: his gingerbread man head and his iced-on mouth shaping its habitual O of petulance. She saw him screaming apoplectically at his underlings. Kissing the bottoms of people who counted. Stealing credit for successes he'd had no part in and assigning blame to others for his own failures.

Be charitable, she chided herself. The poor schmuck's dead. Find something good to think about him.

She groped to remember something, anything—some little kindness or random act of generosity. Okay . . . The last time she'd had the flu, he'd urged her to stay home in bed, even though they'd had to postpone an important meeting.

Although the real reason was that he was just so paranoid about catching germs . . .

I could murder the little prick, I really could. Her words to Warren Doran suddenly replayed in her mind.

And Warren's reply, something about how that would be justice and therefore could never happen in Hollywood . . .

She hadn't meant it literally, obviously. And so there was no reason she should feel even an iota of responsibility.

None at all.

Nevertheless, she did feel a slight nag of something like guilt.

The minute of silence seemed to be dragging on for about an hour. She wondered if anybody was actually keeping time.

After what felt like another infinity, Dick Landower lifted his head. "Godspeed, Cody," he pronounced.

"Go with the angels, buddy," echoed Martin Drake.

"*Shalom*, kid," said Lois. "You didn't stick around long, but while you were here, you grabbed life to the fullest."

"Amen to that," said somebody else.

They all raised their coffee cups in a valedictory salute.

"Okay, let's get down to business." Dick Landower squared his shoulders, placed his palms on the table. "Fact. We are now left without a head of production. We've got to take immediate control of the situation. No way we can look like we're left with our dicks swinging in the wind. We've got to present seamless control, and that means getting on the phone, people. We've got to reach out to all agents, to our top talent. To all our open deals. Make sure everybody understands we're still completely on the ball."

Voices piped up in full support.

"I've got the trades covered," Lois said. "I'll be directing their reporters to you, Dick, for a couple of lines about how we've got terrific management and we won't be missing a beat. The *Wall Street Journal*'s gonna definitely want something."

"How about the networks?" A note of preening importance crept into Landower's voice. "Think they might want to talk to me?"

Jesus weeps, Alicia thought.

"Fox, for sure," Lois said. "CNN probably. I'll get on the others."

"And needless to say," Martin Drake chimed in, "Dick and I will be making calls to all the other studios to remind them that if any of their people try poaching on any of our deals while we are in . . . let's say mourning . . . we will tear their heads from their bodies and stuff them up their freaking asses." He smiled grimly.

Everyone chortled and nodded.

Alicia girded herself: if she was going to say what she had rehearsed on the way over, it was now or never. "Martin, if I could say a word about protecting our projects . . ."

"Go ahead, Alicia." Martin darted a quick look at her.

"I totally agree with Dick. We've got to make sure everybody sees clearly that we're still on top of all our stuff. We've got terrific movies in the works. Under Cody, they were parented by a strong head of production, and it's going to take another strong head of production to keep them on track. Somebody already in the loop, who knows where all the bodies are buried. Someone who's aware of all the stuff that didn't make the memos." She took a breath. "If you're thinking that someone sounds like me, I'm thinking you may be right."

No reaction from either Dick Landower or Martin Drake.

She plunged ahead: "I was Cody's number two. He shared everything with me. If you want seamless continuity, I can provide it. Of course, if you can think of somebody better . . . And who's immediately available . . ."

Still silence. Some of the other production executives wore shit-eating grins. Expecting her to go down in flames.

Then Martin Drake stole a glance at his superior, Dick Landower. The chairman shrugged and nodded.

"Yeah, okay, makes sense to me," Martin said. "For now, Alicia, consider yourself acting president of production. No increase in salary. If it sticks, we'll work out the details later. Got it?"

Alicia was almost too stunned to reply. She caught the breath she'd been holding. "Sure, yes, great! I'll start running down all the open projects right away, to make sure none of them slip out the door. Beginning with our biggest—*Wildwood Murphy*. If it's going to be our tent pole release for next summer, it's got to go into production by the end of next month."

"I can personally attest that Cody was passionate about that movie," Lois offered.

Having now moved on from whatever Cody Takish was or was not passionate about, nobody made a comment. Appetites improved: people began tearing into muffins and bagels and swiping them with butter and jam.

"So here's what I'm going to do," Alicia pushed on. "I'm going to bring Denny Brandt's entire agency over here—from the top brass down to the copy room boys if necessary—and I'm going to close on his deal. Then we can sign a director, and this studio will be sitting on next summer's megahit!"

"Wait a sec, Alicia," Martin Drake said. "Cody told me *Wildwood* was too expensive. And I was inclined to agree with him. In these days, a hundred and seventy million is a big bite to swallow."

Alicia thought fast. "Yes, and actually my very last conversation with Cody *was* about getting the cost down. His idea was to shave something off Denny Brandt's deal. I floated that to his people and got an emphatic no. Denny's got three other major offers on the table. He'd pass on us in a New York minute. But I'm positive that I can get . . ." She paused, rapidly calculating: "At least three points off from the production side. I've already discussed the possibility with Warren Doran."

Martin glanced at Dick who almost imperceptibly nodded.

"Okay, then, I think we're all on the same page," Martin said.

"Alicia, get the concessions from Warren Doran. Resubmit the budget, then we'll nail down Denny Brandt and make this puppy fly!"

Warren Doran received the shocking news about Cody from his personal trainer who arrived at the house at six forty-five a.m. The immense flood of relief he felt caused such a violent quaking of his entire body that he couldn't continue the workout. He closeted himself in the library to watch the t.v. coverage.

He sat through two entire cycles. Two reruns of Cody Takish's shrouded body journeying on the coroner's gurney. Two updates of statements from cops and neighbors. His quaking finally subsided, replaced by a feeling of such buoyancy that he gripped the arms of his chair as if to keep himself from bobbing to the ceiling. It was another hour before he felt he could sufficiently compose himself to shower and get dressed and appear at the WildFilm offices looking, if not appropriately somber, at least not positively ebullient.

It was after nine. The phones were symphonic. No one was sitting—everyone was standing in corridors or darting between offices, feeding off the buzz. Warren's assistant Benjamin waved a sheaf of messages. Warren grabbed them, went into his glass-sided office and closed the drapes. He delivered a couple of celebratory whacks to the punching bag in a corner. Then he collapsed into his swivel chair, clasped hands behind his head and jubilantly gazed up at the ceiling.

"Hey, War?" Thad Miller popped into the office. "What do you think?"

"I think we've won the war! We're the holy Allied army marching into Berlin!"

"We caught a break."

"A hell of a break! I'll tell you, when I met with Tom and Alex to explain the new situation, it wasn't pretty. They were not going for it."

"Didn't think they would," Thad said.

"I was planning to confront Cody today and try to get him to back down. If he didn't, I didn't know what the hell I was going to do. I might have had to kill him myself."

Thad laughed. "Ha, ha, ha."

Benjamin's voice floated on the intercom. "Alicia Chenoweth on two."

Thad flashed a V for victory sign and left the office. Warren snatched up the phone. "Alicia! Staggering news, huh?"

"It's quite a shock. We're all just stunned over here. Funeral's the day after tomorrow. There'll be a memorial but it's yet to be determined where and when."

"Of course, and I'll be attending both. But, uh . . . how long before everything gets, well, reorganized over there?"

"The studio's fully on top of everything, Warren. That's what I'm calling about. I'm the new Acting President of Worldwide Production."

"You are? Wow, well . . . Congratulations."

"A bitch of a way to get promoted, but thanks."

Warren felt that bobbing sensation again. "So everything's back on track, right? No more obstacles?"

"Also what I'm calling about. It seems Cody had already convinced Martin Drake that the budget was out of control."

Warren crashed down to earth. "And . . . ?"

"You're still going to have to give back, Warren. The good news is that it's only three points, not five."

"You call that good news?"

"Actually, I call it reality. Making things work."

"Fuck, Alicia! You're double-crossing me."

"I'm only doing what I have to do, Warren. I can't discuss it now—I have a million and one other calls to make, so we'll talk again later. But I've given you the bottom line. You either take it or leave it."

Warren slammed down the phone. Bitch! He hadn't counted on this.

He had one trump card left with Alicia. He'd been holding it back—but it was more than time that he dealt it.

THIRTEEN

Coincidence. The word struck Mitch Arpino while catching the news on CNN when he woke up shortly before noon.

The coincidence being that within the space of a week the world-renowned movie producer Warren Doran had experienced two dramatic occurrences in his life: number one being the unexpected release of his convicted shoplifter daughter from prison; and number two, the violent murder of the studio chief presiding over Warren's big budget new movie.

So where, Mitch wondered, was he going with this? That Hannah Doran's release was somehow linked to the demise of Cory Takish?

Why not? Through her father, she had only one degree of separation from Takish. Also, she'd spent a summer as an intern at Constellation Pictures, which meant she actually had two links to him. So suppose she'd hooked up with a few other prisoners behind bars and filled them in on the layout of the homes of her rich acquaintances. And once they get out, they go on a looting spree . . .

A kind of an *In Cold Blood* thing with a gender switch.

Or Patty Hearst, twenty-first century style.

Pretty far-fetched. But none of the pieces he'd picked up so far really locked together. Nothing quite added up yet. What was Hannah's business with the Russian procuress? What was the fat-faced private dick looking to dig up? Where really did Warren Doran fit in all this, from the moment his daughter was charged with grand theft . . . ?

Time of a Hail Mary pass. He wondered if Hannah had gotten his card, and if so, had she read the message? Not that he'd expected her to leap to the phone, but maybe it had intrigued her enough that if he showed up, she'd be willing to see him.

He was feeling better—achy, but manageably so. Had kept down all his breakfast and no longer saw purple haze when he got to his feet. He unwound the Ace bandage and applied a muscle liniment he'd brought back from Bangkok that the Thai martial arts guys swore by. Shi-i-t! It was like rubbing habanera chilies on raw flesh.

But the Thai masters knew their stuff—once the sting went away, it worked wonders. He felt alert and alive and ready to hit the trail.

※

"I'm Hannah Doran. I'm here to see my father." Hannah strode briskly past the open-mouthed receptionist who manned the desk in the WildFilm Productions lobby. She continued through the maze of circus-tented cubicles towards her father's beautiful glass-sided office. She could see him inside, talking on a headset, his feet in their black Italian loafers propped on his steel and glass desk. She skirted his assistant Benjamin and barged into the office.

Her father glanced at her and waved an okay to Benjamin. "Something's come up, I'll get back to you," he said to his caller. He removed the headset and swung his feet off the desk.

"I need some money," Hannah said bluntly.

"Going shopping?" He reached for his wallet. "How much?"

"No, nothing like that. I need a lot of money. Fifty thousand dollars."

He smiled thinly. "To give to Benny Davis?"

She gave a start.

"Thad told me you've concocted some scheme to hand over all your money to that coke addict. That guy's bad news, Hannah."

Hannah flushed. "If that's what Thad told you, he was being simplistic. It's much more complex than that."

"Whatever. I dealt with Benny Davis on three movies and most of the time he was out of control. I'd have gotten rid of him after the first *Wildwood* if he hadn't already become too established as the character. But I wouldn't trust him for a split second. He's scamming you for every dime you've got."

"That's absolutely not true! I've done my homework, Dad. But this isn't about Benny Davis, anyway. It's something else."

"What?"

She hesitated.

"Christ, Hannah! You come crashing into my office demanding fifty grand and I'm not supposed to know what it's for?"

"Why do you need to know? It's my own money I'm asking for."

"I'm the guardian of that money. It's something I take fairly seriously."

She paused again. "I'm being blackmailed."

His eyebrows shot up. "By who?"

"It's not blackmail exactly. There was a woman who was with me in Peachrock, another prisoner. She knows things about me. She's said she'll tell me more if I pay her."

"What kind of things?"

"Like about how I ended up in jail. Dad, I think it might not have been my fault. I might not have been in control of what I was doing."

"Yes, we all know that, honeybun." He smiled. "You were hungover. You already tried that one, Hannah, and it didn't fly."

She felt like she'd been slapped. "I'm not talking about being hungover. I mean drugged."

"This . . . person told you that?"

"No, I found that out before. I saw my old boyfriend Shawn, and he told me he put a drug in my drink that day at lunch. The day I was arrested."

"And why would he do that?"

"Somebody paid him to do it. A guy. Shawn didn't know his name. It was supposed to be some kind of treatment to get me to stop drinking."

Her father gazed at her with pity. "You seem to believe anything anybody tells you. Especially if they're trying to get money."

"I'm not stupid, and I'm not that naïve!" she flared. "Please don't treat me that way."

"Okay. May I ask the name of this person who is going to give you fifty thousand dollars worth of information?"

"Valentina Rostov. She was a call girl, and I think she knew a lot of important people. She says she knows things about Mom."

Warren's expression darkened. "What's that supposed to mean?"

"I don't know yet!" she said impatiently. "It's part of what I'm trying to find out."

"Your mother has been dead for over twenty years. There's nothing to know. This woman is playing you, Hannah."

"There's plenty for me to know. You never even bring up Mom's name."

Warren rose to his feet, his face black. "Your mother was a very troubled and extremely confused soul. She'd been allowed to run wild, and she felt she'd made a lot of mistakes. I tried to protect her. Obviously I failed. And now to see you going the same way . . . I can't tell you how it makes me feel, Hannah. It breaks my heart."

"You're wrong, Dad. I'm not like Mom. I've changed, I'm getting my life together. You just have to believe me—this is something I really need to do. If my trust fund is not immediately available, then loan me the money until it is."

"You expect me to write you a check? Just like that?"

"No. I need it in cash."

He gave a harsh laugh. "Do you think I keep that amount lying around in petty cash? Jesus, Hannah. Just hold your horses a few more days. We'll have all your new accounts set up. And then you can throw your money away in whatever scatter-brained way you want."

"You're so wrong, Dad!" She felt so angry she could hardly choke out the words. "Whatever you still think about me, you're totally wrong. And I'm going to prove it to you, with or without your help."

"I hope so, honeybun. I honestly do." He smiled indulgently. "And now I'm sorry, but I really need to get back to work."

As soon as she'd gone, Warren hit the intercom: "Tell Thad Miller to get in here ASAP."

A minute later, his junior partner ducked into the office. "Did I just see your daughter go by?" Thad said.

"Yeah, you did. She came in wanting fifty thousand dollars in cash."

Thad gave a little whistle. "For that Benny character?"

"No. One of her prison mates has some story to tell her. Wants the cash in exchange. When the hell is this parole thing supposed to happen?"

"I just got off the phone with her P.O. Tomorrow morning. Everything's set to go."

"Can't he move it up?"

"I'll bug him again, but I don't think so. But relax, War. No way Hannah's going to get that kind of cash. Not by tomorrow, anyway. And after that, it will be a moot point."

Back in her car, Hannah pounded her fists on the steering wheel.

It was nearly one o'clock. Where else could she possibly get the money? Perhaps from one of her old friends or acquaintances? Shawn used to "borrow" constantly from her before his work started selling. Maybe he'd be willing to pay her back a portion of it?

Fat chance.

Except she didn't need Shawn, she realized. She owned one of his major acrylic paintings. His prices had soared—it should be worth a bundle now!

She raced home and up to a closet in the second bedroom. She'd originally owned two of his paintings: one she'd slashed to ribbons the night she found out about his break-up-by-text. This one she'd stuffed out of sight. She dragged it out from the recesses of the closet. A canvas about five feet by four—a garish female nude with flamingo pink skin and a turquoise gash of a vagina. She lugged it down to her car, where it just fit in the back seat with the top down, and then she headed to Beverly Hills.

Westside Lending Co. A discreetly bland name for a pawn shop that catered to the cash-strapped rich and famous—Hannah had been here several years back, accompanying Crissie Townsend who'd been pawning a tennis bracelet that was a gift from a rejected suitor. Located on the second floor of a discreetly bland office building on Wilshire. She parked in the underground structure and maneuvered the painting to the elevator. On the second floor, she pressed a bell next to a locked steel door, and the rasp of a buzzer releasing the lock sent a shudder through her.

You're not in Peachrock, she reminded herself. *Get a grip!*

She shouldered open the door. It was a brightly-lit space, the walls dotted with impressive works of art—a Warhol, a Renoir, a luminous abstract that could be a Rothko. A Steinway concert grand in a corner. A dark, quiet-looking man in a charcoal Brioni suit presiding behind a display case bristling with Rolexes and diamond brooches. If he recognized her—and Hannah was certain he did—he didn't betray it with even a flicker of an eye.

He examined the painting front and back. Looked without comment at the dedication Shawn had scrawled in paint to her on the back. He chopped rapidly on the keyboard of a laptop. "Sixteen thousand eight hundred."

She bristled. "This is an authentic Serafian. It was presented to me directly by the artist—you saw the dedication. It's got to be worth at least two hundred thousand dollars."

"I can go seventeen even. Final."

His expression told her it was useless to argue. "Okay, fine. I'll take it."

"Cashier's check or cash?"

"In cash. Please."

She produced an I.D., signed a document explaining the terms, waited while the money was counted out in crisp hundreds. It was drastically short of the fifty thousand Valentina was demanding, but with luck, she'd snatch at it and give out her information anyway. Though she was just as likely to turn it down with a withering sneer and vanish forever, and this second possibility filled Hannah with alarm.

The stacks of hundreds, secured by elastic bands, made a surprisingly small stash in the bottom of the tote bag she'd brought. She locked the tote in the trunk of her Mercedes, pulled out of the garage and began to head east in the direction of Hollywood. She was now a bit early—had over an hour to kill. She turned up La Brea, hoping Flora Diner was still in business, happy to discover it was. A combination florist and café, all wood plank floors, tile-topped patio tables with high stools, banks of refrigerated compartments filled with cut flowers. She chose a table by the window, ordered the far-falle with Cowgirl Creamery goat cheese and a double iced espresso and consumed it with sudden hunger, watching the sun-dappled river of traffic surge along the avenue.

After finishing her food, she went over to the floral compartments. "I'd like a dozen calla lilies," she told a clerk. "Don't wrap them, just tie them with white ribbon."

The salesclerk counted out the lilies and brought them to a counter, twined hemp around the stems and began fashioning a white satin ribbon bow. Hannah's attention drifted to a man who was paying for take-out at the register. Beat-up trucking company hat and dorky mirrored sunglasses. Tourist or some local worker.

But something familiar in his profile . . .

He turned and left by the rear exit. Hannah grabbed her bouquet, waited impatiently at the same register to pay, then dashed out the back to the parking lot. A vintage yellow Corvette was pulling out, disappeared around a corner.

Probably just a tourist.

She got back in her car and headed off to meet Valentina.

Mitch had approached the Bougainville from the alley in back, just as the gates of the building's garage were rattling open. Another piece of luck—Hannah Doran's Mercedes emerged directly in front of him and turned onto Wilshire. No trouble following her: Hannah used to have a rep for speeding, but now she was poking along—probably on account of that big old painting sticking up from the backseat. Judging from the screaming-mimi hues of the palette, Mitch was pretty sure it was a Serafian.

A straight shot down Wilshire Boulevard, crossing Doheny into Beverly Hills, and then a left into the underground parking of a high-rise. Mitch hit the brakes, then followed at a safe distance. He rolled past Hannah pulling into a slot and continued down to the next level. He got out and walked back up the winding ramp to where he could watch her from around the bend. She was carrying the painting to the elevator, clutching it by the frame like removing a naughty cat by the scruff of its neck.

She looked amazing. Soft white shirt tied at the waist. Brown hair flowing straight to her shoulders. Like a college kid. Young and smart and heart-achingly pretty.

Cut it out, asshole. Stay on focus.

The thought occurred to him again, stronger than ever: *Who did she look like?*

No mystery about where she was taking the painting. Westside Lending Co., suite 244. An establishment well-known to the paparazzi. Good for nabbing shots of fading stars who needed quick cash for some rejuvenating plastic surgery or to meet an overdue alimony payment.

Bottom line: a pawnbroker. Unloading some lousy art, are we, Miss Doran?

The mystery, though, was why she was taking it to a pawn shop instead of Serafian's dealer who'd put it on consignment for top dollar. Hannah Sebring Doran was worth what?—sixty, seventy million, maybe more?

How come the need for instant money?

He captured a few seconds of her on his Flip cam before she disappeared in the elevator. He continued waiting in the parking structure. Didn't take long—she reappeared in less than twenty minutes. Minus the painting—and from the way she was holding her tote bag, the transaction had evidently been a success.

He dove back into his car and continued to follow as she pulled out of the structure, back onto Wilshire. A turn onto La Brea for several blocks, until she swung into the little gravel parking lot behind Flora Diner. He hovered for several moments, giving her time to go into the café, and then he pulled into the lot. Waited half an hour. His stomach was rumbling. He could really use a bite himself.

He selected a beat-up old trucker's hat from his costume stash and pulled it low over his forehead. He slapped on a pair of heavy, square-framed shades with mirrored lenses. He ambled cautiously into the shop.

She wasn't in the café. Was it possible he'd lost her?

No, there she was in the flower section. Buying lilies, it looked like.

So who died? Could they be for Cody Takish?

Keeping his head turned away from her, he ordered a couple of cranberry muffins and a large lemonade to go. He took the food out to his car and, with the Vette idling, began to wolf it down.

He was gulping his drink when Hannah emerged with her bouquet several minutes later. Gripping the cup with his teeth, he grabbed the wheel, stepped on the gas and shot around the corner.

In her rear view, Hannah watched the yellow Corvette appear from a side street and came up behind her. It was no tourist—it was that photographer, the one who warned her on his card about VR. She could not afford to risk having him scare off Valentina now.

She made several turns at random. The Corvette followed, always keeping two or three cars between hers. Either he was really lousy at this, or he thought she was an idiot—either way, it was going to be easy to lose him. She swung onto Mansfield, a quiet residential street. Some seconds later, the Vette appeared. There were no other cars between them now.

Several blocks ahead, Mansfield intersected with the heavily-trafficked Third Street. The light ahead was green. She approached it at a crawl. As the light turned yellow, she crept up to the intersection and stopped. The Vette rolled up behind her.

The light turned red. She gunned her engine and shot across the intersection. The Third Street traffic immediately began to flow, leaving the Corvette stranded at the red light.

Ha! It had almost been too easy! She sped across Beverly Boulevard, turning onto Rossmore, and then a right on Santa Monica, where she headed through a pair of ornate iron gates in the center of a long block.

The Hollywood Forever Cemetery had a number of famous names buried there, making it a minor tourist attraction, but Hannah knew from the past that at this time of day visitors were scarce. As she cruised the pretty, winding lanes, she passed only a scattering of people: a Filipino family clustered at a newly-laid marker; a gardener training a yellow hose on a bank of azaleas. By the time she reached the far end of the park, there was no one in sight. She parked at the side of a lake—more accurately, a large pool surrounding a mausoleum built to resemble a classical Greek temple. She grabbed her bouquet of lilies, crossed the lane, and walked through the monuments until she came to a white marble stone.

No dates. No sentiments.

Just a name engraved in elegant block lettering: PAMELA SE-BRING DORAN.

She stood at the foot of the grave and stared at the stone. Her mother had purchased the plot for herself just weeks before she had swallowed the insecticide—that fact had been a decisive one in the ruling of suicide. Warren Doran had tried to prevent Pamela from being buried here. He'd begun to make arrangements at the lavish and more socially-correct Forest Lawn, but Hannah's grandfather, Jonas Sebring, had stopped him. Jonas had told reporters that if Warren put his daughter in Forest Lawn, he'd dig her up and bury her where she wanted to be. It had the stirrings of a scandal, and Warren had backed down.

Hannah continued to gaze at the stone, hoping as she always did that it would reveal something. It was cold. White.

As always, it told her nothing.

Her fingers tightened around the stems of the bouquet. Calla lilies had been her mother's favorite flower, so her grandfather had told her. It occurred to her that they resembled her mother, the long slender stem topped with the perfect pale flute of the bloom. Such elegance. Such pristine beauty.

Hannah preferred ornate flowers. Peonies. Frilly parrot tulips.

The lilies suddenly didn't look like flowers at all. They were ghost plants, white and waxy. Furled primly within themselves. They suggested nothing.

They gave nothing away.

Just like her mother. Her damned selfish fucked-up bitch of a mother who'd chosen to end her own life without telling why, without a care for her daughter, without any reason at all, why, why . . .

She was smashing the lilies against the marble stone, violently, again and again, until the waxy heads, bruised and broken off from the stems, lay scattered over the grave. Exhausted by rage, she stood clutching the headless stems tied with the silly white bow.

As she let them drop at the foot of the stone, she had the almost unbearable sense that she had destroyed something innocent.

Watching the Mercedes shoot through the red light, Mitch gave a chuckle. One of the most basic moves in the book. He did a quick eyeball for cop cars. Coast was clear. Leaning on his horn, he hit the gas and barged into the intersection against the light.

Horns blared back, somebody yelled "hey, asshole!" A pickup slammed its brakes inches from Mitch's hood and the driver mouthed something choice in Spanish. But basically the law of self-preservation held steady—the other vehicles stopped or swerved to let him continue through.

On Beverly now, he could see traffic held up at a light several blocks ahead. No Mercedes—meaning Hannah must have turned either right or left. A right would just send her back in the direction she'd come from . . . He swung the first left and gunned it. Gotcha! She was just disappearing around a corner.

He followed at a discreet distance, pretty sure she hadn't noticed his reappearance. Paramount Studios were just a few blocks away—maybe she was heading there? *I'm ready for my close-up, Mr. DeMille . . .*

But then she hooked a right on Santa Monica. When he followed, she'd vanished.

He cruised slowly until he saw the gates in the middle of the block. A cemetery: the Hollywood Forever Memorial Park. He'd heard of it. There were some famous old-timers buried here. Rudolph Valentino, the Sheik of the Burning Sands. Tyrone Power. But dead celebs didn't do much good for him; just the ones still alive and kicking and making spectacles of themselves.

He drove through the gates and glimpsed the Mercedes winding through the park. The place was small enough that he could ditch his car and by cutting across the grounds follow her on foot. He parked just beyond the entrance, grabbed his long lens and started trotting through the graves.

Some were marked by grandiose obelisks and ornate sculptures of angels. Some displayed photos behind glass of the dearly departed themselves. Others were heartbreakingly modest. Every so often, a famous name leapt out at him. He almost tripped over a high-heeled shoe somebody had left in tribute on the flat stone of Jayne Mansfield. And, whoa! Dee Dee Ramone. *Didn't know he was here!* And check the inscription: "O.K. . . . I gotta go now." Mitch snapped some photos as a personal memento.

He kept on walking, keeping Hannah's coasting Mercedes in sight. Finally, she pulled over beside a lake surrounding what looked like a temple to Zeus. She got out, clutching the bunch of lilies she'd bought at Flora Diner. She glanced over her shoulder at the lake, then up and down the drive.

She crossed the drive and started walking directly toward Mitch.

He crouched quickly behind a gray granite headstone. Whoa—another famous name! Jackson Brandt. The original Wildwood Murphy!

It was the perfect eternal resting place for a movie star, Mitch mused. From straight ahead, you got a direct shot of the water tower of Paramount Studios. From the other direction, a picture postcard view of the Hollywood Sign up in the hazy hills. And several hillocks to the right, the triple dome of the Griffith Observatory, forever linked with that other tragically-dead-before-his-time star, James Dean, from the scene of the famous switchblade rumble in *Rebel Without A Cause*.

He peered gingerly from behind the stone. Hannah was still heading straight towards him. His adrenaline surged: should he bolt or stay put?

Then, less than ten yards away, she suddenly stopped. It was at one of the modest grave markers, a small white marble stone. She gazed down at it intently. Her face clouded with emotion.

Mom, Mitch surmised. Pamela Sebring Doran.

As he watched, she began to do a smackdown on the headstone with the lilies. She was pretty damned pissed-off at whoever was down there—and if it was her mother, he couldn't blame her. What kind of monster freaking mom does that to her little kid?

Then the purr of a luxury vehicle coming up the drive from the eastern road. Rolls convertible, late model, top up. Two ladies, the driver in a floppy hat, the other with bushy red hair. It pulled over and stopped. He snapped a few shots of the car, and then of the redhead as she got out.

If Mitch wasn't mistaken—and he never was about things like this—it was the Russian, Valentina Rostov—the corrupter of little girls.

Okay, this was getting extremely interesting.

Mitch raised the long lens of his Canon. He emerged from behind the Jackson Brandt monument and fixed Hannah in its sights.

Zizi and Valentina were early. Hannah cursed herself for still being at her mother's grave: the last thing in the world she wanted to do was to have it desecrated by the presence of Valentina Rostov. She dashed quickly back to her car, popped the trunk and took out the tote bag. She gestured to the Corniche as it rolled to a stop.

Valentina snapped open her door. Zizi Howell stayed behind the wheel.

Valentina came walking towards Hannah, placing one foot directly in front of the other, like a supermodel on a runway. She was wearing high metallic sandals, a short skirt and gold halter. An arrogant orange-glossed smile smeared her face.

Hannah's pulse quickened. She clutched the tote bag tighter.

A dull popping sound came from the Roman temple in the center of the lake.

Valentina seemed to rise slightly on the toes of her shiny sandals. Then she sank to her knees in front of Hannah, slowly, as if moving underwater. There appeared a large bright jewel on the base of her throat, a glowing, expanding ruby, and Hannah vaguely thought: *How beautiful.*

Valentina began to crumple face forward, and instinctively Hannah reached out and caught her in her arms. She heard a loud screech of tires. Zizi in the Corniche shot onto the lawns and raced an obstacle course through the gravesites back towards the entrance.

Something was trickling down Hannah's arms. It was blood, she realized—the blood now surging from the ruby at Valentina's throat.

With a guttural cry, she let Valentina's lifeless body continue its watery crumple to the ground. She scrambled to her feet in a panic, unable to think. She heard footsteps and whirled, and found herself staring down the length of a long gray barrel.

The fact that it was the barrel of a camera and not a gun didn't matter. Either way, she knew that her life was over.

FOURTEEN

It was the money shot.

The producer's daughter fresh out of jail cradling the blood-oozing body of a former hooker and recent prison mate. The snap-shot that would sell for a fortune, solve all his problems: finance the documentary and catapult his reputation into the stratosphere.

Mitch lowered his lens. "Get out of here," he said.

Hannah stared at him without comprehension. She lifted her hands, red and sticky with blood, as if in a futile appeal.

"I said, get the fuck out of here before somebody sees you. You were never here, got that? I'll handle it."

Her lips parted, she tried to say something. Then she turned and fled back to her car. He watched the Benz pull away, speeding unsteadily, wavering back and forth along the drive.

Christ. Was he totally out of his mind?

He popped the memory card out of his Canon and slipped it in a little pocket formed from several pulled stitches in the hem of his jacket that he'd created for precisely such a purpose. He took a fresh card from his bag and clicked it into the camera; then he scrambled back among the gravestones and rapidly shot the Jackson Brandt tombstone from a variety of angles. When he heard a shout, he jogged back to the road. A gardener clutching a rake was sprinting towards Valentina's body. A car braked and stopped, a couple burst out from either side, and the man began bellowing "Call 911!"

The cops arrived quickly. First, two uniforms in a squad car, a disco swirl of lights. They kept multiplying and mutating, like some early form of single-cell organism: more uniforms, and plain-clothes

cops, and coroner cops, and K-9 cops. Then the bosses of the uniform and plain-clothes and K-9 cops. They all asked Mitch varia-
tions of the same questions, and he repeated the same answers: he'd
been taking some photos of the Jackson Brandt gravesite—what
with the redoing of *Wildwood Murphy*, he figured the snaps might
be good for a few bucks. "I heard popping sounds coming from the
direction of the lake. Figured it was backfire or maybe gardening
equipment. Then I saw a late model Corniche convertible driving
hell bent for leather . . ." Yeah, a Rolls Royce, silver mist, silver fog,
one of those Rolls names for gray. The top was up, but he could
make out the driver was a woman, she was wearing a floppy white
hat, oversized sunglasses. He got curious wondering why she was
speeding like that, maybe she'd been assaulted, dragged behind
some mausoleum? "So I wrapped up my shoot and started walking
towards the lake to look for suspicious characters or whatever, and
that's when I saw the woman in the road—at about the same time
as these other people did. I called 911."

End of story.

One of the uniforms recognized Mitch from some paparazzi
dust-up in the past and gave him some hassle, until Mitch proved
his story by showing them the shots of the headstones. A detective
confiscated the memory card.

It turned out the boss of the detectives was a Ramones freak,
and when Mitch mentioned Dee Dee's grave, he and Mitch bonded
a little. Mitch overheard on one of the cops' squawk boxes that a
Rolls fitting the description had been recovered ditched in an alley
down in Little Ethiopia. Finally, the detective boss told him he
could go, but they'd "be in touch" for further questioning.

He hiked back to his car and got the hell out.

At home, Mitch dumped the sticky residue from a Subway cup,
poured a double finger of Cuervo and tossed it down. The cat door,
a relic of a former tenant, snapped open, making him jump. Jesus!
James, the obese orange tom who lived across the street, squeezed
through it and yowled for a treat.

"Not now, buddy." He deposited the cat back outside, then
gulped down another measure of tequila. He noticed with a certain
degree of scientific detachment that a vein in his hand was throbbing and dancing. Doing the lambada under his skin.

The doorbell rang and he jumped again. Goddamned cops
wasted no time.

He flung open the door. Stared dumbfounded.

"Can I come in?" said Hannah.

He nodded mutely and moved aside to let her enter. She took several steps and began to collapse. He caught her in his arms before she hit the floor. He carried her, Rhett and Scarlett style, into the living room, kicked a clutter of books and papers off the couch and deposited her on it. Her skin was pale, her lips parted, brown hair tumbled about her face, she looked like a Pre-Raphaelite painting . . .

Stop standing there gawking and do something! Loosen her clothes.

He untied the tails of her shirt and was starting on the buttons when her eyes shot open.

"What are you doing?" She scrambled to a sit up, pressing her knees to her chest.

"Loosening your clothes. You fainted."

"Don't be stupid. I never faint."

"Maybe you never had anybody shot dead right in front of you before."

"Oh." Her face went ashen. "Oh my god. Valentina. She's dead?"

"Dead as they get."

"Who did it?" Hannah hugged her knees closer.

"No idea. The cops figure it was some kind of mob hit."

"Oh god, the cops! Do they know . . . ?"

"That you were there? Nope. Not yet, anyway. They're looking for the girl who was driving the Rolls." He realized she was shivering the way he'd seen people with malaria in Africa and Asia shiver, the entire body engaged right down to the tips of their fingers. He started out of the room.

"Where are you going?" she asked with alarm.

"You've been through a trauma, you're shaking like a leaf. I'm going to get you a blanket and a stiff drink."

He dashed into the bedroom, yanked a blanket off the bed and one of his nicer shirts from the closet, pale violet linen; he'd always felt a little gay in it so didn't wear it much. He sniffed the pits anyway to make sure it was clean. In the bathroom cabinet, he dug up a vial with a couple of Valium rattling in it, left behind from some forgotten stay-over date, and shook one out. He filled a glass with water and rushed back to the living room.

"Take this. Just low dose Valium."

Her hand was shaking so hard she spilled half the water down her shirt. "Damn!"

"It's okay. It's just water, and your shirt's a goner anyhow."

She looked down and gasped. "Oh my god! There's blood on it."

"I brought one of mine. There's some blood on your jeans, but it's not very noticeable. Lucky, cause I don't think you'd fit any of my pants."

"I'd better not." She forced a weak grin.

"I'll just . . . um, turn around." He faced the other way while she changed shirts. "Okay?" He turned back. She had the blood-ied shirt balled so tightly in her hand he had to pry it from her. "Why don't I just toss this, okay? Try to relax." He handed her the blanket, took the shirt into the kitchen and crammed it into the trash, then gulped a walloping hit of Cuervo straight from the bottle.

When he came back to the living room, she was huddled be-neath the blanket, but no longer shaking violently. "Better?"

"Yeah, some." She tried another smile. Her eyes glanced around the living room. "I kind of figured your place would be a mess."

"It's usually not this bad." He edged a section of newspaper with his heel under a chair. "I've got a cleaning lady, but her day isn't until tomorrow, and I've been kind of under the weather . . ." He scooped up some ossified Chinese take-out from off the floor, realized there was no other place to put the containers, and set it back down again.

"But all these books. That I hadn't figured on."

"They're mostly photo books. And art books . . . I like to look at pictures."

She reached for one that lay on the floor close to her. "Cartier-Bresson. I always loved his work."

"He's one of my gods." Mitch crouched beside her as she turned the pages. "Used a rangefinder with a fast film, but never a flash. He'd wait as long as it took to get exactly the one shot. The split second that tells the entire story . . . He called it 'the decisive mo-ment.' Like this one . . ." Mitch pointed to a photo: two women reading newspapers in a Paris café. "These two women—one is very young, a trendy Sixties schoolgirl. Obviously beautiful, though you can't really see her face through her hair. She's absorbed in her paper. The other's a matron, primly dressed, that dowdy felt hat. She's holding her newspaper, but all her attention is on the girl. She's looking at her with an expression of what? Disapproval? Envy? Concern? Christ, you could write an entire novel from this one shot!" He stopped himself short. "Just what you need. My babbling on about some photo."

"No, it's nice, you make me see what you do. And I'm feeling better." She closed the book, put it back down on the floor.

"Good." He swept a sock, a lens-cleaning cloth and an In Montreal CD case off an opposite chair and sat down. "So maybe we'd better just cut to the chase. What are you doing here?"

"I didn't know where else to go. I can't go home. I mean, look at me, I've got blood all over. What if anybody saw me?" She laughed, a gulping, nervous hiccup of a laugh. "I've been driving around totally freaked, I don't even know for how long. And then I remembered your card. The one you'd left for me at my building.." She dug it out from a pocket of her jeans. "'V R is extremely dangerous' That's Valentina Rostov, right? You said you knew she was dangerous and you could help."

"Oh, yeah, right. Sorry, but that was just a ploy."

"A ploy? What do you mean?"

"I mean, I was just trying to get you to see me."

She stared at him, uncomprehending.

"Look, I made some assumptions. I knew you were mixed up somehow with this woman, Rostov. I knew she was a nasty customer, and that the two of you were in Peachrock together. I was looking for a story. I figured there must be one there."

"A story?" she repeated.

"Yeah. I'm a photojournalist. I mean, I used to be. I worked for newspapers, covered major stories. I got sidetracked with this celebrity shit, and I've been looking for a way out." He shrugged. "A good story."

"Then why did you let me go? Back there, at the cemetery." Her eyes widened. "Oh my god! Did you already get your story? Is that it? You already got the shots, and now you're going to feed me to the wolves?"

"No!"

"Why should I believe you?"

"I don't know. Maybe because you've got no other choice."

For a moment, he thought she was going to bolt out the door. But then she settled back against the couch.

"So tell me about this Valentina," he continued. "What was going on between you?"

"Nothing."

"Obviously something. You two were locked up together over a year. So did the two of you cook something up? Some kind of robbery thing? A plan to steal from people you used to know?"

"Are you crazy?" she shot at him.

"Hey, I can see how something like that could happen. You're locked up in a shithole, rotting away, thinking about all your friends out there enjoying the good life. They're not giving you a second thought. It must have made you furious. I could see where you'd start thinking: Wouldn't it be nice to get back at them after you're out?"

"That's ridiculous!"

"Not after what I just saw happen. It seems like an extremely reasonable explanation. You and a little bunch of your prison mates cook up a scheme of breaking and entering. Maybe one of them gets cut out of the plan. She gets a gun, or gets a boyfriend with a gun, and starts eliminating."

"You're being insane! How can you even imagine something like that?"

"Nobody's got to imagine you involved in stealing. They can read about it in black and white and color."

"Screw you!"

"Hey, you might just get that wish. Because I could be royally screwed, covering up for you like this."

"Then why did you?" she flashed.

"Beats the hell out of me," he said. Except maybe it was for the same reason that looking at her right now, he had the almost irresistible desire to sweep her back into his arms. He shifted his eyes to neutral space. "So am I on the right track?"

"No, you're not. You're not even on the right train."

"Did you know Cody Takish?" he asked suddenly.

"Who?"

"He was the head of production at Constellation. You worked there once."

"The guy who was just killed in the home break-in? I heard it on the news, but I didn't know him. He wasn't at the studio when I was an intern. Why?"

"He was the make-or-break guy at Constellation for your father's movie."

"So?"

"So you're connected to two violent murders right after you're sprung from prison. Is it coincidence or is it Memorex?"

"It's coincidence, obviously. I didn't have any connection to that guy. My father did but it didn't involve me. You're being totally insane." She threw off the blanket and started to get up. "Maybe I should just go."

"Hey, no, I'm sorry. I was just fishing. I'm trying to get a handle on what just happened back there."

She hesitated. "Okay. I'll tell you the truth. The reason I was meeting Valentina was to give her some money."

"Blackmail?"

"No."

"Charity? A handout to a prison pal."

"God, no."

"So what then?"

"In exchange for information. About why somebody wanted me kept in prison. Maybe why I got sent in the first place."

He leaned forward in his chair. "Is there any question about that?"

"I didn't steal anything," she snapped. "On purpose, I mean. You can believe that or not."

"Okay. I believe you. Go on."

"Valentina showed up at my apartment last night. She made it sound like my being in jail was a set-up, and she knew what was behind it. I'd already found out some things. Like, for instance, the day I stole the necklace, it turns out I'd been drugged."

Mitch's brows shot up.

"This guy I used to go with, Shawn Serafian. I saw him at a party a few nights ago and he told me he had put some drug in my drink at lunch that day. Something that made me woozy and sick."

"So that's why you slapped him silly."

"How did you know that?"

"I was there. Watching you. It made my night."

"You bastard!" she flared. "You really have been stalking me!"

"Yeah, well, fortunately, as it's turned out. And if it's any consolation to you, about five minutes later, I proceeded to get royally stomped by Denny Brandt's entourage." He lifted up his shirt and displayed his bandaged midsection.

"Oh! Ow." Hannah leaned toward him with concern.

"It's okay. It only hurts when I laugh."

She drew back. "Serves you right."

"Yeah, it probably does. But enough about me, fascinating though the subject may be. Let's get back to you. Why did Serafian drug you? Some kind of date rape thing?"

"No! God, no! He was paid to do it."

"Paid?"

"He said that one of my friends had hired an interventionist to make me stop drinking. This guy, this interventionist, said the drug was supposed to make me go off alcohol. You know, make me sick at the taste of it. Shawn wanted me to sober up, and . . . Well, he also needed some quick cash. So he agreed to do it."

"A prince among men." Mitch gave a snort. "And who was the fabulously concerned friend who hired the interventionist?"

"Somebody in my old crowd, obviously."

"But according to Valentina, it was a set-up, right? Meaning whoever it was who bribed Serafian probably also made sure you got caught with the bling."

Hannah rested her head back against the arm of the couch. "It's all just too unbelievable. I can imagine one of my friends doing something crazy like hiring an interventionist. But getting me sent to prison?" She shuddered.

"If you had to make a wild guess, which one would you pick?"

She squeezed her eyes shut. "Crissie."

"Cristina Townsend?" Mitch pictured her: America's Sweetheart, all frothy curls and adorableness. Fiancée of his sparring partner, Denny Brandt.

"It had to be. Cris was the one who insisted we all go with her to the jewelry store. I told her I was feeling sick, but Crissie—oh god, she's totally self-absorbed. You could be on your *deathbed*, gasping your last breath, and Crissie Townsend would still expect you to be catering to her."

Mitch gave an appreciative chuckle.

"I've tried calling her, but if she even gets my messages, she's not calling me back. But it doesn't make sense, does it? What would she have gotten out of it?"

"How about Denny?" he suggested. "Maybe she already had her eye on him, and maybe she sensed there was something between the two of you. That would be reason enough to want you out of the way."

"Between me and Denny? Absolutely no way! We can hardly stand each other. You should see us, we always end up fighting with each other."

"Classic, isn't it? Two people who think they hate each other but it's really because of this enormous sexual tension between them. In the end, they fall passionately into each others arms."

"Please. You've seen too many bad movies. That's the worst cliché in the world. There's absolutely no way in hell I would ever get involved with Denny!"

In her anger, her eyes darkened and her jaw set, and in a flash,

Mitch realized who it was she looked like. The resemblance was suddenly so strong, it nearly floored him. But it was ridiculous, wasn't it? It couldn't possibly be . . .

"What?" she demanded. "Why are you looking at me like that?"

"Nothing," he said quickly. "Not important. Let's go back to Valentina. How much money did she want?"

"Fifty thousand in cash. She told me she was about to break parole and leave town, she and her girlfriend Zizi."

"ZZ? Like in ZZ Top?"

"Z-I Z-I. Zizi Howell. She was the one driving the Rolls back there. She was in Peachrock too. She's a car thief, but she used to be a call girl—she and Valentina both once worked for the Malibu Madam, it's where they first hooked up. They were really tight."

"So you agreed to give them the money?"

"Yes, but I couldn't get that much cash immediately. I could only raise seventeen thousand."

Hence the Beverly Hills pawn shop. Mitch decided that this wasn't the optimum time to mention his lurking in the parking garage. "Where's the money now?"

"In a bag in the trunk of my car." She shot him a wary glance. "Why?"

"I'm not planning to steal it, if that's what you're thinking."

"Don't be stupid. It's just . . ."

"Just what?"

She regarded him with an intent frown. "I just can't make out if you're really a bastard or some sort of Boy Scout."

"Maybe a little of both," he said.

She smiled. Then yawned. "I'm exhausted. I couldn't sleep last night, thinking about Valentina and what she might tell me."

"It could be that now you'll never know."

She shook her head adamantly. "I've got to know. I've got to find Zizi. Valentina would have told her everything. There must be a way to track her down."

"She could be anywhere by now. Mexico, halfway to the border of Canada."

"Not Zizi. She could hardly take a pee without first asking Valentina. I think she'd stay somewhere close by." Hannah glanced up. "I've got an idea."

"Yeah?"

"There was a car that picked up Valentina and Zizi from Peachrock. An old Coupe de Ville Cadillac. It had Texas plates. Vanity plates. They said NO REGRETS. We could track that down, right? Find out who the car is registered to?"

"Sure, I can do that easy. But do you want my advice? Let it go. This thing that just happened—the cops are right, it's got all the earmarks of a mob hit. And if it was, they'll be going after this Zizi too. You really don't want to get caught in the crossfire."

"I can't let it go. Don't you get it? I've been through total hell, and if there's a reason for it, I've got to find out why!" She looked up at him, brushing back a tangle of hair. "But there's no reason you need to be involved. If there's danger, I mean."

"Too late. Looks like I already am."

She smiled. Mitch's heart did an extra beat.

Hannah studied him a moment. "So are we going to talk about it?"

"It?"

"You know what I mean. That time we met before."

He smiled wryly. "So you do remember."

"It was at a launch party. For some new perfume."

"Aftershave. Smelled like armpits. It was at the Peninsula."

"Yeah. We were out on a balcony. I was still smoking back then, and you came out and bummed a cigarette."

"I'm pretty sure I had my own."

"Okay," she allowed. "But you looked different."

"My hair was shorter."

"You were skinnier."

"Ouch."

"Just a little." She conceded: "I was too."

He had a vivid memory of the way she'd looked on that balcony—like a kid playing dress-up in a big sister's clothes. Looking over the balcony, her gray eyes searching for something irretrievably lost in the city below.

"I'd picked you out before," Hannah said. "At other times, among all the photographers. You'd always seemed a little detached. Like, you were there, but also not there. Like at the same time you were taking pictures, you were also watching yourself. I'm probably not making any sense at all."

"You're making perfect sense," he said.

"I kissed you, didn't I?" she said.

"Yeah. And I kissed you back."

"Yeah."

"And then you ran off and locked me out on the freaking balcony."

"Yeah, I guess I did." She gave a short laugh. "I hope you weren't out there very long."

"Only all night. Getting soaked to my bones and freezing my butt off."

"Oh my god, you spent the whole night out there? I thought somebody would find you before the end of the party." She tried to suppress another giggle but couldn't. "I shouldn't be laughing. It must have been awful!"

"I've spent worse nights," he said. "But I'd really love to know why you did it. We seemed to have kind of a thing going, and then that?"

Hannah bit her lip. "I don't know, exactly. I mean . . . I remember thinking you were the first person to talk to me in a long time like I was an ordinary girl and not some kind of trashy celebrity. And I remember thinking you were cute."

"Yeah?"

"A little. But then after we kissed, I suddenly realized that you were one of *them*. I mean, I figured the only real thing you were interested in me for was something to sell. It made me furious. Because the thing is . . . I'd started to really like you."

He grinned.

"Are you laughing at me?"

"No, uh-uh. It's just that I really liked you too."

"So you were being a Boy Scout, not a bastard."

"Neither one. I was being me."

She studied him a moment. Then she yawned and stretched back down onto the couch. "At least I know your name now. It's on your card. Mitchell J. Arpino."

"Mitch will do."

"And I know your phone numbers. And your email. By heart."

"You memorized them?" He felt irrationally pleased.

"They stick in my head. Numbers. Whether I want them to or not."

A talent for numbers. He'd heard that before. And not too long ago.

She yawned again, cavernously. "Just how strong was that Valium?"

"Go ahead, get some sleep. It's okay."

"Maybe just a short nap." Her voice drifted off and her eyelids drifted closed.

He waited until she was fast asleep. Then he went closer to her and for some moments gazed at her intently. He bent down so close to her he could feel the warmth of her breath against his cheek. If he brushed his lips against hers, would she awaken like a fairytale princess and flutter into his arms?

But he didn't kiss her. Instead, he plucked out two hairs from the crown of her head. She stirred but didn't wake up.

He went into the kitchen and sealed the hairs in a Ziploc baggie. Then he went out to the large trash bin at the side of the house and rummaged through the garbage, pulling out a shirt he'd thrown away, the shirt he'd been wearing when he got roughed up at the Isis party.

He returned inside, went into his bedroom, and began making calls. The first to a guy who for the low, low fee of only seventy-five bucks would run the license plate in any state in the union.

The second to a former girlfriend whose name was Jennifer Leong.

FIFTEEN

The prevailing etiquette at the Rustic Canyon Mommy and Me was for no parent to acknowledge the status, higher or lower, of any other parent. But Alicia had been aware of a buzz reverberating through the room as soon as she'd arrived this afternoon. Though nobody actually mentioned her new and enviable position, the news had obviously made the rounds. And now as she emerged from the playgroup, people were jockeying to simply exchange a casual word with her.

Basking in this flurry of attention, she momentarily lost sight of her nanny, Marianela, and the twins. She felt a twinge of anxiety. Then she spotted Marianela on the edge of the crowd fussing with the Bugaboo stroller and hurried over to her. "There you are! Where are the girls?"

"I thought they were with you, Alicia."

"No, they're not. Where are they?" Alicia's anxiety skyrocketed to alarm. Her eyes frantically swept the surroundings, the street clogged with cars, the unadorned lawns of the homes on the opposite side of the road. There'd been a thunder shower twenty minutes before: the trees dripped, the grass and ivy glistened moistly, and a faint rumbling could still be heard in the distance.

She thought that if she did not see her daughters in one more second, she would perish.

A sweet rush of relief. There they were, Shane and Laura, the most beautiful, precious children in all of creation. A woman was leading them by their hands—a stranger, a woman with an hourglass figure wearing a skirt designed for a teenager. Alicia shouted the girls' names. They let go of the stranger's hands and scampered over to their mother. She gathered them tightly in her arms. "Sweethearts, where did you go?"

The stranger came up beside her, smiling. "Not to worry. They came with me. I saw that you were busy, so I took them for a little stroll." A Viking blonde, her accent hinting at Scandinavia: Danish, Norwegian. Her eyes were green, quick, and slightly tilted. Like the eyes of a magical creature, Alicia thought. Full of mischief.

"You took my kids?" Her voice was shaking. "I don't even know who you are."

"My name is Sabina. And no, you don't know me, but you do know my friend, Elizabeth. See her? She's over there, waiting by that big purple car."

Whatever residue of relief Alicia had been experiencing evaporated, replaced by sudden horror. The moment she'd been both dreading and expecting for twenty-three years had finally arrived.

Betsy Bell had found her.

She crouched to speak to her daughters. "Guys, I want you to go over to Marianela and stay with her. Don't leave her again, okay?" She waited until she was sure they were secure with the nanny, and then she wheeled with fury back to Sabina. "What does she want?"

"Just to say hello."

"I doubt that very much."

"Then you'll just have to find out for yourself."

"Okay."

Alicia marched rigidly to Betsy who was propped against an ancient Coupe de Ville sedan. Twenty-three years had not been kind to the Malibu Madam. Too many lifts had frozen her face in a fixed parody of a smile. Her hair featured the same jet black Jackie O flip, but was now obviously a wig, badly centered on her head. Her right hand and forearm shook noticeably.

"What do you want?" Alicia demanded.

"Oh, child, is that a way to greet an old friend?" Betsy's molasses drawl was more pronounced than before. Like her frozen smile, like her artificial hair, it seemed a ghastly parody of itself.

"We were never friends."

"No, no, of course not, sugar. Just old acquaintances. You were once kind enough to grace a few of my parties."

"Those parties of the Eighties, they really rocked," Sabina observed gleefully.

Betsy beamed. "Sabina came to me . . . oh my, several years after you did, Alicia. She had such a lovely shape, and she was very popular with my gentlemen. She did very well for herself. And now she runs my establishment for me while I enjoy my retirement in the country. When I come back to town, she does me the occasional favor of driving me around. She's my Morgan Freeman to my Miss Daisy."

Sabina giggled. Her elfin eyes gleamed.

"I've got nothing to say to either of you," Alicia said.

"Oh, child, I don't expect that you do. But you see, I'm an old lady with no grandchildren to brag about, so instead I like to brag about my girls. Especially those of you who've done so well out in the world. I even like to show off pictures of y'all, just like any proud granny." With her quaking hand, she reached into the dowager's handbag that dangled from her elbow and removed a gadget, dropping it on the asphalt. "Now you see that?" she said sadly.

Sabina bent and picked up the device.

"Modern technology leaves me breathless," Betsy went on. "Somehow, with the help of some very smart people, I've been able to get my old home movies sent right onto this little teeny toy. Why, I can even get them sent anywhere I please! It's a miracle, don't you think so, Alicia, honey?"

Alicia glared at her.

"And d'you know, that kind of technology can lead to even more miracles. For example, there's a medical trial here at UCLA for a very promising new drug that I was not eligible for. Too far advanced in my disability, so they told me. Well, I found out that one of the physicians conducting this trial just happens to be one of my former girls. Isn't that just amazin'? And so I sent one of my old home movies right to her cell phone, and it seems she was so touched by the gesture, that guess what? I have now been accepted for that drug trial! I shot right up to the top of the list. Isn't that simply a miracle?"

"What does that have to do with me?" Alicia demanded.

Sabina touched a function on the device and handed it to Alicia. "We thought you'd find this fun to watch."

The device was a miniature media player, and the postcard-sized screen displayed a video of a bedroom illuminated by the unearthly light of an infrared camera. The bed had black sheets, and a girl with long dark hair sprawled on it. She was naked except for a pair of patterned schoolgirl panties. An older man came into view. With a shock, Alicia recognized the Old Goat, her former employer, and her heart began pounding hard.

The Old Goat was naked and had an erection. He lay down beside the girl on the bed, and though there was no sound on the recording, he appeared to be speaking tenderly:

Are you warm enough? Shall I pull the sheet up?

He straddled the girl, fondled and kissed her breasts, let his hands stray between her thighs. He eased the panties down over her knees and untangled them from her feet. Then he opened her legs wide, and the girl gasped and seemed to be making cries as he entered her. His buttocks rose and fell as he thrust in and out. The girl raised her chin and squeezed her eyes shut and appeared to be making sounds in her throat.

The girl who was herself.

Her nineteen year old self. In the bungalow behind the Malibu Madam's party house, having sex with the Old Goat.

For a moment, the world seemed to spin out of all control: she closed her eyes, shutting out the hellish images.

Arms suddenly flung themselves around her legs. "Mommy!"

Alicia jumped. She looked down: it was Laura. "Get away from me!" Alicia shrieked.

The little girl stared up at her with a stupefied look. Her lips quivered, and then she burst into tears.

Alicia thrust the video player at Sabina, then knelt down and cradled her daughter in her arms. "I'm sorry sweetie. I didn't mean to yell at you. You just startled me. I am so really sorry." She saw Marianela approaching with Shane in the double stroller. "Mari, take the girls home *now*!"

"But Alicia, I thought you wanted me to take them shopping for new shoes."

"I changed my mind. Just take them straight home, right now!"

Marianela bundled the still howling Laura into the stroller beside Shane who also looked like she was about to cry. Other parents, attracted by the outburst, were peering curiously at Alicia and her two odd-looking companions. "Get in the car," she snapped at Betsy. "We can't talk in plain sight of everybody."

She took the lead, sliding into the Cadillac's back seat, its leather cracked and reeking of stale tobacco. Sabina helped Betsy in beside Alicia and then slid behind the wheel.

"Drive around the block," Alicia ordered.

Sabina complied, turning into a street of residential estates screened by towering hedges.

"Stop here."

Sabina pulled over and idled the car.

Alicia turned to Betsy. "Okay. What do you want?"

"A favor, sugar. Not for me, but for a very dear friend of mine. Bina, honey child, would you light me up one of my little cigars? You don't mind if I smoke, do you, Alicia?"

"I don't care if you rot."

Sabina lit a long, thin cigarillo with a gold-tone Zippo. Contorting herself, she extended the cigarillo to Betsy. Betsy leaned forward to fit her lips around it, took a dainty drag, and exhaled. "I can't even hold my own little cigars anymore," she drawled to Alicia. "Isn't that simply awful?"

Alicia stared at the two. It was as if she'd landed in the middle of some nightmarish fairytale, complete with a wicked witch and malevolent elf. "Just tell me what you want."

Betsy allowed herself another suck of the cigarillo. "It's really just a simple little favor. According to my friend, you're in charge of a project that's very important to him, and all you have to do is make sure it gets done."

"You mean a movie project?"

"A movie, yes."

Was that it? Some lunatic had a crappy script languishing in development at the studio and had staged all this just to get it going? "What movie?"

"The title is on the tip of my tongue, but all these medications I'm taking make my memory a little fuzzy. Sabina, sugar child, what's the name of the movie?"

"*Wildwood Murphy: The Legend Continues.*" The green eyes danced and sparkled. "I met Jackson Brandt one time, back when I was young, and I thought he was the sexiest man alive! I don't think Denny Brandt is half as handsome as his father was."

"*Wildwood Murphy?*" Alicia was thunderstruck. "But it *is* getting made."

"Well, then you see, there's absolutely no problem at all," Betsy said. "That's all there is to it. Except that I've got to mention one other small thing. The movie has to go ahead according to the original terms of the deal. Yes, that's the most important part." Betsy's voice suddenly turned hard and lost most of its molasses drawl. "You understand, don't you? There's to be no renegotiating the original production deal."

"Who is this friend of yours?"

The molasses came back to her mouth. "Oh child, you know me. The soul of discretion. I never reveal a thing about my friends. Not unless it's absolutely necessary."

"Hey, Betsy, you've got an appointment at the hospital," Sabina piped up. "Don't want to be late."

"So are we clear on all of this, Alicia?" Betsy said to Alicia.

"Yes," Alicia said. "We're clear."

"You agree to my friend's request?"

"Yes. Tell your friend we have a deal."

"Well then, there you see? Easy-peasy. Bina, sugar, you're right, we mustn't be late for my doctors."

"Alicia, you want me to drop you back at your car?" Sabina said.

"No!"

Alicia threw the door open and hurled herself out of the Cadillac, striding furiously until she had turned the corner, out of sight of those two monstrous creatures, until her ankles wobbled, and she was forced to sink to the curb.

Rage and fear swept through her mind. She was being blackmailed! Her children had been threatened. And all for the sake of some movie deal?

Her first thought was that it was somebody at the studio—one of the other executives who'd been blindsided by her nabbing the promotion and was looking to engineer her immediate downfall. But which of them could have known about Betsy?

She flashed on a sudden memory. That first party of Betsy Bell's, the one Alicia's wild child roommate Marcy had taken her to. The one where she'd met the Old Goat, leading to the loathsome scene on the bed with black sheets . . . She remembered how at first she'd stood huddled in a corner, clutching a drink, feeling nervous and awkward and out of place; and how she'd been approached by a skinny young man in aviator shades. A Jersey guy with bushy *Spinal Tap* hair and *Miami Vice* stubble. How she'd found him so appealing in his raw Jersey guy way. How grateful she'd been for his attention.

And then she remembered that Betsy shot him a look—*no, not this girl*—and how she'd noticed that he'd instantly done what Betsy wanted, had immediately slunk away.

In her mind, she cut off his heavy-metal hair and shaved his chin and took away the aviator glasses. She polished the Jersey out of his accent.

And came up with Warren Doran.

It was impossible! It made no sense at all. Warren was one of the major players in Hollywood. She'd known him for years. *Everybody* had known him for years.

What about the fact that he had first rocketed to the top from out of nowhere . . . ?

So what? This was Hollywood. Lots of people came out of nowhere.

But all the strange circumstances of his life: his wife dying under such tragic circumstances; his daughter convicted of a felony . . .

Again, not so strange: early success often led to lives of spectacular disarray.

Alicia thought of something else: how it had been that former roommate Marcy who'd first told her that Hannah had been released from prison, having heard it from the lips of Betsy Bell. And how Alicia had wondered why the Malibu Madam had been the first to know . . .

No mystery now. Betsy obviously still kept in touch with her one-time protégé Warren Doran.

Very close touch.

A centipede of horror crawled up Alicia's spine. It was the only possible conclusion: the charming and effervescent Warren Doran was entirely willing to destroy her career, her reputation, her entire life, for the sake of a few more points in a motion picture.

She'd agreed to the deal—she had no choice. But she wouldn't tell her boss Martin Drake that she was reversing herself—not yet, anyway. Contracts always took several weeks to finalize; she'd drag them out as long as possible.

And in that time, she vowed, she'd find a way to destroy Warren Doran.

SIXTEEN

Hannah opened her eyes and brushed the seaweed of tangled hair from her eyes. Horrific images had threaded and flickered through her dreams: *The gorgeous ruby blossoming on Valentina's throat. The eerie, almost pleased, look in Valentina's eyes as she melted to her knees. The dead weight of her crumpled body*; and for a moment, she couldn't remember where she was.

Then she did remember: Mitchell J. Arpino. Mitch. She smiled to herself.

Delicious smells were wafting from another part of the house, and a cozy clink and rattle of cooking ware. She got up and followed the sounds and smells to the kitchen. Mitch was mashing a greenish paste with a mortar and pestle. The counters were littered with choppings and peelings of garlic and lemon grass and tangerine, and with opened cans and packets of spices. Strips of chicken were sizzling in oil. The kitchen table was set for two: mismatched silverware, festively-painted Mexican bowls. A water glass in the center overflowed with a cluster of fresh-picked flowering quince.

"Hey, you're up!" he greeted her.

"How long have I been sleeping?"

"About an hour and a half. I thought you'd be hungry when you woke up so I popped out to the Asian market down the block."

"You left me here alone?"

"Fifteen minutes tops. Everything locked tight." He deftly flipped the chicken strips. "By the way, the cops called."

"What did you say?" she asked anxiously.

"Nothing about you, of course. They want me to come in to the station tomorrow morning and look through mug books. See if

I can identify the girl in the Rolls. Maybe I can fish out what they know while I'm there."

"Good." She peered into the pan. "What are you making? It smells delicious."

"Green coconut curry. Hope you like Thai food."

"Adore it."

He sprinkled a Halloween orange spice into the mortar, then began chopping green chiles. "Mild, hot, or set your mouth on fire?"

"Somewhere between hot and fire department."

"You got it." He tossed a large pinch of the chopped chiles into the mortar.

"Where did you learn to cook?" she asked.

"Picked it up here and there. I love to eat, and sometimes the only way you can eat well is to make it yourself." He spooned some shrimp paste into the mortar, continued mashing. "A few years back, when I was working for the *Times,* I was embedded with a marine unit in Afghanistan. Out in country, the only thing we had to eat were MRE's. Jalapeño crackers that tasted like peppery dust. And these packets of chili macaroni, you added water and they boiled up like some weird junior high chemistry experiment. We used to spend hours talking about what we were going to eat when we got home. Cheeseburgers. Kentucky Fried. But for me, nothing beats a great curry." He scraped the smooshed paste from the mortar into the crackling chicken and sluiced in half a small jar of coconut cream. "In Thailand, they eat this dish soupy, but I like it creamier. Gives it more mouth feel." He peered into a lidded pot of rice. "So how about you? Are you into cooking?"

"Before I went to prison, I couldn't even boil water. There was a kitchenette in my dorm, and to avoid the horrible cafeteria food, I had to learn some basics. Nothing anywhere near as good as what you're making, though."

"Better not say that until you taste it. Five minutes."

Hannah went over to inspect a row of framed 8x10 photographs hanging on the opposite wall. The subjects were all children, Asian or Latin American. Some were ragged and emaciated. Two of the girls had garish makeup and provocatively sexy clothing. "Is this your work?"

"Yeah. Frame grabs from a documentary I was working on. About kids who are used as slaves. The one in front of you? Her name is Carlita. She's Ecuadorean. Eleven years old, and she'd already been a prostitute for three years."

"She's gorgeous."

"She's also really a boy."

Hannah shot him a glance.

"The kid in the photo next to her, that's Setiawan. Indonesian. Nine and a half in the picture. Assembled circuit boards fifteen hours a day, seven days a week. Couldn't remember ever having been outdoors."

"What happened to the documentary?"

"The funding went bust. Never finished it." Mitch gave the curry a vigorous stir.

"But I don't get it," Hannah said.

"Get what?"

"These photos. They're amazing. They show such commitment. Real passion. How did you go from this to chasing around ridiculous celebrities?"

"Beats me. Maybe the same way you go from being an honors student at Yale to becoming one of those ridiculous celebrities."

She flushed. "That's a shitty thing to say!"

A sudden buzzing made them both give a start.

"My text tone," Mitch said. He picked up his cell from the table and glanced at the message.

"The police?"

"No. It's a guy I contacted to run down that Texas plate. NO REGRETS. Interesting. It's registered to one Elizabeth Bellingham."

"Who's that?"

"You probably know her better as Betsy Bell."

"The old Malibu Madam? The one Valentina and Zizi used to work for?"

"That's her."

"So she was the one who picked them up from Peachrock. And she's probably the friend Valentina said was double-crossing her."

"I gotta believe so." Mitch dipped a wooden spoon into the pan, tasted and added another flick of red pepper. "Look," he said. "I'm sorry about what I said to you before. That was harsh."

"No, I'm the one who should be sorry. You're right, I shouldn't judge you. I've never had to worry about money. At least up until now."

"Why now?"

"I've been having some trouble getting money out of my accounts. Just a temporary thing. My father's partner—his business partner, Thad—he arranged to have the management of my trust transferred to WildFilm, my dad's company. He said it would be more efficient and save me money, not having to pay an outside manager. But he said there was some kind of snag in the transferring. He's supposed to be sorting it out."

"Do you trust this guy?"

"Thad? My father does. But honestly? No, I think I never really did. It's one of the things I plan to do—take control of my finances."

"You definitely should." Thinking about her money—how much of it she had—made him uneasy. He turned back to the stove, checked the rice again. "This is ready to go. Let's eat!"

He mounded rice in two of the Mexican bowls and ladled the curry over it and brought the plates to the table. He watched anxiously as she took her first bite. "Edible?"

"It's really good." Hannah started eating with more appetite than she expected to have.

"Music to my ears." Mitch attacked his own plate. For several minutes, they attacked the food.

"So how do we find Betsy Bell?" Hannah said at length. "Even if Zizi didn't go back to her, she could have a lead on where Zizi could be."

"If we find where her parties are operating, we've got a good chance of finding her."

"Does she still throw parties? I thought the Malibu Madam got put out of business years ago."

"Officially, yeah. But with an operation like hers, it's like whack-a-mole. You stomp it down in one place and she pops up in another. She might not be in Malibu anymore, but she's got to be doing business somewhere. Did you know that Valentina was busted for recruiting girls for her?"

"I knew she'd worked for the Malibu Madam." Hannah flashed on the scene at the cemetery. She shuddered. "Poor Valentina."

"Yeah, boo-hoo."

"My god, Mitch. That's cold."

He gave a snort. "You don't know the whole story. I told you she was a recruiter. The girls she was getting for Betsy Bell were thirteen-year-old kids. Runaways right off the bus."

"To be hookers?"

"They sure as shit weren't studying algebra. She'd cozy up to them like a mama bear protecting her cubs, and then when they became dependent on her, she'd feed them to the wolves. I can be real cold about people who abuse kids."

"I had no idea. I mean, I knew she was bad news, but not that."

Hannah thought of Valentina, her demands. . . . And of the seventeen thousand dollars in the trunk of her car . . .

"No reason you should've known," Mitch told her. He glanced at her polished plate. "Want some more?"

"No, I'm fine."

"Hey, I didn't mean to spoil the meal."

"You didn't. It's just that it's getting late. It's almost nine o'clock. My parole officer can call any time, and if he does, he'll want to know where I am."

"And saying you're with a material witness in the murder of Valentina Rostov might not be such a hot idea."

She hesitated. "I could lie."

He hesitated too. "Probably also not such a hot idea."

"Then I guess I better get back to my place."

He accompanied her to the door. "You sure you're okay?"

She nodded. "But I don't know what I would have done . . ."

"Yeah." He smiled.

"You've got a little bit of sauce . . ." She dabbed at a speck of sauce on his upper lip.

"I'm a slob."

"It was just a speck."

And then in what seemed like the most natural thing in the world, they were kissing, deeply and extravagantly, an extension of the kiss that had begun on that hotel balcony.

Then suddenly she stiffened and broke away. "I've really got to go."

"What's wrong?"

She glanced evasively away. "Nothing. Just like I said, it's getting late."

It was the balcony again. Pull and then push. He tried to cover his feelings. "Okay. If I get any news about Betsy or anything else, I'll call you."

"Yeah. Okay, thanks." Hannah turned abruptly and continued to her car.

Sucker, Mitch berated himself. He was being played again. Maybe he should have taken the shot of her and the Russian corpse in the cemetery, cashed in when he had the chance.

At any rate, he still had a story to pursue.

And in pursuit of that story, he still had things to do that he hadn't seen fit to tell her about.

Hannah began driving, but not back to her own place, heading to downtown instead. Her emotions were in turmoil. It had seemed so natural to kiss him, and yet it was crazy. Absolutely insane. After everything that had happened in the past few days . . . How could she know if she could trust him? How could she know if she could trust anybody?

She turned into the asphalt lot at the darkened Sunlight Center. For some inexplicable reason, she had the feeling she could trust Benny Davis.

Lights were burning in the green and white bus behind the warehouse, and a t.v. muttered from inside the bus. Hannah walked up the wheelchair ramp and rapped at the door. "Benny? It's me, Hannah."

The metal panel slid open. "Damn it, girl, what are you doing wandering around this hood this time of night? Get your ass in here."

She stepped into an open area in the center of the bus that was just large enough to accommodate both her and Benny's wheelchair. She gazed with interest at the rest of the interior. Everything was ingeniously built in, made to fold out or flip up. A queen-sized bed neatly made up was unfolded across the rear. Towards the front, a two burner propane stove was pulled down on hinges above an efficiency sink. Benny's two Golden Globes and his Emmy glowed in a recessed niche.

He clicked off the t.v. that was mounted over the bed. "You look like you been through hell. Something happen out there?"

"No," she said quickly. "I'm just not sleeping very well. I keep having bad dreams."

"I know about that. Thirty years later, I still sometimes dream I'm back inside."

"You were in prison?"

"Yeah. Nine months for possession of cocaine with intent to sell. The hell I was gonna sell it. My *intent* was to snort every last flake of the shit myself."

She said tentatively: "I heard you used to be a cocaine addict."

"Who told you that? Your daddy?"

She nodded.

"He was right. I put every dollar I made up my nose, even after I couldn't walk no more. *Especially* after. But I kicked it going on ten years ago. Now I smoke a pipe but there's nothing in it except tobacco." He gave a wry shrug of his shoulders. "So . . . What's so urgent it couldn't wait till tomorrow?"

"I've brought a donation."

"More of your Versace?"

"Not exactly." She held out the tote bag she was carrying.

He looked inside, and his eyes started from his head. "Holy shit! Is this real?"

"Yeah, it's real. Seventeen thousand dollars in genuine bills."

"Jesus Christ, girl! What are you doing with all these Benjamins?"

"I sold some junk I didn't need anymore. They paid in cash."

"You swear it's legit?"

"I swear. And it's the first of a lot more to come."

"Is it all gonna come in a bag?"

She gave a short laugh. "No. It will all be on the up-and-up. But maybe now you'll take me seriously."

He stared wonderingly at the money again. "I guess I'm gonna have to. But Christ almighty, girl, you could've gotten yourself killed if anybody in this neighb knew you was cashed up like this."

"I'm parked right outside. I don't think it was that much of a risk."

His hooded black eyes took her in for a moment. "Anything else you want to tell me?"

"No. That's it."

"What's that on your pants?"

She looked down and saw the brown stains. She drew a breath. "Just . . . some mud."

He made a "yeah, right" face but didn't press her further. He released a catch on a cabinet and stowed the tote in it. "Actually, I got something for you too." From amidst other items in the cabinet, he pulled out a lidless shoebox crammed with Polaroid snapshots, with several set on top. "You know how boring it gets on sets, waiting around forever till the next shot gets set up. For awhile, I had a Polaroid camera to pass the time. After we were talking the other day, I got hit by nostalgia, so I got to looking at some of these, and I found one you might want to see." He handed her a photo that had been set on top of the stack. "It's kind of faded out now. That's the trouble with old Polaroids."

She looked at it. It showed a towering, Easter Islandish figure made of glass, seated with its legs crossed, a fierce expression on its face. Two very young children, a girl and a boy, were playing on it.

"It's the crystal totem from the third *Wildwood* movie," Hannah said. "*The Judgment of the Shamans*."

"Yeah, out there on the set in Arizona. But check out the kids. They don't ring a bell?"

She scrutinized it closer. The girl whose face was turned away from the camera was about four or five with matted dark curls. The boy was a year or two older with dark blond hair and long-lashed eyes. He was perched on the shoulder of the statue, grasping the little girl's hand as if to prevent her from falling off the statue's lap.

"It's me," Hannah said.

"Yeah. That time your mama brought you out to the set. You were a wild little thing, racing around like a cat with its tail on fire, getting into trouble—you and your best buddy there."

With a shock, she realized who the boy was. "That's Denny Brandt."

"Yeah, Jackson Brandt's kid. The one who's such big box office now. Gonna be the new Wildwood Murphy, so I hear."

"Yeah, he is."

"You and him, you were like glue back then. Mutt and Jeff. Except once in a while something would set the two of you's off, and you'd be wailing the daylights on each other. You don't remember none of this?"

Suddenly she did!

Denny had easily shimmied up the big glass statue and was sitting on its shoulder, swinging his legs. "It's easy, Hanny, come on, don't be a baby." And it was easy for her to climb up onto the lap, but when she tried to go higher, it was too slippery. Denny reached down and grabbed her hand and started to help her, but then she slipped and was sliding off the statue and fell onto a tangle of cords on the floor. And then Denny came tumbling down right beside her. "You stupid!" he said. "No, you're the stupid!" she said back. And then he pushed her, or maybe she pushed him, and then they were hitting and wrestling, in a fight, but they were laughing really hard too.

And then all of a sudden Denny was being dragged away by a very tall and skinny lady. It was his mommy, Hannah knew. Her hair looked like a hat, a shiny, hard, brown hat. "I told you to stay away from her!" she yelled at Denny. "Her mother is crazy and so is she!"

Denny's mommy started to take Denny away, and he looked back at Hannah and stuck his tongue out at her, and Hannah stuck hers out at him.

And then she started to cry. A man wearing a white dress came up to her and picked her up. "Hey, big girls don't cry," he said. "Didn't nobody ever tell you that?"

"I remember you there!" Hannah said. "You were wearing your Dr. Taylor lab coat, right? You picked me up when I was crying."

"Broke my heart. Little kid like you bawling your eyes out."

"I can't believe I blocked all this out. Where was my mother?"

Benny got that shifty look in his eye. "Busy, I guess." He reached for his pipe and a box of matches.

"And so what happened after that?"

"You hung out with me for a while and eventually your mama came to find you. That was the last time I ever saw either of you. We wrapped a week later, and then a couple of weeks after that, Jack Brandt went off a cliff."

"And a month later, my mother was dead too."

He grunted.

"Can I keep this?"

"Huh! For seventeen grand, you can take anything I got!"

Hannah stared hard at the photo again. Somewhere within this timescape, just beyond these black and white borders, her mother, Pamela, walked and spoke and breathed.

SEVENTEEN

Hannah woke up after another restless night, this one punctuated by nightmares. Nevertheless, she'd slept until after ten. She checked her messages—Mitch hadn't called.

Her eye fell on the faded Polaroid Benny had given, propped against her bed lamp. It gave her an idea. If she wanted to talk to Crissie Townsend, obviously going through Denny Brandt would insure it. He was even a bigger star than his fiancée, meaning he would be doubly insulated from contact. Still, it was worth a try.

She had sixteen listings for him in her phone's address book. All labeled for various types of entourage—except one listed under "CELL." But whose cell? And would it still be in service after all this time?

She gave it a shot.

A drowsy male voice answered. "Yo."

"Denny?" she said with astonishment.

"Yeah?"

"It's me. Hannah."

A pause. She thought he would hang up, but he didn't. "Yo, what's up?"

"I'm trying to reach Crissie. It's important. Is she with you?"

"Nah. We had a fight last night and she took off."

"Where did she go?"

"Don't know. Don't give a shit."

"It's incredibly important I get hold of her. Can you give me her cell number?"

"Won't do you any good. That phone's history. I rammed it down the disposal. It's a casualty of war." He chortled. "Hey, you know what Cris Townsend is like without a phone? Nonexistent. Like ectoplasm."

"Look, Denny, if you hear from her, make her get in touch with me," Hannah said forcefully. "I'm not kidding, I've *really* got to talk to her."

He stopped laughing. "Hey, are you okay?" His voice had a catch of genuine concern. "You sound kind of strange."

For a second, she weighed the idea of confiding in him. He liked to play the airhead actor. It was disarming; probably made him appealing to his younger fans. She knew it was an act that he could turn off and on at will. Maybe she should tell him everything that had been happening since her release, and how totally freaked she was about it all . . .

She caught herself. No matter how natively intelligent he was, Denny was still a spoiled and unpredictable movie star. "I'm okay," she said evasively. "Just still trying to adjust to being back home. But hey, Denny? Can I ask you something?"

"I guess."

"Do you remember as a kid ever going to the set of *Wildwood*? The third one, *The Judgment of the Shamans*?

"Sure. Last time I ever saw my dad."

"Really? Wow." She hesitated. "So do you remember me being there too? On the set, I mean?"

"Sure."

"You do?"

"Yeah, we ran around together until my mom said not to play with you. She said your mom was crazy and should be locked away and you were crazy too."

"Do you know why? Why your mom thought mine was crazy?"

"Well she was, wasn't she? Everybody said so."

Hannah felt a flash of anger. But at the same time, she wondered if he were right.

"Hey, Hanny, do you want to hook up?" Denny said. "I'm here all by myself."

"You're never by yourself."

"I mean except for some posse. Why don't you come on over. We can still play together."

"We're not little kids anymore, Denny."

"I know. Why do you think I'm asking you over?"

"For godsake, Denny, it's not even noon. And anyway, I'm not interested."

"How come?"

"You've never been my type."

"Bullshit. You know there's always been something between us."

She hesitated. "You'll get back with Crissie. You always do, don't you?"

"You're right. She'll come crawling back and I won't have the strength to resist. So why don't you come over and rescue me from that?"

He was so damned arrogant. So infuriatingly sure of himself! "Just get Cris to call me," she told him and hung up.

She went to the kitchen and grabbed a golden plum from the refrigerator, part of the stash of produce that Thad Miller had brought. It was staggering to imagine it was less than a week ago. It seemed like a lifetime. A week ago, she had not known that Shawn Serafian had spiked her drink in a supposedly botched intervention, or that Valentina and Zizi might have been paid to keep her from getting parole. And she'd never seen anybody murdered right before her eyes.

A week ago, she did not know who Mitch Arpino was. And she'd thought she had stopped questioning about her mother.

Everyone said your mom was crazy . . . She thought of Denny's words again, and a memory flickered in her mind:

She was at her grandfather's house and she'd woken up in the middle of the night. There was a strange sound coming from outside. Like coyotes they sometimes heard howling, but not really like them—this was a different sound. She got out of bed and went to the window. There must have been moonlight because she could see her mommy standing in the garden. She was wearing a long blue nightgown and her face was lifted to the moon, and she was the one making the strange howling sound.

Her mother was howling at the moon.

The memory suddenly seemed vividly real. Hannah could visualize the liquid drape of the nightgown against her mother's long body, and her silvery hair pouring down her back. Her pale howling face turned upwards to the paler moon.

Was that it? Was that why she'd killed herself? Simply because she was out of her mind?

She couldn't—she wouldn't—believe that.

Valentina had insinuated that there was more to know. Maybe she'd been just bluffing. Her usual swagger. But some instinct told Hannah that it wasn't.

She finished the plum and tossed the pit. The enormous windows offered a panorama of a vast city, but suddenly she'd never felt so alone.

She had the enormous urge to call her father. She wouldn't ask anything from him this time. She just wanted to make a connection. They were the only family each other had—and in those many long months in prison, she had come to realize more and more that the connection to real family was what counted most.

She headed to where she had put down her phone.

There was a sudden pounding on her front door. She went to the peephole and saw the concierge, Eddie's face. Her heart froze as she recognized her parole officer, McAuliffe, looming behind him. McAuliffe was flanked by two police officers, one male, one female, clutching armfuls of papers and files.

Eddie was preparing to fit a key in the lock. He jumped when she opened the door. "Didn't think you were home," he muttered.

"Compliance check, Doran," McAuliffe said.

She felt a jolt of alarm. "Already?"

"We're acting on some information."

"What information?"

He ignored her question. "Is there anybody else here on the premises?"

"No. Just me."

He nodded to the cops, and all three marched briskly into the penthouse. "Sorry about this," Eddie said and slunk back to the service elevator. The female officer, a wiry black woman with a humorous face, turned to Hannah. "You're gonna have to come down and wait in the car."

"I want to call my lawyer."

"You can do that afterwards. Just come with me, please."

"Can't I at least put on some shoes first?" Hannah indicated her bare feet. "There's a pair right by that table."

"Go ahead."

"Wait!" said the other cop. "Let me see those shoes."

Hannah's heart began to pound. They were the espadrilles she'd been wearing the day before. She'd kicked them off the minute she returned home last night. As the cop picked one up, she could see that its rope soles were splotched with dried blood. She watched, breathless with terror, as the cop experimentally rattled the shoe, then ran a finger inside the toe.

He appeared to be satisfied. He tossed it back on the floor and repeated the action with its mate. "Okay." He moved away.

Hannah let out a breath. But she was shaking as she put the shoes on her feet. Willing herself to be steady, she accompanied the female cop down to the street. The cop ducked her into the back of a patrol car and then headed back up to the penthouse.

The backseat felt like a little cell. The doors were secured, the front seat grilled off, and there was the smothering unwashed-body smell of a lock-up. Hannah suppressed a surge of panic. Every prisoner in California knew the state was famously harsh about even the most minor parole infractions. The running joke was you could get shipped back for spitting out your gum on a sidewalk. If they found anything in her apartment—anything at all—she could be swiftly sent back to a real cell.

What if she hadn't taken that tote bag to Benny Davis? How could she have explained away a bag stuffed with cash?

Don't think about that. Another rule from the unofficial Peachrock handbook: Deal with situations as they came up. Don't dwell on what might have been or try to second-guess the future. She closed her eyes and tried to shut out the claustrophobic car.

She tried to think of nothing.

༄

Jennifer Leong, USC doctoral candidate in biomolecular engineering, had the large lustrous eyes, silky ink-jet hair, and endless legs of a pageant queen. Three years back, Mitch had found these attributes an irresistible turn-on, but now they paled in comparison to the soft brown hair and smoke gray eyes of the girl he had just kissed.

Hannah . . . He felt a wild rush of elation.

He walked up to Jennifer. Wearing a white lab coat, she was bent rather lovingly over a glass tank in which a five inch furry tarantula was devouring a cricket. "Hey," Mitch greeted her.

"Mitchy!" She whirled. They pecked each other demurely on the cheek.

"How's the genetic sequencing of the creepy-crawly going?" he asked. "What's it called again, your spider?"

"Grammostola rosea. Also known as Chilian rose hair tarantula. And it's going great—we'll have the entire sequencing mapped by the end of the year." She tapped on the case, and the spider, having swallowed its meal, began a creepy crawl toward the glass. "See how friendly she is? They make pretty good pets, you know."

"I'll take your word for it." Mitch glanced at the diamond ring on her left hand. "So who's the lucky guy?"

"A nice Korean boy, just like my parents always wanted. He's a lecturer in astrophysics. And brilliant and handsome and totally adorable."

"Okay, I'm intimidated. And happy for you."

She blushed. "Thanks."

He held out the grocery bag he was carrying. It contained the shirt he'd pulled out of the trash and the two of Hannah's hairs. "So here are the samples I told you I'd bring."

"You *do* know there are lots of public labs that will do DNA testing?"

"Yeah, but I need a certain amount of discretion. And pedal to the metal."

"But you won't tell me what this is about?"

"Sorry, I really can't."

She pursed her lips. "Why do I get the feeling it's something either illegal or unethical?"

"It's not, I swear. It's just to satisfy some curiosity. And your name will never come into it."

"I don't know, Mitch . . . It sounds pretty fishy. And besides, my time is like completely crazy right now. Finishing my dissertation and planning the wedding and all. I'm getting about two hours sleep a night."

"Yeah, I can imagine. So when is the wedding?"

"August."

"Hired a videographer yet?"

"We've interviewed a few. But we're still browsing."

"Those guys are pricey, aren't they?"

"For somebody good."

"I'm good. Amazing, in fact."

"You do a wedding? That'll be the day."

"I'll do yours. No charge."

She regarded him skeptically. "That's a bribe, right?"

"Reciprocal favor."

Jennifer debated with herself a moment, then snatched the bag. "Okay, I've got to pull some all-nighters this week anyway. I'll see what I can do." She peered inside. "Yikes, Mitch! Is this blood?"

"A friend of mine cut himself shaving."

"He must have sliced a jugular. Mitch, you've got to tell me what this is all about."

"I will, I totally promise, just not yet. How soon can you get me the results?"

She did this blowing-through-pursed-lips thing that he remembered well. One foxy bio-chemist. "*If* I can extract the variable DNA from the samples, and assuming it's not too degraded or been too contaminated . . . And depending on how many other people are on line for the thermal cycler . . . Maybe in a week."

"Make it three days and we've got a deal."

After leaving the campus, Mitch headed to the Hollywood police station, and while flipping through mug books under the guise of trying to identify the driver of the Corniche, he pumped a couple of the detectives. They were wavering about the Russian mob angle: Valentina Rostov had been a pimp and a pros, but always for homegrown operators like Betsy Bell. Her name had never been flagged by any L.A.P.D. gang specialists.

He stood an especially chatty sergeant to a burger and a beer at a nearby tavern. Casually turned the conversation to the Malibu Madam.

"You looking for some professional booty?" the sergeant grinned.

"Something like that," Mitch grinned back. "I always heard that Betsy Bell's ladies were the best. I guess she's closed up shop though, huh?"

"Not totally. She went back to where she came from. Buttfuck, Texas. But she's got one of her old girls running the show. A Salina or Sabina."

"Still in Malibu?"

"No way. It's a small-time operation now, and Malibu real estate's got far too pricey. I'm hearing Chatsworth. The boonies." The cop gave Mitch a jab in the shoulder. "There's far better tail around. Talk to the guys in vice, maybe they can set you up."

Mitch returned to his car, debating his next move. The Nextel on his dash crackled.

"I hear you were an eye witness to that Russian ho murder!" Ajay Nayar's voice had that boa-constrictor squeezing-his-guts gasp.

"How did you hear that?"

"Source in the L.A.P.D. Get any close-ups?"

Freaking ghoul. "Yeah, I got plenty of nice, oozy snaps of the corpse," Mitch lied. "And there's more. Did you hear that there was another car that drove away? Rolls Royce convertible, girl at the wheel. I was an eye witness to that too."

"Sweet! You got photos?"

Mitch expanded his lie. "You bet. And check this out. Police don't know yet, but the chick who was driving is a celeb."

"Who? Tell me!"

"Can't yet. The cops don't even know. My shots are out of focus, everything happened fast, but I'm at USC right now. Got a friend in the cyber department who's gonna digitally enhance them."

"I get the exclusive, right?"

"You joking? You canned me, you dickwad. You won't even return my calls."

"Come on. *Mitch!* What do you want?"

Grinning, Mitch edged into traffic on the 10. "What I want is for you to find out where the Malibu Madam's currently running her parties and get me in."

"You need to get laid, bro? Just come on over to my crib. I've got plenty of hot babies hanging around."

Mitch gave a snort. Ajay seemed to regard the show *Entourage* as a lifestyle template—always had a dozen or so half-naked starlets free-loading around his pool, while he strutted around in a Speedo, popping Provigil tabs like M&M's. "Can you get me connected with Betsy Bell's parties or not?"

"Okay, okay, I'll work on it." The Nextel went quiet.

Almost immediately, Mitch's cell rang. When he looked at the I.D., his heart skipped a beat.

EIGHTEEN

Better than sex!

Getting a green light on a big budget studio film was a high like no other, Warren Doran reflected. Heroin, coke, and ecstasy rolled into one. Winning triple gold at the Olympics; summiting Everest; scoring with a supermodel: it was all of these things combined, plus an avalanche of money.

The calls, texts, emails and faxes began before dawn and continued into the night. He'd heard from people he thought were dead. People he *wished* were dead.

People he knew wished *he* were dead but who were now desperate to do lunch.

Between meetings and meals, gloating and schmoozing, he barely had time to accomplish a fraction of everything he needed to do. Denny Brandt was now officially signed, and the choice of a director was now his biggest priority. It was going to be tricky—it had to be a director young enough to deliver something fresh and hip, but also experienced enough to keep a world-class whacko of an actor like Denny Brandt under control. In the meantime Warren found it intoxicating to have every top agent in town kneeling at his feet, offering their A-list director clients like virgins to a volcano god.

In fact it was because he was coming from a powwow with the head of Intertalent who'd been groveling so delightfully that Warren could hardly tear himself away that he was late for his current meeting—to plan the press event that would announce *Wildwood Murphy: The Legend Continues* to the world.

It was being held in Alicia Chenoweth's office, formerly Cody Takish's, in the Constellation Pictures executive building. As he stepped out of the fourth floor elevator. he felt a familiar searing bubble of acid burst in his esophagus—the first time since he'd gotten the go-ahead for the movie.

Why now? Everything was back in gear. As soon as all the i's were dotted on his contract, Constellation would cut him a check for twenty million dollars. Half of that would go to the men in the blue suits as their share, plus another five to pay back what they'd advanced him.

The remaining five million would keep his own company, Wild-Film, through the coming months of production. He was practically home free.

And once the movie was wrapped, there'd be more money flowing in from many different sources. A veritable Niagara Falls of revenue. Everything would get paid off. Everybody would win.

So what did he have to worry about?

Alicia.

Warren paused before rounding the final corner to her suite. Alicia Chenoweth was nobody's fool. She'd have figured out by now that he was the one behind Betsy Bell's little proposal, and she'd be desperately looking for a way to retaliate. He had to be prepared for anything she threw his way.

Fuck the bitch, he told himself. There was nothing she could do. He had her by the short and curlies. *Actually, sort of literally*, he thought, with a chuckle. She was dragging out the finalization of his contract, he could see that, but that might buy her maybe a week, two at the most.

Bottom line: she couldn't touch him without totally destroying herself as well. And like he'd just told himself—Alicia Chenoweth was no fool.

There was his other worry: Hannah.

Thad swore he'd have everything taken care of with her by the end of today. But if he didn't? If she continued to be demanding money and raising questions . . .

The acid brushfire leaped from Warren's esophagus to his throat.

He popped a purple pill dry, swallowing it dry, grimacing as it made its way down his enflamed throat and lodged stubbornly at the tip of his stomach. He made certain no trace of his agony showed as Alicia's secretary ushered him into the office.

"Sorry I'm late, folks!" He spoke with his customary brio, creating a bustle as he shook hands. There were four people beside Alicia waiting for him: Denny Brandt's manager, Jon Ayler, who had a face like a choir boy but who'd be willing to suck your blood with a straw if necessary. Denny's agent, Roddy O'Neill, who was Skeletor-thin. The Botoxed-to-a-death-mask Head of Marketing, Lois Dubosky. And Thad Miller, with his trendy little beard, looking way out of his league.

Warren took a swig from a bottle of tepid water. It eased the recalcitrant purple pill into his stomach. "So fill me in. What have I missed?"

"Lois has just informed us the press event is scheduled for Friday," Alicia said. She sat directly under that bizarro upside-down painting that used to be Cody's. The only thing freakier than that topsy-turvy screaming guy, Warren thought, was the expression on Alicia's face—all smiling and serene.

Could it be possible she actually didn't suspect him?

Disconcerted, he took a seat on a sofa besides Lois Dubosky. "So. Friday . . . ?"

"Yeah, we're taking over a space between some of the sound-stages and turning it into a *Wildwood Murphy* set," Lois said. "We're going to have all the exhibitors in the country for two days on the lot and we'll be screening clips from all our forthcoming releases. We'll be wining and dining them and they'll all be in a fantastic mood. It's the perfect opportunity at the end of the second day for a big wrap-up. A bang-up cocktail party, mingling with the stars, and then the announcement about *Wildwood*."

Warren cleared his burning throat. "Before we proceed any further, I'd like to tell you all how I envision this event."

"Go ahead, Warren," said Alicia.

That spooky agreeableness.

He avoided looking at her. "We want the world to know that Wildwood Murphy is back, right? And I mean the *entire* world—after this event, we want every damned Bushman in the Kalahari Desert, every monk on every top of every damned mountain in Tibet, to be aware that Wildwood is back. So what we need to give 'em is an old-school show business moment!"

All eyes were fixed on him.

"So . . . Everybody's gathered at sunset. They're eating, they're drinking, we've got girls giving out cigars, extras in costumes—mummies, witch doctors—and members of the old cast, and they're all working the crowd. We've been feeding the blogs misinformation about Denny maybe having dropped out of the role, so everybody's on edge. They're all agog: Who's going to be the new Wildwood?

"Then, suddenly, a biplane comes swooping overhead, and there's a motorcycle on the wing. It gets closer and we realize it's Wildwood Murphy on his bike! He's got the goggles on, his blond hair whipping in the wind, the bike's his famous Indian with the silver star. And then he guns the bike. It leaps off the wing and a parachute opens. It sails through the air and lands behind the set backdrop. Everyone's holding their breath . . .

"And then *wham!* The bike comes crashing through the backdrop, shoots onto a ramp right down the middle of the press corps, and whips a wheelie at the end. Wildwood lifts his goggles. And, ladies and gentlemen . . . It's Denny Brandt! Denny Brandt *is* Wildwood Murphy!"

"Whoa, love it!" said the agent Roddy O'Neill.

"Everyone's gonna want to run the footage!" enthused Lois Dubosky.

"I think Denny will go for it," pronounced the manager Jon Ayler. "He'll love the dramatic reveal."

"Um, Warren." Thad jiggled his foot. "I think I ought to mention that we might have some problems with Denny's insurance. For a risky stunt like that, I mean."

Warren looked at his junior partner. All his doubts and anxieties came rushing up in a wave of acidic bile and crashed onto Thad Miller. "Jesus freaking christ, you moron! Obviously it's going to be a stunt double jumping off the plane. He'll change places with Denny behind the backdrop."

"Oh, yeah. Of course." Thad ducked his head, his face crimson.

"Though of course Denny prefers to do his own stunts whenever he can," Jon Ayler said in a prickly voice. "When the insurance allows."

"Of course he does, Jon," Warren soothed. "We all know that."

Lois Dubosky piped up: "I think this idea's a winner. We're gonna own the media for a week!"

"I've just got one concern," Alicia interrupted.

Warren allowed himself a glance at her.

"It sounds expensive." There was now a purr of something dark and dangerous in her voice. For the briefest of moments, their eyes locked. "So my question is, Warren, do you really think that all this you're doing is worth the cost?"

"Yes, Alicia, I do," he said levelly. "Absolutely worth the cost."

"All right, then." Her voice purred so low it was scarcely audible. "Go for it."

※

In the mirror of her office's private bathroom. Alicia contemplated herself intensely.

She was wearing a fifty-four hundred dollar Valentino silk jacket and skirt and a pair of seven hundred dollar Louboutin pumps. She was about to set off for a lunch with George Clooney and his manager, and last night, she'd attended a ten thousand dollar a plate fundraiser for the governor of California. She could call anyone in the industry—in practically *any* industry—and her call would be immediately taken.

What need we fear who knows it, if none can call our power to account?
Oh yeah? So how did that work out for you, Lady MacBeth?

She, in fact, had plenty to fear. Constellation Pictures was a family-oriented motion picture studio. PG-rated animations were its bread and butter. Plus, thirty-five percent of it had recently been acquired by a Bollywood corporation; and in Bollywood, actors weren't even allowed to kiss on screen.

So how would her Constellation bosses react to the news that one of their major executives had been caught pumping tang on camera?

Not well, she strongly suspected. Didn't matter at what tender age she'd been when the footage had been shot. Even one frame of it finding its way out into the world would spell sudden death for her career.

And every time she summoned the image of that hideous elfin Sabina taking her children by the hand, her knees gave way and her lungs constricted so tightly she could hardly breathe.

If she'd had a gun stashed in her desk, she might have taken it out and shot Warren Doran right between his smiling, charismatic eyes.

But there were other forms of death beside the actual one; and for someone like Warren, the figural kind was probably worse than the real thing. She thought of the appointment she had made for tonight: it was not with a governor or a movie star or any industry mover and shaker; but it could well be one of the most important appointments of her life.

Lady MacBeth-like, she scrubbed her hands. She reapplied a matte of apricot lipstick, spritzed a mist of volumizer over her hair, and minutely adjusted the fit of her exquisite jacket.

She regarded herself again, satisfied that she looked like who she was: a wealthy and successful woman, with connections and resources. A woman with power.

And one who intended to use it.

⚜

Thad Miller slammed a Melissa Etheridge CD into the dashboard player and gunned his muscle car out of the lot, startling half the remaining life out of the doddering guard in the security booth. That arrogant prick, Warren! He'd always treated Thad with an infuriating degree of condescension, and ever since *Wildwood* had been green-lighted, it had become worse. The way Warren looked at him . . . Sneered at him . . . Or totally ignored him. Like Thad was some bumbling hick. Or a twenty-year-old intern with his head up his ass.

The fabulous creative visionary, Warren Doran. What a joke!

Thad's cell phone rang. He honked a pokey PT Cruiser out of his way, then answered it.

"McAuliffe. The compliance check was clear."

"What do you mean?"

"We just left the place. It was clean."

"That's impossible. You sure you searched the living room couch?"

"My officers were thorough. Tossed the entire place."

"Okay, I don't know what went wrong. Give me a day to set it up again."

"I'm out of this," McAuliffe said. "Lose my number." He hung up.

Bitching hell! Thad spoke the name "Roger Lopez" into the voice-activated dial of the phone. "You're fired, you useless asswipe!" he barked. "As far as collecting the rest of your fee, you can go suck your own dick." He cut off Lopez's squeals of protestation.

There was more than one way to solve a problem.

Thad made an abrupt U-turn and headed south, in the direction of the airport.

The motel was off Sepulveda, a dirty-putty two-story structure that blended with the yellowish haze of the air to the point of invisibility. Thad bounded up a metal staircase to the second floor and rapped the heel of his hand on the door.

It cracked open. Cherry Morrison's face appeared in the crack. "Hey." He opened the door wider.

Thad entered warily. The room was as characterless as the exterior.

"I thought you were gonna be somebody else," Cherry said. He gnawed on the take-out barbecue he was holding.

He was expecting company? Thad thought in amazement. "Yeah? Who?"

"Dude bringing me a new pistol. I had to ditch mine."

"Why? Did you shoot somebody?"

"Yeah. A couple of ho's."

Thad regarded his old pal narrowly. "You joking?"

Cherry gave a short laugh. "No, I am not."

"How come you shot them?"

"They were getting chatty. Talking about stuff they weren't supposed to talk about."

Thad wasn't sure whether to believe this or not.

"So whassup?" Cherry made a chip shot of the rib bone into the Styrofoam container on the floor.

"I got rid of Lopez. He fucked up. The compliance search was a bust."

"Did you tell your boss yet?"

"You mean Warren?" Thad's lip curled. "Maybe you don't get it. This is my show."

"Your show, huh?"

"You bet. If it wasn't for me, Warren Doran would be a washed-up nothing right now. He'd be bumming spare change on Hollywood Boulevard."

Cherry licked a bit of sauce from his fingertips. "You think?"

"I know." Thad settled on the edge of the bed. "Two years ago when he hired me to do his books, he was going down fast. He'd invested everything in that stinker of a movie, *Tale of Two Cities*. Big-time flop. But he was still strutting around town, picking up checks and throwing cash around like Mr. Big. It didn't take me too long to find out the real story. I was doing the books, but I was also browsing around in all the back files. Reading the fine print. Putting two and two together."

"You come out with four?"

"Not exactly. Warren Doran's two plus two didn't equal four. It came out to about twenty. Didn't add up at all." Thad got up from the bed and began pacing. "So I started digging deeper. To make *Tale of Two Cities*, Warren borrowed fifty-five million from a venture fund in Seattle, and he'd put up his own company, WildFilm as collateral. The movie bombed and suddenly he had to pay back the fifty-five with interest. There was no more money in WildFilm, it all got spent on production. So he had no more collateral. How did he pay back the venture fund?"

"Got money from the tooth fairy?" Cherry grinned.

Thad ignored the sarcasm. "He created all these fancy financial instruments. So tangled up with each other, it took me a little while to untangle them. But I did. And guess what I found out? This time he borrowed on his daughter's trust fund. Meaning one of two things—either Hannah's proxy firm had signed off on the loans, or the signatures were forgeries."

"Which one was it? The suspense is killing me." Cherry lit a cigarette.

"Forgeries, obviously." Thad made a "duh" face at Cherry. "I knew her proxy firm. Conservative as hell. No way they would have signed off on betting a client's entire fortune on something as iffy as a movie project." Thad sat down on the bed again. "Give me one of those, will you?"

Cherry tossed him the pack and a book of matches.

"So typical of Warren's freaking ego," Thad went on, lighting up. "He could never imagine his precious Charles Dickens movie would be anything less than a huge success. But after it flopped, he had nothing left to juggle. All those fancy funds were about to start pulling money out of Hannah's trust. His forgeries were going to be uncovered. He was going down hard."

"And here you came to save the day!" Cherry gave another sarcastic grin.

"Goddamned right I did." Thad took a meditative drag on the cigarette. He had known at the time that Warren was cooking up a new project—to revive the Wildwood Murphy franchise with Denny Brandt taking his dead father Jackson's role. And even a guy as low down on the Hollywood food chain as Thad Miller could recognize this as pretty much a sure thing. If Warren could just buy enough time, it could still all work out brilliantly for him.

But Warren had been out of time. And that's where Thad had come in.

"I discovered a catch," he told Cherry. "I found out that if Hannah should become incapacitated—lapse into a coma, say . . . or get herself incarcerated . . . Warren had power of attorney to make all decisions for her. Including the ability to fire her proxy and name a new one. Which, of course, could be himself. If we could get Hannah out of the way for a couple of years, we could use her money until the *Wildwood* movies started to pay out. And nobody would ever discover his frauds."

"Nice plan."

An almost insane plan, Thad reflected. He'd known that once he brought it to Warren Doran, it would either get him immediately fired, or it would make him Warren's partner.

He coughed hoarsely. He wasn't used to smoking anymore. "I saved Warren's butt twice. First, I bought him the time he needed to get this movie going, and second, I introduced him to the Cantorellas. I've set up every single step of this project. And Warren treats me like a lousy stock boy."

"Pretty shitty," Cherry agreed. "Did you come here to cry on my shoulder?"

"No. I've got a new problem. Your P.I. fucked up and Hannah is still out free." His anger turned abruptly from Warren to his daughter. Goddamned rich brat! It all should have worked out beautifully. Her arrest and incarceration had gone like clockwork. There was always the threat that she'd make parole, but here Warren had used some ingenuity. His witchy old friend Betsy Bell, the former Malibu Madam, had a couple of her old girls locked up in the same institution. It had been easy to bribe them to make sure no parole would be forthcoming.

But Hannah got out anyway. Shitty, crappy luck!

"We've got to figure out something else to do," he told Thad. "And we've got to do it quick."

"Like the Bible says: 'The way shall be made straight and the path shall be made smooth.'"

"What the hell? "You becoming some kind of religious nut?"

"No, I'm not, Thad. I'm saying that when obstacles are in the way, I remove them."

"Like in Brentwood?"

"Exactly right. Like in Brentwood."

"You really overstepped there." When Thad had consulted with Cherry on the problem of Cody Takish, that prick of an exec at Constellation who was jeopardizing the entire project, Cherry had been all over it. *Rough him up a little and he'll back down like a whipped bitch.* "You were just supposed to rough the guy up. In case you've forgotten."

"He had an attitude. What kind of dumb motherfucker gives attitude to a guy who's broken into his house in the middle of the night? If he'd had a weapon, now that would've been different. That

I could've respected. But he's standing there giving me attitude, and he's holding nothing but his dick."

"Jesus, Cherry." He was essentially a junkyard pit bull, Thad reflected. He should've *expected* him to bash Cody Takish's brains out. Attack and kill—that's what pit bulls do. "Let's get back to the business at hand. The parole office, that guy McAuliffe, he's spooked. We can't count on him to do another search."

"Already know that. And I'm already on it."

"You already have another plan?"

"Yep."

Something about Cherry's tone of voice made Thad recoil. "No drastic measures, you got that? She goes back to jail, not to the morgue."

Cherry crushed his cigarette butt. "What makes you think that's your call?"

A queasiness churned in Thad's stomach. What made him think that, indeed? "Because I hired you, that's why."

"Did you? Did you really, Thad, old friend?"

Now Thad felt a real jolt of fear. It suddenly all became clear. Crystal clear. It had been no accident he'd bumped into Cherry Morrison after that first Vegas meeting. It had been a set-up: Cherry had been assigned to babysit him.

When he'd brought Warren into the orbit of Tom and Alex Cantorella, Thad had known precisely what he was signing him up for. Thad had grown up with these sorts of men. He had no illusions. He should have realized they'd protect their money. No way they'd leave anything to chance—or to the half-assed manipulations of a Thad Miller.

Cherry had always been the one handling Thad, not vice-versa.

Christ. How could he have been so stupid not to realize that immediately?

And why didn't he realize the men in the navy blue suits would get rid of anybody who stood in the way of their profits? Anybody, from a studio boss to the daughter of one of their own business partners.

He sprang to his feet. He just wanted to get the hell out of this room. "I guess you're going to do what you're going to do."

"You got a problem with that?" With a smirk, Cherry made a gun out of his fingers and pointed it between Thad's eyes.

"No. I've got no problem. See ya later, man."

Cherry pulled the trigger on his finger gun. "*Poom.*" He grinned again.

★   ★   ★

Outside, in the motor court, Thad passed Cherry's Escalade, a black hulk of machine, blacked-out windows and Vegas dealer plates, all the chrome removed. Might as well have a sign on the door: MOB CAR.

Oh yeah, Thad told himself. *You knew it all along.*

Except out here in the brilliant L.A. light, with no shadows anywhere, even the borders of the asphalt motor court splashed with bright petunias, he felt better. If the men in the blue suits were protecting their money, logically it meant that they were protecting Warren's, and ultimately Thad's, money as well.

Which further meant he didn't have to worry about Hannah Doran anymore. The problem was off his shoulders: he could—he had to—leave it to the pros.

NINETEEN

I t looks like fireworks." Hannah, lying naked on the canopy bed beside Mitch, gently traced the starburst scar below his left clavicle. "Does it still hurt?"

"Twinges. There's still a few scraps of shrapnel in there." He smiled, drinking in the tenderness in her beautiful gray eyes.

After getting her call, he'd reached her building in fourteen minutes flat. She was calm as she told him about the compliance search. She'd called her lawyer and he'd been blasé: "As long as you follow the rules we've got nothing to worry about." But Mitch could tell she was more upset than she was letting on. He gathered her in his arms to reassure her.

And then it seemed the most natural thing in the world to go upstairs and tumble into the canopied bed.

The first time they made love it was hungry, clutching, quick. The second time was slow and amazing. Now they lay quietly, contentedly, feeling sealed from the rest of the world.

Hannah pressed her lips on the starburst scar, then let them travel in little kisses down his chest. She stopped at the bandage around his abdomen and touched it gingerly. "What about this? Still hurt?"

"It's not pain I'm feeling," he laughed.

He pulled her on top of him and she thrilled to feel him hard against her. This time, when they made love their bodies fitted together so effortlessly that it seemed as though they'd known and needed each other all their lives.

Afterwards they went down and raided the refrigerator. Mitch found the makings for a pasta and a salad and together they worked smashing garlic cloves, tearing prosciutto, pitting olives. They ate by candlelight looking out over the downtown skyline, and they couldn't stop talking. They had a lifetime of things to tell each other.

It became their pattern for the next couple of days: cooking, eating, and chattering nonstop. They flooded the penthouse with music, from Vivaldi to Amy Winehouse. They danced, wildly and uninhibitedly, slow and close; and then they made love again, on the stairs, in the shower, and long and luxuriously in bed.

Mitch was toasting fontina cheese sandwiches for a light supper when his text tone sounded. He'd been ignoring his phone, but now, after glancing at the I.D., he read the message. "It's from Ajay—the guy who owns the agency I work for. I asked him to track down Betsy Bell's parties."

Hannah glanced up from stirring a pan of sautéing red onions. "Has he found them?"

"Yeah. There's one tonight, out in Chatsworth. Starts at midnight." Mitch glanced at the clock "It should take about forty-five minutes to get out there, and I've got to go home and change first. So I'd better leave soon after we eat."

"I'm going with you," Hannah said.

"No way. Technically, these parties are criminal activities. You'd be violating your parole."

"It's a chance I'll have to take. You don't even know what Zizi Howell looks like."

"Hey, I've had some experience smoking out people who don't want to be seen. In fact, I'm actually pretty damned good at it."

"Maybe," she conceded. "But I'm going, Mitch, like it or not."

"I don't. I don't like it at all. Besides, if you come with me, it will look very suspicious. Couples don't attend these events."

"So we can go in different cars. That way we won't look like a couple."

"No. It's too risky."

"I promise, if anything seems at all risky, I'll get out quick. But you've got to understand, Mitch. I need to do this."

He knew her too well by now to argue further. "Okay, then I'll come back here after I change. We'll go in separate cars but in tandem. And while we're there, you make sure I'm always in sight."

She rolled her eyes. "I *can* take care of myself. I've been managing damned well for a while now."

He wanted to protect her. To keep her far away from any kind of harm. He figured it would be a mistake to say that.

He turned back to the sandwiches on the grill and flipped them. "You're right. We'll watch each other's back."

⁂

Working in the bright fluorescent light of the Bougainville Condominiums parking garage, Cherry Morrison had efficiently completed most of his task. The sealed canister was packed beneath the driver's seat of the silver blue Benz convertible, and the seat bolted back in place. Timer superglued onto the undercarriage. All he had to do now was connect the timer to the ignition wire.

He got a little kick out of the timer he'd picked out—blue plastic Scooby Doo digital watch. He'd loved that bitching show when he was a kid.

"Scooby-Dooby-Doo!" he growled, doing the voice. It still made him laugh.

At the sound of the elevator opening, he dropped to a crouch behind the Benz. Fucking hell. It was the girl. What was she doing going out on the town at midnight? Like, what part of being on fucking parole didn't she understand?

He grabbed his tools and scuttled sideways to his Escalade parked in front of the fire stairs. He should've done this last night, but yesterday he'd gotten itchy for some action, so he'd drove out to one of the Indian casinos intending just a couple of hours. But he'd started kicking ass at Texas Hold'em. There were a couple of chicks, he was buying drinks. Then his luck went south, the girls vanished, and he'd crawled out barely even at 3 a.m.

Now he remained scrunched, not twitching a muscle, until Hannah got into the Benz and drove out of the garage. Then he leapt behind the wheel of the Escalade and followed.

⁂

The Chatsworth address Ajay had provided was in a neighborhood of newish estates constructed in the frenzied height of the housing boom. McMansions on steroids, was Mitch's take. You get rattlesnakes sunning at your pool and tumbleweeds meandering across your browned-out lawn, and every ten years it all burned down anyway; but in the meantime you can live like a sultan for a fraction of what it would cost in Bel-Air.

The entrance to the party estate was heralded by a pair of

twenty-foot high steel gates, suitable to maybe Valhalla. Hannah's tail lights were just disappearing up the drive as Mitch approached, and the gates of the Nordic deities were slowly creaking shut. His car was flagged by a detail of ninja-wannabes, black-on-black jump-suits chicly accessorized with a pair of snarling pit bulls.

A ninja face scowled at Mitch's window. "Can I help you, sir?" It sounded like *can I slit your throat?* These goons made Denny Brandt's security look like second-graders.

Mitch spoke the password Ajay had given him: "Sugar Plum Fairy." Winced as he said it. Couldn't be right. They *were* going to slit his throat.

But apparently, it was right. The ninja started to wave him through. But then another pair of headlights, mounted high on a huge SUV, loomed behind Mitch. The SUV braked. Reversed fast back around the bend in the road.

Wanna-Ninja now glowered suspiciously at Mitch. "Step out of the vehicle, sir. We've gotta search it, search you."

"Hey, come on. I gave you the password."

"Outta the car or fuck off."

"Okay, okay. Don't get your thong in a twist." Mitch grudg-ingly slid out of the Vette and assumed the position for a pat-down.

Cherry slammed his breaks. He hadn't expected armed guards.

He whipped in reverse back around the bend, too pissed-off to care if he slammed into anyone or anything coming the other way. When he was out of sight of the guards, he pulled off onto the scrub at the side of the road and killed the lights. Settled in for what could be a long wait.

Hannah entered into a series of cavernous rooms, all sixteen-foot-high ceilings and marble floors. The din of voices and oldies pop music was amplified by the hard surfaces. The lighting was gas-blue, overlaid with a smog of tobacco smoke. The crowd was mostly middle-aged Asian men, all of whom seemed already drunk. The party seemed confined to the first floor. The hall leading to the stair-way was blocked by a black-clad guard.

She walked with attitude, swinging her hips. The heels of her sandals were perhaps too low. She hadn't wanted to be teetering in stilettos. Not tonight. Otherwise, she blended in: she'd gathered her hair up in an unkempt beehive and her dress was a strappy or-ange frock with a scoop of cleavage. She'd bought it, she recalled, on a shopping spree with Crissie Townsend. In fact, they'd bought the identical dress and worn them to a tennis star's party that night, posing for the cameras with arms around each other's waists and kissy faces. Best Friends Forever.

No point in thinking about that now.

She circulated briskly. There were only perhaps a couple of dozen other women, all very young, all glitteringly dressed. None of them Zizi Howell. She accosted several of them: "Hi, could I talk to you a moment? Do you know a girl named Zizi? About five-six, brown skin and short black curly hair?"

They had no interest in talking to another female. "Maybe she already went upstairs," one said abruptly, before giving Hannah the cold shoulder.

"Hello, baby. I have been waiting for you all night." A stocky man with a loose hanging tie lurched up to Hannah. His breath was an assault of whiskey and dental decay. "You want somethin' drink?"

"No, thank you. I'm here with somebody."

"Yeah, baby, that's right. You are here with me." He lurched closer, backed her against a wall and nuzzled his nose into her cleavage.

"Get off me!" She shoved him hard, and he went reeling into another customer who shoved him again.

Hannah made her way to the guard at the stairway. "There's a guy over there causing a lot of trouble. He's been trying to grope all the girls. I couldn't get him off me."

As the guard made for the drunk, she darted up the stairs. They gave onto a dim hallway with embossed silver wallpaper lined with closed doors, each door numbered like a hotel. She tried several before finding one unlocked and pushed it open.

It was almost a cartoon version of a bordello bedroom: Red-shaded lamps and lavender walls. White shag carpeting. A circular bed with black silk sheets was placed dead center on the white car-pet, like a chocolate cake on a doily.

"You're early, dumpling." A voice lilted from the connecting bathroom.

The door opened and a naked woman stepped out.

Hannah stared at her transfixed. The woman wasn't young, perhaps forty, but her body was almost shockingly sensual: volup-tuous breasts; a shaved vagina; a high, plump behind.

She stared back at Hannah with raw shock. "What are you doing here!" she gasped.

"I'm looking for somebody," Hannah said.

The security man came bolting in from the corridor. "Sabina?"

"It's all right, Duncan," the woman said. The lilt in her voice was the residue of a Scandinavian accent. "Please wait outside, and when my client arrives, tell him I'll be ready in a few minutes."

The man retreated back to the hall. The woman turned back to Hannah. She seemed regally unconcerned about her nakedness. "Who are you looking for?" she demanded.

"Zizi Howell."

"Who is that?"

"Don't play games," Hannah snapped. "If you work for Betsy Bell, you know very well who she is."

The woman walked to a chair on which a pink peignoir was draped and picked it up. "Why are you looking for her?"

"That's my business. Is she here or not?"

"Of course not. She worked when Betsy was still entertaining in Malibu. That was a long time ago."

"How can I find her? Who else here would know where she is?"

"I think it would be better if you would just leave now."

"Not until I get some answers."

"I can call my man back in. He can make it rough for you."

"You know who I am, don't you?" Hannah said. "You recognized me as soon as you saw me."

Smiling, the woman leisurely put on the peignoir. It was sheer, revealing shadows of the creases and folds of the flesh underneath. "Yes. I know who you are."

"Then you'd know there'd be a lot of trouble for you if anything happened to me. My people know where I am." Hannah moved pointedly to be in the focus of a camera secluded in a corner. Just a pin-prick of light that only somebody who'd become acutely attuned to surveillance would notice. "You're not the first person to try to bully me. You wouldn't even have been the first naked person."

Still smiling, the woman lowered herself into an armchair. "Please, sit down, dumpling. Relax a minute."

Hannah stubbornly remained standing.

"There's nobody here except me who's left over from those old days. Our party operation is very small right now. We do most of our business online. Craigslist."

"Then where's Betsy Bell?" Hannah demanded. "She picked up Zizi from prison. I was there, I saw her get into a car that was registered to Betsy."

"But Betsy wasn't in it. She is sick, very sick. I was the one driving her car. I picked up two ladies and left them at a restaurant in West Hollywood. I gave them each a thousand dollars and that was the end of our relationship."

"One of those ladies is dead," Hannah said. "Valentina Rostov."

"Yes, I heard that. A terrible thing."

"Maybe Zizi has contacted Betsy. How can I get hold of her?"

"You can't. Nobody talks to Betsy, except through me." The woman had green eyes, and when she smiled, the outer corners tilted up toward her brows.

Fairytale eyes, Hannah suddenly thought with a shock. She was struck by a distant memory—a memory of somebody who looked like Tinker Bell and who called her "dumpling" in a voice that sounded like a song. "Do I know you?"

The woman's green eyes danced. "Maybe."

"What's your name?"

"I'm Sabina." She gave a sly smile. "I used to be called 'Bina.' When I was much younger than I am now."

"Bina," Hannah repeated. A feeling like dream-walking came over her. "That was the name of the au pair who was working for us. Back then, when my mother died."

"Yes, dumpling," the woman, Sabina, said.

"Was that you? You were the au pair!" Hannah stared at her in utter amazement. "I don't believe it! This can't be just a coincidence."

Sabina continued smiling sardonically.

"You were there that night . . . That I found my mother . . ."

A curt nod.

"I never saw you again. What happened to you?"

"After that? Well that night, I was in hysterics, you can imagine. I forgot even how to speak English. When the authorities came, I could only babble away in Danish, and they had to put me in a hospital and give me drugs to calm me down. And then the agency, the one that placed me with your family, they were going to send me back to Denmark, but I didn't want to go. So your father brought me to meet Elizabeth. Betsy Bell."

"My father? He knew Betsy Bell?"

"Sure he did. Everybody knew Betsy back then. Everybody who counted, I mean. There were lots of girls dying to get to meet

Betsy but didn't have the connections. I was lucky your father was so nice to me."

"I don't understand. What did my father have to do with a place like this?"

"But it wasn't like this. Back in those days, it was nothing at all like it is now. It was the very best place to be. What you see here now, these affairs are nothing, really. Shabby shit. But back then, oh, you can't imagine! It was like being at the most fabulous party every night. All the most wealthy and famous men! It was a wonderful opportunity for a young girl like me."

"An opportunity?" Hannah repeated scornfully.

"Oh, don't give me that judgmental look! Girls fuck rich and famous men all the time, and mostly they do it for nothing. The smart ones like me grab something for themselves as well. And why not? We all weren't born with a big fat silver spoon in our mouth, you know." Sabina folded her arms across her breasts and preened herself. "Do you have any idea what a man pays to be with me? Four thousand dollars an hour! Like a supermodel." She frowned. "Oh, there's that criticizing look again!"

"You're wrong, I'm not criticizing you," Hannah said. "I really don't care whatever it is you do. But I don't believe my father would bring anybody to a place like this."

"No, *not* like this. Pay attention, please!" Sabina's irritation made her pale body heave beneath the peignoir like a voluptuous sea. "I'm trying to tell you that it used to be the best of everything. The best, and the very best drugs. And by far the best girls. The very cream of the crop."

"Like you, you mean?" Hannah said sardonically.

"Sure, like me, especially back then. And before me, like your mother."

Hannah gave a start.

"Ha, I knew that would get your attention. Sure. Pamela Sebring, the crème de la crème."

"You're full of shit! My mother was rich and beautiful. She had no need for money, and she could meet anybody, rich or famous, that she wanted to."

"Sure, just like you, rich and beautiful. And it didn't stop you from making a spectacle of yourself, did it?"

"You're disgusting! I'm not going to listen to this!" Hannah edged a step toward the door.

"Oh-oh. Now you look just like you used to when you were

little and about to have a tantrum. But that's okay. I understand how this could be a little bit shocking for you. It was shocking for me too. When I first started working for your mother, I was in such total awe of her. She seemed so perfect, like a goddess, you know? But when I found out she wasn't always so perfect, it made me think of her even better. More like a real person."

She was lying. She had to be: it was too absurd. "I don't believe a word you're saying!"

Sabina gave another sly smile. "Did your father ever tell you how he met your mother?"

"Of course. It was at a party, on a beach in Nantucket." Her mother had been walking in the surf, he'd always said, and when he first saw her, he lost his breath. He said she looked like a dazzling mermaid who'd just risen out of the sea."

"Maybe it was on a beach," Sabina said. "But not in Nantucket. It was at one of Betsy's party in Malibu. Your father, Warren Doran, was Betsy's right-hand man back then. A nobody kid on the make before Betsy took him under her wing and gave him the necessary connections. And your mother . . . It was the usual thing, the spoiled rich girl going through a wild streak. All very cool and rebellious, you know. Until she killed that poor man."

Hannah's face registered shock. "What?"

"Oh *ja*, it was quite a cover-up. Pamela Sebring sliced up one of Betsy's clients with a piece of broken glass. He bled to death, the poor man."

"What man?"

"A client. Nobody important. It was easy to move him someplace far enough away where he could be found and not connected to Betsy. And then your father made sure that Pamela Sebring was never suspected."

"This is all bullshit! You weren't even there, how would you even know?"

"No, I wasn't there. But I've seen photos. And video tapes. Betsy is a brilliant lady. She always made sure everything that went on in her house was well documented." Sabina's tilted eyes gleamed with malice. "Pamela Sebring always looked beautiful in photos. Even when she was cutting somebody up."

"Stop it!" Hannah took a menacing step towards her. "You're lying. Shut up your filthy mouth!"

A tap on the door. "Sabina? Everything cool?"

"Everything is fine in here, Duncan. My guest is just leaving." Sabina stood up. She suddenly stepped close to Hannah and enveloped her in a hug, her body exuding a swampy sweetness. Hannah jerked away, but Sabina gripped her tight, speaking low in her ear: "That girl you're looking for, Zizi, she's already dead. Like the other one, Valentina. Don't go looking any further, you're in a lot of danger."

She placed a kiss on Hannah's temple and released her. "Now you'd better go."

☙❦❧

The ninjas had taken their sweet time, patting Mitch down far too thoroughly, the pricks, then painstakingly searching the car, popping the hood and trunk and giving a scrupulous once-over to the undercarriage. Fifteen minutes elapsed before the Thunder God gates finally parted and Mitch got the thumbs up to proceed.

He parked at the end of a long line of cars and trotted another eighty yards to a huge pinkish-painted house. There were two main rooms downstairs where the festivities were taking place. Sure as hell wasn't the glamorous, coke-fueled, movie star-studded frolics that Betsy Bell had been legendary for. This was a crowd of pasty-faced salarymen in cheap suits, lurching drunkenly to a sound track of Hootie and the Blowfish.

Hootie? What year did these guys think they were in?

Mitch rapidly circumnavigated both rooms without finding Hannah. He made another round-trip, feeling a mounting alarm. Maybe he ought to call in a fire, get the place swarming with firemen and cops . . .

To his relief, he sighted Hannah in the crowd. "Hey, where were you?" he said, sprinting towards her. "Jesus, did any of these guys . . . ?"

"No, nothing like that. But let's go. I've got amazing things to tell you!"

☙❦❧

Waiting down the road in his Escalade, Cherry was startled to see Hannah's car come jacking back so soon, followed by the boyfriend's Vette. He gave them a few seconds, then joined the parade.

Something must have happened behind those gates—the girl was driving like a maniac, hell bent. Maybe she'd smack herself up, making his job a little easier.

Then suddenly she pulled off beside some grease joint. Had a neon sign. Probably once spelled out GINO'S or GINA'S. Now it said GIN 'S. Good one!

The Vette swung into the dirt lot next to the greasy. Cherry cruised over to a dark spot across the street. Watched both the chick and the dude head inside. He held back five minutes, then approached the place. Cautiously poked his head in the door.

The two of them, hunkered down in a booth on the side. Cute couple.

He ducked back out, went to the Benz. He had a little time but couldn't count on a lot.

He was quick, yanking the ignition wires, clamping them to the detonator wires with a couple of razor alligators. Then he set the Scooby-Doo watch timer to fourteen seconds which he considered his lucky number.

He finished everything up in seven minutes flat—maybe hurried a little too much, he might have fucked up the oil pan or something.

But this vehicle wasn't going to need anymore oil anyhow.

⊰W⊱

"Talk to me," Mitch said, blowing on a cup of scalding coffee. "Tell me what happened."

They'd pulled up to a roadhouse on Reseda Boulevard that dated from the Seventies. With a little effort you could imagine it in its heyday, the Faces of that era—the Ben Gazzarras and Farrah Fawcetts—crowded into one of these red vinyl booths, twirling spaghetti carbonara on forks, while Mel Tormé wove velvet from the jukebox. But now the faces belonged to barflies; the booths were cracked, the once-jazzy linoleum worn to a grimy checkerboard, and jukebox crooners had given way to a t.v. blaring over the bar.

"Oh god, you're not going to believe it!" Hannah said. "I sneaked upstairs, and there were all these doors with numbers on them. I went into one of them. It was a bedroom with red lights and a round black bed, like a whorehouse. And then a woman came out of the bathroom. She was nude. And really startled to see me."

"Yeah, I'll bet."

"No, wait. She covered up herself with a peignoir, and I asked her about Zizi. She said she was the one who'd picked up Valentina and Zizi from Peachrock. She dropped them off in town and gave them a thousand dollars, and then she claimed she didn't see or hear from them again."

"Did she tell you her name?"

"Sabina."

Mitch nodded. "She's the head girl. The one who runs the place."

"But here's the really freaky part. I used to know her! When I was a little kid, she was my au pair. I called her 'Bina.' And she was there, the night my mother committed suicide."

Mitch froze, the cup halfway to his lips. "Are you serious?"

"It's unreal, isn't it?"

"Are you sure that's who she really was?"

"Pretty sure, yeah. I sort of remember her eyes. I used to think they looked like Tinker Bell's."

"Tinker Bell?"

"Yeah, like in *Peter Pan*. Green and kind of slanting up." Hannah took a sip of coffee. It had an undertaste of burnt egg. "And then she started telling me things—crazy things about my mother and father."

"Like what?"

"She said my father when he first came here from New Jersey was Betsy Bell's right hand man. And she said he met my mother at one of Betsy's parties. Can you imagine? My mother at one of *those*?" She gave a shudder.

"They were different back then," Mitch offered.

"Yeah, that's what she said too. There was more." Hannah's voice grew less steady. "She told me that my mother slashed a guy to death with a piece of broken glass. He was a client. She said it was all covered up. The guy's body was moved to somewhere far away, and my father covered it all up for my mother." She looked at Mitch with confusion. "It can't be true, can it? It's got to be all lies."

"Why do you think she'd be lying?"

"I don't know. Maybe she used to be jealous of my mother back when she worked for her. Or she could have been secretly in love with my father. He was a famous, glamorous producer, and she was just this little au pair, and maybe he never even noticed her. So now she has a chance to get revenge by making up stories about them both."

"I don't know," Mitch said. "This can't all just be coincidence."

"What do you mean?"

"Valentina and Zizi and your old nanny, all working girls for Betsy Bell. Valentina said she knew some things about your mother. Maybe this is what she was going to tell you."

"You mean that my mom was a whore and my dad was a pimp?" Hannah flashed. "And they all hung out at a whorehouse? You think I'm going to believe that?"

"Just listen for a minute, okay? Say your mother did go through a wild streak, rebelling against her background and all that. She might have hung out at Betsy Bell's. It wasn't just a whorehouse, it was a real scene back then. From what I know about it, it attracted everybody—players from every rung in Hollywood and rock and roll, and rich kids and top business guys and well . . . everybody. It wouldn't mean your mother was actually turning tricks. It certainly doesn't mean that she sliced up one of the patrons. That part of the story could be exaggerated."

"Or totally made up."

"Maybe. And as for your father . . . Well, a kid coming from nowhere on the make, it's possible that's where he'd go. And your father, Warren, he knew how to hustle and also how to blitz the charm—it's easy to see how he'd make himself indispensable to somebody like Betsy Bell. It was the quickest way to get to know everybody." He reached for her hand. "I think we've got to consider every possibility, no matter what."

Hannah held his hand, silent a moment. She thought about Valentina in her apartment, picking up the little photo of Pamela: *You think she is your madonna, pure as driven snow . . .* "I don't know, Mitch. I just don't know what to believe anymore."

"Maybe there are some things you shouldn't know. Maybe it's time to let the past rest. Drop all this and get on with rebuilding your life."

"I can't. I can't just drop all this. There are too many things I've got to know. I thought you understood that."

"Okay," he said quickly. "I do understand. It's your call. We'll keep on looking for Zizi."

Hannah shuddered. "That was the last thing Sabina told me. She said Zizi was dead, just like Valentina."

"How did she know?"

"She didn't say. But the *way* she said it—she grabbed me tight and whispered in my ear, I guess so the guard outside couldn't hear or if the room was bugged. I got the feeling it was true." She gave a little shrug. "So where *do* we go from here?"

"We're not going to figure everything out tonight. You need to get home. You've already pushed the limits of your curfew."

"Yeah, you're right. You'll come back with me?"

"As long as you want me. Yeah."

He dropped some bills on the table, and they headed back outside. A wind had come up, heavy gusts that flapped their clothes and spat grit into their faces. As they approached Hannah's car, Mitch noticed a ripple of something orange on the asphalt directly beneath the bumper.

"What's that?" He squatted to examine it.

"It's a reflection of the sign from the restaurant," Hannah said. "In a puddle."

She was right—it was the reflection of the neon roadhouse sign rippled by the wind, but in a puddle of something thicker than water. "It looks like oil." He tested it with a finger. "There must be some oil leaking from your car. You shouldn't drive it if there is."

"Let me turn the ignition. I'll see if the warning light's on."

Hannah slid into the driver's seat. Mitch peered at the Mercedes' undercarriage. It was really too dark to see a leak . . .

As she turned the ignition key, a green diode blinked on under the car. The number fourteen.

It blinked to thirteen . . .

Mitch sprang to his feet and grabbed Hannah by the hair. He shrieked as he yanked her out of the car and, still half pulling her by her hair, dragged her away from the Mercedes and behind a parked delivery van.

He let go of her. She turned on him in a rage, slapping and pummeling him, as he tried to grab her wrists. "Hey . . ." he started to say.

But then it didn't matter: there was a shattering explosion, and the force of the blast knocked them both unconscious.

TWENTY

He was back in Afghanistan, with the convoy jolting down the desolate, rutted road maybe seventy klicks out of Kabul. The flash, the ear-splitting bang; the sensation of the world becoming suddenly soundless and a split second of ecstatic weightlessness. And discovering himself unable to move, there was something wrong, no feeling on the left side of his body. And knowing, immutably, that somebody else was dead.

Then the present came rushing in on him. He was lying on asphalt and wind was blowing gravel and grit in his face. He heard a sickening whoosh, lifting his head just in time to see Hannah's Mercedes erupt in flames. A car alarm was whooping nearby, and people had begun edging out of the roadhouse to see what was going on.

Mitch picked himself up and looked wildly around for Hannah. She was sitting on the ground nearby, dazed but alive. Her hair had tumbled down around her face and she was staring through wisps of it at her burning car. He raced over to her.

"What happened?" She groped for her bag that had flown from her shoulder. "Where's my purse?"

"Somebody put a bomb in your car. Whoever it is, they're probably still around."

"What?" Still dazed, she kept searching for her handbag. It was at the curb, flung open. She began hunting for the scattered contents. "Where's my phone? My wallet."

"Never mind that stuff, we've got to get out of here! Come on!" He yanked her by the arm and pulled her to his Vette, unlocked it and pushed her into the passenger seat. He ran to the other side and jumped in beside her.

"Mitch?" Hannah felt a stinging on her forehead. She touched it and saw blood on her finger. "Oh my god! Am I hurt?"

"Just a scrape. Nothing serious." He gunned the motor, slamming out onto the street.

"There was a bomb?" She was beginning to focus. "Oh god, Mitch! Are you okay?"

"I think so."

"You sure it was a bomb?"

"Yeah, I saw the timer when I looked under your car. Shit!" Glancing in the rearview mirror, he saw a car pull out behind them, a monster of a black SUV, like some prehistoric creature. Driving with just its parking lights. "We're being followed."

Hannah turned to look. "Do you think that's him? The guy who put the bomb?"

"I'm not going to stop and ask for an I.D."

"Can we lose him?"

"I'm gonna try." Mitch down-shifted to second and floored the accelerator, feeling the power of 350 horses stampeding beneath him and the intoxicating smell of burning Eagle F-1 rubber. Traffic at this time of night was sparse and Reseda Boulevard stretched nearly deserted ahead. With an eye on the tach, he redlined, then shifted, third, then fourth. The speedometer edged above eighty.

He glanced back in the mirror. The SUV was suddenly ablaze with lights. About ninety of them, it seemed.

"Faster!" Hannah urged.

All streetlights ahead glowed green: Mitch speed-shifted to fifth and the speedometer nudged ninety. In spite of himself, he felt a thrill. The thrill of the chase—the super-intense, heart-jolting, E ride of the celebrity chase, the only part of the job he relished; except this time it wasn't in pursuit of some drug-dazed pop princess: this time he was racing for his life.

"You okay?" he shouted to Hannah.

"We're losing him. Don't slow down!"

She felt it too, he knew—the exhilarating high of the chase that momentarily dispersed both panic and fear.

He jumped a yellow light going ninety-five, but now the intersections ahead were blinking successively into red. Slamming the brakes, he fish-tailed a right into a residential neighborhood—one of those flat and monotonous housing tracts that spread over this part of the Valley like a board game.

"Watch out, there's a cul-de-sac!" Hannah shouted.

Coming up fast, a dead end semicircle of stucco bungalows

fronted by shrubbery and neat patches of lawn. Mitch threw the wheel hard, and the car went into a spin. Hannah let out a scream as they slid up over the curb, taking out a hedge of hibiscus and a strip of newly-mown grass, coming to a full stop on the middle of a lawn.

A window flew up: "Calling the police!" somebody yelled.

Mitch glanced at Hannah. Her face was ashen, but she nodded. "I'm fine."

He jacked into first, throwing up sod as he hit the accelerator. He turned back on Reseda Boulevard, just as the monster SUV raced by in the other direction. "Shit, I thought he'd be past us by now. Do you think he saw us?"

There was the sound of furious honking. Hannah swiveled to look behind. "He just made a U-turn right into traffic, so I'd have to say yes. Your car is kind of hard to miss."

"I'm trading it in for a Prius, first thing."

"The hell you are! If you had a Prius, we'd be dead by now."

True, Mitch mused, which brought up certain questions about fate, and predeterminism. Questions he definitely didn't have time to ponder now. They were heading south, back towards the city, and traffic had become heavier, it was harder to keep up the speed. The SUV loomed suddenly again.

"It's like a ghost car!" Hannah said.

Yeah, and why? Mitch wondered. Why did it seem like a ghost car?

Because it had no chrome! It was stripped of any reflective surface. No ornament, no logos. Bumper and wheel spokes painted black, all windows tinted near-black.

The ghost of a killer whale, and now it was threatening to swallow his minnow of a Vette.

"Hold on!" He shot into a narrow gap between two caravanning trucks, then, swinging around the lead truck, redlined back up to ninety. Cross streets flew by in a blur, a dark expanse of a park on the left.

They were coming up to Victory and Reseda . . .

Gotcha, you bastard!

"I know how to lose him!" He whipped a right onto Victory Boulevard. "There's a motel somewhere down here. A kind of historic place, the Adobe something. Used to be where celebrities could come to dry out in private, before rehabs got popular."

"Up there on the left . . . The Adobe Siesta?"

"That's the one!" It was fronted by adobe Taco Bell-ish arch. A low arch, meant mainly for show, but, Mitch happened to know, with enough clearance for a nine-year-old Corvette C5 to pass under.

But not enough for a freaking humongous ghost of an SUV.

He made the left, cleared the arch, and sped through the courtyard, tires kicking up twin waves of sand.

Hannah laughed. "He'll never get through that!"

"No way." He whipped out the alley in back and began zigzagging through back streets. "I think we're okay. But where do we go now. We sure can't go back to either of our places tonight."

A sign for the 101 loomed ahead. The Ventura Freeway.

"Get on the freeway!" Hannah exclaimed. "Take it south."

He knew immediately where she wanted to go.

⋑⋇⋐

The arch was too low! Cherry slammed the Escalade brakes and violently threw the wheel. The vehicle careened left, then center, and then, tilting on two wheels, jumped the sidewalk and wrapped around a parking meter, wheels still spinning.

A face peered in at his window. "Whoa! You alive, dude?" Teenage hipster asshole.

Cherry grabbed the gun he'd lodged in the cup holder and jammed it at the kid's face. The kid's eyes popped. "Whoa, take it easy, dude." He backed away.

Cherry jacked the stick into reverse. A scream of metal on metal as the Escalade pulled away from the parking meter. He sped around the block to the rear of the motel, but the Vette was long out of sight.

TWENTY-ONE

He definitely looked the part of a shady private eye, Alicia thought, opening the door to Roger Lopez. Middle-aged, dumpy, sporting a short-sleeved shirt and shiny tie. A furtive but cunning air about him.

And for absolute authenticity he reeked faintly of urine.

She took a step back to put a purifying distance between them. "Thank you for coming, Mr. Lopez. I'm sorry it had to be so late."

"Not a problem," he said. "A lot of my clients find this kind of hour more discreet."

It was past midnight: she'd returned only twenty minutes ago from a benefit at the Peninsula and was still wearing the little Christopher Kane number that had set her back over three grand. A deceptively simple dress. But this Lopez was not fooled: his eyes appraised it knowingly.

It was Marianela's night off, and the babysitter she'd hired had just left. The twins were sound asleep in their rooms, with intercoms connected to the kitchen. Should either child awaken, she'd hustle this slime ball out of the house before he could blink twice.

She led him into the kitchen and motioned for him to have a seat at the breakfast bar, watching his eyes take in the room. Limestone counters, cherrywood cabinets with crayoned drawings, telephone trees, and snapshots taped onto them. Expensive toys scattered on the wide-planked floors. Counters cluttered with boxes of Mini-Chex and Fruit Roll-ups, a glittery tiara, a caged gerbil.

He'd have done his homework; she was sure he knew exactly who she was. And exactly how much she was worth.

"Mind if I ask how you got my name?" he said.

"You used to work for the investigator Marco DaSilvio, right?"

"Correct."

"Before he was sent to jail, DaSilvio was very helpful to a friend of mine during her divorce. My friend remembered your name from that time. She'd thought you'd be somebody who could, well . . . work outside the box."

"Also correct."

"Okay, good." Alicia started to sit, thought better of it, and remained standing. "I've never used somebody like you before, so I don't really know how this is supposed to work." *Just how many clichés could she pack into this little encounter?*

"It's pretty easy. You tell me what you need. I tell you if I think it can be reasonably done. You agree to my fees, pay me a retainer, and we get the show on the road."

"What are your fees?"

"A hundred and fifty an hour including drive time, two hundred after six p.m., plus any additional expenditures."

Alicia walked to the other side of the kitchen and picked up a manila envelope from a counter. "I have five thousand dollars cash in here. Would that be enough for a retainer?"

"Works for me."

She stood for a moment uncertainly, gripping the packet.

"Hey, could I trouble you for a glass of water?" Lopez said. "With ice?"

"Oh. Yeah, sure." She set the envelope back on the counter, filled a glass from the ice water dispenser on the door of the stainless SubZero and handed it to Lopez.

"Thanks." Lopez took a long, slow slurp. He wasn't really thirsty, but with clients as edgy and likely to call it quits as this one was, getting them to serve him a drink helped to keep them on point.

"I want to have somebody investigated," she ventured. "A man."

He lowered the glass. Looked respectfully attentive.

"It's not somebody I'm involved with romantically. It's not a case of finding out if somebody's cheating on me. Sexually, I mean." She paused. "I'm looking for something bigger. Something that, um . . . if I needed to, I could use against this person."

He decided to be blunt. "You want me to dig up some dirt."

"I suppose that's the way to put it."

"You're pretty sure there's something to dig up?"

"Yes. No . . . I mean, I don't know exactly, you might have to go way back to his past."

"You want to give me a name? In the strictest of confidence, of course."

Alicia hesitated. This character was a creep of the highest order, but who else could she get who wouldn't be? "Warren Doran," she told him. "The film producer. I'm sure you've heard of him."

Lopez almost gave a start. For composure, he sucked a piece of ice into his mouth and swirled it with his tongue. "Yeah, sure, I've heard of him."

A child's cough hacked faintly from the intercom. Alicia froze, listening, but there was nothing further. "I don't know. I'm sorry, Mr. Lopez, maybe this all isn't such a good idea."

He glanced greedily at the manila envelope. He'd been stiffed on his last bill and he'd already floated some checks, counting on the payment. They were all going to start bouncing like boobs with no bra. "What if I gave you something useful on Warren Doran right away?"

It was her turn to give a half-start. "Like what?"

She was keeping a distance, he noticed. Didn't blame her; he'd packed on a few pounds and was now back on the no-carbs, and the ketosis that came along with it, he probably smelled like a walking urinal. He shifted his bottom on the stool. "I know for a fact that he's been bugging the apartment of his daughter—the one who was just sprung from the Peachrock prison. Plus, he's been having her followed."

"How do you know this?"

"That's confidential."

"Okay. So *why* is he doing it?"

Lopez shifted his glance away. "Could be for many reasons. Maybe for her protection. She spent over a year inside a state institution with some pretty tough customers."

"That's interesting. But not extremely useful."

The ice cube in Lopez's mouth had reduced to a frigid stiletto. He let it melt behind his teeth, a cool trickle down the back of his throat. "Okay, I'll level with you. He wants her sent back to prison."

She became raptly still. "What makes you think that?"

"He had his people hire a professional to plant a stolen item in her place. A necklace, like what she stole before. It was concealed down in a sofa. The cops were supposed to turn it up in a parole search, but the daughter must've found it first and got rid of it, because the search was a bust."

"Was that professional you, Mr. Lopez?"

"That would be totally confidential."

She remained silent.

"But this professional . . ." he added. "He was the one who'd also placed the bugs in the daughter's penthouse. He also put one in the daughter's cell phone. In addition to the home bugs. Nobody knows about the phone bug except him. The professional, I mean."

Alicia picked up the envelope and placed it down in front of him.

"Consider yourself on the clock," she said.

After he'd gone, Alicia hurried to her daughters' room and made sure they were still sleeping soundly. She kissed their warm foreheads and tucked their blankets and smoothed locks of their hair.

And then she returned to the kitchen and picked up the glass that Roger Lopez had been drinking from and dropped it in the trash.

TWENTY-TWO

The familiar route, the Ventura Freeway merging into the 134, then across the old Pasadena Bridge with its clusters of Victorian lamps spanning the Arroyo, and emerging onto Orange Grove, the famous intersection where the Rose Bowl parade kicked off every year. Hannah felt a swell of emotion as they turned down a wide, leafy avenue of estates enclosed by tall stone walls. Her eyes misted as they turned into the ornate gate with the letter S entwined in the ironwork. It had been a year and a half since she'd last seen it.

"So this is your grandfather's estate?" Mitch said.

"Yeah. Though technically it belongs to me. My great-grandfather Henry Sebring left it to my mother, and when she died, she left it in trust for me. In some ways, it's always been my real home."

Mitch was gazing through the gates at the sweeping grounds. There was a look on his face she couldn't quite interpret. "Press the code on the call box," she told him. "5-2-60. My mother's birth date."

He tapped in the code and the gates yawned open. They drove down an avenue lit by dim lanterns through broad lawns dotted with live oak and sycamore. The grass needed cutting and was strewn with dead leaves and twigs.

"Kind of overgrown," Mitch remarked.

"I don't know why. A gardener always used to come every day."

Mitch pulled up to the end of the drive. The house loomed dimly—a rambling, rectilinear structure painted moss green.

Hannah began rummaging in the glove box.

"What are you doing?"

"Looking for cigarettes."

"You know I don't really smoke any more."

She pulled out an almost empty pack of Camels.

"Okay, maybe one or two a day, and sometimes on stakeouts, to pass the time. But I thought you said you'd quit."

"It's not for me. It's for my grandfather. He'll probably be up wandering around, and it will be the first thing he'll ask for. He's not allowed to smoke anymore."

"Why not? At his age, how much could it hurt?"

"He tends to start fires."

Mitch shot her a glance.

"Not on *purpose*. He's got Alzheimer's, you know." Hannah dug again in the glove box. "Is there a lighter in here too?"

"Should be. So he just accidentally starts fires?"

"Yeah. He usually nods off in the middle and drops the butt. The first time was about three years ago. He caused a small fire in the dining room. Then Gloria, one of the couple who takes care of him, called me at Peachrock last year and said it happened again. Some workman left a pack behind, and Nonny got hold of it, and this time it did some damage to the house."

"So why exactly are we giving him these?"

"Because he'll throw a fit if we don't have any for him." She found a plastic lighter and tested it with a click. "It'll be okay. We'll watch him."

"Yeah. Like a hawk."

They got out of the car and began walking towards the house. It was larger than Mitch had first thought, with carved wooden beams curving out from the eaves, like arms trying to grasp the crescent moon. "Looks kind of Japanese," he said.

"It is. Japanese Craftsman style. My great-grandfather adored Japan. He was an amateur architect, and he designed it for his family's summer place. In the winter, they lived in Lansing, Michigan, but in May they'd pack up everything, six kids and trunks and dogs and servants, and they'd come out in their private railroad car. My grandfather's the only one left. He was the youngest and the only one to survive past his forties."

"How come he didn't inherit the place?"

"His father considered him a screw-up. Nonny could never settle into a career. Tried med school and architecture. Even acting for awhile—he was incredibly handsome when he was young. But mostly he just hung out with society people and chased women. He had four wives. Five, if you count the one he married twice. So my great-grandfather disinherited him and left it all to my mom."

Mitch turned towards the front door. Hannah stopped him. "It will be locked, and I don't want to ring the bell. The couple, Gloria and Tomas, who takes care of Nonny live in the chauffeur's apartment over the garage, and I don't want them to know we're here." She glanced at him. "In case anybody comes looking for us."

"So how do we get in?"

"I've got a secret way."

She guided him to a path around the side of the house, past a trickling stony-sided pond and an untended tangerine grove. They came to a service alley cluttered with trash bins, rotted-out boxes, dead leaves and fronds and scattered branches. A fresh gust of wind rustled the sycamores, carrying an intoxicating scent of roses and jasmine.

A low window faced the alley. "This is to the old servants' quarters," Hannah whispered. "It never really locks because the window doesn't quite meet the sill. But if you just jimmy it a little . . ." She grasped the frame, jiggled it and edged it partly open. "I figured this out when I was a teenager and wanted to sneak out at night."

She boosted herself with one knee on the sill and squeezed through the opening. From the inside, she hoisted the window further, and Mitch climbed in after her. Hannah groped for the light switch and flicked it on.

"Oh my god!" she gasped.

"Jesus," Mitch echoed.

A room, once a compact bedroom, was now charred almost beyond recognition. Fire had eaten at the furniture and bed, the carpet was blackened, the ceiling a burnt-out maw.

"This must have been where the last fire started . . ." Hannah's voice broke.

Mitch reached for her.

"It's okay," she assured him. "Let's keep going."

She led him out to the hall, flicking lights on the way. The hallway was stained with soot and mildew and the adjoining butler's pantry was in ruins. "Oh my god," Hannah breathed.

"It looks like the damage was contained to this wing," he said.

"But why hasn't anything been done about it?" She continued leading through a maze-like series of corridors that had been untouched by the fire. They emerged into the main section. She flicked another switch. A chandelier illuminated a paneled foyer with a wide staircase curving up from it.

"Nice," Mitch said.

"It is, isn't it? It's listed on the Historical Register. All the carving and joinery was done by hand. The chandelier was designed by Frank Lloyd Wright."

"Jesus."

"Look at the living room." She led him into the adjoining room, switching on a floor lamp. It wasn't overly large, but exquisitely proportioned, with a coffered ceiling and two airy walls of tall, rectangular windows. Built-in bookshelves gracefully flanked a fireplace carved from a burnished dark wood. Stickley furniture. American Impressionist paintings on the wall. A pale antique carpet floated on the oak plank flooring.

"You never told me you lived in a work of art," Mitch said.

There was that look on his face again. "A lot of it is in terrible shape," she said quickly. "After my grandfather dies, I'm not sure I'll keep it."

It still felt suddenly awkward between them.

She moved towards one of the bookcases. "There's something I want to show you. There's a secret compartment behind here."

"Yeah? You pull on a copy of *Wuthering Heights* and it slowly creaks open?"

"Close. Except it's not a book. It's these knobs."

A row of ornate brass knobs ran across the middle shelves. Hannah twisted the two center knobs in opposite directions until something clicked. She slid out a narrow panel connected to a metal rod and turned the panel like a key. There was the sound of a latch snapping, and then the entire middle section of the bookcase opened outwards on runners.

"Holy shit!" Mitch exclaimed. Both interior sides of the section were lined with guns. Handguns, rifles, shotguns, all neatly arrayed on racks, with boxes of ammunition stacked on the bottom. "That's a lot of fire power!"

"My grandfather was a collector. Some of these go back to the Civil War."

"Hey, a Gestapo gun!" Mitch reached for a small pistol, a Walther P38 with a brown Bakelite grip. "Is this real?"

"Yeah, it's real. It was always one of Nonny's most prized pieces. But we're going to need something a little more modern." She ran her hands down the racks, then selected one of the handguns, a Glock semiautomatic.

He grabbed her wrist. "What the hell are you doing?"

"What does it look like? We need something to defend ourselves."

"If you get caught with a gun, you'll get shipped back to jail immediately."

"For godsake, Mitch! Somebody's trying to kill us. I'd rather take the chance of going back to prison than being dead." She took the gun from its mounting.

"Do you even know how to use it?"

"Enough. I used to shoot skeet with my grandfather."

"This isn't a skeet gun." He grabbed it away from her. "I'll carry it."

"Do *you* even know how to use it?" she flashed.

"As a matter of fact, I do." He searched the stacks of ammunition and found the appropriate clips. He expertly released the slide stop lever on the Glock and fed a magazine into it, then snapped it closed.

Hannah gave a surprised laugh. "Where did you learn that?"

"Back in Kabul with the unit. There were always long stretches of downtime. Out there in the desert, nothing to do, nothing to look at except dust, you go stir-crazy. We spent a lot of time shooting at rocks."

Footsteps sounded behind them, and they both whirled.

An old man emerged from the gloom like an image developing in a Polaroid. He wore a mustard cashmere robe that swamped his frail skeleton and velvet slippers.

"Nonny!" Hannah flew towards him.

"Hello, my darlings!"

She threw her arms around him. "Oh, Nonny, I'm so incredibly glad to see you!"

"I'm happy to see you, too, my darling. Would you happen to have a cigarette on you, by any chance?"

"Yes, I've brought you some. A whole bunch of them." He seemed so much frailer than the last time Hannah had seen him. Her heart constricted. "Mitch, this is my grandfather, Jonas. Nonny, I want you to meet my friend Mitch."

Jonas Sebring extended a hand. "I'm extremely pleased to meet you."

Mitch jammed the Glock in his waistband, gangsta-style, and grasped the old man's hand. "Pleased to meet you too, sir."

Jonas tightened his grip on Mitch's hand. "Did you hear that my daughter died?"

"Yes," Mitch said. "I'm very sorry for your loss."

"She killed herself. She swallowed some insecticide. It's an excruciating way to go, so I've been told."

"I know. I'm really sorry." Mitch wondered how he could extricate his hand without pulverizing a few ancient bones.

"My daughter, Pamela, died. Did you hear that she died? She killed herself."

"Yes, sir, I heard."

"Nonny." Hannah tugged at her grandfather's arm. "Remember, I've brought you some cigarettes? Come on, let's sit down over here and have a smoke."

The old man relinquished Mitch's hand. "Benson & Hedges, by any chance?"

"They're Camels, Nonny. Would you like that?"

"Yes, please, I'd love to. It would be my great pleasure. Thank you very much, my darling."

Hannah coaxed him to a club chair while Mitch swung the bookcase closed. She shook a cigarette from the pack, gave it to her grandfather and lit it for him. He held it elegantly between crooked index and middle fingers, savoring the inhale like a rare wine, exhaling slowly from a corner of his mouth. Fifty years seemed to melt away; his voice acquired a jaunty society drawl: "Well, I'm thrilled to have you here, my darlings. Can I offer you both a drink? Please, help yourselves, there's a bar in the game room. I could use a g. and t. myself, Bombay Sapphire if we've got, otherwise Tanqueray will do fine, with maybe just a splash of grenadine." He waved the cigarette like a conductor's wand, conducting a mini-symphony of conversation.

Mitch gave Hannah a questioning glance. She shook her head: "There's been no alcohol in this house for years."

"Are we out of Tanqueray?" Jonas Sebring piped up. "That's criminal. I've been having some trouble with the help lately. I suppose I'm going to have to speak to them."

"It's okay, Nonny." Hannah knelt on the floor beside his chair. "Finish your cigarette. We'll have a drink later."

Mitch's text tone vibrated in his hip pocket. At one o'clock in the morning, it had to be from somebody pulling an all-nighter in a lab.

He was right: Jennifer Leong. He stared hard at her text:

bro & sis 1 parent in common 85% accurate
wtf??

"What is it?" Hannah was watching him anxiously.

He hesitated.

"Ow!" She flinched. Jonas Sebring had nodded off, his freckled head drooping over the collar of his robe, and the cigarette had dropped from his fingers, grazing Hannah's arm.

"Are you burned?" Mitch stuffed the phone back in his pocket and hurried to her.

"Not really." She plucked the cigarette off the floor, stubbed it out against the sole of her shoe. "But I'm so exhausted I might just pass out myself."

"Get some sleep. I'll watch your grandfather."

"He'll be okay here for a while. He might wake up and wander around some more, but then he'll go back to his own bed. We can both go up to my room and sleep for a few hours." She gazed at her grandfather with emotion. "He's deteriorated so much, Mitch. He looks so much older and frailer." Her eyes blazed with anger. "All that time I could have spent with him was stolen from me. No matter what happens, I can never get it back. He needed me. And now he doesn't even have a clue who I am!"

"I know." He took her arm. "But you have to get some rest. We both do."

"Yeah, you're probably right." She turned from the old man reluctantly. "Let's go upstairs."

As they ascended the curved staircase, the smell of an old house became more apparent. Traces of dry rot and mildew mingled with the lingering odors of generations of people and their pets. The upstairs rambled in several directions. "My room's down this way," Hannah said. "That hall to the left goes to my mother's. She glanced in the direction, as if feeling a magnetic tug. "Do you want to see it?"

"Are you okay with that?"

"Yeah. I'd like to show it to you."

The door faced inwards at the end of the corridor. A spacious room, with graceful furnishings made of a light wood. A four-poster bed with a spotless white coverlet. Pale blue satin drapes shimmered to the floor, framing a bay window with a faded cushioned seat. The wallpaper, a pattern of chrysanthemums against pale blue had also faded, but this seemed to enhance the charm of the room.

"It's a gorgeous room," Mitch said.

"I love it. Everything's pretty much the same as when my mom was alive. The bedding's been changed, of course. And there used to be a rug. A Chinese rug. Blue and red, I remember. And I remember one night I was in here with my mother, and I was trying to walk in a pair of her high heels. I fell over onto the rug, and she picked me up. She was laughing. I remember both of us being happy." She shrugged. "It's my only real memory of this room."

"Nothing about that last night?" he asked tentatively.

"Not really. Just a bug with wings. It must have been on the insecticide package, but in my mind it's huge, like the size of a dog. And then somebody pulling me away by my hair. It must have been Sabina. It hurt like hell, and I think I must have been screaming. Maybe we both were."

"That explains it."

"Explains what?"

"Why you went ballistic on me when I pulled you out of your car. By your hair."

"I'm sorry. I guess I kind of over-reacted."

"I'll try not to do it again." He turned to a photo in a tarnished silver frame from a bed table. Pamela, in jeans and a khaki shirt, holding a gray-eyed baby. Behind her a low-slung red Ferrari.

"I was about five months old in that picture," Hannah told him.

"Nice wheels."

"My father's Ferrari. He owned it until I was about ten or eleven. It made this growling sound like a bear. I always knew when he came home, even late at night, because I'd hear that growling bear." She crossed to the other side of the room and opened a pair of double doors. "This used to be a separate room, but my mother had it converted to a walk-in closet. Old houses like this weren't built with any closets at all."

Mitch set the photo down and followed her into it. The racks and shelves were crowded with clothing and accessories. There was a spectral whiff of mothballs and old perfume.

"You've still got all her clothes?" he said.

"Yeah. I always meant to go through it all. There are some fabulous designer pieces that should be in a museum. Halston. Christian Louboutin. I really should get around to going through them."

"How about in that box?" Mitch pointed to a cardboard packing box, closed, but not sealed.

"Nothing much. Movie memorabilia. From the *Wildwood* films."

"Yeah?" He knelt and opened the lids. "Hey! This is great!" He began rummaging happily through an assortment of props and wardrobe associated with the legendary character: pairs of motorcycle goggles and driving gloves; heavy, lace-up boots suitable for tramping through the ruins of mythical cities; a snakeskin belt embossed with skulls. "This whole house is full of bitching toys!"

Hannah sat down cross-legged next to him as he explored the box. She reached in and took out a frayed white photo album.

"What's that?" he asked.

"A scrapbook that my mother put together before I was born. It's full of pictures of her and my dad together." She handed it to Mitch and he opened it. "I've never looked at it much because it made me kind of sad. And kind of confused. My mother looks so happy in these photos."

Mitch turned the pages. They had cellophane pockets filled with photos clipped from magazines and newspapers: *Variety*; *The L.A. Times*; *People*. Each clipping featured either Pamela, or Pamela and Warren together, posing at various events. In a restaurant, seated amidst a group of other glamorous people; on a red carpet, grinning for the camera as other celebrities streamed by. "I wouldn't have pegged your mother as the scrapbook type."

"Yeah, it's funny, isn't it? Everybody thought she was this icy cold person, but I think this shows she wasn't. She must have had a very sweet romantic side." Hannah yawned suddenly and rubbed her eyes with her palms. "I really am wiped. I think I will go lie down for a couple of minutes."

"I'll join you in a second. I just want to look at some more of this stuff."

Mitch continued looking through the memorabilia. It was corny, he knew, but hey—he'd grown up with Wildwood and all these props brought back memories of being a kid. At the bottom of the box was a beat-up black leather bag. He took it out with a little thrill of excitement. Wildwood Murphy's authentic courier bag! Probably just one of about two dozen that had been made for the movies . . . But still! Way cool!

He wiped the dust off it. It was divided into two zippered compartments. He opened one, found it empty. He unzipped the other. It contained a sheaf of documents.

He took them out. A contract of about a dozen stapled pages and some half-dozen legal memos. A birth certificate for Pamela Allison Sebring, born May 2, 1960. A passport issued in 1987 for Pamela Allison Doran.

And a photo. An 8x10—it looked like a frame grab from a low-quality video.

And what was being depicted in the frame made Mitch's blood run cold.

He pulled out a last document. An official-looking paper from the government of Haiti, embossed with an ornate seal. Written in French, which he didn't read—but he presumed the word "divorce" meant pretty much the same thing it did in English.

He replaced everything in the bag and stepped out to the bedroom. Hannah was curled on her mother's bed, already fast asleep.

On an impulse, he turned and went back into the closet. He picked up the album of clippings and examined it again, this time with greater scrutiny.

And then this too he placed in the courier bag.

He suddenly knew exactly why Pamela had compiled it.

TWENTY-THREE

Warren Doran's eyes shot open.

Since getting the green-light from Constellation, he'd been springing out of bed before dawn to pack in his grooming rituals before the deluge of daily event, leaving Tracy in a comatose, snuffling heap in bed (something about the resculpting of her nose caused snuffling and snoring in her sleep); but the clock face now glowed 4:13—early even for his current super-regimen. What had awoken him, he realized, was a two-note phone chime. Somebody ringing at the front gate.

He groped for the intercom, muttered: "Who is it?" and from the squawking reply made out the word "police."

Tracy peered from between slitted lids. "War? What's going on?"

"It's nothing. Go back to sleep."

He struggled into a robe and headed downstairs, nearly colliding in the front hall with Hernando, the young Guatemalan who was his whatever-the-politically-acceptable-word-for-houseboy. "It's okay, I've got it," Warren told him and strode to the door.

Two plain clothes officers flashed badges. One a short, rather delicately-built, Latino. The other was older, grizzled, beefy, with a boozer's complexion. You'd never cast these two in a buddy cop flick, Warren thought fleetingly. Too goddamned clichéd.

"Mr. Doran?" said the Latino. "Is your daughter Hannah here with you?"

"No, why would she be? She's got her own place."

"Have you heard from her in the past twenty-four hours?"

"No. Would you please tell me what this is all about?"

"Her vehicle was destroyed by an explosive device several hours ago."

Warren blinked. "What?"

"Her car was bombed," the grizzle head cop said.

"Bombed?" Warren wondered if he were sufficiently awake to be accurately processing information. "When did this happen?"

"Rough estimate, three hours ago, outside a roadhouse in Reseda. We don't think your daughter was in the vehicle at the time. Explosion was followed by a fire, so it's not a hundred percent sure yet."

"Jesus." A dozen thoughts flashed through Warren's mind, none of them coherent.

"Mind if we come in?" said the Latino cop.

"No, please . . ."

He ushered them into the living room that opened onto the foyer. Hernando flickered in the hallway.

"Can I offer either of you gentlemen coffee?" Warren asked.

"We're good, thanks," said Grizzle Head. Warren waved Hernando away.

Both cops began peppering him with questions: When was the last time he'd heard from his daughter? Did she sound distressed in any way? Mention being in any kind of trouble? Is there any reason he could think of why she would be in the northwest Valley at one o'clock in the morning?

He gave terse replies. He'd last seen her at his office the day before. She'd shown up unexpectedly, and unfortunately he'd been extremely busy and couldn't really talk to her. They were planning to get together for lunch. No, he didn't know when, he'd have to check his calendar, Hannah was going to make the date through his assistant. Yes, she'd been fine when he saw her. Normal. Normal, that is, for her which was always a little high-strung. No, he couldn't think of any reason she'd be in such a neighborhood. No, he didn't know the names of any of her friends who might reside in that area.

"Did she ever mention someone named Valentina Rostov?" asked the Latino.

A bubble of corrosive acid burst in Warren's esophagus. "I don't think so. Who's that?"

"Woman who was in prison with her. They both got out the same day. Rostov was murdered on Monday."

"Good god! Do you think Hannah is mixed up in it?"

"Do *you* think she might be?" There was a challenge in the Latino cop's tone.

"I honestly don't know. To tell you the truth, I've been a bit estranged from my daughter. I'm sure she felt I could have done more to prevent her from going to prison. Pulled some strings to get her out of it. Or paid somebody off." He made a wry grimace. "She didn't understand that behavior has consequences. Of course, I take some responsibility—it was my fault for spoiling her. She was always overindulged, and that was my mistake. But now that she's learned some important life lessons—now that we *both* have—I'm hoping we can be reconciled."

"Which is why you're having lunch on a day you can't remember when?" There was a crude note of sarcasm in the older guy's voice.

Warren adopted a humble tone. "I know how that must sound to you guys. But honestly, I was hoping we could have a fresh start." His esophagus was on fire. He tried not to swallow. "This news is extremely upsetting. I mean, I'm extremely worried. I really wish there was something more I could tell you."

The Latino snapped out a card. "If you hear from her, contact us immediately. If nothing else, she's in violation of her parole. She's spent a night away from her place and didn't check in with her P.O."

"So what would that mean?"

"There'll be a bench warrant issued for her arrest. Better if we talk to her first."

"Of course, gentlemen. If I hear anything—anything at all—I'll be in touch. And please, let me know immediately if you locate her."

He showed them out. Then he marched rapidly to his study, locked the door, and called Thad Miller.

Thad answered in a sleep-fogged voice: "Hello?"

"Hannah's car was just blown up."

"What?"

"You heard me."

"Oh my god! You mean she's dead? That's terrible. I can't believe . . ."

"She wasn't in it."

A split-second of silence. "So where is she?"

"I don't know. The police were just here. She's disappeared."

"Well, thank heavens she's. . . ."

"Cut the crap, Thad. What's going on?"

"What do you think's going on, Warren?" Thad suddenly sounded fully awake. "Our investors are protecting their investment."

"What the hell are you talking about?"

"I'm talking about our financial partners. They're getting rid of all obstacles between them and their profits."

"Christ almighty, Thad. Are you serious?"

"Why don't you cut the crap, Warren? Who did you think we were dealing with, the Boy Scouts of America? Once you take these people's money, they don't dick around forever. They do what's got to be done. You've been going along with it every step of the way, so don't come whining to me now that you didn't know what you were getting into."

Warren was momentarily taken aback by this new tone of authority in Thad Miller's voice. "I wanted her to go back to jail, not to the morgue. Christ, Thad, this is insane."

"It's the way it works. Get used to it."

"Okay, okay," Warren said. "Just for argument's sake, let's say for a moment that what you're implying is true. Then 'these people' as you call them no longer have anything to worry about. My daughter is in serious violation of her parole. She's going to be arrested and sent back to jail. So mission accomplished. 'These people' can stand down."

"Doesn't work that way, Warren. Things that are put in motion stay in motion. They're going to find her, so get used to the idea."

"I refuse to even comment on that!"

Thad gave a harsh laugh. "So how about telling me what it is you do want to happen? To go back to the way you were before? Dead broke, your career down the crapper? Maybe it can still be arranged, Warren. Just say the word. We pull the plug and it all goes away."

Warren was silent.

"Yeah, I thought so," Thad said and hung up.

⊛

A C.O. was conducting a strip search on her. A male C.O., fat, hairy, his chest naked, covered with a matted rug of hair. Hannah was naked too, completely exposed to his probings and fondlings. He had complete access to her, inside her mouth, her vagina and anus, between her breasts and fingers and toes. "I found it," he said, and his voice gurgled with glee. Someone in a corner was watching. A whiteness, indistinct, beautiful. It was her mother, it was Pamela. "Yes." Her voice was a faraway chime. "Yes, yes, I see." The chime now so faint it almost couldn't be heard . . .

Hannah tossed in terror and the nightmare dispersed.

It gave way to another dream, this one even weirder. She was in her mother's bedroom in Pasadena, with its satin drapes and chrysanthemum wallpaper, lying fully clothed on top of the bed. Mitch Arpino was in the room too, wearing nothing but boxer shorts. And in this dream, Mitch was pointing a gun at her grandfather, who was flapping his right wrist up and down and whimpering in distress.

Except it wasn't a dream. It was really happening!

She sat bolt upright. "Mitch? What's going on?"

"I woke up to find your crazy grandpa with a gun stuck in my face—that's what's going on!"

"You lying, thieving, son of a bitch!" Jonas Sebring spat at him. He flapped his wrist.

"Did you hurt him?" Hannah demanded.

"No! He was going to shoot me, so I hit his wrist to knock the gun away."

"I'll kill you," Jonas hissed.

"You see?" Mitch said.

"Put that down, he's not going to hurt you." Hannah slipped off the bed and went to her grandfather. "Nonny? Are you okay?"

"You don't have to stay with him, Pamela. Come back home and I'll protect you."

"Nonny, it's me, Hannah. I'm *Hannah*."

Panicked confusion swept over the old man's face. He peered at her, then at Mitch, whose near-nakedness seemed to increase his confusion.

"I've brought you some cigarettes, do you remember, Nonny? I brought you a pack of Camels. Would you like to have a smoke? We could go downstairs and have a cup of coffee and smoke a cigarette."

The sun peeped out from behind the clouds in Jonas Sebring's eyes. "Yes, thank you, my darling, I'd love that. That's incredibly kind of you."

"Why don't you go on down to the breakfast room, and I'll be there in a minute and bring some cigarettes, okay?"

"You'll be down soon?"

"I'll be right behind you. Just let me freshen up."

"Wonderful, my love!" He was rubbing his wrist, but absently, as if he'd forgotten about the pain. "Of course, freshen up, by all means. I'll wait for you downstairs. Please don't take too long." He retreated out the door, the soles of his flannel slippers slapping his heels.

"Holy Christ." Mitch sank down onto the bed.

"What the hell, Mitch? How did he get hold of the gun?"

"I left it on the nightstand. How was I supposed to know he'd come waltzing into the room like that?"

"I told you he roamed around at night."

Mitch shot her a look.

"Well at least nothing actually happened." Hannah tried futilely to smooth the creases on the bed spread, glancing at the window. A faint gray light had begun to suffuse the sky. "What time is it?"

"Just after six."

"We've got to get going. The Espositos might already be up."

Mitch began pulling on his jeans. "What about your grandpa? Isn't he going to tell them we're up here?"

"Sure. He'll tell them that my mother is upstairs and that he tried to shoot my dad. And Gloria will say that's swell, Jonas, and then she'll feed him a delicious breakfast." She went to her mother's closet, took out a pastel Calvin Klein shirt and a pair of khakis and put them on, rolling up the sleeves and legs. She hung up her sexy orange dress from the night before and concealed it among the other garments on the racks.

Mitch quickly finished dressing. He stowed the Glock in the leather courier bag and shouldered it. And then they were creeping down the narrow back staircase to the burnt-out servant's quarters and squeezing themselves out the window with the faulty latch. They scurried as quietly as they could back around the path to the car. Mitch tossed the bag in back and they pulled out.

In the restroom of a Chevron station, Hannah scrubbed off the vestiges of last night's makeup. It was an act that brought back all the nightmarish events and revelations of the night before and rekindled the sensations of the actual nightmare she'd had just before awakening—the horror of feeling utterly helpless and violated, and her desolation at the fading bell-like chime of her mother's voice. She splashed cold water on her face, jolting herself back into full wakefulness. Her thoughts turned to Mitch and her spirits revived. Funny how things seemed almost okay as long as she was with him.

But why? she asked herself. How could she be sure he wasn't just using her for his own purposes?

What made her so positive she could trust him?

Because I love him.

The thought roped her by surprise. She threw it off with a resolute little shake. *Get a grip! You don't know what the hell you're talking about.* Just a few days ago, she'd thought she might still be in love with that serpent, Shawn Serafian. Now the very thought of him made her gag.

Forget about these kind of feelings, she told herself, patting her face with a rough paper towel. If she did love someone, they'd promptly leave her, the way her mother had. Or knife her in the back, like Shawn, and like her former Best Friend Forever, Crissie Townsend. Or throw up thick walls between them, like her father always had.

You've got no business mooning over love and romance. Right now, your job's just to try to keep your ass from being blown to kingdom come.

At least long enough to get answers to what had really happened to her life.

Slotting the gas pump into the Vette's tank, Mitch reviewed his current situation. It was 6:58 in the morning. He was at a gas station somewhere in the outskirts of Pasadena, on the run from a murderous person or persons unknown. He was in possession of a handgun not registered to himself, and he was aiding and abetting a convicted felon in violation of her parole.

In other words, life was good.

He dug out his phone and checked the local headlines to see what coverage Hannah's blown-up Mercedes had inspired. There were plenty. Headlines galore. But it was a different item that gripped him. He was immersed in reading this one, when a touch on his shoulder made him jump.

"It's just me," Hannah said.

"We've got to get away from here." Mitch replaced the pump and snapped the cap shut. "Get in the car."

"What's the matter?"

"I just checked the news. What that woman Sabina told you last night—she was right. Zizi Howell is dead."

Hannah gasped. "How?"

"Shot, just like Valentina. She'd swapped that Rolls she was driving for a Carrera. Twin turbo GT. The cops hauled it out of a ravine off Mulholland. She was shot dead at the wheel."

Hannah felt her knees go watery. "Is there any connection to me?"

"Oh, yeah. The cops are definitely considering a connection between your car being bombed and your two dead jail mates. They're looking for you, and they'll be knocking on your grandfather's door pretty soon, if they're not there already. And if he's been babbling about how he's just seen his dead daughter upstairs, it's suddenly going to make a little sense. We've got to get out of this area." They slid into the Vette and Mitch plugged his iPhone into the charger. Hannah grabbed it and began punching a number.

"What are you doing?" he said.

"Calling my father."

He snatched the phone from her and ended the call.

"Mitch!"

"He's not going to help you," he told her.

"Yes he will. He has to. I know what you think of him, Mitch. That he hasn't been the greatest father in the world. But nevertheless, he's still my father."

"No, he's not, Hannah." He turned and looked steadily into her eyes. "Warren Doran is not your father."

TWENTY-FOUR

What are you talking about?" Hannah said. "Of course he's my father."

"No. I was going to tell you last night, but after everything that happened, and you were so exhausted . . ."

"Tell me what? Mitch, you're not making any sense."

"Okay, listen to me. Your mother, Pamela, before she killed herself—she'd been having an affair. With Jackson Brandt."

Hannah gave a short laugh. "How could you possibly know that?"

He reached behind him for the courier bag and took out the white scrapbook album. "Look through these clippings again. In every single one of them—tell me who you see."

"I already know. My parents."

"Besides them. Either in the background or together with them. Or just with Pamela."

"For godsake, Mitch . . . !"

"Just look at them. Closely. Okay?"

She took the album and began examining the clippings. Her face grew pale.

"It's Jackson Brandt, right?" Mitch continued. "He's always there, somewhere in each photo. Even when Warren isn't."

"Yeah," she whispered. "You're right."

"That's why your mother made the scrapbook. It was her way of keeping pictures of Jackson without it being obvious."

Hannah shut the album. "It doesn't prove anything. It could just be coincidence."

"Think of all that stuff in the trunk. It's not just random

memorabilia. It's only things that Jackson would have worn while playing Wildwood. Personal effects. Your mother was in love with him, Hannah. They were having an affair. And that's who your real father was. Jackson Brandt."

Hannah was ashen. "I swear to god, Mitch, if this is a joke . . ."

"It's not. I've never been more serious about anything."

She shook her head wildly. "It can't be true. My parents were the perfect couple, everybody always said so. They were desperately in love. My father's never gotten over her. Look how he keeps trying to replicate her with other women . . ."

"Listen to me," he interrupted. "I proved it. Definitely."

"How?"

"I had a DNA test done."

"They've both been dead for twenty years. How could you possibly test their DNA?"

"Not with theirs. It was Denny Brandt's and . . . Well, with yours."

She stared at him speechlessly.

"I had the shirt I was wearing when I punched Denny in the nose at the Isis party. It had his blood all over the sleeve. I took it with a few of your hairs to a friend of mine who's in biochem at USC, and she ran a DNA test on the samples. That text I got last night? That was from her. She confirmed it. You and Denny are half-siblings."

"You did it without telling me? Without my knowing?"

For a moment, he thought she was going to slug him. Instead, she burst out of the car, and began walking blindly along the road.

He jumped out after her and grabbed her by the shoulders. "I'm sorry. I shouldn't have done it behind your back."

She shook him off. "I suppose you thought it would make a great story. You'd get some kind of scoop and cash in big-time. You're as sneaky and rotten as any of them!"

"Hey, you know that's not true. If I'd wanted to cash in on you, I'd have done it already." He tried to stop her again, but she yanked away and walked faster. He caught up with her. "Okay, I'll admit, I started all this looking for a story and a way to cash in. But it's got to be obvious that that's changed. You can't think I've been pretending my feelings for you for the past few days."

She whirled on him. "Then why are you telling me these things?"

"Oh I don't know. Maybe because they're true?" He grabbed her arm firmly. "For Christ sake, stop being so damned stubborn for once in your life, okay?"

"Is there anything else you've done that you've neglected to tell me?"

"Not recently. No."

She shook her head. "But it's just so impossible! Denny and me? I mean, we can't be related. We're nothing at all alike. We're complete opposites. God, we hate each other."

"Come on, you know that's not true. I think you're a lot more alike than you want to admit. Did you ever notice, for instance, you've both got tempers that go off like Stinger missiles?"

She gave a dry laugh. "Maybe."

"Once I made the connection, it became obvious. The test just confirmed what I'd already figured out. You look a little like Denny. But you really look a lot more like Jackson."

She stood for a moment, absorbing all of this. "Oh god . . . !" she whispered. "My father . . . I mean, Warren . . . I've spent my entire life trying to win his attention, wondering why he never seemed to really love me. Always thinking I wasn't good enough. That I could never live up to his expectations. But maybe all this time he knew . . ."

"I think he's probably always known—that you weren't really his daughter."

"Do you think," she said in a low voice, "that he could be the one behind all this? Everything that's happened to me?"

"Yeah," Mitch said. "I do."

She was dead white now. "Because of my money, right?"

"My guess."

"But he could have had it anytime. I would have given it to him."

"It hasn't been yours to give, has it? At least not for a few more years. And he needed it immediately."

"He's a monster. All my life, I've been trying to please a monster!"

"Hey, as far as you knew, he was your dad. You couldn't have done anything else." A siren whooped on a road close by. Maybe an ambulance or fire truck, maybe the police. "Come on, we've really got to get out of here. Let's get back in the car."

They returned to the Vette. "Where can we go?" Hannah asked.

"I'm thinking the desert. Palmdale. Then we can figure out what to do." He handed her the courier bag, then started the car. "There's a photo in there you need to see," he told her. "It's a frame grab from an old video. You'd better brace yourself—it's not easy."

She looked in the bag, took out the 8x10. She drew a sharp breath. There was her exquisite young mother holding a jagged-edged broken glass in her hand. A young man was writhing on a black circular bed. Screaming, blood streaming from his face. "Oh my god! It's true, then. She did kill this man!"

"That photo makes it look like she did. Unless we saw the whole video, there's no way to say for sure." He pulled onto a main road. "There's another document in there. It's got a big gold seal. It looks like a divorce decree from Haiti. Do you read any French?"

"Enough." Hannah found the document and read it quickly. "Yes. It's granting my mother a divorce from Warren Doran. It only has her signature, not his." She looked at Mitch. "It's like she got this divorce on her own, in secret. So she was probably going to leave Warren and run off with Jackson."

"That could be. And maybe Warren found out and he sprang this photo on her. He told her he'd expose her for murder if she tried to leave him."

"I wonder . . ." Hannah began.

"What?"

"If that's true, if she was planning to run off . . . I wonder if she was planning to take me."

He glanced at her. Then back at the road as a vehicle shot out from around a corner, cutting them off. Green 4Runner, covered with dust. Handicap sticker on the windshield.

"Son of a bitch!" Mitch slammed the brakes and they skidded to a stop. He snatched the Glock from under his seat, leaped out of the Vette and threw open the door of the SUV. It was him, Fat Face, frantically trying to dial a cell phone.

Mitch yanked him out, slammed him out onto the asphalt. The cell went flying into a patch of weeds.

Mitch pointed the Glock at the back of Fat Face's head. "Who are you?"

"Nobody. Just a P.I." The guy wriggled like a plump bug, struggling to get up. Mitch put a foot on his back and crushed him back down.

The cell phone in the weeds began to buzz. Mitch backed toward it, stooped and picked it up. He tossed it to Fat Face.

"Answer it," Mitch told him.

About a dozen people were nestled in the capacious, kumquat-colored leather seats of Constellation Pictures' executive screening room. The sleek 3D glasses that bisected their faces gave them the look of a crack team of downhill skiers peering over the top of an icy mogul, rather than who they actually were—a director, a couple of producers, and a clutch of the studio's production executives. They were gathered to view the director's cut of the studio's forthcoming Christmas release, a hundred million dollar animation about a planet inhabited by walking and talking vegetables.

Alicia Chenoweth, seated dead center in the third row, adjusted her glasses on the bridge of her nose. Two seats down was the director, a first-timer squirming with nerves. He had reason to squirm, she reflected. Advance word from Editing was that he'd gone overboard with the action—his movie apparently had so much slicing and dicing of the veggie characters, it looked more like a Veg-O-Matic commercial than a PG-rated family film.

The lights dimmed, and the audience rustled expectantly. On screen, a 3D whirl of stars coalesced into an angel whose wings unfurled directly into the audience's eyes. And then the words CONSTELLATION PICTURES rose to the swelling of a celestial chord.

Which clashed with a ringtone of Carly Simon's "Tired of Being Blonde."

The audience rustled again. Some pathetic loser had forgotten to kill their phone! A head was going to roll! The lesser executives smirked and cast sidelong glances at their neighbors.

Until it became apparent that the head belonged to Alicia Chenoweth, and all smirks vanished abruptly.

Alicia began edging her way out of her row, aware of a squawk as she trod on the director's foot. "Tell them to freeze the print for five minutes," she commanded a V.P. and continued out into the bright corridor. She walked rapidly down the hall to a secluded area where she wasn't likely to be overheard. She pressed return call.

Roger Lopez answered. He sounded stressed.

"It's me," she said crisply. "Did you find her?"

"Yeah. Fact, she's right here."

"Really? Let me speak to her."

She heard Lopez mumble something, followed by a man's voice. Then Hannah on the phone, warily: "Hello?"

"Hannah, it's Alicia Chenoweth."

"Alicia? Who's this man?"

"An investigator. I'm sorry, I had you followed. There are things you need to know. I think you might be in danger." Alicia lowered her voice, speaking close to the phone. "From your father. He wants to get you back in prison."

A low laugh. "I think it's more than that. I think he wants me dead."

"What? What makes you say that?"

"Haven't you heard? I mean, about my car blowing up?"

Alicia listened dumbfounded as Hannah filled her in on what had happened. One of the V.P.'s appeared at the end of the corridor with a questioning look. She held up a finger, and he withdrew. To Hannah, she said: "I can't talk right now, unfortunately, but I can meet up with you later. Get Lopez to stay with you. He can at least provide some protection. Do you know a safe place you can go to?"

"Actually," Hannah said, "I think I do."

◦◦◦

"Is it the curse of *Wildwood Murphy*?"

The question was brayed by a puffy-lipped blonde with a mike who'd shoved her way to the front of the media pack that was clogging Warren Doran's entrance into the WildFilm building. He stopped and addressed her with a patronizing smile. "A curse? Of course not. Curses are very real in the plots of my movies, but they don't exist in real life. There's no such thing as the Wildwood Curse."

The reporter persisted: "Jackson Brandt is dead. Also Emma Lockhart, Ken Motolla . . . The screenwriter Ron Tobias . . . And Benny Davis is paralyzed . . ."

He cut her off. "There were hundreds of people involved in the making of the *Wildwood* movies. It's an unfortunate fact that out of those hundreds, a few were bound to have bad things happen to them. Statistically, it's almost certain that some of them would even die. That doesn't mean there's a curse or any sort of black magic at work."

"Do you think Hannah is still alive?" someone shouted from the back of the pack.

"I expect to find my daughter alive and well."

"Two women who were in prison with her have both been murdered. Was Hannah involved with them in any way?"

"I really have no idea. You'd have to ask her that."

The redhead thrust herself forward again. "As her father, wouldn't she confide in you?"

"My daughter has always possessed a sturdy independent streak. I can't speak for everything she does. I'm afraid that's all I can say right now."

They kept bellowing questions—"Was she abducted? Is there a ransom demand?"—which he ignored, finally pushing through into the sanctuary of the WildFilm building. Here too everybody was abuzz, but the buzz died quickly at the sight of the boss. Warren kept a composed smile on his face as he continued to his office.

His cell had been ringing all morning, but he hadn't picked up. Now, as he walked, he scrolled through the I.D.'s of missed calls.

His assistant, Benjamin, flagged him. "Thad Miller in your office."

Shit. He continued briskly in. "Make it short, Thad. I'm running triple overtime."

"Have a seat, War."

He lifted a brow. Thad Miller inviting him—no, make that *commanding* him—to have a seat in his own office?

Warren pointedly remained standing. "What do you want?"

"I've been on the phone all morning to Vegas."

"*You've* been on the phone?"

"Yes," Thad said implacably. "And they're pretty damned concerned, I don't have to tell you. They want some assurances that you're going to make the right play when it comes to Hannah."

"And what is that supposed to mean?"

"Meaning that you're not going to go soft. I think I've been pretty successful convincing them otherwise, but we're going to have to show some results soon." Thad got up from his chair and faced Warren, looming a good five inches above him. "You better let me know the truth. Are you protecting her?"

"Don't be a fucking ass."

"So you've had no contact with her in the last couple of days?"

"No, but I will. She'll call me soon."

"What makes you so sure?"

"Because she's got no other options. I'm the one she's always turned to in a fix. I'm the only one she has."

Thad's lips curved in a mocking grin. "I've got news for you, War. She's picked up somebody new. A boyfriend in a yellow Corvette."

Warren almost asked "how do you know?" He stopped himself. He no longer wanted to know how Thad Miller acquired information. "What's his name?"

"Mitchell Arpino."

"Arpino?" Warren took out his cell and scrolled through the missed calls. "Well then, you see? She's called me already. From this guy's phone." He showed the I.D. to Thad.

"Outstanding. That's all I need to know."

TWENTY-FIVE

"Dickless in Sun Valley."

The L.A.P.D. Cold Case officer on the other end of the line gave a disgusted grunt. "That's what they used to call him. He fits your bill—body dump of a white thirty-year-old male, mid-Eighties. Discovered maybe five, six days after T.O.D. Case never closed."

"Sweet," Mitch said wryly. He was ensconced in Benny Davis's office inside the hive of energetic activity that was the Sunlight Center—if you could call a rolltop desk an office. But he had at his disposal a MacBook, a quality printer and scanner, and a phone with three lines, so he pretty much had everything he needed. He'd spent the past couple of hours tracking down leads, burrowing through layers of the L.A.P.D. until finally hitting pay dirt—a desk sergeant in the Foothill Division, friend of a friend of a connection of Mitch's *LA Times* pal Ken Wozensteig who'd directed him to the right old-timer in Cold Case.

"Oh, yeah, Dickless in Sun Valley. Haven't heard noise about this one in maybe twenty years."

"So I take it that the body had its dick cut off?"

"Correct. Slashed clean off and not found on the scene. Also had cuts to the hands and face. Bled out from the do-it-yourself castration maybe a couple of hours before the dump."

Mitch took a gulp from a Styrofoam cup of a beverage that resembled coffee sort of in the way Kool-Aid might resemble a '99 Dom Perignon. "You got a real name for Mr. Dickless?"

"Joel Steven Pressler. Failed actor, big surprise. Hailed originally from San Diego, had been living the swinger's life in Marina Del Rey. No wife or kids, parents deceased. How he ended up a dead eunuch out in the sticks never determined. But according to the file, there was more than one perp."

"How did they know?"

"The cuts on the face and hands? They were superficial. Made in the heat of emotion, slashing out quickly and at random. Using something with a jagged edge, a piece of broken glass or chinaware. DOA could've survived those, if that was all."

"So the. . . . dismemberment? That was done different?"

"Apparently, yeah. Skilled butchery. Smooth, sharp blade, carving off the prime cut. So to speak. *That* perp knew exactly what he was doing."

"Whoo. So what was the blade? Like a carving knife?"

"Nah, something smaller. Switchblade category. Nice little knife, does the trick every time. So what's your business with this? You got a lead?"

"Maybe I do. If so, you'll be the first to know." After dangling this juicy hint, Mitch added casually, "I could use a picture of the crime scene. If I give you a fax . . . ?"

"Yeah, I could do that."

Ten minutes later, Benny's ancient fax machine spat out the photo. Medium-close shot of the body sprawled face up in a thicket of scrub. Nice-looking guy, though what with the dirt and leaves, not to mention all those slashes across his face, it was a little hard to tell. Longish dark hair, well-cut. Miami Vice fashion look, black T-shirt under Italian jacket. White pants pulled down to the knees. Pants were soaked in black blood that had issued from the mess of gore at the groin.

It certainly jibed with what Sabrina had said. Except for the castration part. That was news. And it wasn't exactly the kind of detail you'd be inclined to omit.

So had Pamela Sebring Doran actually killed this man?

"What's that?"

He swiveled quickly as Hannah came up behind him. She'd pitched in with the lunch prep, and now her face was flushed from steam, her brown hair falling damply into her eyes. He'd never seen her look more beautiful.

His instinct was to hide the gruesome photo from her, but he knew she'd want to see it. "An L.A.P.D. crime scene photo of a body dump in 1985. I think it's what that Sabina was talking about."

Hannah examined it, exhaling slowly. "This is the man my mother killed?"

"I don't think she killed him," Mitch said. He recounted his conversation with the Cold Case officer.

"So he was attacked by two people, not just by my mother?"

"It's possible. And it would have been the second one who actually killed him. It had to be somebody pretty skilled with a blade. Maybe one of Betsy's security guys. Or even another of the johns."

"Or one of the other girls. When I was up for probation I got turned down because Valentina had planted a switchblade inside my mattress. She and Zizi used to joke about cutting people. I'll bet a lot of the girls who worked for Betsy Bell carried knives and knew how to use them."

"It seems easier to imagine than someone like your mother."

"Maybe she never knew," Hannah said. "She might have been crazy with guilt thinking she'd killed that man. And then, after Jackson crashed his bike, maybe she just couldn't stand living anymore."

"Could be."

"I'll probably never know for sure."

"Maybe," he said. "But we're not done yet." He took a sip of coffee and made a face. "This stuff is poison."

"Benny says he keeps a pot of real coffee brewing in his trailer."

"Lead me to it!"

Alicia Chenoweth, picking her way gingerly through the broken glass, shredded newspaper, and discarded fast-food containers, the cigarette butts and crumpled packets, the dog poop and god only knew what else, paused in front of the rusty green and white bus. She was captivated by the sight of the young couple through the rolled back door of a handicap entrance. The pretty girl with wide-set eyes and rippling brown hair holding a cup; the broad-shouldered young man with the rumpled shirt and tousled curls pouring coffee. She noticed how the girl's face was lit with a glow, and the way the young man's body seemed to curve protectively around her even while engaged in this simple task.

And for a moment she was struck by an almost overwhelming sense of envy.

"Yo, 'Licia!"

She turned. It took her a second to realize that the unshaven African American man rolling in a wheelchair towards her was Benny Davis, the suave actor she usually saw in a tuxedo at fundraisers in the ballroom of the Beverly Hills Hilton.

His hooded eyes took her in sardonically. "Don't guess you're here to help with the lunch serve."

"No," she admitted. "I'm here to see Hannah."

"Did she call you?"

"I spoke to her," she said evasively.

"What in the hell you got to do with all this, Alicia?"

"Nothing, really. Except that I've known Hannah for a long time and I'm very concerned for her."

"Cut the b.s. The first time I see your overpaid ass anywhere near this place, it's gotta be for something more than just out of the goodness of your bleeding heart." He tamped a polished red pipe and began filling it. "It's that movie, isn't it? That goddamned cursed movie. You worried the girl's daddy is gonna send it off the rails, put your precious job in jeopardy?"

She hesitated. She decided it would be better to be straight with him. "It's actually more personal. I'm being blackmailed, Benny. By, as you put it, that girl's daddy."

He stopped fiddling with the pipe and shot her a stunned look. "You serious?"

"Very."

"Huh. What's he got on you?"

"That's something I'm going to only share with Hannah."

"Huh," he grunted again. "Well, okay. If you need me, I'll be back there in the food truck."

"Okay, thanks. And oh, Benny?"

He swiveled.

"You were . . . you are, one of the greats. If you ever wanted to come back to work . . . There are parts, you know. Character roles . . ."

"You mean for Angry Wheelchair Guy?"

She smiled. "It's a guaranteed Supporting Actor nomination."

"That's probably a fact. Tell you what . . . I'll keep it in mind."

He turned his chair again and headed off. Alicia continued toward the bus. "Hello . . . ?" she called.

Hannah lit up at the sight of her. She quickly jumped down to greet her. "Alicia! You're here!"

They hugged. Alicia glanced at Mitch.

"That's my friend, Mitch Arpino. He's a brilliant photographer. And he saved my life."

Alicia raised her brows.

Mitch shook it off with a wry grin. "How about some coffee, Alicia? Jamaican Blue beans."

"Who'd have guessed Benny Davis would be a secret coffee snob?" Hannah laughed.

"I'd love a cup. Black."

Mitch poured her one and stepped out of the bus. They settled at a weathered picnic table set in front of it.

"Why don't I be straight, Alicia?" Mitch began. "Hannah is inclined to trust you, but I'm not. I think you're here because of Warren Doran."

"And you're right. But it's not what you think. It's not about protecting the movie."

"Then what?"

Alicia smiled grimly. "I'm being blackmailed by your father, Hannah."

The couple exchanged glances.

"Does it have anything to do with the Malibu Madam?" Hannah asked.

Alicia felt a shock. "Yes. How did you know?"

"We'll explain. But you first. What was your connection to her?"

"When I was nineteen years old," she said, "I was taken to one of her parties by a friend of mine. I ended up in a bedroom with one of her clients and . . . Well, I ended up having sex with him. I was young, broke, and drunk, but that's no excuse. I went back a second time and did it again. The second time was the last, but it was enough."

"Are there photos?"

"Yes. Or actually, a video."

"And Warren showed it to you?" Mitch put in.

"No, it was Betsy. Betsy Bell. She waylaid me several days ago as I was picking up my kids from their preschool, and she confronted me with a video on a portable player." Alicia struggled to keep her voice even. "It was from back then. It showed me in bed with a man. One of her clients. It shows everything, even him paying for it afterwards. Betsy threatened to make it public."

"In exchange for what?" Hannah asked.

"I'd been trying to renegotiate Warren Doran's deal. I wanted to get him to accept a lesser up-front payment. The condition Betsy laid out was to restore the deal to what had been originally negotiated."

"Did you agree to it?"

"Yes, I did. I felt that I had no choice." Alicia tightened her fingers around the handle of her coffee mug. "The idea of that obscene thing ever getting out . . ."

"You'd lose your job," Mitch said.

"Probably. But that's not the worst thing. The worst is thinking that my daughters might ever see it . . . I'd do just about anything to stop that from happening."

"Yes," Hannah said vehemently. "I understand."

Alicia nodded. "Good. And now it's your turn. How did you know it was about Betsy Bell?"

"My mother, too. We think he'd been blackmailing her, as well."

"Your father had?"

"That bastard's not her real father," Mitch growled.

Alicia looked at Hannah. "Is that true?"

Hannah nodded.

"Then who is?"

"Jackson Brandt," Hannah said.

Of course! Suddenly, with very little imagination, Alicia could picture the face of the biggest box office star of the Eighties in the features of the girl across from her. Just as suddenly, everything made perfect sense. "Your mother also attended parties at Betsy's place, didn't she?"

"Yes. We just found out. We've got a photo."

"And it's also taken from a video," Mitch added. "They're in that leather bag on that bunk behind you."

Alicia reached for the courier bag. She rifled briefly through its contents and pulled out the 8x10. She stifled a sense of horror. That familiar room, the black waterbed and the red-shaded lamps. An exquisite silver-haired girl brandishing a broken glass. The howling man on the bed clutching his bleeding face. "My god! Who is this man?"

"A guy who used to hang at the parties," said Mitch. "Name of Joel Steven Pressler. Aspiring actor."

"Did she kill him?"

"He ended up dead. His body was dumped out in the middle of nowhere. But he didn't die from getting his face slashed. He bled out from getting his penis cut off."

Alicia drew a constricted breath.

"We're pretty sure my mother didn't do that last part," Hannah said quickly. "But we can't prove it. We only have this photo, not the original video."

"So obviously we have common cause," Alicia said.

"It still doesn't explain what brought you here," Mitch said. "What do you want from Hannah?"

"An answer," Alicia said. She leveled a glance at Hannah. "Why does Warren want you sent back to jail?"

Hannah lost all color. "What makes you think that?"

"That investigator, Roger Lopez. He'd previously been hired by Warren's partner to bug your apartment. He was supposed to get something incriminating on you. When he failed, he was fired, and according to Lopez, they replaced him with a serious thug."

"Serious enough to try to kill us," Mitch said.

Alicia gave a sardonic grimace. "It's about that damned cursed movie. That's how Benny put it, and I'm beginning to think he's right. Hannah, does Warren control your trust fund?"

She nodded, her face still ashen. "He got control of it when I went to prison. I've been having trouble getting any money since I've been out. We think he might have stolen it."

Looted his daughter's trust. Alicia's hunch had been right—it was how he managed to keep his company afloat after the financial debacle of his last movie. "May I ask what happens to your estate if you die?"

"The trust passes to my grandfather for the duration of his lifetime. But because of my grandfather's Alzheimer's, Warren would still be the administrator."

"At least that's what he thinks," Mitch put in.

"Do you have a reason to think differently?"

"My mother had divorced him, but I don't think he even knew it. She went to Haiti and did it on her own."

Alicia nodded. "Haiti is one of the few countries with no mutual consent requirement."

"So it would have been legal?"

"A unilateral Haitian divorce would be acknowledged in some jurisdictions but not in others. I'm not sure about California. How did you find out?"

"There's a divorce decree in the bag," Mitch told her. "And there's a batch of legal documents. They mostly seem to do with *Wildwood*, so maybe you should take a look at them."

Alicia opened the bag again and pulled out the sheaf of documents. A name leapt out at her from one of them. Silver Bike Holding Corporation. "This looks like a contract. Have you read it?"

"We haven't gone through everything yet," Mitch said.

Alicia read it through, with growing excitement. "It is a contract," she told them. "You know, of course, that before any movie is made, the lawyers thoroughly research the chain of title. To make sure that whoever is selling the script really owns the script, as well as all the underlying rights—any previous book, for example. So when we negotiated with Warren to make a new *Wildwood* movie, our legal did a title search. They were satisfied that the original film was made from a script written by Ronald Tobias."

Hannah nodded "The alcoholic who died choking on his own vomit. It's part of the official *Wildwood* curse."

"What about him?" Mitch asked.

"The script had been purchased from Tobias, along with all sequel rights, by a company called Silver Bike Holding Corporation. Warren filed the appropriate documents with our legal, but with one very crucial difference. In his documents, Silver Bike was a company owned jointly by himself and by your mother, Hannah, Pamela Sebring Doran. But according to this contract, it was Pamela's money that had bought the rights." Alicia scanned the pertaining paragraphs again. "Warren's name is not here at all. The document he filed with our legal must have been forged."

"So what does that mean?" Hannah asked.

"It means the whole game is about to change. If this contract is genuine, Warren does not hold the rights to *Wildwood Murphy*. He's got no claim on them at all."

"They belong to Hannah, then," Mitch said.

"That would be the case. And if so, Hannah, you are now the recipient of all fees and payments from the studio."

Hannah stared at her, too amazed to speak.

"She'd get back the money that bastard stole from her?" Mitch said.

"I'd think so and maybe even more. I'm going to put my legal on this right away. They'll go over these documents with a fine tooth comb. And as soon as possible—hopefully by tomorrow morning—we'll have new contracts drafted for you to sign.

"Just like that?" Hannah said.

"Pretty much. It will all be kept strictly confidential until everything is signed and notarized."

"It's amazing! But what about you?" She glanced at Alicia.

"You can use this as counter-blackmail," Mitch suggested. "You could turn him in as a forger."

"Yes. I could probably use this as effective leverage. But I really want to get my hands on that video, and I have a strong feeling that Warren is the one who has it."

"Why?"

"Something that Betsy said. About a friend keeping them safe and sound. The same friend who'd sent her to blackmail me."

"Yes," Hannah said quickly. "That would make sense. My father . . . I mean, Warren . . . When something is important to him, he needs to keep complete control. Like my mother, obviously. And like his movies, he always tries to keep complete control of them."

"That's a well known fact. He drives directors crazy.

"So he'd have them someplace close at hand," Mitch said. "Maybe in a storage facility, or a bank vault nearby."

"Oh my god!" Hannah clapped her hands to her face. "I think I know where they are! They're at the house."

"Warren's house?" Alicia said. "Would he really do that?"

"He's got a home office. It's in an addition that was built about a year after my mother died. It has a whole bank of built-in filing cabinets and they're always kept locked. But one time when I was about ten or eleven, I wandered into the office and found one open. It contained video cassettes."

"Did you play them?"

"No, I didn't bother. Cassettes were always being sent to the house for my father. There'd be trailers and dailies and rough cuts of his films, or other things he needed to take a look at. I didn't think anything of it."

"That's just what they might have been."

"Maybe. But a maid caught me in the office and she must have tattled to my father, because he yelled at me. He was madder than I'd ever seen him before. Told me never to go in there again. And then sometime later, a locksmith came and worked in the office. Probably putting on better locks."

"That's where we could start," Mitch said eagerly. "If I could get in at a time when he's not there, I could probably break the locks."

"I have a better idea," Alicia said. "Let Lopez do it. He's a professional. And I can guarantee a time that Warren won't be at home. Tomorrow, at the *Wildwood* press event. He'll be on the Constellation lot from four o'clock until at least seven. That should give Lopez time to make a pretty thorough search."

"There'll be other people at the house," Hannah said. "Staff, and probably his girlfriend Tracy. If I go with Lopez, I can make up some pretense for being there."

"It's too dangerous for you to go anywhere right now. Especially Warren's house."

"Then I'll go with Lopez," Mitch said. "I don't trust that guy to tie his own shoe laces."

"He may be better than you think."

"Tell him I'm going with him." Mitch was adamant.

"Okay," Alicia conceded, "I'll get him set up." She looked back inside the courier bag. "Anything else in here I should know about?"

From the bottom, she drew out a miniature audio cassette. "What's on here?"

Hannah and Mitch exchanged puzzled glances. "No idea," Hannah told her. "We didn't even see it there."

"It looks like it's from an old answering machine. I can get somebody to transcribe it for you."

Hannah hesitated. "I think maybe I should listen to it myself first."

"Okay, then I'll try to hunt up an old machine for you. Right now, the main priority is to keep you safe.

Thad Miller had barely managed to keep himself together through the frenetically-paced schedule of his day. Returning home to the classy little modern house with killer views in the slopes of Sherman Oaks—the perfect starter place for a rising young Hollywood player—he was enraged to find his carport occupied by the Escalade, forcing him to park his Audi A5 convertible coupe at the curb where a swerving vehicle could ding it.

Inside, his new roommate had made himself thoroughly at home. Cherry Morrison lounged on Thad's Roche Bobois leather sofa. He was sporting Thad's black velour robe with the Ralph Lauren crest woven on the breast. Guzzling Thad's single malt Scotch straight from the bottle, while a basketball game blared from Thad's 52" Sony LED.

"That's eighteen year old Glenfiddich, you asshole," Thad snapped at him. "Hundred twenty bucks a bottle."

Cherry's response was to upend the bottle for another lengthy chug. He wiped his mouth with the sleeve of the velour robe.

Thad could hardly keep a lid on his simmering rage. He'd squeezed the last ten grand out of his Platinum Card so that Cherry could bribe a guy—some sort of high level snitch at the DEA with the ability to track cell phone activity. "Everything go okay with the cash?"

"It's delivered," Cherry said. "Just left my man an hour ago."

"So how exactly is it going to go down?"

"Short answer. My man gets his people to pull the calls made to your man's cell phone. He narrows it down to the one that counts. And then they pinpoint the location of the caller through the GPS."

"So what if Hannah made the call from a phone that doesn't have a GPS."

"Then we're screwed.

"Fuck."

"Hey, calm yourself, okay? Every phone comes equipped these days."

"So how soon is this going to happen?"

"The hell I know? In the *first* place, my man's gotta wait till his people get back to work. He's gotta have *access*. To equipment and stuff. Nothing's going to happen tonight, so you might as well relax."

Thad paced nervously. He'd had very different plans for this evening—to entertain an ambitious young publicist with honey hair and a stunning pair of C cups. A far cry from hanging around like a tool at home while Cherry Morrison decimated his liquor cabinet. "My ass is on the line here, you know," he grumbled.

Cherry placed his feet on Thad's Thos. Moser Edo–style coffee table. "Your ass and mine, Thad Boy. If I don't finish the job, I'm going to have to catch the next plane to Bolivia and spend the rest of my life fucking goats. And if you know what's good for you, you'll come with me."

Thad grunted with disgust. He stalked over to his twenty-bottle wine fridge and uncorked a Cakebread Cellars Cabernet. Sixty-eight bucks a bottle. At least his wines were safe from Cherry Morrison. Cherry thought drinking wine was gay.

TWENTY-SIX

The suite at the Beverly Wilshire was lavishly appointed, every luxury from steam shower to baby grand piano. The service was extravagantly discreet: a gentle knock on the door, a flicker as someone set down a tray or hung items in a closet. Alicia, via the studio's services, sent changes of clothes, cosmetics, toiletries. Mitch didn't want to speculate on the tab that Constellation Studios was picking up—but if you had to hide out, he reflected over a room service dinner of Chilean sea bass, it was better to do it in style.

At noon the next day, Alicia appeared with a clutch of lawyers, a bundle of contracts, and a notary public. They huddled with Hannah for several hours while all documents were read and explained and duly signed and notarized.

And then Alicia clapped her hands. "It's official! Hannah, you're now the sole owner of all underlying rights to the *Wildwood Murphy* movie franchise, with a t.k. deal as Executive Producer of any and all forthcoming films." She and Hannah hugged.

As the lawyers and notary took off, Alicia's phone jangled. She spoke briefly. "That was Lopez. He's in Brentwood now." She glanced at her watch. "It's 3:45. The house should be clear. My marketing people told Warren to be on the lot by four, so if he hasn't left already, he will very shortly. And his girlfriend is out. My p.r. people got her invited to a Proenza Schouler trunk show at Saks. Very exclusive—she jumped at it."

"So I'll meet up with Lopez at the house?" Mitch said.

"No, a couple of blocks away. At the corner of Sunset and Rockingham." She began gathering her things. "If I want to make this event on time, I'd better scoot as well."

"I can't thank you enough, Alicia," Hannah told her. "For everything."

"Hopefully we're both profiting, here," Alicia picked up her crocodile tote. "Oh, wait, I almost forgot." She reached into the tote and removed a small brown plastic appliance. "A Panasonic answering machine. Seventies vintage. Our props people were able to dig one up right away."

Finally alone, Mitch and Hannah regarded each other a little awkwardly. "So . . ." he said. "It looks like you're going to be rich again."

"Looks like it." She smiled. "Do you mind?"

"To be honest? It's kind of intimidating."

"You always knew I had money."

"Yeah. But until I saw that spread of yours in Pasadena, I guess I never realized just how much."

"I could give it all away," she said teasingly.

"It's a possibility," he grinned back.

"Some of it, anyway. If that would make you like me better."

"Know what? I think I'd like you either way." He reached for her. "You can be swimming in money, or flipping burgers at Chili's."

"Okay, now you're making me hungry." She playfully licked a corner of his mouth.

He gathered her closer and kissed her deeply. With an effort, he broke away. "Hey, not fair. You know I've got to go meet up with Lopez."

"Mitch?" she said, suddenly serious.

"Yeah?"

"Be careful."

"Count on it," he said.

After he'd gone, Hannah paced nervously. She switched the t.v. on and off. Picked out a Philip Roth from a bookshelf stocked with hardcovers, tried and failed to concentrate on its pages. Put a jazzy CD into the player, then turned that off as well.

A cell phone laying on the piano rang. Not her Cyndi Lauper ringtone—it was Mitch's basic trill. Their phones were identical—he must have grabbed hers by mistake. She had the urge to answer it. At least have somebody to talk to. She read the name on the caller I.D.: Ajay Nayar. Mitch's photo agent.

Business. She shouldn't interfere.

She suddenly remembered the Panasonic answering machine

that Alicia had brought. And just as suddenly, she couldn't wait to listen to the little cassette. She dug it out from the courier bag and fitted it into the device.

Her heart beat faster as she pressed PLAY.

The machine's robotic voice: *First new message. Sent today at 5:46 p.m.*

A man's voice, unmistakably Warren Doran's. Shouting over an airport hubbub. "Pamela, where the hell are you? The damned flight's been delayed, I'm not going to get in until after midnight. And tomorrow I'm going to be running like mad, so I probably won't get a chance to call again . . . Are you there, Pam? Pick up!"

Beep.

Second new message. Sent today at 6:25 p.m.

"Yeah, Mrs. Doran? It's Vinny from Superior Roofing. Your special order shingles just came in, so we can get going on your roof on Monday. Let me know if that's okay."

Beep.

Third new message. Sent today at 10:16 p.m.

A tick of silence. Then another male voice. A soft baritone with a Western inflection. A famous voice: "Hey, it's me. You there?"

The click of a receiver being picked up. "Yes. I'm here." Hannah felt a cold shiver run through her. It was her mother's voice: low, musical, slightly out of breath.

"Are you alone?"

"Yes. Daddy's away and Hannah's in bed."

"How is she?"

"Oh, beautiful! We played hide and seek tonight, and she came up with the most amazing hiding place, this tiny, tiny space under the stairwell. I'd never have found her, except she couldn't keep from giggling and giving herself away."

"Sounds like fun. I wish I'd been there."

"I wish you'd been here too." A long, soft sigh. "Oh god, Jack, I miss you."

"Me too. I'm going crazy. Listen, I'm coming down tomorrow night, okay?"

"Yes," Pamela said. "Yes."

"I already reserved the suite at the Langham. This time it's under Ricky Ricardo."

A silver bell of a laugh. "I'll be your Lucy. We'll be Ricky and Lucy forever and ever."

"Loo-cy! You got some splainin' to do . . ."

The ruthless machine guillotined the rest of the conversation.

No more messages, spoke the robotic voice.

Hannah played the tape again, her emotions coursing violently. Those voices: her mother's and her real father's and also Warren's, from twenty years ago—hearing them, stirred something in her, a memory of that terrible night she'd tried all her life not to think about.

The growling bear made her wake up. She got out of bed and went down the hall, happy that her pajamas had feet so it wasn't cold to walk. Mommy's light was on and she was on her bed. Her mommy had beautiful mermaid hair was like Princess Ariel's, and it was hanging all over her face. But she was twisted up and not moving, and there was throw-up everywhere. Hannah ran to find Daddy. She knew he was there because she'd heard his car come home.

Except he wasn't there, only Bina. And when she showed Bina, Bina pulled her down the hallway by Hannah's own hair that was brown and rough and not like a mermaid's at all.

It seemed startlingly vivid. The look of the room. The shape of her mother's body . . .

She desperately needed to talk to Mitch. She grabbed his phone and called her own number, and got the electronic mailbox message. Shit! She'd turned it off, and he probably didn't even realize he was out of reach.

She hit replay on the answering machine and listened to the voices for a third time. The turmoil she was feeling became more intense.

She had to do something, or she would explode.

She went into the bedroom of the suite. She reached deep under the mattress of the bed and removed a tiny gun. A Beretta Bobcat pistol, scarcely five inches long.

It had been Zizi Howell who'd taught her how to palm an object. An ace. A spoon. An apple. *"You see? Magic!" Giggles bubbled on Zizi's lips as she turned her palm over and then opened it. The little red cell phone she'd been holding had disappeared.*

Hannah had practiced what Zizi showed her: you straddle-grip the object with five fingers, turn your hand over briskly while at the same time thrusting it forward to make the object slide up your sleeve. It had been easy for her to palm the Bobcat from the gun racks when she was showing them to Mitch. She'd hated keeping it a secret from him. But she'd had no choice.

She tucked the pistol in her purse. Then she picked up Mitch's cell again and called another number that, having called it once before, she knew by heart.

Pick up, Denny, she silently pleaded. *Please please please, pick up!*

❧

Mitch climbed into the PacBell truck idling at the Sunset corner of Rockingham. Lopez was wearing a uniform with a laminated I.D.—for one Rick Sandoval who only vaguely resembled Lopez—clipped to his shirt pocket.

"Where do you get the truck?" Mitch asked.

"A pal lends it to me. I give him a few bucks for his risk." Lopez made a U-turn and headed towards the Doran residence. "I was here forty minutes ago. I got to the street box and dirtied up the land lines. Then I talked to Doran's butler and told him the whole block was reporting problems with their phones. He let me check out the central brain system in the garage. I said there were shorts in it. I'd need to go through the house and uncouple some of the receivers, plus a lot of technical blah, blah. So he's expecting me."

"You sure Doran is gone?"

"Watched him pull out about ten minutes ago."

They arrived at the house. Lopez rang the buzzer. "PacBell," he announced and the truck was buzzed in. He parked in front of the opened three car garage.

"So what about me?" Mitch asked. "You got another one of those jumpsuits?"

"Nope. You sit tight here. I'll get to the location and pop the locks. If it's pay dirt, I'll come back and we'll both bring boxes. With you carrying a box, it won't look so suspicious if you're not in a uniform."

"How long are you going to be?"

"Lickety-split." Lopez fastened a tool belt around his waist, got out and went into the garage.

Mitch waited edgily. Five minutes. Six.

Screw it. He jumped down from truck, headed into the garage and cautiously opened the door to the house. He was in a service area leading to a kitchen. A dishwasher churned, and somebody was whistling tunelessly—probably the private chef. He rehearsed his story—if he ran into any of the staff, he was Lopez's assistant and he was looking for his boss.

He skirted the kitchen and walked through a passage to the main hallway. Hannah had said the new addition was in the back of the house, which would be to the right . . .

Behind him, he heard the front door opening. Jesus! He ducked into the nearest room, the dining room.

A man's voice shouted: "Hernando?"

Footsteps came down the hall. Goddamned modern house. All rooms were open, no doors to hide behind. Mitch flattened himself against a wall.

He watched, scarcely breathing, as Warren Doran walked briskly past.

"Hernando, are you back here?" Doran called. "I'm empty on Nexium. I need another packet."

Mitch heard footsteps scurrying above him, a muffled voice. Then footsteps hurrying down a stairway. A conversation.

Warren was heading back past the dining room. Mitch dove for the floor, flattened himself. Rehearsed his story about looking for Lopez. Then why was he lying on the floor? No good reason he could think of.

A cell rang. Mitch heard Warren answer and continue talking. From the floor, Mitch watched his legs go by. He waited until he heard the front door open and slam shut. Then he picked himself up and practically jogged toward the back of the house.

A room that actually did have a door to it! Mitch pushed the door open onto a sleekly furnished office. Lopez stood in front of a bank of opened file cabinet drawers, a lock pick in his hand.

"What's taking so long?" Mitch said.

Lopez jumped. "Christ almighty! You startled the shit out of me!"

"It's been longer than five minutes."

"These locks were pretty fancy pin tumblers. Took me a few minutes longer to pop them. Doesn't matter, though. It's a swing and a miss."

"Nothing here?"

"Mostly empty. A couple of them got scripts, but that's it."

"You've checked them all?"

"Every one. I guess Doran moved the cassettes to someplace else."

Mitch looked around the room. Same luxurious modern furnishings he'd noticed in the rest of the house. And yet the room had an unused feel. Metaphorically dusty.

He turned back to the cabinets. The scripts were stacked in the lower drawers. "Were these locked too?"

"Those were the only ones that were locked. The empty ones weren't."

Mitch took out one of the scripts. He flipped to the title page. *Blind Date With An Alien*, by Jason Fedderman. Dated 9/13/90

"This was written back in 1990." He replaced it, looked at another. "This one's from 1993. A bunch of dated screenplays."

Lopez picked one up. "This one says '90.'"

"So what's so valuable about these old screenplays that they've got to be kept under lock and key?"

Mitch did a quick shuffle through the pages of the script he was holding. Then he grasped it in both hands, weighing it. He held it by the edges of the front cover and shook it.

"What?" Lopez demanded.

Mitch opened the back cover and unfastened the arms of the brass binders. He opened the fold of the back cover. "Pay dirt!" he said. There was a thin strip of metal taped beneath the fold.

"A flash drive!" Lopez said. "Doran must've digitalized the cassettes."

"It makes sense. You can probably store about two hundred hours of video on one of these babies." He started gathering an armful of scripts. "Go get your boxes. We've got to get these out fast."

⁂

When the call came in that the cell phone in question had been activated and could be geographically targeted, Cherry was out the door in a shot. Traffic was constipated on Sunset, so he swung down to Santa Monica, which was no NASCAR speedway neither, and inched another thirty-five minutes into B.H. Fancy hotel, valets jumping like fleas the minute you pull up. He tossed his keys to one of the blood-suckers and charged into the lobby.

Lunged for a house phone. "Give me Hannah Doran's room."

"I'm sorry. We have no guest of that name registered."

"How about under Arpino?"

"I'm sorry, sir. We have no guest . . ."

Cherry slammed the phone down. They didn't register under their real names, so what was he supposed to do? Knock on every door in the hotel? Or sit here in the lobby with his thumb up his ass hoping she'd come walking by.

Which, to his stupefaction, she suddenly did.

His eyes nearly popped out of his head: Hannah Doran had just come out from the elevator bank and was walking fast towards the main door. For a minute, he thought maybe he was just hallucinating or something. But it was her okay, in a lame disguise, big old hat and shades. He began sprinting across the lobby, an obstacle course of sofas and little tables and jungle plants, but by the time he got outside, she was sliding her ass into a limousine and then it pulled away.

He flagged the main valet. "Where's my car?"

"Your ticket, sir?"

Cherry jammed the ticket into the guy's outstretched hand.

"Fifteen dollars, sir."

"I was only here five minutes."

"It's a set charge, sir. There's no grace period."

Cherry could smash this creep's smirky bean-eating face like a soft pie. Instead, he threw him a twenty, snatched the five in change. If he was expecting a tip, he could blow himself. "So where's the car?"

"It will have to be retrieved, sir. We'll bring it up as soon as we can."

Forget smashing the face; Cherry had the almost irresistible urge to take out his gun and blow brains all over a stretch of Wilshire Fucking Boulevard.

TWENTY-SEVEN

Hannah felt increasingly jumpy as the limo slinked through the west gate of Bel Air and began snaking up among the exclusive estates. She sat tensely on the jump seat, tightly gripping Mitch's cell in her hand like a talisman. It seemed to vibrate constantly with texts and calls, but none were from Mitch.

At the crest of Roscomare, the car swung briefly onto Mulholland and then up a private lane that gave onto a sprawling traditional-style home. The driver leapt out to open the door, and Hannah heard the trademark squeak of Crissie Townsend's voice: "Why did they send a limo and not an SUV? You can never make a really good entrance getting out of a limo, all folded up and all . . ."

"We needed a limo 'cause we're bringing somebody else," Denny's voice said.

"What somebody else? Is it Shia?" Crissie came ducking into the car, a froth of chiffon and tousled strawberry-colored hair, the famous five carat pink diamond glowing like a sunrise on her left hand. At the sight of Hannah, she froze in the exact jackknifed position she'd wanted to avoid, and her eyes, already celebrated for their size, widened to colossal blue moons. "You!" she gasped.

"Yeah, me," Hannah said with a cold smile.

Crissie unfroze herself and plopped sullenly on the opposite seat.

Denny slipped in next to her. "Hiya, Hanny." He was dressed in the renowned Wildwood Murphy outfit: beat-up leather bomber jacket, fly boy cap with goggles pushed up over it, and his auburn hair had been streaked with shades of wheat and straw.

It was amazing! Hannah thought. More than just the clothes and hair: it was his expression, his body language, the slight lopsidedness of his smile—he had completely absorbed the character created by his father. Even the purple bruise on his nose left over from Denny's fist fight with Mitch added to his Wildwood swagger.

"Why didn't you tell me it was her?" Crissie snapped at Denny.

"Didn't have time to tell you. She needed a lift."

"Relax, Cris, it's just a ride," Hannah said. "Once we get there, I'll leave you alone."

Crissie crossed her stunning legs, and raked a pair of crystal-studded sunglasses through her hair, and slapped a smile on her gloss-plumped lips. "Oh, Hanny, don't be a goose. We're happy to have you tag along. Just like old times, right?"

Old times. Not quite, Hannah thought wryly.

An enormous Samoan with a shaved skull wedged into the passenger seat beside the driver. The limo pulled away, trailed by a white Explorer conveying the rest of Denny's entourage.

"So Hanny, what the fuck gives?" Denny said, "I heard your car got bombed?"

"Yeah, what's going on?" Crissie echoed. "Some people were saying you were dead."

Yeah, you wish, Hannah thought. "I don't know what happened. That's for the police to figure out."

Crissie produced a mock sigh of concern. "It's so weird that you're in trouble again. It's, like, you just can't keep yourself out of it, can you?"

"Lay off, Cris," said Denny. "She's been through a lot."

"Yeah, but why is she dragging us into it? Baby, we could be in danger just having her with us."

"Relax, Crissie," Hannah said. "Nobody even knows I'm with you."

"I don't give a shit if they do or not," Denny said. He slouched casually on the seat. "You need a ride, I'm happy to give you one."

Crissie narrowed her eyes at him. "What's that supposed to mean?" She shifted her eyes back to Hannah. "What's going on here?"

"Going on where?" Denny said.

"You don't think I see the way you're looking at her?"

"For Christsake, Cris. It's a lift. Drop it."

Crissie beamed the cold blue rays of her eyes onto Hannah. "I think there's something else going on. Maybe you think that just because she's some kind of jailbird now, that makes her hot."

"Back off, Cris," Denny warned.

"Trust me, Crissie," Hannah said. "Denny and I are never going to hook up."

"Never?" Denny turned a teasing smile to her. "That's not very flattering."

"Never," she said firmly.

"Give me one good reason." He leaned toward her, joking but seductive.

Crissie linked a proprietary arm through his. "Cut it out, Denny. This isn't funny anymore."

He unlinked his arm from hers. "No, wait—there really is something weird going on here." He studied Hannah. "There's always been this kind of attraction between us, but now suddenly you're acting like I'm poison. So what's changed?"

"What attraction?" Crissie glared at Hannah. "What have you been doing behind my back?"

"I told you to back off, Cris," Denny told her. "This is between me and Hannah. I just want to know what's going on here?"

"It's something I found out," Hannah said.

"Yeah? What?"

She hesitated. "Haven't you ever wondered about certain things? I mean, like how much alike we sometimes seem to be?"

"Oh for godsake!" Crissie groaned. "You think the two of you are soul mates or something?"

"No, not soul mates. But it's sometimes spooky, isn't it, Denny, how alike we are? Sometimes down to the kind of expressions we make, or the way we say things . . ."

"Yeah, maybe. So?"

"So what I found out is, well . . . we're related."

His brows shot up. "How?"

"Well . . ." Hannah gave an uneasy laugh. "Okay. I found out you're my half-brother."

"Oh, please!" Crissie scoffed. "What kind of bullshit is that?"

"Shut up, Cris." Denny glanced back at Hannah. "Are you serious?"

"Yeah, I'm serious. My mother, Pamela, was having an affair with your father. It went on for years, I think from the time they first met. He was my father too. Jackson."

Denny's expression was stunned. "Are you sure?"

"Yeah. Totally sure."

"You believe that?" Crissie snapped. "I don't believe a word of it! It's the most ridiculous thing I ever heard."

"No," Denny said. "I think it's true."

"Come on, she's delusional!"

"I *used* to be delusional," Hannah snapped. "I used to think you were a human being, Crissie. But this happens to be true."

Crissie rolled her eyes. "Come on, Denny, it's totally insane. She doesn't look a thing like you. Or your father either."

"Nah, she does," Denny said, his eyes fixed on Hannah. "We've got the exact same chin. It's amazing, I never noticed."

"Actually, I think I look more like Jackson," Hannah said.

"Christ, yeah! Your eyes, that same smoky gray. With Dad, I remember he smoked a lot, like he had a cigarette going twenty-four/seven, and I used to think the smoke somehow got caught up in his eyes." Denny shook his head. "It's freaking amazing. Unreal."

"That's because it's *not* real!" Crissie's voice rose to a pitch above high C. "Can't you see she's playing you, Den? I mean, how can you believe somebody who lies and steals like she does?"

Hannah resisted the urge to slap America's Sweetheart's perfect heart-shaped face. "I don't steal, Crissie. If anybody should know that, you should."

"Please. *I'm* not the one who just got out of jail."

Hannah decided to bluff: "But you should be. For what you did to me."

Denny's eyes narrowed. "What's that mean?"

"Why don't you tell him, Crissie? How you set me up to look like I shoplifted that necklace."

Denny whipped his head to look at Crissie, causing the goggles over his forehead to tilt down over one brow. "What is she talking about?"

"Nothing! I told you, she's delusional."

Hannah continued the bluff. "Shawn Serafian told me all about it. That day at lunch before I was arrested. He told me he put a drug in my drink and then it was *your* turn. To get me to the jewelry store."

Crissie shot an appeal at Denny. "You see how crazy she is?"

"What was that about Shawn?" Denny said to Hannah.

"He was paid to drug me so that I'd feel dizzy. And then it was up to Crissie to get me to Charles Gray and sneak that necklace into my purse." She glanced at Crissie. "Shawn got six thousand bucks. What did you get out of it?"

Crissie hesitated a split second. It was true, then! Hannah tried another bluff. "You got to pick out something for yourself, in return, right? Something not to borrow to wear to the Emmys but to keep."

Crissie opened her mouth. Nothing came out.

"Jesus, you actually did it!" Denny exploded.

Crissie instantly realized her error. "It was all just supposed to be kind of a joke," she said desperately. "It was just shoplifting. What's the big deal? I mean, who's never done any shoplifting in their lives? Everybody steals sometimes."

"You stole fourteen months of my life, you skanky bitch!" Hannah flared.

"I didn't know!" Crissie whined. "I thought you'd get out of it. I didn't think it would stick. Your father's rich and famous, he's the one who should've got you out of it. I mean, Denny, you know what I'm talking about, right? He could've made everything go away."

Denny fixed her with an impenetrably black stare. "I guess I always knew you were a bitch. I just never realized how much of one." He grabbed her wrist. "Give me back that ring!"

"No way!"

He began yanking at the diamond and twisted it off her finger.

"Give it back!" she screeched, grabbing for it.

Holding it out of her reach, Denny rapped on the partition. "Hey, driver, pull over to that bus stop."

"What? What are you doing?" Crissie demanded.

The driver cruised the limo to the curb. An elderly homeless woman was encamped in a bus shelter, two heaped-up shopping carts at her feet. Her body was encased in an Arctic layering of rags. Two long white braids straggled from a balding center part on her scalp.

Denny rolled down his window. "Ma'am? Here, catch!"

He tossed the ring into the woman's lap. Suspiciously, she scooped it up and examined it.

Emitting an unearthly shriek, Crissie Townsend threw herself out of the limo and lunged at the woman.

"Hey, toss me your phone," Denny said to Hannah. She did and, switching it to video, he focused it out the window. Crissie was grappling with the woman over the ring, savagely yanking her by the braid as the woman flailed at Crissie with her fists, until all four of Denny's entourage erupted from the limo and SUV and pulled the kicking, shrieking Crissie off.

Denny stuck his head out the window. "JoJo, tell the guys to make sure Cris gets home okay? And how much cash you got on you?"

"About two grand, Denny," the Samoan said.

"Give it to that lady. See if she thinks it's a fair price for that goddamned ring."

"Will do."

Denny rolled the window back up and tossed the phone back to Hannah. "I got the whole thing on video. Put it on YouTube."

"I think I can do even better than that." Hannah pulled up the number for Mitch's photo agent, Ajay, and uploaded the video to him. "Crissie Townsend's finally going to do some good for somebody else."

The Samoan, JoJo, slid back into the front seat. He tossed the pink diamond ring to Denny who pocketed it and the car began to roll.

He and Hannah looked at each other, hardly knowing where to begin.

"So, wow," Denny said. "I've got a sister. I feel like Jane Eyre or somebody."

"Actually," Hannah grinned, "we're more like Leia and Sky-walker."

"Nah, they were twins. We're only halvsies."

"Still . . ."

"Yeah, still . . ." He smiled at her impishly. "So what if you and I had actually . . . you know, hooked up?"

"It was never going to happen," Hannah said firmly.

⟨✺⟩

The flash drives contained about sixteen hundred hours of blackmail, Mitch figured, as Lopez tossed the duffle into the Pac-Bell truck. He removed his tool belt and gave it back to the P.I.

"I'll call Chenoweth and tell her what we got," Lopez said. "We can't be a hundred percent sure it's what she's looking for, but the odds are pretty good."

"The odds are outstanding."

Lopez turned to get into the truck. Mitch grabbed him by the shirt, yanked him around and slammed him up against the door.

"Hey!" Lopez said.

"I just want to say. If I ever see your bloated ass anywhere around Hannah again, I'm gonna kick it to fucking China. Are we clear?"

"Yeah, sure, no problem. Hey, she's got bigger things to worry about than me."

"What do you mean? The guy in the black Escalade?"

"For starters."

Mitch released him. "You know who he is?"

"Sort of, yeah. Cherry, he's called. He's the guy who took over surveillance from me."

"Describe him."

"Ordinary. Maybe thirty. Military haircut. Usually wears a blue jean jacket. Hard ass killer, if you ask me."

Mitch flashed on an image: in the roadhouse, right before Hannah's car blew, the two of them sitting in a booth, and a guy coming in the door. Ordinary. Denim jacket. Next time Mitch had looked, he recalled, the guy was no longer there. "This Cherry—he was hired by Warren Doran?"

"Yeah. Though not directly. It was the other one, the younger partner, Miller."

"Thad Miller?" Mitch knew the name. The junior partner . . . The one who'd been so nice to Hannah, bringing groceries and whatever.

"Yeah, he's the one. He's from Vegas, right? Got a connection to a Vegas organization."

"What do you mean? The mob?"

"Don't know. Never asked, don't wanna be told. But if I was a betting man, I'd say it's the connection who's really calling the shots. The connection's not gonna tolerate somebody getting in the way of their payout."

Jesus, Mitch thought.

"I'll tell you one other thing," Lopez said. "These killer types like this Cherry guy, they don't stop. They're like cats on a scent. They get blood in their nose, they keep on going till there's a kill."

"You better hope for your own sorry ass that doesn't happen."

Mitch slammed him again, just for good measure. Then he headed back to his own car, pulling out his phone.

Except it wasn't his phone. He must have grabbed Hannah's in his hurry to meet up with Lopez.

He called the hotel suite. No answer. He tried his own number, exhaled with relief when he heard her voice. "It's me. Where are you?"

"I'm with Denny." Bad connection: she was barely coming through. "We're heading to the Constellation lot. I've told him everything, Mitch! About my mother and Jackson and about how we're half brother and sister . . ." She faded out, then in again. ". . . about you. I told him all about us. Denny says he promises not to hit you again."

Mitch stewed on this a moment. If memory served, *he* was the one who'd busted Denny Brandt's nose, not vice-versa.

"Mitch? I think this battery is going."

"You've got to get back to the hotel, Hannah. I mean immediately!"

"Don't worry, I'll be at the studio. It's got more security than the Pentagon . . ." The connection was breaking up.

"Hannah?" he yelled. "Can you hear me?" He cursed as the other line went dead.

He threw the Vette into gear and began heading to Constellation Studios. If Hannah was with Denny, they were going to the *Wildwood* media event—meaning she was obviously planning to confront Warren. She had no idea about Thad Miller's part in the whole thing—no clue of what danger she'd be in.

He calculated: it would take at least twenty minutes to get over to the Valley, and once at the studio, how the hell was he going to get in? More security than the Pentagon . . .

Almost no exaggeration.

His Nextel crackled. "Arpino?" Ajay Nayar hollered. "This is some amazing shit you sent me! I mean, whoa! Crissie Townsend beating on a bag lady!"

"What are you talking about?"

"This clip you just sent me, it's freaking dynamite. This is gonna bring in six figures, broheim, and I mean high six!"

Mitch was struck by a sudden idea. "Hey, Ajay! I need you to do something for me. There's a media event at Constellation Studios just about to kick off."

"I am aware of the fact. But it's closed to the likes of you and me."

"Yeah, okay, but here's what I want you to do. Get it out on all the feeds that Denny Brandt is definitely going to be the new Wildwood. That's what the studio is going to be announcing. And leak it that right after the announcement Denny is going to marry Cristina Townsend, right there in one of the soundstages."

A gargle from the other end of the line. "Is that true?"

"No, it's not true, you moron! That's why I want you to put it out to everybody."

"But . . ."

"Just do it!" Mitch yelled and jumped a light to cross north on Melrose.

TWENTY-EIGHT

Denny Brandt's limo was waved immediately through the star-crested arch of Constellation Studios East Gate and wound through the lot, snaking around the rear of the two dozen airplane-hanger-sized soundstages. It stopped behind Number 6. An assemblage of people who'd been anxiously awaiting Denny's arrival swarmed it, engulfing Denny the instant he stepped out of the car. Hannah emerged from the other side. She was given brief scrutiny, determined not to be Cristina Townsend, and then ignored.

She paused for a moment, getting her bearings. Amplified music and excited, chattering voices waxed and waned on the freshening twilight breeze from an area in front of the neighboring soundstages. For a moment, she faltered. This could be the craziest thing she had ever done. If she had even an iota of sense, she'd stick here with Denny's entourage and forget this idea entirely.

No, she couldn't forget it.

She began walking around the dun-colored soundstage to the front. The party area was screened by a row of towering potted palms and through the thick fronds she could glimpse the event. An entire space between four of the soundstages had been turned into the mythical junglescape from the first *Wildwood* movie, with its rainbow-colored foliage twittering with birdsong and latex snakes coiling around the trunks of weird-looking trees. A twenty foot backdrop featured Jackson Brandt posed in silhouette on his silver star bike. Music blared, and waiters dressed as creatures from the film circulated amidst a crowd of several hundred.

She edged cautiously between the palms, into the thick of the crowd. She was pretty sure she wouldn't be recognized by most people, now that she no longer looked like the trendy blonde of her celebutante days. But here and there she spotted faces she recognized—Benny Davis in his wheelchair, wearing his Toke Taylor lab coat; Alicia Chenoweth social-kissing a cheek. She veered quickly to avoid them.

And then suddenly, on the other side of a wide ramp that bisected the party, there he was. Her father.

No, not her father, she reminded herself. Her *real* father was the famous figure on the silver star motorcycle depicted on the huge backdrop behind her.

The man she was looking at now was just Warren Doran.

She stood rooted, studying him. The man she'd spent her entire life desperately trying to impress. Ceaselessly striving to attract his attention. Win his love.

But now it was like she was seeing him for the first time: a stranger in a crowd.

How obvious he appeared. The way he squeezed a shoulder here, engaged eye contact there. Dispensing charm like a New Year's Eve drunk flinging confetti.

Courting the approval of these people because he thought they counted.

He was nothing really. A marionette jerked by the strings of his own ambition and love of power.

She needed only one thing from him. Once she got that, she'd be free.

"Croquettes of wild-caught salmon tartar with egg-free aioli garnish?"

She turned with a start. A waiter sprouting turquoise tentacles from his head was proffering a tray. "No, thanks," she murmured.

When she looked back at Warren, he had been swallowed by the crowd.

※

Freaking hell! Thad Miller craned his neck to make sure he wasn't mistaken.

Yep, it was her, all right. He scuttled to the fringe of the party, slapping his phone to his ear and covering the other against the bedlam.

"She's here!" he hissed to Cherry Morrison. "I just saw her! She's just waltzed right in!"

"I'm already on it. Picked up her location on the GPS. Give me five minutes and I'm there."

"Yeah, okay. But don't use the main gate. Use the East Gate, around the corner on Oakwood. I'll call in a pass. They'll want to see an I.D. What've you got?"

"I got a Wyoming license for a Harvey Smith and a California under José Estevez."

Cherry Morrison looked about as much like a José Estevez as a Rottweiler did. "Use the Wyoming," Thad said.

*

Alicia paused in the midst of the party to watch Warren Doran soaking up the adulation of the people around him.

Let him enjoy his last hurrah, she thought. At the end of the event, she was planning to drop the bomb. Roger Lopez had called back a moment ago—he'd viewed a few of the flash drives on his computer and confirmed they were the incriminating videos from Betsy Bell's. She would apprise Warren of the fact that she had them in her possession. And then she'd let loose the sweet, oh-so-sublime death charge. *Guess what, Warren, old chum? You're history!*

Oh yes, it was going to be sweet.

She took a celebratory sip of Sauvignon Blanc. She reeked of cigar smoke, the sleeve of her Jil Sander mulberry silk jacket sported a chocolaty smear and her hand felt like raw meat from squeezing too many other hands. But she was floating on air.

Over the rim of her glass, she suddenly imagined she saw Hannah Doran. Just for a second—and then disappeared. Couldn't have been, Alicia decided.

"Alicia, there you are!" Martin Drake appeared with a squat, balding man in tow. "I've been hunting all over for you! Ernie's got a few questions for you."

Ernie Krenowski, head of United Cinema. He controlled about thirty-eight hundred screens in the Northeast corridor. He had the power to decide if your movie would open on two thousand of those screens or just a lousy two hundred of them, and whether your movie would then stick around on those screens for the next couple of months or be booted off the following Friday.

Tugging her jacket down to reveal just a hint of cleavage, Alicia fastened her beautiful earth-mother eyes on him. "Anything you need to know, Ernie," she said in an intimate murmur. "I'm at your complete disposal."

*

Mitch heard them before he saw them.

The muscle cars and tricked-out SUV's racing at breakneck speeds towards the main entrance of Constellation Studios. Horns blaring, tires squealing. His plan had worked! Every paparazzo within twenty miles was surging to the studio, crazy for a shot of the rumored Denny Brandt-Crissie Townsend marriage vows.

Taking a corner on two wheels, Mitch positioned himself in the middle of the pack. He whipped into the wrong lane to pass a brace of Mustangs, overtook a CelebShot Brazilian driving like a maniac in a Landrover LR3, then cut back in front of a Lexus SUV with a video camera mounted on the hood like a streamlined ornament.

His adrenaline surged. The rush! It almost made it all worthwhile.

A logjam already at the studio gate, a strident orchestra of horns and obscenities. A guard babbled frantically on the phone, as more vehicles piled up, blocking all access to and from the studio. There was a crash and the shattering of a headlight. A cop car whooped and yipped, trying to nudge through the pack.

The guard shouted: "Okay, we're letting you all in. Have your photo I.D. ready, and pop all your trunks for a search."

Mitch dug out his driver's license. Then he took out the loaded Glock semiautomatic and jammed it back in his waistband, figuring the search wouldn't include dropping his pants. Going through the routine was slow; by the time he made it inside the lot, the visitor's parking was almost full—cars were fruitlessly circling for free spaces.

So now what? There was a smaller parking lot reserved for the studio's top execs and stars, but you had to access it from the East Gate on Oakwood. There'd be no way he could get through security at that entrance.

But who said he had to go through the gates?

He K-turned and drove onto a paved walkway, sending script girls and development boys scrambling and a go-cart careening onto a border. On a normal day, every uniform on the lot would be screaming down his ass, but this was no normal day. He navigated the Vette down the narrow footpath between two rows of production Quonset huts and emerged finally in the second parking lot.

Yes! A free spot marked for Kyle Deckland, an actor currently doing three weeks in rehab for sex addiction. Mitch pulled into the slot, killed the engine and jumped out.

Then froze.

The vehicle next to him was a black Escalade.

So what? The town was lousy with black SUVs. Lots of them steroidal Caddies.

Mitch flashed on the chase of two nights ago—the spook car, stripped of all chrome and ornament, its windows tinted black.

Just like this one.

The back of his neck prickled. He was here—the guy Roger Lopez said was called Cherry. Killer eyes.

Mitch could hear the chatter and music of the party drifting from the soundstages adjacent to the parking lot. He began sprinting toward them, wondering if he was already too late.

TWENTY-NINE

The fire raging in Warren Doran's sternum had been intensifying throughout the party. It made no sense. This was a triumphant occasion: it should be dousing the flames, not pumping gasoline on them.

He was confident, though, that he'd managed to conceal his pain. If anything, it had forced him to be at the top of his game. He'd read somewhere that the mark of a social genius was to make other people feel like they were social geniuses; and to judge by the way the people around him were pulsing like supernovas, he was succeeding brilliantly.

Who was going to be the new Wildwood? It was the question on everybody's lips. And he was teasing them: "We kicked around the idea of Russell Crowe, but he's a little long in the tooth. Matt Damon wasn't available. And Hugh Jackman . . . well, too Hugh Jackman. But okay, if you really want to know. . . ." They leaned in close to him, breathlessly. "It's Hilary Swank!"

Hearty laughter. Warren laughed with them and felt a roil of acid. Pain blurred his eyes—so much so that for a moment he thought he saw a ghost—the ghost of Jackson Brandt, that cocksure sneak thief of an actor. Standing some yards away. Staring at him with pitiless eyes.

The acid fire spat up into his neck and the side of his jaw.

This is bullshit, he told himself.

The ghost began moving towards him. He was right: it was no phantom. It was his flesh and blood daughter, Hannah. The same gray eyes, the two of them.

He summoned every atom of self-control to maintain a smile.

"If you'll excuse me, folks . . ." he twirled his glass jauntily, "I need a refill. Stay tuned, I'll be right back."

He walked quickly to intercept his approaching daughter. "What the hell are you doing here?"

"Looking for you, of course," she said. "I want to talk to you."

"Not now. For Christ sake, Hannah! I'm busy. I don't have time for your nonsense now."

"You're always busy. Now is the perfect time."

Thad Miller suddenly loomed beside them, wearing a grin. "Wow, Hannah, am I relieved to see you! You gave us all a hell of a scare. Where've you been?"

She looked at him. His bland good looks and trendy little beard and stylish clothes. She saw it clearly for what it was: a disguise for something despicable. "You've been in on it too, haven't you?" she demanded.

"Whoa, somebody's being a little paranoid here."

"Bullshit. You've been there all along. Pulling my strings. You knew my money was gone. You were probably the one who arranged to steal it."

"Come on, I'm just trying to help out here . . ."

"Step back, Thad," Warren snapped. "I'll handle this." Warren clamped his hands on Hannah's shoulders, whirled her roughly around and started marching her towards the outskirts of the party.

Thad stood motionlessly, watching until the two had disappeared behind the screen of palm trees. He pulled out his cell phone.

Arriving at the first of the soundstages, Mitch was stopped by a cordoned-off area. Behind the orange rope, Denny Brandt was mounted on a huge black motorcycle with a silver star—Wildwood Murphy's famous Indian bike. Several dozen people fussed around him, girls in cigarette jeans, guys in porkpie hats. Some chattering into headsets. Some tweaking last minute adjustments to Denny's costume. The bike was poised at the end of a ramp that led directly into a huge paper backdrop bordering the party.

"Hey, Denny!" Mitch yelled.

Denny revved the bike. With his helmet on, he wouldn't hear a thing.

Mitch became aware of a faint drone in the sky. He looked up. A biplane appeared in the distance flying in a direct line to the studio. There was some object on top of the left double wing— looked like some Mothra-sized insect. The plane banked and began to circle in a wide loop like it was trying to shake the Mothra thing off.

Denny continued to rev the bike. Mitch tried to duck under the cordon.

A guard in a cop-blue uniform blocked him. "Area's off limits, sir."

"I've got to talk to Denny."

"You've gotta go around the other side of the stages to the party entrance. They'll check you off."

The security guard morphed into triplets, forming a human barricade in front of Mitch. "Either go around or we'll remove you from the lot," the first one said.

"Okay, okay!" Mitch turned and jogged back to the executive parking lot. He considered getting back in his car and barreling through the walkways again, but it was too risky—this time he'd be sure to be stopped by studio cops.

Okay. Try some creative thinking.

If he took an angle to the left, go through the working sets . . .

He could see the constructions of the sets from here: the saloons, the general store and church of the Western town, the water tower and brownstone roofs of the Bowery set, the Mansard rooftops and Gothic spires of the Parisian street. It would be navigating a maze, but it beat the hell out of jogging a half mile around the massive stages.

But that's what Cherry must have done too, Mitch realized. If you're a loco-killer packing major heat, no way you're going through a main-entrance check-off point.

In a sprint, Mitch headed off into the maze of the sets.

Warren pulled Hannah to an area screened by the palms and shoved her roughly down onto a bench. "Just what kind of stupid stunt do you think you're pulling?" he demanded. "You've got no business being here."

"I already told you. I want to talk to you. I need to get some answers."

"I can have eight security cops here in an instant and have you tossed out."

She stared up at him defiantly. "And I'll make a huge scene, right in the middle of your big event. Do you really want me to spoil it like that?"

An amplified voice rose above the music and chatter from the party: *Ladies and gentlemen, can I have your attention? I've just received information that a plane is heading directly toward this studio. I'm told it's carrying a very important cargo, and it will be coming out of the northwest sky.*

Warren glanced briefly up, then back at Hannah. "Do whatever the hell you want. I really don't have time for your nonsense."

"This time I think you do." She reached into her purse and took out the Bobcat pistol.

He stared at it. "Are you totally crazy?"

"Maybe. It's very possible. You can't believe how crazy you can get when you're locked up behind bars for over a year."

Warren winced at a fresh spurt of corrosive pain. It was that, more than the sight of the gun, that made him sink down on the bench beside her. "Okay. What do you want?"

"Just some answers. There are some things I already know. Like, I know that you stole all my money."

"Don't be ridiculous. I didn't steal your money, I invested it. I did what I thought was best for you. Don't forget, I'm your father."

"No, you're not," Hannah said. "Jackson Brandt was my father."

His face twitched, partly from surprise, partly in revulsion. "Jackson Brandt was nothing but a lousy little thief."

"My mother was in love with him. But you wouldn't let her go, right? You had the photos from Betsy Bell's. Photos that showed her slashing that man's face with a broken glass."

"That guy was a prick. He deserved it."

"Why?"

"He took Pam into one of the bedrooms, told her he had some coke. She thought they were just going to do a line. But then he pulled down his pants. When she tried to back off, he went rough. Forcing her. She was just defending herself."

Hannah felt a rush of relief. "So that's all she did? She just cut his face."

"She did what she had to do."

"But you let her believe she'd murdered him. Who actually did? Was it you?"

"Me?" A deep shudder ran through him. "No, that was Betsy. Always carried a little knife. She finished him off before I was in the room. I was the one who got Pamela out of there and made sure none of it caught up with her."

The amplified voice from the party climbed to a fever pitch: *There it is, ladies and gentlemen! It's a biplane! And oh my god! Oh my god! There's something on the wing!*

Warren glanced up again.

"What happened the night my mother died?" Hannah pursued.

"She took poison. You know that, Hannah."

"Did you make her do it?"

"What?"

"I know you were there that night. I remember hearing your car."

"No. I was on the set in Arizona. Everybody vouched for me."

"Your Ferrari could go a hundred and fifty miles an hour through the desert. You could have driven from the set and been back in time to make an early call. Nobody would have even known you were ever gone."

"Don't be stupid," he said sharply.

She released the safety on the Bobcat.

He jumped. "Okay. Yes."

"You were there?"

He nodded.

"Why?"

He felt suddenly crazed with pain. It was in his neck, his arm, his jaw. It mingled with the buzz of the approaching plane and the frantic roar of the party. "I'd found out she was planning to sneak away. To take you and leave the country. I was actually going to plead with her. Beg her to stay. But she turned on me. She been drinking a lot, but this time she was totally sober. And the things she said, the way she said them, so incredibly cold, I never realized . . ." He shuddered again. "I never knew how much she hated me. So I told her I'd killed him. That lousy little thief—I told her it was her fault he was dead."

Hannah stared at him, ashen. "Jackson, you mean?"

"Yeah." Warren gave a mirthless laugh. "I knew they'd been meeting in secret. So that last night, I followed him. Fucking hotshot on a motorcycle. It was easy."

"How?" she whispered.

"I was in a car. He was just on a bike."

"So you forced him off the road. And the bike went over the cliff."

"Easy," Warren repeated. "I told Pamela it was her own goddamned fault. And it was." He shook his head. "It was her own fucking fault."

Hannah pulled the trigger of the gun.

He flinched violently. Only when the wave of agony had subsided did he realize the gun had not gone off.

"It's not loaded," she said coldly. "I'm not like you. I'm not a killer. If you'd ever known me at all, you'd have known that."

She tossed the Bobcat scornfully at his feet.

The electronic voice rose to a shriek: *Something's happening, la-dies and gentleman! Oh my god, he's jumped! Wildwood has jumped his motorcycle off the wing of the plane!*

Warren glanced up to see the motorcyclist plunging through a sky streaked with vivid pennants of gold and pink. A parachute suddenly bloomed above him, jerking the bike upwards.

Warren rose unsteadily to his feet. "I've got to get back now, honeybun," he said almost tenderly. "It's important. I've got to get back to my movie."

Hannah watched as the man she used to think of as her father disappeared back behind the palms. It had always been about the movie, she thought.

His own movie and no one else's.

She gazed up at the billowing parachute descending now in the direction of the party. Something closer caught her eye—a figure standing on the ledge of the Western set saloon. A man with scruffy blond hair in a blue jean jacket.

The gun he aimed at her caught the red gleam of the setting sun and seemed to be made out of fire.

⚜

Mitch raced back between the production Quonset huts and sprinted diagonally into the working sets. A mock city street. Chicago, circa 1932: a row of brownstones, each with three steps and a stoop; a barbershop with a candystick pole; a movie theater, The Odeon, with a glitzy marquee.

The party now seemed to echo from several directions at once. He needed a vantage point. He hoisted himself up onto the rungs of a fire escape that dangled against the façade of one of the brown-stones and climbed it to the top of the false front construction.

From up here, he had a view straight across the other sets to the party site. A voice was squawking indistinctly on a mike, and then everyone at the party appeared to crane their necks and gaze up at Mitch. He had the strange urge to wave to them.

Then he realized they weren't looking at him, but at the sky be-hind him. The biplane was flying straight toward the studio through the vermilion and gold of a spectacular sunset. Mitch could now clearly make out the object on the wing. It was Wildwood Mur-phy—a stuntman in costume straddling a silver-starred motorcycle that was a duplicate of the one Denny Brandt had been revving down below.

Mitch glanced back towards the party. In between was another set—The Old West town. A man suddenly appeared in the deserted Main Street. Denim jacket. Close-cropped hair. It was him! He began loping down the street, like John Wayne heading for a showdown, his shadow stretching the length of the cobblestones.

Mitch followed warily on top of the brownstone. He watched Cherry take a phone from his jacket pocket. Cherry listened, replied, then snapped it back into his pocket. Then climbed a winding set of stairs to the roof scaffolding of the saloon. Shading his eyes with both hands, he stared out in the direction of the party. Then he glanced down at something directly below him.

A sudden roar erupted from the party. The amplified voice began hollering: *Oh my god, he's jumped, ladies and gentlemen! He's jumped off the plane!*

Mitch kept his eyes fixed on Cherry. Watched him reach inside the denim jacket. Metal gleamed red in the sun.

This was no phone—it was a gun barrel. From the length, it looked like it was fitted with a silencer. Cherry took aim at whatever he'd been looking at below him.

"Hey!" Mitch yelled.

Cherry whirled and fired. Mitch felt a hornet sting. His left leg crumpled and he went down.

He struggled to get up. His leg was refusing to cooperate. Dragging himself along the top of the brownstone construction, he fumbled for the Glock in his waistband. There was a water tower at the end of the roof. If he could get to it, it would cover him . . .

A bullet zinged, ripping a chunk off the cornice at Mitch's feet. The tower was yards away, and his entire leg was now numb. He saw Cherry aim at him again, confident of a clear shot.

Something large, like a racing cloud, suddenly passed directly overhead. It encased Mitch briefly in shadow and headed directly toward Cherry. Cherry looked up, his mouth agape.

And in the second that he did, Mitch, having been expertly schooled by the 3rd Marine Unit during long, sun-pummeled afternoons on the road from Kabul, aimed the Glock and shot his assailant efficiently between the eyes.

Alicia jumped at the pop of what sounded like a gunshot.

But then the *Wildwood Murphy* theme song began to blare, and the gleaming Indian motorbike came crashing through the paper backdrop. The cyclist shot up the ramp and threw a full wheelie stop, throwing his goggles up over his tousled blond locks, and the

M.C. shrieked: "Ladies and gentlemen, I give you Denny Brandt! Denny Brandt *is* Wildwood Murphy!" The audience was going gaga.

The shot probably came from some production running overtime, Alicia decided. The working sets were just fifty yards away. She glanced towards them and through the whooping, cheering crowd, saw Warren Doran come walking toward her.

Warren swam slowly through the jubilation. People embraced him; they grabbed his arm and pumped his hand and pounded his back. Every gesture just intensified the excruciating pain that now inflamed every nerve on the left side of his body.

Why were they torturing him like this?

And now here was Alicia Chenoweth, planted directly in front of him. Those big brown cow eyes lit with triumph. "Guess what, Warren, old chum?" Her voice acid in its glee. "It's over for you! Remember those precious movie rights that you thought were going to shoot you right back to the top of the heap—you didn't even own them, you asshole! You're ruined, old pal! You can kiss it all good-bye!"

"Huh?" It was all he could manage.

Through some trick of the setting sun, her eyes seemed to have acquired a reddish light. "Let me tell you one more thing. Anybody who comes after my children, I'm going to crush them like a bug. Just like I've crushed you. So enjoy the party, Warren. There's not going to be many more for you in your future."

He turned and began shoving past people, wanting to get away from her as fast as he possibly could. Almost blinded by agony, he stumbled out of the confines of the party and back through the alleyways of the lot. A miracle to find himself back at his car. As he clicked the BMW open, someone emerged from a sleek silver car at the end of the row.

It was one of the men in navy blue. The smiling younger one. Alex.

An all-encompassing jolt of terror. Warren collapsed behind the wheel. With a peculiar amount of difficulty, he fitted the key into the ignition. It couldn't be Alex. He was just being paranoid, it was somebody else. Some V.P. of marketing or a flack from the p.r. department.

Maybe he should see a doctor. There was a hospital not too far away, St. Somebody-or-other, right off Burbank Boulevard. He steered out of the lot and drove for several blocks, then tried to turn onto Burbank. But his left arm had gone suddenly rigid and his right arm seemed too weak to cooperate.

His car was drifting up onto a sidewalk, angling to a stop in front of a shuttered Greek café. With a brief flash of something like humor, the thought came to him that, all this time, it hadn't really been heartburn. It really had been just plain old heart.

With eyes wide open, he slumped lifeless against the wheel.

THIRTY

Once again, a powwow of top Constellation Pictures executives were gathered around a conference table. Faces were somber, but there was an underlying mood of celebration. A war had been won! There'd been casualties, sure, and that was regrettable, but in the end it was a victory; and everyone was digging into the catered Chinese lunch with appetite.

The marketing chief Lois Dubosky, swallowing a mouthful of ginger-glazed black cod, clinked her water glass with her fork. "I'll kick things off by stating the obvious. The announcement of Denny Brandt as the new Wildwood Murphy has gotten us more media coverage than any other film this studio has ever made!"

The studio chairman Martin Drake plucked a sliver of shiitake mushroom with his chopsticks. "But not all of the coverage was, shall we say, perfect." He placed the vegetable between his teeth.

"No, it wasn't. But like the wise man once said, there's no such thing as bad ink except for your own obituary. And according to our overnight poll, awareness of the remake of the *Wildwood* franchise is now a whopping 92 percent!"

Alicia, sitting opposite, a cup of green tea at her lips, mused on another popular adage of show business: "Death is a great career move." *Yes and no*, she thought. Death had been a fairly bad move for Cody Takish. But a pretty damned good one for Warren Doran: instead of being exposed for a bankrupt fraud and a blackmailer, he'd now be forever memorialized as a legendary Hollywood producer.

One of the greats.

The chairman of the parent corporation, Dick Landower, glanced briefly down with dismay at a speck of catfish on his azure silk tie. "So you're positive, Alicia, that all the underlying rights are now firmly secured?"

"Legal has triple checked the chain of title. Pamela Sebring Doran had purchased the original script with her own money, meaning Warren had no real claim to the rights, even under community property law. With the added factor of the Haitian divorce, there's no question that the rights are included in Hannah's trust."

"And you've closed a solid deal with her?"

"Air-tight." Alicia paused for a sip of tea. "And naturally, we'll be throwing our full weight into clearing her name and parole violations. "

"I think we're all comfortable with the official story," put in Martin Drake. "That Warren Doran left the rights to his daughter, Hannah. As basically the only thing he had left in his estate."

"Except everybody now knows she wasn't really his daughter," chimed in Lois.

Martin Drake showed snow-white teeth. "But he had raised her as such and always considered her his beloved daughter. And now she'll carry on his legacy. It's a heart-warming ending, really."

For a cold-blooded reptile. Alicia fought to keep her expression blank.

"What about Warren Doran's money people?" said Dick Landower. "What do we know about them?"

"Not much, and frankly, I think it's best if we keep it that way," Alicia said. "Warren's former partner, Thad Miller, is negotiating a deal for us to buy them out of their position."

"So is Thad gonna keep on working with Hannah now?" said Lois.

Alicia suppressed a shudder. "No. Apparently he's leaving the film industry to return to his roots in Vegas."

There was a pause as several people refilled their plates from the communal platters, a clink and scrape of spoons and chopsticks. Martin Drake slurped some noodles, then dabbed his chin with a paper napkin. "To recap the, um, incident on the lot yesterday . . ."

"We got it totally under control," said Lois. "A crazy with a gun managed to get through security while it was overwhelmed by a storming of paparazzi. This guy, this Conrad Morrison, we believe he was a paranoid-schizo. He had the idea that *he* was the real-life Wildwood Murphy and he thought we were stealing his life story. So first he murdered Cody Takish." Lois lifted her eyes heavenward. "Rest easy, kiddo."

"Are we sure he was Cody's killer?" said Martin.

"L.A.P.D. has confirmed that the forensic evidence is a match," Alicia said. "It was definitely the same man."

"So after eliminating Cody, he goes after the producer, Warren Doran, through his daughter," Lois continued. "Tries to kill her by blowing up her car. Yesterday, god only knows what kind of blood bath he was planning. He could've murdered us all if that photographer hadn't taken him down."

"This photographer," said Dick. "His name . . . ?"

"Mitchell Arpino," Alicia supplied.

"He got shot and wounded in the process. The studio might have a certain liability."

"He's not going to press charges," Alicia said. "After all, he was carrying a gun not registered to himself."

"Any difficulty with the police there?" Martin asked.

"We've already made it go away. It seems that the gun actually had once been registered to Jackson Brandt, and Mitch Arpino was intending to present it to Denny as a gesture. Where he'd acquired it . . . Well, we didn't ask."

"And it just happened to be loaded," Martin said.

"Yes," Alicia said without a blink. "Fortunately, as it turned out."

Dick Landower crossed his chopsticks on his plate and pushed the plate slightly away. "It still leaves the problem of what this all looks like for Constellation. We let people with guns get on the lot, psychos murdering our executives . . ."

"It's not the studio, Dick," Lois interrupted. "It's the curse of *Wildwood Murphy*."

Landower raised an eyebrow.

"There's been a longtime rumor that the *Wildwood* movies had a curse on them," explained Martin Drake. "There's been an uncanny amount of people associated with the movies that ended up dead or injured."

"The curse is all over Twitter and LinkedIn, and ET's gonna run a bit on it tonight," continued Lois. "Everybody's gonna be watching like a hawk all through production, wondering who's gonna drop dead next."

"It'll keep that awareness flying high," said Martin with something like glee.

Death is a great career move. Alicia drained her sweet tea.

"So we're all comfortable with the explanation of events?" said Dick Landower.

"To the best of our knowledge, this is the correct story," said Lois.
Every expression around the table remained perfectly deadpan.
"Okay, then," said Landower. "I'm comfortable with it too."

"Now that everything is pretty much in place," Alicia said,
"I'm going to take the next week off to be with my daughters. And
I mean off. No phones, no texts. No messengers at my door."

"You've earned it, Alicia," Martin said.

Yeah, she supposed she had. She regarded the table, all the triumphant faces. *Well, we all make deals with the devil.* Betsy Bell was
back in Texas, a phalanx of Alicia's lawyers having made it crystal
clear that should she ever threaten anyone again, she'd spend the
rest of whatever life she had behind bars. And Alicia had the flash
drives secure, possibly to be destroyed.

But the electronic web was forever. Who knew how many of
those images were still floating around out there?

She pictured the rosy faces of her daughters. No matter how
high she rose and how much power she accumulated, how could
she ever protect them from all the predators in the world?

Particularly the ones with money in their voices and candy apple smiles?

Dick Landower rose to his feet. "A toast." He raised his porce-
lain cup. "Here's to *Wildwood Murphy: The Legend Continues* and to
its sequels and all such good things."

All cups were elevated, and Alicia murmured "To all good
things."

⚜

Thad Miller stood trembling in a room that offered sweeping
views of the skyline of Las Vegas. The room itself, though opu-
lently appointed, offered no evidence that it was for actual human
usage. The mirrored surfaces were preternaturally devoid of marks
or smudges. The carpets once stepped upon retained no footprints.
The furniture was upholstered with the hides of beasts that might
have been slaughtered just hours ago, so immaculate were they.

The two men who occupied a deuce of those spotless chairs
didn't exude an impression of great humanity. Dressed in hushed
and costly navy blue suits, one was smiling, the other wasn't. Both
waited expectantly for Thad to speak.

His mouth was dry as crackers. "I've reached a deal with the
studio," he managed. He tried to gesture forcefully with the file he
clutched in his hand, but it resulted in a quaver. "This contains

the broad details. Basically, um, they're willing to buy out your position with ten percent interest." He hacked his throat. "No questions asked."

"That's the best you can do?" the unsmiling one, Tom, asked gruffly.

"I uh, um, think so. Since Warren's ownership of rights had been, um, uh, tenuous to begin with, I, uh, think it's not a bad offer."

The smiling one, Alex, smiled a little wider. "I'm inclined to agree."

Thad glanced at him warily.

"Go ahead and close the deal. Good work, Thad. In fact, I have to commend you on your work on this project in general."

Was it sarcasm? Thad wondered. A spasm of fear nearly brought him to his knees.

"It showed a good deal of creativity and initiative," the smiling Alex went on. "We're impressed with that."

"We're giving you a job," grunted Tom.

No! Thad shrieked silently.

"Since your father's retirement, we haven't found anyone to fit his place," Alex said. "You've been the obvious candidate all along. Welcome aboard."

Thad felt an almost liquid relief, replaced almost immediately by another sensation: the numbing realization that his father's life was now about to be his as well. There'd be no bright lights; no rare wines and honey-haired starlets. If he toed the line, he'd pull down middle-income wages, and wear off-the-rack suits, and live in some shitty middle class development. He'd marry an average-looking woman and his average kids would go to mediocre schools; and for this privilege, every day of the rest of his working life, he'd have to bow and scrape to these men in hushed blue suits.

Basically, he was about to become a slave.

"Thank you," he said. He knew it would be the last free remark he'd ever be permitted to make.

⚬⚬⚬

Mitch was going stir-crazy.

The bullet from the .45 had passed clean through the fleshy part of his thigh, miraculously missing a major artery, adding a new scar to his battle collection. The surgeon promised that in six weeks he'd be fit to travel; Ajay Nayar had pedaled the video of Crissie Townsend brawling with the homeless woman to a German tabloid for two hundred a grand, and Mitch's forty percent was enough to let him finish shooting his doc. If his recovery was on target, six weeks from now he'd be heading to the diamond mines in Sierra Leone.

But at the moment he was restricted to Hannah's canopy bed, the wounded leg propped on cushions. Despite the pals who'd trooped in with beer and deli, and his cell phone constantly buzzing, after just three days he was ready to climb the walls.

Hannah had been out all afternoon. He heard her come in downstairs, tossed aside the remote with which he'd been irritably surfing the cable, and struggled for the crutches propped against the wall.

"Stay put!" she commanded, appearing in the bedroom. "You know you're not allowed to walk for another four days."

"I'll be certifiably insane before that."

"Then I'll pad the walls. But you're not moving until then." She climbed onto the bed and stretched herself out beside to him. "At this point, I'd happily change places. It's been a long day!"

"Which lawyer was it today?"

"Bankruptcy. Warren left behind a real rat's nest. It's going to take months to straighten it all out and dissolve what's left of the company. And did I tell you Tracy is threatening to sue for palimony? Wait till she finds out there's absolutely nothing left."

"It shouldn't be your problem."

"In the eyes of the law, I'm still Warren's next of kin." She kicked off her shoes and wriggled her toes. "After the lawyers, I went to see Benny. We're going to start structuring a non-profit as soon as the *Wildwood* money starts coming in."

"It sounds a hell of a lot more interesting than my day."

She snuggled into his encircling arm. She looked the way he liked her best, no makeup except for a pale peach lipstick, her brown hair rippling loose over her shoulders. She kissed his cheek, then continued the kisses down his neck.

He groaned. "If you don't want me to move, maybe you shouldn't do that. I won't be able to keep off you."

"In a few more days, I'm not going to let you keep off me." She withdrew a little. "You know, it's funny. I can't stop thinking about Warren. After everything I found out about him and what he did, I really hated him. I was practically ready to kill him. But then when I heard he actually was dead, I felt . . . I don't know . . . Grieved, in some peculiar way."

"Yeah, I can understand that. He was a cold and ruthless son-of-a-bitch, but he was the only father you ever knew."

She reached for his hand. "I'm going to miss you terribly while you're away."

"If you want me to, I could postpone going for a while."

"No, you need to finish your film. I'll be fine, don't worry."

"I'll be thinking of you all the time."

"Me too. Every second."

They lay in silence for some moments, just holding each other's hand. Hannah caught an oblique glimpse of herself in the mirror above a dresser: a girl with brown hair and gray eyes lying beside a guy with tousled curls in drastic need of a shave. He'd be leaving for several months, and he would always be restless. And she would continue to be grappling with demons.

But right now, just the feel of his warm, dry palm against hers made her almost dizzy with joy. "It's strange," she said.

"What?" he asked.

"I don't know, exactly. Strange, maybe, to feel happy."